The Mistake

AND THE

Lycan King

BOOK 1
HEALING FATE SERIES

ASHA NYR

ISBN: 978-1-64184-892-3 (ebook)
ISBN: 978-1-64184-893-0 (paperback)
ISBN: 978-1-64184-894-7 (hardback)
ISBN: 979-8-98853-500-3 (hardback with dustjacket)

Copyediting by Misha Carlstedt, Verity Ink Editorial

This novel is dedicated to Marsha M. Linehan, Ph.D., whose DBT tools saved, and continue to save, my life.

Content Warning

Dear new readers, this novel contains adult content with scenes describing explicit language, explicit sex, sexual assault, and suicide ideation. Reader discretion is strongly advised.

The Mistake and the Lycan King was originally exposure therapy for the sexual assault I survived. Due to popular demand, I've decided to publish it. More information is provided in the Author's Notes about why this was written. Please note that includes spoilers.

Acknowledgments

As this book started as my first foray into exposure therapy, I would never have imagined it having a page for acknowledgments. I never intended to publish. Since starting this, irreplaceable individuals have flooded into my life, each like a singular breath of sustaining air.

First, before all, I must thank Renee Sanguinetti, my therapist. It took years to find the right person to help treat my trauma, and I believe she saved my life. I got to this seemingly impossible place because of her encouragement and the life-changing DBT tools she taught me.

Next, I must thank my readers, but you must know that they're more than readers—they are my friends, and they are my family. From the day I submitted chapter one online, they responded unknowingly to the need I had of not being alone with this form of therapy. When they told me a chapter made them cry, little did they know that I'd cried while writing it. When they told me a chapter made them laugh, I too had that same experience. I thought that being on the road to recovery was going to be cold and lonely, but I was quickly joined by people who either understood what I'd gone through or offered their compassion because of it.

Nurse Moon was one of the very first to join my journey and has amazingly stuck with me since then. Her sense of humor and passion for predicting the answers to questions made the entire writing experience much more fun than I'd ever anticipated. Ultimately, she became a dear friend and an endless font of support—and laughter. I always look forward to her getting my jokes. Honorable mention to both her house wolves, Marilyn and Lola—fine, upstanding sub-pack members!

Callie H. was there too. I eventually grew to anticipate her commenting first on almost every single chapter I'd ever written. If anything, she was the reader who was always there and constantly validating the emotional experiences I'd been exploring. Honestly, her presence unknowingly got me through some rough nights after submitting a chapter.

Gigicup joined my shifter family later, and their support didn't end at enjoying my novels. They not only encouraged me but also validated my value as a human being. I've often been nearly moved to tears by their kind words. They also helped scan this novel for issues when I did a shoutout for help, and together, it's all more than I could have ever asked for.

Suzanne was a steady column of support. I looked forward to reading every single review she'd written because she made my book feel truly read, thoroughly experienced, and genuinely appreciated. This was an individual who recharged my depleted batteries. She also helped catch so many little typos, one in particular that made me laugh.

Manon Leah van der Veen lit up my comment section with guiding sunshine. She is not only heartfelt and detailed in her validation but also generous with any help she gives. It was a clear, sunny day in my heart when she joined my little shifter family. I especially must thank her for aiding me with the synopsis. Summarizing is incredibly difficult for me, and she helped me vault over that challenge.

Julie came along like a beautiful tornado, sweeping through all my books and catching a plethora of mistakes. Such was my delight and gratitude, I asked for her continued assistance, and she read this novel more times than I could believe. Undeniably, she is like a true beta— genuinely dedicated and a joy to have in my life. Beta Julie.

I also need to extend sincere gratitude to Hunter Ambrose—an author with an impactful vocabulary and a natural proficiency for writing in a variety of voices—who I consulted and relied on for several things. His feedback was critically helpful, and my novel is better for it. His kindness and articulateness made communication a delight. I am glad to add him to my long list of friends created by this project. Thank you, Hunter.

And to Logan Black, an incredible, erotic mystery author, who swooped in to educate the heck out of my brain. Thank you so much for all you've taught me. You continue to sit on my shoulder as I type, pointing out what I can do to improve my writing. Or at least I hope you are; otherwise, I should be seen about that voice in my head.

To the team who helped me publish this book, know that I am grateful for the safe space you've allowed me to work in. Starting the publishing process was terrifying, and you made it easier than I imagined.

Starlight preserve you all, especially the hundreds of followers who lift me up daily. You have my love and gratitude, so much that I could fill a book with it.

Love,
Author, artist, musician, and unyielding survivor,
Asha Nyr

Chapter 1

Ragna

I wish I had known to leave before that day. My human eyes would not have noticed the difference, but to our inner wolves, it was the day the sun lost his confidence, and the stars lost their shine. Even the sky, in its unwavering silence, seemed to struggle to maintain a space for order. The moon, most of all, lost her luster, her spirit.

I'd moved into the pack's apartments the week prior. I was about to make my eighteenth migration around the sun, and—per our custom—it was time for me to move from my family's home. I'd be considered an adult and ready to take on larger responsibilities. I had a thirst for knowledge and wasn't certain about how I wanted to contribute to our pack, so I kept my options open. It meant pursuing further training with the warriors, helping our healers, and studying with our scholars, but I'd been ready for it.

I would've been training with the warriors on my birthday the following day, but I'd been excused for a very specific reason. I was preparing for the stroke of midnight, for I was about to come of age. My she-wolves had gathered with food and drinks to celebrate the awakening of my inner wolf, who was expected to make her appearance.

Hekla arrived first—the beautiful she-wolf from my childhood and my first friend. She was as confident as the midnight sky and just as soothing. All she-wolves were beautiful, but she was one to be admired with the Queen of Night tulip shades of her velvety skin and glossy hair. Her umbral eyes sparkled in excitement when she embraced me. She had as much spirit as beauty and was wise beyond her years. She was the guiding light of our group of friends, our sub-pack.

Soley arrived next, rapping on the wooden door in a spritely fashion. I embraced her in turn, breathing in her sweet scent of roses as her pink cheeks and ember-red curls brushed my face. She was smaller but strong—not strong in the body but in the mind. She was our font of knowledge, our living library.

Rakel was last—late, but for a reason. She was fierce, bold, a force with which to be reckoned. Her lean, deeply tanned arms were wrapped around large bundles of food. Chuckles rang from my throat when I untangled her long, moon-blonde hair from the overripe plantains peeking from a tote bag. The fruit would be good fried but less so with her hair still attached.

I'd been happier then and laughed easily.

That night, before everything changed, was warmed by swaying candles, the glow of the woodstove, and the love of my friends. The air was seasoned by the sizzling roast and steaming vegetables. My beautiful she-wolves were just as excited as me—perhaps more so as they knew what was coming to me. Their inner wolves had all awakened, and I was the last to be blessed. That night, our sub-pack would truly be complete.

We formed a circle on the floor, clasping hands of different sizes and colors with giddy grins on our faces. My cheeks hurt because I'd been smiling so much, but it was a pain I relished. My friends' wolves peeked through their eyes as midnight drew near. They were as excited to meet my wolf as their human counterparts were. Hekla's silvers glimmered like starlight. Soley's turned copper, warm as the sun himself. Rakel's wolf had light eyes like a gold coin. All but the harvest moon herself was put to shame.

I didn't recall the transformation as much as I recalled my friends' faces moments before it happened. All I remembered was a snap in my mind and chest like a weathered lute string that'd been tuned too tight. The pain was so powerful, the shock so great, that I almost didn't feel it.

Bones had stretched and rearranged, some broken, others splitting to form new ones. Tendons had pulled and organs shifted. Growing pains and menstrual cramps were insignificant in comparison. I knew my friends worked to stabilize me during my first shift, but I hadn't been able to feel them—my nerve endings had been too distracted elsewhere. Nausea and aching were the least of my symptoms, and all I'd been able to do was yell, sob, and screech. I couldn't properly explain what it felt like. Perhaps a poet could, but I was no poet.

Upon the last change, my trembling body collapsed. A muscle cramped occasionally, and my bones throbbed, but most of the pain had gone. I recalled panting through my wolf's lungs and trying to ease through the fog of shock. I blinked slowly to clear my vision, which had become quite sharp, and the smallest movements in the room startled me. My friends cooed and fawned over me, and their love brought me strength.

"Ragna, you are beautiful," Soley said.

"Brown fur, so soft," Hekla admired. I felt her gentle strokes upon my wolf's neck.

"Eyes like spring grass," Rakel noted as she brought our foreheads together.

They waited patiently for my wolf to speak, running their fingers through our fur and offering water to quench our thirst. I tilted my wolf's head to lap, which felt like a strange new way to drink. A wolf's tongue worked a bit like a ladle, and I was grateful for guiding instincts.

Are you there?

Those words were the first she'd ever spoken to me. Though uncertain, they somehow comforted me. My wolf's soul was prodding me as I was her, dancing about each other like two autumn leaves.

My human, I found you.

If I'd been in my human form, I would've sobbed upon her greeting. I hadn't known there'd been such a lonely, empty spot until she came along.

I'm here! I'd thought back to her, then I'd pulled my friends into our mind-link. *I'm Ragna. I'm so happy. I never knew I missed you.*

If I'd been human, I would've been crying and laughing in jubilation. My friends embraced me—embraced us—and swiftly joined in our bonding.

Trail, she said back. *My name is Trail. My heart is full, my human.*

Trail, I gasped to my friends with happy tears gracing my heart. *Her name is Trail!*

"It's so right, Ragna," Hekla said. "Like a deer trail in the woods. She looks like the woods—so suitable for our tranquil forest child."

"Earth and bark. Leaves and grass," Soley giggled, wrapping her little arms around our neck and nuzzling. She breathed us in, digging her nose into our fur. "You smell like autumn, my beautiful Trail, like the crisp fall air!"

Trail perked up at that point, feeling the love and sense of belonging that our sub-pack offered. I smiled in my mind, feeling her tail wag as she leaned into and then jumped onto our friends in excitement. We were tired, but adrenaline had been coursing vibrantly through our bloodstream. She'd just woken from her long eighteen years of slumber, and I'd waited eighteen long years for this moment.

"Are you ready, Ragna? Trail?" Rakel asked, ruffling the fur between our ears. "Shall we have our first run?" She was practically vibrating with her desire to shift.

Trail yipped and pranced in her race toward the door and crouched playfully, waiting for someone's hand to turn the handle.

Three pairs of feet and one set of paws burst out into the wild night, slapping through the damp grass of the pack grounds. Dewdrops dampened our fur and skin, making our awkward Soley slip on occasion. The she-wolves' laughter rang out amongst the starlight as they stripped and shifted, allowing their inner wolves to take the lead.

Hekla's ebony wolf, Eventide, pranced and jumped on my wolf. Trail stumbled and nipped at her, feigning offense. Soley's small red wolf, Noon, rolled onto her belly in submission when Rakel's polar wolf, Wax, leaned over her in a whimsical display of dominance. After tumbling and playing, we were itching to run. We loved our pack, but we were high on our little sub-pack. That night was just for us. That night was for Hekla, Soley, Rakel, and me. The ground beneath our paws was for Eventide, Noon, Wax, and Trail.

I wished I had known to leave then. That moment, that perfect moment in my life, was the last time I would ever experience that kind of joy.

Chapter 2

Ragna: Eighteenth birthday

We were taking a direct route to the woods through the center of our community when we noticed males jogging up to us. Trail and I became uneasy, and our sub-pack slowed at their approach. We backed up behind our stalwart Rakel, feeling like something was wrong when we noticed their dilated eyes, their flushed cheeks, and the tension in the air. They were all staring at me.

"Mate! Mine..." one of the younger males announced, grinning and kneeling before me. I froze and took a step away from him. My she-wolves moved to offer us space, and their animated chatter filled our group's mind-link. They were congratulating me on finally finding my mate and were happy it happened as soon as it was possible, upon my eighteenth birthday—my wolf's awakening.

Trail and I felt some excitement, but the moment was dampened with a sense of apprehension. My heart sped up, and my body responded in an expected but embarrassing manner. The male before me growled, sensing my slight arousal, and came closer to sniff us, but something was off about the moment, like I was expecting more. They smelled good, but I couldn't quite make out what it was. This wasn't matching any recognition story I'd ever heard. If this was my fated mate, the one given to me by the Moon Goddess, I should be able to smell more. I should be feeling more.

Additional growls arrived from different directions, and the male before me was ripped to the side. "What are you talking about, Emil? Ragna's my mate!" the other male snarled, and I retreated several more steps. They began to bicker, and it wasn't long before they started grappling. It was embarrassing and a little frightening. I hadn't wanted to cause a scene or get anyone in trouble.

S-stop! I shouted through the pack's open link. *Don't hurt each other! L-let's talk!* Nervous whimpers escaped Trail's throat as other males approached.

What's happening? Hekla and Rakel asked in unison.

You have multiple mates? That's crazy! Soley exclaimed, sounding bewildered.

An intimidating grey wolf approached us from behind and attempted a sniff under Trail's tail. She yelped in surprise and stumbled forward, moving her hindquarters away from him. *Wh-what?* I protested.

Who are these other males? Come with me, mate! The slightly older male in his wolf form snarled at us and moved to our flank, trying to separate us from the growing crowd. Rakel noticed his herding, and her wolf squeezed aggressively between us, growling.

This is becoming a problem, Ragna, Soley whined nervously, watching Rakel's attempt to intervene. The red wolf's tail was slightly tucked between her legs, and her ears were flattened in fear.

I don't understand this. Let's get some distance, Hekla ordered, and her wolf began loping along the quickest route out of the community. I was grateful for her taking the lead because after the shift, Trail and I were already fighting mental and physical exhaustion.

More males of different ages approached me, shouting to wait and that each was my mate. Our distress elevated, and Trail ran to hide behind Hekla's Eventide. It was pointless because they could smell me, but hiding gave us a small sense of security.

At this point, we noticed the rest of the pack coming out to watch the commotion. Some were frightened or confused, but others looked downright furious. Some young females who caught my name on the wind narrowed their eyes at me. I could see their jealous fury flash in the darkness, and I shuddered at the intensity. The hatred in their gazes frightened me more than the males' pursuit. For the first time, I felt like I was in danger. That was when I shouted into the pack link for someone to find our alpha. If anyone could sort this out, it was him.

I don't understand. This is impossible! I gasped as more males joined the fight over me. *I'm scared, Hekla.*

Something is wrong, Rakel decided. *I don't know what it is, but something is terribly wrong.*

She slowed to growl at another male wolf approaching us. Her wolf's hackles were raised, and Wax did the best she could to appear larger than him. She was quite big for a she-wolf, but males usually had the advantage in size and strength. I was so grateful for her bravery, though. She was buying us time.

The pheromones in the air became cloying, choking. There were so many scents that they merged into one revolting cloud that dulled my senses. Trail gagged and nausea roiled through our belly.

I didn't do anything! I swore to my friends. *I swear, I don't know what's wrong with our males!* They could have so easily assumed I was the culprit for this incident, and I was terrified they'd turn on me too.

We believe you. We'll figure this out, Hekla soothed, but she sounded terse, anxious. I prayed to the Moon Goddess that she believed me. I prayed they all believed me.

The males grew violent with my she-wolves as they fought to get past our ornery Rakel. It wasn't until I heard her Wax's yelp of pain that my distress turned into panic. A wolf had bitten her neck trying to get her out of the way, and another snapped at her ankle.

Rakel! Fall back! I begged desperately.

No! she snarled.

A group of she-wolves approached our retreat from the left, growling. *What have you done to our unmated males?* one demanded. *You can't have them all! What have you done?*

Was it witchwork, Ragna? another hissed and lunged to snap at our heels. *Fae magic? What?* Trail yelped in fear, dancing away from her maw. I knew her. She was Mela, my neighbor's daughter. Trail bumped against Hekla's wolf, who circled around and put herself between me and the raging she-wolves.

I didn't do anything, I swear! I begged them to understand. *I just turned eighteen at midnight, and they started acting like this! I don't know what's going on! Please, let's find Alpha! I'm sure this can be figure—*

A female I knew as Valorie lost her patience and tried to dart around Hekla. Hekla intercepted her but could not stop another from digging her teeth into our shoulder. Trail cried out in pain and tried to buck her off us. Another she-wolf raked her claws down our back, and louder yelps erupted from Trail's throat. We were slammed from our right as another she-wolf tried to topple us. She was going to try to rip our belly open; I knew it. She lunged to attack, but a male wolf intercepted her.

Mangy bitch! Don't touch my mate! he raged and went for her throat. She managed to squirm out of his reach and run, but a female took his distraction as an opportunity to dig her teeth into our right thigh. When another male yanked her off, her teeth shredded through muscle. We cried in pain, and warm blood ran down our leg. Trail and I were overwhelmed with injuries, and she was having a hard time keeping up with our shifter ability to heal.

Ragna, we need to run! Trail sobbed. *We're going to die!*

I glanced over to see my sub-pack members in various states. They were all trying to fight off wolves, even little Soley; bless her. Out of all of them, I was terrified about her safety the most.

You need to leave, Hekla concluded in a tone thick with grief. *We'll try to slow them, but... if you don't leave, you're going to be killed.* Neither Soley nor Rakel spoke their opinions. Even though none of us were in our right minds, I knew we were in agreement, me included.

I'm sorry... I'm so sorry, Trail and I choked out in unison, and we scrambled away from the females as my she-wolves redoubled their efforts to free me. Trail ran as fast as she could, ignoring our leg injuries. Our back right thigh was potentially going to cost us our life if my sub-pack couldn't hold back the she-wolves. I knew more would be coming. I could hear them.

Trail finally entered the woods and raced through the underbrush. There was no point in hiding; everyone knew our scent by now. Even if the females didn't know our smell, all they had to do was follow the unmated males. I wished I could go home, but I couldn't bring the violence back to my mother and father. Would I ever see them again? A pang shot through my heart at the thought.

Trail said we were losing a lot of blood, and I was terrified that we weren't going to make it out of our sprawling territory.

Did she cut the femoral artery? I asked her as she ran deeper into the woods. *I don't know where that is in a wolf!*

I don't know! It's just bleeding a lot! I'm losing energy to heal us. I'm so tired...

My mind raced for ideas, but panic and fatigue made for terrible advisors. We didn't have time to stop and look at the injury. I couldn't even recall if any bodies of water were nearby. Perhaps we could've traveled up a creek to hide our tracks or coat our body in mud to suppress the scent. If we could only hide and rest for a moment...

Trail's pace slowed, her chest heaving as she gasped for air. As expected, dozens of she-wolves caught up to our heels and snapped viciously.

I'm sorry. Trail sobbed in our mind. *I'm sorry I failed us.*

It's not your fault, Trail, I replied, devastated. *We are one... no matter what. I don't know what happened, but... at least I got to meet you. I love you. I couldn't believe that we were about to die before we'd been given a chance to live.*

I love you too.

She stumbled, and our waning strength was snuffed out like a candle flame starved of air. Her shrieking yelps filled the night as she-wolves descended and tore into our flesh.

"STAND DOWN," our alpha's voice boomed, and the she-wolves melted off me in submission. I barely noticed the pressure emanating from our leader because Trail had begun to choke on her own blood. She tried to gulp it down and take short, rattling breaths between swallows, but it was difficult. One of the wolves had punctured her throat, but neither Trail nor I could tell how bad the damage was.

"Hans, fetch several unmated males. Try to find the calmest ones you can—we don't need extra trouble here," Alpha Erik ordered, and I caught sight of our beta running off in my peripheral vision. "Females, back to the village!"

I felt several hands rotate Trail off her back and onto her belly. She leaned forward to let the blood drain out our mouth instead of into our lungs, but it wasn't very effective. It felt like an eternity had passed under the alpha's silence before I heard an approaching group. I barely heard the males calling me their mate before rushing to aid me.

"You all will give her strength to recover, then you'll return to the village. Is that clear?" the alpha asked, pressuring the males with a firm command. There were reluctant responses as hands landed on Trail's body. Tingles from the fated mate bond sparked across our skin from every finger and palm that stroked us. We were too tired to feel the pleasure of being touched by our so-called mates, but I sensed Trail was recovering. She could finally put some energy into healing our wounds as the males surrounding us murmured with comforting, loving noises. They urged our recovery to completion, then left unhappily for the village. Several had a harder time tearing themselves away from us and had to be handled by the alpha.

"Shift, Ragna," Alpha Erik ordered, and I attempted my first shift back into my human body. We yelped until our cries turned into human moans of pain. I finally lay panting on the damp forest floor and pushed myself into a sitting position so I could look up at the alpha.

"Was that your first shift, Ragna?" he asked, with his arms crossed over his chest and an inscrutable expression on his face.

I nodded in response, too afraid to speak.

"What happened?"

I closed my eyes tight and balled my hands into fists, trying to gather what little courage I had left. He was a good alpha, so maybe he'd believe me. "I had my coming-of-age celebration tonight with Hekla, Soley, and Rakel. I shifted a little past midnight, and we went to have the traditional run. As soon as we left my home, males began to approach and declare I was their mate... Then there was fighting, and the she-wolves..."

I gulped, having a hard time accepting the sudden change in my pack's behavior toward me. It was incredibly painful and shocking to see females that I was on neutral or good terms with suddenly attack without giving me a chance to prove my innocence. They almost made me believe I was guilty, and I questioned my sanity.

Don't think that! I was there. We are not insane, Trail said. She was firm, even with her fatigue.

"P-please," I begged of the alpha, hanging my head. "I didn't plan anything. This wasn't intentional. I don't know what happened. I swear on my life!" I groveled, letting my fingers sink into the spongy detritus. I would have prepared for the worst, but the alpha allowed me to be healed. As much as that decision gave me hope, I knew the situation still looked bad.

"If you had a history of causing problems, I'd be less inclined to believe you, but you do not," the alpha said thoughtfully. "However, I don't know if you understand how much of a catastrophe this is. The reports on my way here suggest this is packwide now. Any unmated male who's seen you has put their claim forward in a panic, and the females are issuing complaints—and the night has only begun, Ragna.

"Regardless of whether you actively caused this or not, you might've usurped every single unmated wolf's potential mate bond. I must investigate further, but there is no way that I can allow you to stay here." My breath stopped at those words, and my vision blurred from brimming tears. "Not only would the fighting among the males continue, but you'd have a target on your back every single day."

My body shook, finally giving in to my wrecked nerves. "I-I'm so sorry." I sobbed. "I didn't... I swear..." I prostrated myself at his feet, but I knew his decision had been made. He squatted in front of me and placed a large hand on my back.

"I am not unreasonable, Ragna," he said in a calmer voice. My head shot up, along with my hope. "Every member of my pack is important, so I have an offer for you. You can camp outside of our pack's territory while we investigate this disaster, and we will bring you supplies and news once a month. If we fix the issue, I will reverse your banishment. If we do not make progress with the issue after a year... I would recommend you find a new place to call home. What is your decision?"

"I'll camp! I'll camp outside the territory! Thank you, Alpha! Th-thank you so much!" I cried, rubbing my eyes. I never would've believed that there'd be a day when I'd be happy about an option like that.

"You will be on your own, though, Ragna. You will provide for yourself, and there will be rogues. I will not allow others to join you either. I must protect every member of my pack accordingly."

"I underst-t-t-tand!" I met his eyes and put on a determined face. "I'll be fine!"

The alpha nodded, sighed, and stood. Turning to his beta, he ordered, "Get her parents. Tell them to pack a bag with whatever they think she'll need. Spare clothes, medicine, and the like."

Once again, Hans took the role of messenger and left to fulfill his errand. I pulled my knees up to my chest and wrapped my arms around my legs. I was used to seeing others undressed, but I was surprisingly uncomfortable with my own nudity. Maybe it just compounded with the vulnerability I had already experienced. I supposed I would eventually get accustomed to it, not that it would matter once I was banished.

The silence was deafening as we waited, and every second had me worrying that the alpha would change his mind. "Is th-there anything I can investigate on my own while I'm banished, Alpha Erik?" I asked.

He was looking back to where his beta had gone, and I wasn't sure if he'd heard me. Perhaps he was mind-linking someone. I was about to ask in a louder voice when he answered, "We will let you know in a month's time, but it would be safer if you didn't go wandering off trying to find answers. If you step foot into another pack's territory, they won't be nearly as generous as me. They will probably execute you on the spot."

I shuddered and nodded, feeling the smallest shard of defeat settle in my heart. Nausea was quick to follow.

It's not over yet, Trail declared stubbornly, emboldened by our second chance at life. I nodded again but found little comfort in her certainty.

"How is your wolf?" Alpha Erik inquired, his expression unreadable.

"A lot less scared than I am..." I whispered hoarsely and wiped away two more tears that escaped through my eyelashes.

"If you are innocent, Ragna, hold on to that. Take care of her, and she'll take care of you. I realize you just got your wolf, and it's all very new, but trust me. She'll be the most important factor for you staying alive."

He turned away again, hearing people approaching us. My mother and father came into sight, and I ran toward them, bawling like a pup. I stammered through the evening's events, and they held me. Father was looking drawn, and Mother was inconsolable, but at least they believed me. Mother helped me get dressed while Father went through what they packed.

"You've got spare clothes, a medical kit, some canned food, protein bars... Uh, lessee here. I grabbed your hunting knife, flint, rope, tarp, and s-some other stuff," he listed, his voice getting progressively more emotional as he went through the items. He pulled something off his back, and I gasped when he handed me the bundle. A wave of guilt passed through my belly.

"Father... I can't possibly take Grandpa's shortbow..." I protested and looked up at him worriedly. I gripped the quiver tightly, paranoid an arrow might slip out.

"You will. Let it be used for what it's supposed to be used for. Not negotiable, little Trailblazer." He hugged me tightly and hid his tears in my shoulder. I crumbled a little at the use of my nickname. It summoned memories of a childhood spent exploring the woods with him.

"Trail's my wolf's name." I laughed through a sob, and Mother came behind me, sandwiching me with a hug.

"Appropriate," my mother said through her weeping. I could hear in her voice that she wanted to laugh but just couldn't manage it. "I wish we could get to know her." It broke my heart that Trail didn't have the courage to greet our parents. So deep was her shame that her arrival had cost our parents their pup.

"We won't give up, Heidi," he said, gripping my mother's shoulder and squeezing. "We're going to bring her home, ok?" Mother nodded aggressively and shut her eyes tight, forcing more tears down her chin.

I wanted to prolong the goodbye, but the alpha's presence unnerved me. I didn't want to make him wait too long. I didn't want to push my luck. I said my final farewell and turned to our leader. "I-I'm ready," I announced in a voice I wished sounded stronger. Alpha Erik nodded and motioned for two wolves to flank me.

"We'll escort you to the border," he said in a low voice. We walked off, leaving my mother to wail in my father's arms.

Chapter 3

Ragna

The alpha watched me leave the pack's territory after proclaiming my banishment. The snapping of the tether that connected me to the pack was traumatizing. Like getting Trail, I discovered a place inside of me that I never knew existed, except this place was a hole where the pack bond used to be. It felt like someone had removed my organs. I was a hollow shell of a shifter. I could tell Trail was equally distressed, choosing to stay quiet except for pointing out possible camping sites.

I was numb, unable to believe that the past several hours had occurred. I knew my mind, and I knew it wasn't a dream, but I desperately wanted to wake up to a world where none of this had happened.

I finally decided on a campsite. There was a large, slanting boulder jutting from the earth that provided a little coverage. I didn't bother pulling the tarp out because the weather was clear, and I was tired. I was cold, however, so I dug a pit, grabbed whatever dead wood I could find, and pulled my flint out to start a fire.

We're going to have to find water tomorrow, Trail realized. I nodded, pulling my jacket tighter around me.

"We should get some rest." I sighed. "We'll have to find a better site tomorrow and keep a nose out for packless wolves."

I woke around dawn, delirious, not understanding where I was or how I'd gotten outside the pack grounds. Trail had to calm me down and remind me of last night's events, breaking my heart all over again. As I leaned against a tree, struggling to slow my breathing, I realized that the alpha had been quite right—I needed my wolf more than I realized.

"How do you do it?" I asked her, preferring to talk out loud. I was already feeling lonely, and I'd take the sound of my voice over silence any day. "Aren't you feeling the trauma?"

She snorted. *You know how you're afraid of the dark when it's just you, but when you have a friend who's afraid of the dark, you're not afraid because it's overridden by protectiveness? That's how. Don't get me wrong. I'm shaken, but right now, I can be your rock. If we hadn't gotten that second chance... I'm determined to live, Ragna, and you should be too.*

"Thank you." I sighed and shrugged on my pack. I was too overwhelmed to properly express my deep gratitude. I kicked dirt onto the dying embers and went off in search of water.

Gonna really suck to be banished and afraid of the dark, though, she said wryly, and I surprised myself by laughing. She wasn't wrong. Last night would've been bad had I not been in shock.

"We have a lot to get used to, Trail," I replied, keeping my ears open for the sound of water. I tried not to get too far from the pack's border, but there wasn't any sign of a creek or river. There was a valley way in the distance; we'd probably have to go as far as that. I couldn't tell how many miles, though—maybe ten. I sighed. This wasn't looking good.

Isn't there a creek in our old territory? Maybe it runs all the way through? Trail asked.

"Should we just follow the pack border, then?"

It's as good a plan as any.

It wasn't until early evening that we heard water trickling in the distance. Excited, I stumbled down a steep, fern-ridden slope toward the precious resource. I was almost in tears as I drank my fill. It was stupid to not have asked the alpha where I might find water.

Stop berating yourself, Trail snapped, annoyed. *It's not like I thought of it either, and I'm no dumb butt.*

I apologized and filled my canteen. I wasn't used to my thoughts being so on display. Trail cackled gleefully at my realization.

Better get used to it too. I'm going to be around for everything, even sexy time!

I placed a hand over my face, blushing madly.

I'm going to see e-v-e-r-y-t-h-i-n-g, she teased. *And I'm going to be quality control, so if your choice isn't big enou—*

"Oh, great goddess, Trail! What is wrong with you?" I gasped, scandalized.

Someone has to cancel out your timidity. Hehehehe.

"Ahem... Either way, it's probably not going to happen, Trail, but I'll keep that in mind." I wrinkled my nose but froze when I spotted movement. Several large ferns bobbed as though something had just moved past them.

Did you see that? I asked Trail. *Is it a wolf?*

I can smell them! she answered, her playfulness disappearing in a heartbeat.

I started when my eyes settled on several wolf faces peering at me through the undergrowth. Fear washed over me, and I gripped my canteen so hard my hand threatened to cramp. My heart drummed in my ears, and my breathing turned shallow. There was something in their gazes that made me uneasy. I'd never been looked up and down like that before, and I felt like they were undressing me with their eyes. Maybe not, but...

Trust your instincts, Ragna, Trail advised. *I don't like the look of them.* I tried to swallow, but my mouth had gone dry. *Don't run,* she added. *They'll chase. I think they're packless. Rogues.*

Not all rogues are bad. I whimpered.

These aren't great, she murmured.

Before I knew it, they turned and lazily departed. Trail and I let out a collective sigh, and I resisted the urge to crumple to the ground.

We can't let our guard down, I said, biting on a nail.

Tonight's gonna suck.

We decided to set up camp a mile from the creek, and I outright stopped talking out loud. I grew progressively more nervous once night fell and huddled in front of the fire pit.

What should we do if they attack? Should we stay clothed and use our bow? Should we undress and get ready to shift? Should we stay shifted? I don't like the thought of being naked with those creepers out there, though. I began to nibble on another nail, my eyes darting from one distant shadow to the next.

I vote we put our pack on real tight and sit naked until you finish that bar. I am not eating that. Then we shift and keep our pack on. We need to secure the bow and quiver better, though. Those arrows are gonna fall right out.

I nodded and tied them up with some of the rope in my bag, bundling them the best I could. They were a priceless commodity because I had no idea how to make more.

I wish we had time to go hunting, I thought, staring into the popping fire. *I don't want to go through these protein bars. They make for better emergency rations.*

We'll hunt tomorrow—early, when the game is out, Trail said quietly. We were both on edge, keeping our senses tuned for intruders.

I ate the bar as fast as I could, but before I could shift, three wolves burst out of the woods. I tried to scramble away, but they pinned me down into the dirt. I struggled to push them off, but they shifted into their human forms and secured their grips. Tingles spread wherever their skin touched, and I screamed in outrage. They were unmated. I snarled and spat at the male in the middle who was straddling my waist, but he just laughed. He was bulky, with oily blond hair and a face riddled with scars. I could feel Trail panicking in my mind as I fought for freedom.

"Get off me!" I yelled at the top of my lungs.

I knew I was alone, but a small part of me hoped that a pack member working the border would hear and come to my rescue. The male to my left immediately clamped a hand over my mouth. I tried to bite it, but his hand was cupped, and I couldn't reach his palm with my teeth.

"Ahh," the blond said, "Finally, we have our mate. Unusual that we three have the same one, I know. But we don't mind sharing. It's easier this way. Only one female to keep an eye on." He grinned, elongating his long, sharp canines. His nostrils flared as he leaned forward.

"Moon Goddess must be apologizing for getting us kicked out of our pack," the male on my right said, leaning over to bury his nose in my neck. I shuddered and tried to lean away from his face, repulsed by his proximity. I clenched my teeth and glared at the blond, then tried to kick him in the balls with my thigh, but he was sitting too far up my body. He laughed at the bucking of my hips, only swaying with my efforts.

Should we? I asked Trail, hoping she could focus.

The answer must have been yes because we immediately started shifting, but the male on my left put his hand on my throat and squeezed. I choked and Trail stopped, reversing the process and cursing up a storm in my head.

"So young! What a fresh thing. I'll mark her first."

"No, I will! I saw her first," the one on my right asserted, and I stared wide-eyed as he swapped places with the blond to spread my legs. I bucked again, trying to break free, and my mind raced in desperation for an idea. The male tucked his dark hair over a shoulder and brought his hand down to his cock. It was already erect, but he stroked it feverishly while staring at my body. Nausea roiled in my stomach as he grunted.

Strength is out. Use my brain, use my brain, use my brain, I rambled to myself. A thought came to me. *Trail? Rejecting a mate hurts a lot, right? Like it'll stun 'em for a moment?*

Trail finally broke her silence. *Yeah... Yeah, you're right! It does.*

Can we use that to our advantage?

Reject them, and I'll boost your arm and leg strength. Kick 'em off, and we'll do a full shift!

I need to get that hand off my mouth first... I have an idea, but it might make me throw up, I said to Trail. *Alright, we're doing it.*

I nearly jumped out of my skin when the rogue dipped his finger between my folds and into my core. I screamed in my mind to Trail, shocked. I writhed and attempted to get away from his invading digit. Trail shuddered and whined. I wanted them dead. I wanted them all dead!

"Ugh, she's as dry as stale bread," the male complained, and I held back a cry of pain.

"Can you blame her? Looking at Joe's carved-up face?" the male on my left guffawed, and Joe sneered, showing off a long canine.

"Shut the fuck up, Henri," Joe snapped.

The sparks from his touch made my body respond favorably, and I averted my eyes in shame. He chuckled at my sudden wetness and said, "I think she's recognizing who owns her now."

My face scrunched up in revulsion, wanting to cry from the violation, but I pushed my emotions aside.

"She's almost ready. Such a pretty thing."

I waited for him to stop talking, took a deep breath, and forced an erotic, aroused moan out of my mouth. Loud enough for them to notice but low enough for it to be frustratingly muffled against the male's hand. That got their attention. They turned to look at my face, and I shut my eyes again. I arched my back and let out another low moan, hoping it sounded like the real thing. I'd never made a sound like that before in my life, but I had heard it on occasion. I hated myself in that moment.

Please, for the love of moonlight, let this work.

"Get yer filthy hands off her mouth, Henri. I want to hear her," the dark-haired male said and slid a second finger inside me. I jolted, not expecting that, but it spurred me into action.

"I, Ragna Rhydderch, reject you all as my mate!" I yelled as fast as I could, and the three males staggered, clutching their chests. I was expecting pain too, but I didn't feel much. Trail's power flooded my limbs, and I ripped myself away from them. I shifted, and Trail bolted like her tail was on fire. We didn't waste a second to look back; they were either recovered or not. Trail was screaming and laughing maniacally while I slipped back into the recesses of my mind. I could still feel their hands on me.

It worked in bulk, it worked in bulk, it worked in bulk! Three for one! What a steal! Trail cackled as she zipped through the trees. I watched her route silently, not sure where we could go. They could track us, and that was going to be a big problem. I might have rejected them, but there was no way they'd accept it. They were going to keep coming.

Trail ran at top speed for several miles, at which point she began to get winded. I listened through her ears, searching for any sign of pursuit.

We should assume they're tracking us, I cautioned. *We need to hide our scent somehow.*

Trail chuckled. *Should I find some bear shit to roll in?*

Or mud. Better than being r-raped.

Trail slowed to a lope and kept her nose open for helpful scents. The forest floor turned into an incline, and we found ourselves at a cliff. *Pupsie daisy,* Trail muttered. *Dead end.*

But there might be a stream down there in the canyon. We could roll in some mud. Let's go check it out. There's gotta be a path down somewhere, I pointed out, and Trail agreed. She was tiring fast. We hadn't slept or eaten much and had just run nonstop for miles.

Trail followed the cliff at a brisk pace, skittish now and shaking with fear. When three wolves trotted out of the woods, our heart sank into our stomach.

The one in the middle let out a low growl. His face was covered in scars, and I had no doubt that it was Joe. Trail darted to escape, but one of the wolves leapt into her path. The other two approached from different directions, and we looked toward our right. The bottom of the canyon was a long, long way down.

We just can't win, can we? I murmured. Trail didn't reply. *We're not fighting our way out of this one, and that trick won't work twice.* Trail backed up until our back paw was inches from the edge. *This is no way to live, Trail... but I'm not sure I'm ready to die. What do we do?*

Trail still didn't answer. Her heart was pounding so fast that I was worried it would burst. The wolf behind us tried to squeeze between her and the edge to push us back into captivity. Joe shifted back to his human form and lifted Trail by the scruff of her neck, making her yelp in pain. She snapped her maw, saliva flying in all directions.

"Certainly won't be boring with you around, little mate." He grinned and backhanded Trail's face. It didn't knock us out, but it made our head swim. Trail whimpered and kicked with her hind legs. I tried to help her out of her daze, but she was losing too much steam.

"Let's just bring her back to camp where we can tie her up proper this time," Henri said after he shifted back to his human form. Joe grunted and held us against him with one hand wrapped around our muzzle. "She'll have a harder time leaving once she's marked."

He hadn't made two steps before he was sent sprawling to the ground, shredded and bleeding. Trail bolted out of his reach, and I gasped. A black shadow tore through Henri and the third rogue. The males fell, their throats ripped out of their necks. We stared in shock at the scene before us. Trail's legs shook violently as she whimpered in terror. Her bladder finally gave out and released urine. I was expecting a swift death—until I got a better look at the assailant.

The figure was a wolf around my size. She was black with sparkling silver eyes. There was no mistaking her, but what was she doing here? How had she gotten here so fast? How did she take on three males at once?

She looked like Eventide, my dearest Hekla. How was she here? How...

The black wolf came closer, and I noticed a strange aura about her. Something was different. Something was... borrowing her. I'd never heard of anything like it before in my life, but it was what my gut was telling me.

Hello pup, the thing mind-linked me. It had Hekla's voice. *We need to talk.*

Chapter 4

Ragna

I stared in shock at the wolf who looked like Hekla. She smelled like her and sounded like her, but something was wrong.

I don't know if I can run anymore, Ragna. I'm so tired, and this pack is getting heavier by the minute, Trail admitted, and I felt a pang of guilt, wishing I was stronger and faster so I could take over our fleeing. If Trail could hear those thoughts, she didn't admonish me like she normally would've.

I made a judgment call and shifted back to my human form. Exhausted, I crumpled to the ground and removed my pack. Whoever was before me said they wanted to talk, so I gambled and dropped my defenses—mostly. I opened my bag and withdrew my hunting knife, never letting my gaze wander from the black wolf who was waiting patiently for my response.

"You look like Hekla, but you're not, are you?"

You're half right. This is her body. We needed to borrow one, and she fit the best, the black wolf said.

"She's not a shoe," I growled, bristling at their strange admission. "She's my best friend. Now, who are you? A demon? A witch? Let her go, and face me yourself!" I was an average fighter at best, but my emotions were all over the place, scattered like dandelion seeds on the wind. I was terrified for her safety and furious that something had so casually used her body.

We're the wild blue yonder and the stars that guide your wander. We have no color and all colors. We hold the stage where the sun and moon perform their duties and duets. The wolf paced toward the edge of the cliff and stared over at me. *We are the Sky Gods.*

"Plural?" I blurted out, though it really wasn't the most pressing question I had.

The wolf looked up toward the diamond-peppered void. *There is far too much work to be done up there for one mind, Ragna. So many other planets... Let Us offer you proof.*

My mind was reeling, and I felt a headache bloom in my temples. My body had never been under such stress, and it was affecting my ability to think. I half wished that the arrival of such gods meant that I was going mad, but I feared I was still lucid.

There. Look, Ragna, the wolf announced, turning its head up and towards the right.

I followed its gaze to see a shooting star streak through the night sky. I grew wary when it didn't burn up in the atmosphere and came closer to our location. When it fell into the canyon, unexpectedly close, I started and yelped. My eyes flickered over to the black wolf in fear. That was such a casual show of power. What else was it capable of doing?

Come with Us.

The Sky Gods went straight to a game trail we hadn't noticed before and guided me down to the bottom of the canyon. We walked along a stream, and the rocks beneath my feet dug painfully into my heels. I needed to build some calluses as soon as possible. I'd probably forgo my boots in the future unless absolutely necessary.

We stopped by a modest crater where a small, dark-brown rock nested. *Take it,* the gods prompted. *It's not hot.*

I crouched and poked the rock. It was barely warm, so I picked it up to scrutinize. When I gave it a perfunctory sniff, the gods laughed, startling me.

That is a lunar meteorite, They said. *Also known as a lunaite.* I gasped and nearly dropped it. This was a piece of the Moon Goddess?

"I sh-shouldn't have this!" I stammered, now holding the rock like it was the most fragile object in the world. "This is a part of the Moon Goddess! It's not mine to take or yours to give!"

I stared wide-eyed into my best friend's silver eyes. Would I be punished for this? I wasn't sure if Trail or I could handle much more punishment.

Unfortunately, the gods replied, *the Moon Goddess is not around to give Her consent.*

"What do you mean?" I asked with a confused frown. I pointed up at the sky, toward the gibbous moon. "She's right there."

Do you not think the moon looks different tonight, pup? the gods inquired patiently. I furrowed my brows and studied the moon a second time. The longer I looked at it, the heavier my dread became. It certainly didn't seem as bright as normal and had a bit of a dull orange tint to it, almost like it was dirty. I shivered and wondered if I would have noticed if the last several days hadn't been so life-altering.

"It... almost looks sick," I noted in a quiet voice, then worried at my lower lip and looked down at the rock in my hand. Would this rock have looked different days ago?

She's missing, the gods said, and I almost dropped my knife.

"What do you mean?" I stepped closer to Them. "How could She be missing?"

A breeze blew through the canyon and ripped another shiver from my tired body. I placed my pack on the ground and dressed, no longer able to tolerate the cold with Trail being so drained. Then I sheathed my knife and slid the scabbard through my belt. I'd almost dropped it a minute ago, and losing a toe was the very last thing I needed.

We saw the commotion in your pack and grew concerned. When We went to check on Her, Her domain was in shambles, especially Her workspace. We think someone took Her when She was in the middle of sorting out your mate bond. There's no way She'd pair up one wolf to every unmated male in the world, the Sky Gods said. I swallowed hard, and cold sweat beaded my skin. The dual revelation was staggering. This wasn't my fault, but how could a goddess just disappear?

"E-e-every male? In th-the w-world?" My body trembled as the shock settled into my chilled muscles. "I f-figured the pack and the rogues were... no... Maybe I knew. I just can't. I can't process..." I stared into nothing as my heart slammed against my rib cage. I let out a quivering breath and grazed my face with icy fingertips. "This can't be real."

You need to hunt Her kidnappers, Ragna. You're the last one She was working on. Your soul's scent may still linger on Her. Combined with that lunaite, you may be able to track Her, They bade.

I was almost afraid to ask, but I did it anyway. "Do you think, if I found Her, She could fix the mate bonds?"

Of course. We have no doubt She will. She'd be aghast at the state of things. All you pups, Her children, are in trouble.

"Wh-where would I even start? I'm in danger all the time. I was r-raped tonight!" I gritted my teeth, willing my tear ducts to hold fast. I detested saying it. The words were vile on my tongue. Saying it made it so much more real. If it'd stayed in my head, perhaps I could've pretended it was a nightmare.

And We're sorry We couldn't get Hekla there in time, the gods responded.

I couldn't tell if They were actually sorry, such was Their even tone, but I would accept the apology. Now that Trail and I were alone, I'd take anything anyone was willing to give me, no questions asked.

You start by asking questions. Go to the witches, the fae... In the meantime, We'll help protect you. Do you, Ragna, accept a blessing from the Sky Gods?

"Yes!" I blurted, desperate for any boon. "I accept."

The gods stared, motionless, but I knew They'd begun some process that seeped into me. A cold chill first settled in my bones. I shivered miserably, and no matter how close I pulled my jacket, I couldn't muster a hint of body heat. I sat and pulled my legs up against my chest, trying to fight the invasion. It was like frost was forming in the marrow of my bones. I was cold. I was so cold. My skin prickled, and I was swathed in goose bumps. A minute later, the ice thawed, and the night air warmed. I shuddered the rime off like snow, sighed, and rubbed my arms. "What was that?"

The sky is a cold place, They explained. *Stay out of direct moonlight at night, pup, and you'll be invisible. This is Our gift to you. Use it to rest and recover. Many hunt at night.*

I breathed out a long sigh and felt a weight drop from my shoulders. "I can't tell you what this means to me." I lowered my head in homage, gratitude pouring out of my heart in waves.

Yes, We heard you were afraid of the dark, They said wryly. I pressed my lips together, not sure if I was feeling the urge to laugh or protest. *We must go now, but We will get Hekla home safe. We will find and consult with the Sun God. Starlight preserve you, Ragna. We will meet again.*

I stared after Hekla's retreat into the darkness and slowly brought a finger to rub an aching temple. There were likely a million more questions I could've asked, but my brain had stopped functioning at some point. I winced, suspecting I was going to regret not being more present throughout the encounter.

First, though, I needed to sleep. Come morning, I'd have to begin my search for the Moon Goddess.

King Zorian: Five years later

"What do you mean you lost her again?" I gritted out between my teeth, my voice dripping with rage. These were the best in my kingdom? Were the gods having a laugh?

The captain maintained a straight face. "We've been tracking her, but every time we catch up, she disappears like a ghost. We can smell her, but she's not there! It's like she abandons her scent and runs off. Her previous alpha had no explanation for us," the male reported.

"Except she's not a ghost, Captain Rudi," I growled, leaning forward from my throne. "She's a wolf. How can one young she-wolf evade an entire squad of lycans? It's been over four fucking years of searching! Do you not understand how dangerous she is? What a threat she poses?"

The captain took in a breath and held it. I could see his jaw working as he tried to formulate a response that wouldn't get him killed. "We understand the weight of our task, Your Majesty."

"Do you, though? Because it seems to me that if you did, you'd have secured her the first time you caught her scent," I seethed. "Tell me, Captain, how much power does one mate hold over another? Humor me." I placed my elbow on an armrest and rested my chin on a fist.

"A significant amount, Your Highness."

"Explicate," I ordered.

The male cleared his throat nervously. "Their death could permanently weaken their mate's will to live or kill them outright. A mate would normally do anything for their other half, so they would be a prime target for hostage situations. Mates are very territorial, so sharing is impossible. We saw that report from her original pack. It's lucky that no one was killed."

"So, you understand that this person is the exposed jugular of every single unmated in our kingdom. Every lord, every officer, every alpha. Every single person of power. If she falls into the wrong hands, it could mean mass death and destruction. She is a disaster waiting to happen!" I roared, and my voice echoed throughout the chamber.

"Yes, Your Majesty," the captain acknowledged with a flinch.

"So, what is your next strategy, Captain?" I tapped the fingers of my other hand against the armrest, scowling at him. I was prepared for disappointment. This team had been disappointing me for far too long.

He swallowed. "We have not discussed one yet, Your Majesty."

"Rudesind!" I barked.

My grand beta and second-in-command came to my side. His jaw was set, but there was a flicker of concern in his brown gaze. He knew me. We'd grown up together, and he saw that I was done. This absurd game was over now.

"Demote this male. While I am gone, I expect you to find me a better captain to lead that team," I growled and left my throne, boiling with anger. I stomped up to my study and yanked the door open, only to completely pull it off its hinges. I snarled and threw it into the hall, nearly hitting a maid with an armful of linens. She shrieked and retreated in the direction she'd come. Perhaps, long ago, I would've felt bad about that. My world was different now.

I flopped down into my chair and raked my hands through my hair.

You need a trim, my lycan said. *You'll never get a mate looking like a ragdoll.*

Shut the fuck up, Spine, I snapped. When we shifted, he was a terrifying lycan—a pale-furred half-wolf on two legs. His red gaze froze our enemies, and his claws rent them asunder. Worse yet was his canine maw, a bone-crusher.

Little did our enemies know, he was also an immature asshole.

I flipped through the paperwork someone had placed on my desk, but I couldn't bring myself to read any of it. I was too irritated to focus.

"What did you mean when you said you'd be gone?" my beta's smooth voice said from the doorway. My gaze rolled up to see him studying the hinges where the door used to be. "Perhaps you're picking up a new door? Spruce things up a bit? Get it? That's a carpentry joke. However, I recommend ebony to match your charming disposition."

I snorted in response, bemused but not wanting to show it. If any other lycan had spoken to me like that, I'd have ripped off their good arm. I threw the paperwork off the desk, and the sheets fluttered to the stone floor. Rudesind raised an eyebrow and sat on the leather chair facing my desk, crossing an ankle over a knee.

"You know, I was just thinking that the maids didn't have enough to do around here," he quipped, eying the mess. He put a finger to his lips and stared at me. "So, where are you going?"

I leaned back in my chair and returned his stare. He was also the only one who could do that without me taking it as a challenge. "I'm going to get a scout to take me to her last-known location so I can find that young bitch myself."

His blond eyebrows shot up in surprise. "The Alpha of all Alphas, the great Lycan King, is dropping all his royal duties to go fetch a twenty-three-year-old she-wolf? Are you joking?" His face was incredulous, but I didn't give a shit.

"This twenty-three-year-old she-wolf has evaded my troops for years," I growled and crossed my arms over my chest. "Either our troops are incompetent, or someone is helping her. I'm not wasting another precious resource on this godsforsaken wolf hunt. It's been over four years!" I curled my upper lip in a snarl and closed my eyes to calm myself. "At the very least, it's making me look incompetent. Our people are waiting for results!"

"Oh, so is that what it is? You're throwing your duties away because your pride is hurt?" he said with a scoff, and I glowered.

"No. You watch yourself, Beta." His head lowered slightly in deference, and I felt a pinch of regret using my dominance against my best friend like that. I sighed. "If no one can do it, I'll have to do it myself! You know it's not just an innocent little she-wolf. She's a situation that must be controlled!"

Rudesind rubbed at his temples. "Ok, so let's say you do find her. What then?"

"We kill her," I said in a flat voice. My beta jolted in his seat.

"What? Why? I mean, imprison her at the most!" he protested, leaning forward and gripping the armrests.

"You and I have killed for less, Rude. She's too dangerous."

"It just doesn't seem like the punishment fits the crime," he rebutted. "There's a large number of individuals from her old pack that swear this wasn't an intentional act."

"Intentions don't matter here, Rude!" I snapped. "What matters is protecting my fucking kingdom—my people! The longer she stays alive, the more likely it is others will die because of her. This is about minimizing the damage."

"And what happens when you meet her, and the bond grows between you? You know she's as much your mate as mine. Wouldn't you be putting yourself in danger spending time with her?" he yelled back at me. "What would happen to you if you get attached and you kill her anyway?"

"A half-baked mate bond will not take down the Lycan King," I snarled, glaring at him for thinking such an absurd notion. Rudesind looked astounded.

"King or beggar. In the end, Zorian, you're just a male, a walking cock."

"Oh please, I have plenty of self-control."

He burst into laughter, his face completely baffled. "You know alphas have less control regarding their mates than anyone else. You're all emotional and hormonal as fuck. You're going to do something you'll regret," he said, becoming less irate and more petulant. He'd accepted that I was not changing my mind. "This is a terrible idea, Zorian. That's where I stand on the issue. Don't do this."

"You know when your mate dies, the Moon Goddess, in Her eternal compassion, may grant you another. Don't you want a second-chance mate?" I asked him quietly, tilting my head. This was what everyone else seemed to want.

He looked away, shut his eyes tight, and pinched the bridge of his nose. "That's not fair, Zorian. I don't want my love life to come at the cost of an actual life."

"Well, you may change your mind someday, and I don't think the masses are wanting to wait." I stood up and walked around my desk to place a hand on his shoulder. "I'm the one willing to make the sacrifice, Rude. This is for our people. She is a mistake. She's the moon's mistake. Don't humanize her. That'll make it harder for you."

I stopped at the doorway and turned back to watch him put his head in his hands. "Assign coverage for my daily work and make sure my departure is need-to-know only. I shouldn't be gone long."

I left my office to go pack. It was time to take matters into my own claws.

Chapter 5

Ragna

I flopped in exhaustion onto the cold ground by a tree and stared up at the stars twinkling through the swaying branches. I wondered if the Sky Gods were watching. Closing my eyes, I put a hand to my heaving chest and tried to catch my breath after escaping the moonlight. I had strayed a little too far from the tree line tonight.

That was a close one, Trail muttered. *We should have waited to get water.*

I just thought that since most of the troops had left, it'd be safer, I explained in dismay.

Well, it was Muttons they'd left behind, she retorted, and I clapped a hand over my mouth to hold in a laugh. She'd been the one to give the soldier that nickname.

Did you see that look on his face when we poked him from the shade? I asked, my shoulders shaking with suppressed laughter. *I've never seen a male move like a startled chipmunk.*

Next time, you should poke him in the cock. I want to know what he's packing.

I grimaced. *Ew, no, Trail. Gross. I'd be happy if I never touched a cock in my life.*

Ooh! Before that, we should put a sign up in the woods that reads, "Warning: Randy Ghosts," she added, ignoring my protest. I kept my hand clamped over my mouth, terrified that Muttons would hear me chuckling from wherever he was.

I think we're aging the poor bastard, I mused. *His mutton chops have grown quite grey over the last two years. I'm concerned we're going to give him a heart attack someday.*

I should think he'd be grateful. She-wolves like salt and pepper.

I snorted quietly and opened my pack, looking for the rations I'd managed to steal from our unwanted guests. I bit into the cured meat and closed my eyes in bliss. I missed seasoning. Compared to the bland foods of the wilderness, the strips were bursting with flavor.

Let's switch so we can get some distance. I think I heard a river a couple of miles east. We'll get good and muddy and follow the river, then find a place to sleep. I'm bone tired. Pups and at 'em! Trail prodded.

One thing I appreciated about Trail was that she wasn't a procrastinator. I probably relied too much on her to get my butt going sometimes.

I finished my snack, secured my pack, and shifted into my wolf form. Trail took off as fast as she could but sacrificed speed for stealth whenever we got spooked. As long as we stayed out of the moonlight at night, we were safe. I'd lost count of how many times that had saved our lives and my virginity.

The last five years had been a disaster, and I desperately hoped there would be a change in our luck soon. With all the obstacles, I was terrified we'd never make progress in our search for the Moon Goddess. It was one thing to avoid pack territories and rogues but another thing entirely to elude the soldiers who showed up one day to hunt us. We'd done the best we could to dodge them, but for some reason, someone had put a price on our heads. Whatever their aim was, it was serious. They had been chasing us for over four years; it seemed like an obsession—like they thought we were mass murderers or terrorists.

This is going to put us back yet another day. I sighed. *We're never going to reach the Lunar Coven at this rate.*

I don't know, Ragna, Trail said thoughtfully. *I mean, the soldiers have finally left—except for Muttons, obviously. Maybe the next time he gets close, we can tie him up?*

And leave him for wild animals or rogues to attack? You know I don't have the heart to do something like that, Trail.

I think you're going to have to toughen up, Ragnu. Who's to say these people won't end up killing us?

Maybe my innocence is all I have left! I snapped, losing all control of my emotions. *We're suffering enough as it is. If I hate myself, then maybe I won't want to save myself the next time I end up at the edge of a cliff!*

Trail fell silent, and I knew I'd gone too far. I slipped back into our shared consciousness and blocked out everything. Hibernation was all I had to escape our cruel reality.

I peeked out hours later to find that we'd ended up by the edge of a river. Trail was asleep, so I couldn't see out her eyes unless I forced myself into control. I didn't like doing that, though, and Trail needed the rest. I used her ears to listen instead. Crickets, rushing water, and the occasional hoot of an owl seemed to be all that was out there. She must have done a good job rolling in the mud because our skin felt crusty and stifled.

I stayed awake for a while longer, listening for threats, but it seemed like we'd left Muttons far behind us. Poor Muttons. Didn't Mr. Muttons have a Mrs. Muttons and some Mutton pups back at home? What a sad existence to have to chase a female around the woods for years. I hoped he was at least getting paid well for all the trouble we gave him—not that he wasn't returning the favor.

⚜

Once dawn broke, Trail continued to follow the river until we spotted a rabbit.

Trail! I exclaimed. *Breakfast! Get it!*

Don't have to tell me twice, she said and stalked closer to it.

Just go, the wind's shifting! I urged her, and she darted after the rodent. *Crap, should've taken the pack off,* I lamented as the rabbit outmaneuvered her.

No, no, no, we got this, she replied frantically but almost fell over herself when the rabbit started and ran back toward us. Something huge lurched in the woods, a mass of white fur behind a tall thicket, and it nearly scared the pee out of Trail. She scrambled to snag the rabbit and kill it before we turned tail and ran.

What was that? I shrieked. *It made a bloody rabbit run toward us!*

It smelled like another lycan! she gasped.

How'd they find us so fast? Muttons needs to sleep, right?

That didn't smell like our friend, Mr. Muttons. It smelled stronger. It felt stronger—stronger than Alpha Erik! Didn't you feel that—that crushing dominant aura? I wanted to submit right then and there!

But there's no way an alpha would be out wandering the woods. It must be a rogue! I speculated.

Your dismissiveness is going to get us killed someday!

I sighed anxiously. *It's just wishful thinking! Adding an alpha to the mix... I'm scared. Let's get some distance from whatever that was. We're still covered in mud, so we just need to minimize the tracks we're leaving. Once it's safe, we'll stop, and you can eat. Just try to keep the fur intact this time. I want to make another mitten.*

Only if the mitten is for Muttons, Trail cackled nervously.

Why? Are you smitten with Muttons? I teased, trying to ignore my shot nerves. *Smitten like a kitten? Enough to give him a mitten?*

Hey, he's the only male around! I mean, we've basically been courting for years.

Oh, Trail, you reek of desperation.

Trail pushed herself hard for miles and plopped into the cool grass when she couldn't even maintain a lope. After she ate, I shifted into my human form and continued at a brisk pace. The mud had been flaking off and was nearly gone. I needed to add more soon.

I hear a waterfall, Trail informed me sleepily.

It only took me a couple of seconds to figure out where it was. I climbed up some boulders and squealed with joy when I found a small swimming hole fed by a modest waterfall. The mud around the ferns and weeds was plentiful, and the fresh, falling water meant I could take a quick bath first. I wanted to remove as much sweat as possible before reapplying the mud.

Shh! Trail admonished, and I winced.

Oh, oh! Sorry, I got too excited, I apologized bashfully. I took my pack off and looked into the clear water. *Think there are any critters in there? I don't want my bottom to get bitten by a fish.*

Well, that would be the most action we've gotten in—

Trail, stop... please.

I'm sorry...

I frowned, my good mood completely spoiled, and lowered myself into the cold water. Shuddering, I made my way over to the waterfall and rinsed as much of the mud off as I could. I longed for soap, but I'd run out of that ages ago.

I used an old rag I'd found years ago to scrub my skin until it was pink. Having to coat myself in mud or whatever detritus I could find made hygiene a struggle. All I could do was try to enjoy my bath before I'd have to crawl out and cover myself up again. I rinsed my hair the best I could and detangled it before finally allowing myself a moment to relax.

I leaned back and floated in the water for a while. It was a beautiful day with a royal-blue sky and white, fluffy clouds. I waved at the sky, wondering if the gods were hard at work. The moon was up there too, dull and silent.

"I don't want to leave," I whispered quietly to myself. "I'm so tired of running." My eyes stung with tears. "Where did you go, Moon Goddess? Why did you abandon me?" I said hoarsely to the moon. "I'm trying to find you... but everyone... I..." I stumbled out of the water, leaned against a sun-warmed boulder for comfort, and burst into tears.

King Borian

"At ease," I said to the bowing soldier when I approached him in the clearing. "What's your update?" My escort settled and opened his canteen to take a long draw from it. It took several days to get to this site, and I hoped to be back home in several more.

"I found her at the creek to the east after the troops went home. It was early in the night, and there was enough moonlight, but once she hit the tree line, I lost all visibility. She disappeared again. I suspect she headed west toward Lowell River. Looking at her previous locations, I believe she's trying to skirt around the Quarter Moon Pack territory."

I eyed the male as he handed me his map. "Name?" I asked. The lycan was probably in his middle years and had grown some rather bold sideburns.

"Olev, Your Majesty," he responded with a professional, straight face.

"Is nighttime the only time she magically disappears?" I asked dryly, looking at the route the soldiers had outlined on the map. He was right. It did look like she was trying to find a way around the territory.

"Yes, sir."

"So why can't you catch her during the daytime?" I inquired, raising an eyebrow and studying his face over the edge of the map. His lips pressed into a thin, grim line.

"She gains a lot of ground when we can't track her. Once she disappears at night, she works to thin out her scent and then tries to lose us over bodies of water. If we had an unmated male, they'd be able to scent her bet—"

"We cannot have unmated males on this hunt, Olev, because we cannot trust them to bring her back. You know this," I reminded with a scowl.

If Olev was about to point out that I was unmated, I would have gladly shoved his head up his ass. I glared at him, daring him to say something, and he lowered his gaze. I folded the map, looking in the direction she would have gone.

"Go home to your mate and pups, Olev. Take my escort with you. I'm taking over from here."

"I..." Olev began to say something but then quickly dropped it. "Yes, Your Majesty." He started walking back but paused and turned to face me. "I don't believe in ghosts, Your Majesty, but... please be careful." His eyes darted over to the woods, and he grimaced.

"Get the fuck out of here!" I growled, pointing in the direction of the castle. I stormed away from him. "Ghosts? Oh, for fuck's sake..."

The best of the best, Spine sniggered.

"I have to do everything my fucking self," I grumbled, heading toward the river. I loosened my backpack. "Spine, what do you say we catch up to this bitch?"

I removed my clothes and shifted into my lycan form. Spine stood tall and proud in the open field. He opened his arms wide and turned his wolf head into the woodland breeze.

Ooh, I needed a good stretch, Spine said, his furry tail swishing eagerly. *This wasn't a bad idea, Zorian! A nice break from signing papers all fucking day. Goddess, I'm tired of that shit.*

And a nice run in the wilderness. Won't need to worry about running into people begging for our attention every five minutes, I mused.

Only thing I need now is a fresh kill and lycan lady to warm our lap.

You are not to, under any circumstance, think about sex on this hunt. Is that clear?

It's almost as if you think I'm not a lycan, he replied, a smirk in his voice.

I'm not joking!

Let's get going.

I growled. He'd avoided answering me, and it pissed me off. He'd better not cause any problems. He knew what we were here for, and everything needed to be done nice and clean.

Spine ran into the woods where she was last spotted and caught her scent immediately. *Oh goddess, that is the most mouthwatering, delectable scent I've ever smelled!* he gushed, speeding up to follow the trail. *She smells like... It's like... all the good spices the cooks use in the fall. Cloves, nutmeg, oh, and hot apple cider. Oh goddess, if I could fuck a smell, I'd fuck this one right here!*

Gods almighty, what is wrong with you? Get a grip, Spine! I snapped, grateful only I could hear my lycan's embarrassing commentary.

I steeled myself, knowing full well that the scent was also driving me to distraction. I would never admit it, though, not in a million years. I'd known this would happen, and I was mentally prepared for the lure.

The smell is a lie, the smell is a lie, the smell is a lie.

Spine was almost in a frenzy to find her, and I counted that as worrisome but positive. It meant we'd get home sooner rather than later. I'd just have to make sure he didn't stop me from killing her. He'd been such a little baby about it the entire way here from the castle. This was the same lycan who'd slayed hundreds, if not thousands, on the battlefield. The same lycan who'd bathed in the blood of the fallen and danced on their corpses. He'd better not disappoint.

We got to the river in no time and followed it south as the smell grew stronger. There was an outcrop with mud and wolf hairs scattered below the rocky overhang, and Spine bent to investigate.

She must have slept here last night, I said. *Let's keep going. We're catching up.*

We followed a less potent trail since she appeared to have rolled in fresh mud, but there was no mistaking where she'd gone. A loud scuffle drew our attention, and Spine approached the commotion, creeping to hide behind a thicket. We watched a brown wolf chase after a rabbit, struggling to keep up with the turns due to the heavy backpack she was carrying. If my objective wasn't so grim, the whole scene would have been endearing and comical.

Mate... Spine said, swallowing hard. *Mine.*

No, stop that, Spine. We're here to kill her. Do not get attached.

Goddess, that's the prettiest little she-wolf I've ever seen in my life. It's like someone dusted her coat with cinnamon. I wonder if she tastes like apple pie. We should lick her.

Spine! There will be no licking! Is that clear? Under no circumstan—

Crap! Spine ducked and retreated.

What?

I think she noticed us!

We're here to kill her. It doesn't matter if she notices us! Go after her!

But I don't want to scare he—

OH MY FUCKING GODS, SPINE, JUST FOLLOW HER!

Spine pursued the she-wolf from the shadows, and I groaned, knowing that he was absolutely not going as fast as he could to overtake her. He stealthily followed her at an easy pace for miles until the wolf collapsed from fatigue, still blissfully unaware of our presence.

Aww, look, our little mate did catch the rabbit. Look, she's eating, Spine said with more affection in his tone than I cared for.

Who are you? I interrogated, but I was not expecting an answer. I didn't think he could even hear me. His eyes were riveted to the she-wolf who was scarfing down the rabbit like it was her last meal. Well, I suppose it would be. *Would you feel better if we killed her in her sleep so she won't have a chance to be scared?* I couldn't believe I was offering him an option.

Oh! She's shifting! Spine reported in a giddy voice.

I groaned. *Spine, she's a fake. She's a mistake. She's not our real mate, and she needs to die. How many times must I say this?* I turned my mind away from his vision, not wanting to look at her out of sheer stubbornness. My lycan might be a peeping, horny bastard, but I certainly wasn't. There was no point sitting and staring at a female that I was going to execute.

Hahahaha! Spine started laughing after a minute.

What? What's so funny?

Zorian, she's so your type. Bahahahaha! Oh goddess, you're so unbelievably fucked.

Spine?

Hahahaha... ha... What?

I really need you to shut the fuck up now. I was getting angrier by the second. Was everyone but me completely incompetent? We could have ended this by now. No, I was going to end it right now. I shifted back into my human form, only to discover that she'd disappeared.

Where'd she go? I asked Spine. *She was just here!*

Go sniff her out yourself. I ain't helping your dumb ass, Spine retorted.

I curled my lip up in a snarl, irritated to no end. I suppressed my dominance to keep my approach undetected, then I tightened my backpack and stalked around another outcrop, following that cursed scent.

The smell is a lie. The smell is a lie.

She'd clearly gone to the water source here. I could hear the small waterfall trickling merrily behind the boulders. I circumnavigated the site, staying behind trees and undergrowth to discover where she'd gone.

The smell is... a...

My canines lengthened, and I gritted my teeth so tight I wouldn't have been surprised if I'd cracked a molar. My claws elongated, and I dug them deep into a tree to steady myself. I was furious, my blood absolutely boiling. I could barely control my breathing, and I felt like my heart was going to burst out of my chest. I held back a deep, rumbling growl as my anger threatened to turn into something unacceptable.

Like I said. Spine's irritatingly smug voice pierced through my foggy mind. *You're so fucked.*

Chapter 6

King Zorian

I struggled to maintain my composure and sanity while watching the scene before me. The she-wolf bathed naked in the pool tucked behind a large outcrop. My vision tunneled as it raked over her body where she stood under the waterfall. She closed her eyes as she turned her face up to the water, running her long, delicate fingers through her waist-length hair. Her lips, albeit chapped, parted into a pleased smile.

Pulling an old rag from her backpack, she scrubbed at her skin until it flushed pink. I watched the rag slide over her neck and shoulders, and I tensed, involuntarily picturing how my mark would look on the soft flesh there. I dug my claws in deeper, shredding chunks of bark off the tree. I was instantly and uncomfortably erect.

The she-wolf arched to scrub her back, and I glowered. She deserved a hot bath with exotic oils and sea-salt scrubs, not that disgusting old rag. She deserved servants to bathe her, braid her hair, and clothe her in the finest silks. She deserved elegant cuisine, a soft bed, and a male at her side to either make love to or fuck wildly—whatever she craved in the moment.

She dragged the cloth down to her bosom, and I swallowed heavily, adjusting my position under the discomfort of my throbbing member. The rag tugged at her luscious, buttery breasts and blushing nipples. I was enthralled by how they bounced from her ministrations, and my cock twitched again. I wondered how those soft globes would feel in my palms.

She drew the cloth down to her belly, and I frowned again. She was too skinny in some areas. She needed to be fattened up, not abandoned to the luck of the hunt. My lip curled in irritation. She had exceptional childbearing hips, but I wanted to see more meat on her bones. I flushed, and my abdomen cramped with desire when my eyes fell on the cinnamon curls between her legs. I stared for a while, curious about how she'd taste and felt saliva build in my mouth. My eyes finally slid down to her slender legs. They looked strong, but they needed fattening up too. I wanted to feed her, damn it.

Laughter in my head roused me from my drunken inspection.

Who's the peeping, horny bastard now? my lycan ridiculed.

I clenched my teeth in fury, embarrassed about my lack of discipline. I was a fucking king! Falling prey to the mate pull was beneath me, especially the pull from a false mate—a mistake.

I am most certainly not peeping, I seethed, wishing for the hundredth time that I could rip my lycan's head right off his shoulders.

Oh please, spare me. Spine chuckled darkly, his voice dripping with disdain. *I can hear everything you're thinking loud and clear, Your Majesty.*

I'm— I began, but the she-wolf started talking quietly, and I froze, tuning my ears to listen.

"I don't want to leave," she was whispering. "I'm so tired of running. Where did you go, Moon Goddess? Why did you abandon me? I'm trying to find you… but everyone… I…"

She stumbled out of the pool and began to cry on a rock. She looked utterly defeated, and an emotion I refused to recognize flared up in my chest for just a moment.

What is she talking about? Why is she talking about finding the Moon Goddess? Spine wondered.

Our people have been crying about the Moon Goddess leaving us for years. Haven't you been paying attention at meetings?

Meetings are boring.

You were one of the first to notice the darkening of the moon, Spine. Don't play stupid.

Doesn't mean She's missing. Maybe She's depressed.

Whatever it is, this she-wolf may know more about what happened than we thought. I figured the claims of her innocence implied she was clueless. Maybe she's not so innocent after all.

That little treasure is as innocent as it gets, Spine snarled at me, and I blinked at his aggression. How the fuck would he know?

Well, if she doesn't know anything, I can just kill her, right? I said angrily and took a step forward to wrap up my bloody errand. I was unexpectedly hesitant, but I tried to hide that from my lycan. My legs froze as Spine forced partial control over me. He had never, ever pulled a stunt like that before.

SPINE! YOU ARE OUT OF LINE! I roared, unable to comprehend his defiance.

Let's just enjoy her presence a little longer. We're not in a rush, and she's not getting away from us. We're the fastest, biggest, baddest, strongest shit in the land.

What, you enjoy watching a female cry? I argued, utterly confounded. *We're just putting her out of her misery.*

I get to enjoy my beautiful mate's living, addictive scent, and you get a chance to get more information out of her. You can't pull knowledge out of a dead body, idiot.

I clenched my teeth again. *First of all, she's not our mate. Second, I know you're just buying time, lycan.*

No, I'm keeping you from doing something stupid, he bit right back at me. *All your blood is in your dick right now. Your brain is a fish out of water, human!*

I'll compromise, I growled. *I'll wait 'til nightfall, and if she doesn't say any more, I'll end her in her sleep. I'd say that's more than generous.*

Not good enough, he replied stubbornly.

I raked my hands through my hair. I couldn't believe my lycan was actively defying me. *Unbelievable. You're walking on thin ice, Spine,* I warned but settled down where she couldn't see or scent me.

The day passed by at an agonizingly slow pace. We watched her skin the rabbit and build a wooden frame with some sturdy branches and twine. She threaded the pelt and stretched it tight inside the frame but furrowed her brows in scrutiny.

"Wish we had some salt," she murmured quietly. A moment passed, and she spoke again. "Yeah, it is pretty salty. I guess we could try."

She must be talking to her wolf. We watched her rummage through her backpack and pull out some cured meat. Those looked like our soldiers' rations.

Oh look, she's a thief too, I pointed out with disgust.

Weren't you just begging for the chance to feed and fatten her up? Goddess, you're such a yo-yo.

I curled my lip but didn't deign to reply. We watched her rub the cured meat across the pelt, but she stopped and growled in frustration.

She has a sexy growl.

Shut up.

"Trail, I think I'm just ruining it." She sighed and set the frame against a boulder. She pulled a tiny book out of her backpack, took a peek, and shoved it right back in her bag. Ragna then pulled out a pair of panties and walked toward the pool.

Oh, thank goddess she's getting dressed, I thought to myself a little too loudly, and Spine snickered. She pulled the underwear on, but I paled when she slathered mud all over her smooth skin. No, no, no. I needed her to stop that immediately, but my gaze was frozen. I was rock hard again, and my hand twitched, wanting to grab my shaft. I furrowed my brows and drew on anger to wash away the lust. This bitch would not make me lose control. She was nothing. Cheap.

I suffered the rest of the afternoon watching her, enduring her nudity. She was letting her guard down too much. Had my soldiers really been this slow? Granted, I was a good tracker, but she shouldn't be this comfortable staying in one place for so long. It was also a watering hole, and there were bound to be rogues that frequented this location—unmated ones. Spine growled at the implication.

Night fell, and she picked up her bag and pelt frame. She walked toward a large tree and disappeared.

What just happened? Spine shouted, and I stood up slowly, trying to get a better vantage.

She literally disappeared. My soldiers weren't exaggerating. She must be using magic, I said in surprise. *She could be more dangerous than anticipated. Maybe she did do something to the Moon Goddess or the unmated males. Maybe she's conspiring with witches.*

I'm telling you, she's innocent, he snapped. *I just know.*

I ignored him, slipped some pants on, and crept to where she'd gone. I stayed low and downwind, listening intently. She was still there. I could hear both her heartbeat and breathing. The organs worked at a slow and steady pace, so she hadn't detected us. I decided to stay where I was until she fell asleep, which wasn't long. She must've been exhausted.

After I was certain she was slumbering, I walked toward the tree and followed her footsteps. Her scent—despite the mud—was getting stronger even though I still couldn't see her.

She's invisible, I muttered thoughtfully and looked for any depressions in the ground that gave away her position. When I came upon a patch of flattened leaf litter, I studied it.

There she is, Spine said in awe. *Our mate is remarkable, so fit to be our queen.*

I reached down slowly to look for her neck, but my hand found a mud-caked breast instead. I nearly hissed, then grimaced and yanked my hand away, causing Spine to erupt into laughter. I moved my hand higher to try to find her head so I could break her neck.

Spine stopped laughing.

Don't do it, he warned in a flat voice. I moved slower, trying hard not to wake her so she could die in peace. Could I really do this?

Don't do it. Spine began to growl, and he fought for control over my hands. I pulled out every ounce of willpower and dominance to regain control of my arms, but he fought me every step of the way.

DON'T DO IT! he roared as I broke through his hold.

Ragna

My body lurched out of sleep as Trail forced control over me. My mind reeled, and I struggled to orient my mind. She forced me into a run, screaming.

The lycan is in our camp! The lycan is in our camp! He went for our neck!

I took control back once I was fully awake and suppressed a screech of terror. Tears rolled down my cheeks because I knew, I just knew that this was the end. It didn't matter how fast or strong we were. We couldn't take on an alpha lycan.

I was only able to race through the woods for about thirty seconds before he tackled me. My forehead hit a tree root, stunning me. The smell of fresh wood shavings and almonds filled my lungs as I tried to blink away the blood that was trickling down my brow.

He... could see us? I asked Trail in a daze, and she didn't respond. All I could feel from her was defeat. She'd given up the fight. From the intense, pleasurable tingles spreading across my back, I could tell that he was unmated. That gave me only one option, but I feared it'd only offer me an extra minute of life. I was so dizzy that I didn't think I could stand even if he rolled off me. I opened my mouth and slowly mumbled, "I, Ragna Rhydderch, reject y—"

I was distracted and interrupted by his rumbling laughter that made my toes curl without my permission. "As if you have any say," the male sneered into my ear in a low voice. I struggled to breathe under his weight and tried to crawl away, but he gripped my hips and dragged me back under him.

His pelvis pressed hard into my butt for just a moment, and I whimpered. When I felt his ragged breath caress my neck, I cringed and begged my body not to respond. I pressed my thighs together, and he growled, stood, and yanked me up with him.

I was dragged forcibly into a clearing where he shoved me down into the grass. I cried out when my side hit a rock, sending white-hot pain into my chest. Had a rib broken? Tears dripped from my nose and chin as I tried to sit up and look at the male who was about to kill me.

He was colossal, and I nearly wet myself from fear. Muscles flexed and rippled across his hulking frame as he stared down at me like I was the most disgusting sight in the world. The white hair didn't match his age, which could've been anywhere from late twenties to early thirties. It was probably the color of his lycan. It fell to his chin, shone under the dim moonlight, and cast dark shadows over his menacing face. His deep-set burgundy eyes narrowed, and his handsome features were distorted into something ugly. His lips curled up in a sneer as he studied me, and I shivered under his examination.

"Do you know who I am, little Mistake?" he said in a quiet, threatening voice.

I shook my head and tried to silence my sobs. No matter how hard I gripped my arms, I couldn't stop shaking.

He stepped forward and leaned into my face, flashing his long canines. "I am King Zorian, king of the lycans and all you wolf-shifters."

Our king... My face paled and nausea threatened to empty my stomach. I placed a hand to my throbbing, bleeding head and fought off a wave of dizziness. I wanted to ask what he wanted, but the waves of dominance he was exuding kept me pinned to the dirt. Why did he come after me himself? Were the soldiers who had been chasing me his?

"Tell me, Mistake, what have you done to the unmated males?" he inquired and pulled back some of his dominance so I was able to respond.

"I d-d-didn't do anyth-thing," I answered between sobs. "I w-went with my f-f-friends on a r-run after I g-got my wolf, and..." A wail escaped my throat, and I dug my nails into my arm, desperately trying to control my shattered nerves. "And... all the males s-started fighting over m-me!" I closed my eyes tight, wishing he'd just kill me and get it over with. When I opened my eyes again, I found him staring at me. If he was who he said he was, he could tell if I was lying.

"And what about the Moon Goddess? What did you do to Her? Consort with witches? Are you part witch? What else can you do other than turn invisible? Answer me, Mistake," he snarled.

"I... You w-wouldn't believe me if I t-t-told you," I answered morosely, lowering my head in deeper submission.

"Try me," he growled. "If you don't give me an answer, your life is forfeit."

"Isn't it already?" I looked up at him. "You went for my neck. You t-tried to kill me in my—"

"ANSWER ME!" he spat, forcing me to reply with an alpha command.

I gulped and ducked my head lower. "After I was b-banished, the Sky Gods prevented a second r-r-r-rap—" I couldn't get the sentence out of me. It hurt too much to revisit. "The Sky Gods came to m-me and s-said someone kidnapped the Moon Goddess. They tasked me with finding Her and g-gave me the power to disappear at n-night if I stayed out of the moonlight. They wanted to p-protect me while I t-tried to find Her. I don't have any m-magic. I'm just a wolf." I was convulsing with how bad my shaking had become, and it took all my willpower to keep from having a full-blown panic attack. I was getting extremely tired, and the ground was beginning to tilt.

"Let's assume all that garbage is true. It's been five years, Mistake! Where's your progress?" he asked and began to pace slowly while watching me. His eyes flashed in the dark, and his fists clenched and unclenched.

"Any t-time I make progress, I'm chased away by rogues or these soldiers who keep hunting me!" I explained, digging my fingertips into the dirt to stop the world from spinning. "I can't rest or eat regularly, and w-winters are a s-struggle."

He frowned deeply and studied me. I could almost see his rage. It was practically radiating off his scarred chest and shoulders. Why was he so mad at me? "Th-the Sky Gods s-said They'd t-talk to the Sun G-God and come back to me, but They h-haven't yet..." I gave him everything I had so he could just end my misery. I wiped blood from my eyelid and sniffed.

It was several long moments before he responded. The silence was utter torture, more so than my swirling and pounding head.

"Under my authority as the Lycan King, I am taking you into custody for interrogation at the capital. You are now my prisoner." The great lycan male reached into his bag and pulled out a collar and chain. I whimpered and scooted backwards without thinking, but he growled a warning. I froze, and he approached to slip the collar over my head. I felt something bite into my skin, and I yelped in pain.

"Stop moving. There's hardly any silver in this," he hissed and snatched my wrists with a hand so he could tighten the restraint with the other.

I cringed and tried to create some space between the collar and my skin to ease the searing. It was so painful. I'd never felt silver before, and it was much worse than I'd imagined.

A thought occurred to me when he turned to leave. "P-please... c-can I g-get my backpack? My g-grandfather's bow... I c-can't leave it. Please," I begged. Everything in that bag was all I had left in the world. If there was a chance I could survive this, I needed those things. Most of all, I had to retrieve the lunaite.

"You're in no position to make demands." He scoffed. "A mistake needs nothing."

"Please!" I pleaded and prostrated myself before his feet. "I'll do anything you want! Please, I need my bag. Please, please, please, please! It's all I have left of my f-family!"

I could feel his stare on the back of my neck while I submitted. I leaned and pressed my injured forehead into the dirt, wincing in pain. Should I roll onto my back, or would that look stupid? I squeezed my eyes tight, praying through my teeth to any god who was listening. The silence dragged on for several more minutes, but it felt like hours.

"And if I asked you to get on your hands and knees?" his voice asked coldly. I grimaced and felt a flare of rage, then fear. It mixed with humiliation and nearly resulted in a nervous breakdown. I joined Trail in her defeat, held back a sob, and caved. It'd only been a matter of time, hadn't it?

"Then I'll s-spread m-my legs, Y-Your Majesty," I whispered hoarsely, and the frigid chill of misery seeped into my bones. "Please... please..."

He was quiet for another moment, and then I felt a yank on my collar.

"Let's go," he ordered quietly.

I tried to get to my feet, but the world tilted one last time and went dark.

Chapter 7

King Zorian

The lead attached to her collar tugged, and I heard my prisoner hit the ground. I turned to see her sprawled across the turf and crouched to investigate.

She's unconscious. What the fuck did you do to her? Spine demanded.

You should be grateful I decided to prolong her life, I countered and patted her cheek to try to wake her. I ignored the pleasant tingles when our skin met and focused on the problem. She had a large gash on her forehead. It was possible she'd been concussed when I tackled her during her invisible retreat. I couldn't be sure.

She needs rest, Spine decided.

She needs nothing.

She needs her bag, he insisted, growling. *You said you'd get it.*

I said nothing of the sort, I snapped. *But if you're so concerned about it, you do it. You can carry her too.* I stripped my pants off and shifted into my lycan form. I watched Spine worry over the she-wolf until he eventually picked her up and went to retrieve her backpack. He laid her down gently on some soft grass and removed the rabbit pelt from the frame. He rolled it up and removed a shirt and pants to make room in the bag. When he began to dress her, I grew irritated at his doting.

What are you doing? Let's head back.

Our mate is going to get cold, he said, becoming aggressive again.

She's not our mate. She's nothing.

Spine put both backpacks on and cradled the she-wolf in his arms before making the long trip back to the castle. He reveled in the tingling sensations, while I merely tolerated it.

Answer me this, Zorian. Why'd you demand sex from her when she said she'd do anything? You keep insisting on not getting attached, Spine said in a flat voice.

Oh, I think he knew exactly why, and he just wanted to hear me say it. I would not give him the satisfaction of squeezing it out of me.

What? You were very vocal about it earlier. Can't you easily control your unmanageable alpha urges? Can't you restrain yourself? he persisted, poking at a very sore spot. *I thought you were above the pull of the mate bond—the very fake mate bond.*

I stayed silent, wishing that there was an effective way of punishing him. I would not discuss my fears of an ambush before getting her behind bars. He knew as well as I what could happen, and yet he prodded at fucking everything.

I suppose you're just that magnanimous, offering your royal cock to females you're not attracted to. How very gener—

We are king, Spine! I snapped, letting my anger get the best of me. *We can fuck whoever we want, whenever we wish.*

Spine snorted in disagreement, calling my bullshit, and that only fueled my rage.

If I feel the urge, I don't need to masturbate when there are females to relieve me. Believe me when I say I can very easily fuck a female without getting emotionally attached! She's lucky I let her live and gave her the option.

I didn't know what I was saying anymore. Spine knew how to push my buttons, and he was doing it with abandon.

You gave her no such option. You made her choose between her only familial possessions and sex. And you think I'm the beast? Don't get me wrong, I'd love for you to fuck her for us, but at least I can be honest about why.

We're done discussing this, I said in a cold voice.

For now.

We traveled in silence for most of the day, and Spine spent much of it looking down at the she-wolf he was carrying. It meant I was forced to look at her too unless I turned away and crawled back into the recesses of my mind.

All I could do was stay angry. I had a duty to my people, and I needed to sort out the best way to serve them. If what the little female said was true, I needed a hell of a lot more proof and a place to start. Obviously fixing the mate bond catastrophe was more beneficial to my people than subjecting them to second-chance mates by killing her. It was a rare enough blessing as it was, and who knew if the Moon Goddess could even provide that. Already my people were suffering from bad morale. Many had saved themselves for their fated mates, and now they believed it was all for nothing. They deserved better.

Night fell, and we decided to eat and rest. I secured the chain attached to the wolf's collar, but I wasn't concerned about her escaping if she woke. I could find her easily. I would derive great pleasure from returning with her after my soldiers had fumbled for years. I would have to review how they were being trained—their performance had been an embarrassment.

⁂

Spine and I woke to the sound of crunching. We spied the she-wolf chewing on a bar, the morning sun highlighting bits of copper in her cinnamon-brown hair.

Mate's awake! Pretty... Spine said eagerly.

She's not our mate, and she's a total mess, I grumbled.

My lycan jumped up and moved to hug her, but I shifted into my human form to prevent that. She was startled and prostrated herself before me as if expecting punishment, shaking like a leaf with her food abandoned in the dirt. I frowned at her while I turned to rummage through my bag for a pair of pants.

"Symptoms," I barked.

"I-I'm better, Your Majesty."

"Then you can walk and carry your bag," I replied flatly. "I've confiscated your hunting knife and bow until further notice." I picked up my backpack and slung it on without waiting to see her reaction.

She shouldered her bag, picked up her bar, and blew the dirt off it. She should be eating more than that and certainly not food that'd touched the ground. She deserved bet—

I shook my head in irritation and tugged on her chain to get her walking. She cried out in pain and grabbed her side. I decided not to yank the chain again. I didn't need her fainting on me. That was the real reason. My lycan snorted.

By late afternoon, Spine and I noticed movement off the trail that suggested stalkers. They scented like rogues, thick with exile's wild smell. I looked back to the female to see if she'd noticed their sloppy hiding attempts, but I couldn't tell. She looked just as tired and distressed as earlier. I led her to a decent safe spot, a fallen tree by an outcrop, and leaned close to her.

"You are not to move. If you leave, I will find you immediately, and you will be punished. Is that understood?"

Her eyes widened, her face paled, and she nodded. She squeezed herself back so she could crouch between the sheltering branches and rock wall.

I stepped away and called out into the woods. "I know you're there. Let's not waste each other's time. I have things to do, so just attack already!" I thundered.

A long moment passed before seven wolves and a lycan approached from their hiding places, growling. There were no introductions as the criminals surrounded me, somehow thinking they had a chance. Perhaps there was some madness here. Their dark eyes held little depth, and their drool was foamy.

I didn't bother with talking or shifting. I just dove headfirst into combat. The air was alive with snarls, yelps, and blood splatters. I tore through the assailants, slashing and breaking necks. It had been too long since I'd fought real foes, and I welcomed the familiar rush. The bloodlust pumped through my veins, bringing with it the high that only came from battle.

The rogues got in a swipe or two, but I savored the pain. This was what made me feel alive, truly alive. I grinned and spun, ripping through the throat of the lucky wolf who managed to graze my lower back. I kicked a wolf away while I slashed into the lycan, slowing him down until I could reach his neck. He was dead in an instant.

A wild laugh burst through my lips as I dashed toward the last two wolves. They turned and tried to run, but I dispatched them with a few well-placed strikes. I let out another laugh and howled at the top of my lungs, reveling in victory as my body hummed and pulsed with the adrenaline.

I turned and marched back toward the female, letting out a feral snarl. I saw her sitting among the dead rogues, and my libido exploded when I realized she was trying to hide the scent of her arousal with their dead carcasses. The adrenaline from the battle instantly changed places with a different chemical.

I couldn't remember my plan. I couldn't think, and I didn't care. I was taken over by a primal instinct that blinded me with its intensity. I wasn't sure who I was other than the most dominant alpha. I wasn't sure who the female was other than a needy she-wolf. I only knew that I didn't have the fight to ignore the call, and I needed her on all fours immediately.

Ragna

When King Zorian led me over to a nook created by an outcrop and a fallen tree, I tucked myself away as much as possible in hopes the rogues would overlook my hiding place.

The king walked out and shouted a challenge to our stalkers, and I winced.

Great goddess, look at those back muscles, Trail murmured in appreciation.

Trail! You're awake! I've been so worried. I hugged myself, sighing in relief.

I'm sorry. I tried to take the blunt of that blow to our head. It took me a while to heal, and I was extremely tired.

I love you so much, Trail. Thank you. You saved—

My conversation with her was interrupted by the sight of eight rogues converging on the king. My heart skipped in fear for just a second before I remembered that this was the Lycan King. I'd heard stories about his accomplishments and battle prowess, so I shouldn't have been nervous... But I was still nervous.

When he started grinning and laughing, I was taken off guard by how attractive he was, and I became very uncomfortable between my legs. It was like how other unmated males had affected me but... much stronger. I was unprepared for it. My abdomen cramped and fluttered while the intimate flesh between my legs throbbed with heat. I shuddered and tried to calm myself somehow before he was done fighting. I didn't need the embarrassment, and I didn't want to give him even more power over me.

It's too bad he's so grumpy all the time. Trail sighed. *He's thrilling... The most beautiful male in the world when he's not scowling. Look at those dimples.*

I don't know why he's so angry with us, I remarked sadly. *Why the strongest shifter in the region came to kill or retrieve us, I don't know.*

All I know is that if I had a choice, I'd pick this one, Trail said with a husky voice. *He could protect us the best. He really provokes my instincts. I don't remember the last time we've been so turned on.*

I didn't feel very protected when he tackled me...

I stared at his flexing muscles and dance-like movements. He was graceful but barbaric, and the resulting combination was captivating. He didn't even flinch when a rogue managed to slash him—he just laughed. This wasn't a battle; this was a game, and he did it all without shifting into his lycan form. I squirmed with arousal, and it mixed poorly with my anxiety.

He's almost done, I noted worriedly. *I need to hide my scent, Trail. He's going to smell my response.*

Try sitting by that dead lycan. It smells something fierce.

I dashed out to the dead body while his back was turned and knelt by the lycan with my thighs shut tight. I tried to calm my breathing and make it look like I was just waiting here for him to finish. Surely, he wouldn't punish me for coming back proactively.

He executed the last two wolves and whirled with a snarl. When his eyes locked on mine, his pupils dilated until his irises became a sliver of red.

Uh-oh, Trail mumbled as the king stalked toward me. *He doesn't look mad, but I think his bloodlust turned into lust-lust. Don't run, Ragna.*

I shook at the sight of his wild-eyed advance and flaring nostrils. He could smell me. I lowered my head, hoping that if I averted my eyes, he'd ignore me, and we'd keep walking.

"Submit and present, female," he growled, leaving no room for argument. I'd already agreed, but my heart sank. His voice seemed different, wilder. When a wave of his dominance washed over me, I whimpered in defeat.

Good luck, Ragna, Trail said fearfully. *I'll heal you when it's over.*

I turned away from him so he wouldn't see the tears brimming in my eyes. I'd tried so hard to save myself for my fated mate, and I was heartbroken to have my innocence taken like this—by a male I didn't know. With an audience of dead bodies.

I undid my pants, slid them off, and knelt on the softest undergrowth I could find. I closed my eyes as I leaned forward to support myself with my hands and knees. My heart was pounding almost painfully in my chest, and I clenched my jaw tight, waiting for his approach.

At the sound of a belt unbuckling and hitting the forest floor, I spread my legs a little bit and tensed. His chest rumbled low in approval, surprising me a little, and gripped my hips hard with his hands. With his strength, I was terrified he'd hurt me. I'd just watched him tear apart an entire group of rogues.

His left grip tightened when his right hand slid over my bottom to my folds. I heard his breath catch when his fingers found me ready. I jerked unintentionally from the tingling mate touch hitting my sensitive flesh, and he snarled at my sudden motion.

He wasted no time. He dipped a finger between my folds and slid it inside me. I bit my lip, remembering the sensation I'd experienced before when those other rogues had raped me. I tried not to think of them and forced my eyes open to keep myself in the present. As much as I loathed to have to pick, I'd rather be in the present with the king.

Don't think of them, don't think of them, don't think of them.

He added another finger and pushed in deeper. I whined through gritted teeth, wishing he'd get it over with already. What was he doing? This was humiliating and uncomfortable.

He curled his fingers and removed them from me. I heard the slick sound of his fingers sliding up and down his cock before he lined the tip against my entrance. I held my breath as he parted my folds and pressed against me. My body resisted him, and I tensed even more, but then I realized that he wouldn't fit. I wasn't big enough. There was no way he could get inside me! I relaxed and nearly laughed in relief, but he jerked my hips back while slamming his forward to impale me.

I screeched and scrabbled at the ground to get away from the pain. Had he cut me? He roared at my disobedience and dug his fingers into my hips, elongating his claws in a threat.

He pulled hard on me again and slammed his hips flush against my butt, bottoming out inside me. I cried out again, sobbing from the sharp pain. It burned, it stung, and it stretched well past the point of discomfort.

He pulled himself out almost all the way and rammed back down into me. I narrowed my eyes, unwilling to close them and return to other memories. Tears ran freely down my face, and I braced myself for his next onslaught. He pulled out quicker and pushed back in immediately, grunting in approval.

His pace sped up until he was pumping into me like a starved male. I held on to the ground for dear life as every rapid, forceful thrust threatened to make me lose my balance. I jolted and jerked, but all I could do was cry and mourn the loss of my innocence. The air was full of the sounds of his pelvis and sack slapping against me, the squelching of my juices, and his rhythmic grunting.

He accelerated and snarled breathlessly, pushing my shoulders down until my upper body was flush against the ground. I coughed into the dirt and shifted my grip on the ground to keep from sliding forward.

When would he finish? Whatever hadn't been hurt initially was starting to get rubbed raw. I wished I could shut out the pain. The pleasant, sparking tingles from his touch hardly dampened it.

I could feel him tightening in his feral frenzy. He punctuated his last two thrusts with guttural growls before releasing a howl of ecstasy. He pulled out, and I saw him spill his seed onto the grass next to me. I collapsed from exhaustion, my body unable to hold me up without his grip. Ropes of cum poured from his cock as he fisted his length, pumping out the last of his desire. Sweat streamed down both our bodies, and our warm breaths came in foggy puffs as the day cooled.

He shook his head like he was trying to clear it and blinked hard several times. As he caught his breath, he froze and brought his bloodied hand to his face. I'd bled all over his cock, and he hadn't noticed. Had he also not noticed me screaming and crying? He scowled, staring at the crimson that had stained his grip. He glowered at me, looking slightly paler than normal.

"You were a virgin," he stated coldly. Though there was a slight waver in his voice, it wasn't a question, and I averted my eyes because his gaze was too intense. I didn't want to talk to him. I didn't want to talk at all. I felt ruined. I felt dirty. I felt empty. I stared at a little ant making its way across a leaf. I bet it was still a virgin. Go home, ant. It's getting cold out here.

The king stood and grabbed a cloth from his bag. He poured water from his canteen over it and wiped the blood off him. He then put his pants back on and threw mine at me. I caught them and struggled to stand. My hip joints were stiff, my knees were scratched, and my thighs were shaking. Worst of all was the pain between my legs. I desperately wished for a cloth and some ice, but even if I had those things, I'd be afraid to see what I looked like down there. I was scared to know the truth.

Hi, Ragna, Trail's soft voice said soothingly. *I've got you now. I'll take care of you. I'll start healing...*

Chapter 8

King Borian

I wanted nothing more than to spend my seed into the female before me, the one who was meant to be mine, but a clawing in the back of my mind warned me of something. My instincts skirmished with whatever self-control my brain was trying to exert. The conflict jarred me enough to act as a brutal reminder.

Just in time, as the warm, tingling flood of my climax swept through me, I angrily forced myself out of her to release onto the grass. My roaring cry carried both satisfaction and deep frustration. The air was not as warm as her, and it did not hold me the way she did. I loathed having to pull out, and it'd taken all my remaining control to make sure I had. My body was still disappointed.

I knelt to catch my breath and process the flurry of emotions bludgeoning me. I had an excruciatingly hard time shaking the feral fog this time. I hadn't anticipated it being that intractable; it'd never been that bad. It had been years since I last fought, and I'd forgotten the impact battle had on my other instincts when there was an unmated female nearby.

Following so much death was the insatiable urge to create more life, and our last war had left our population wanting. As a virile alpha, that urge was nearly impossible for me to resist. I'd resisted before, but...

As the haze of my post-battle mating frenzy was fading, my mind slowly returned to me. By the heartbeat, I became more grateful I'd retained enough clarity to pull out of her. The fated mate response had been stronger than I'd ever imagined. Just remembering it was enough to make my head spin.

Despite the haze, I remembered every second of taking her. She'd behaved for the most part, and my feral mind had been more than pleased. Despite my desire to fatten her up a bit, her body was exquisite—by far the most pleasing I've ever enjoyed, including what had become available to me once I'd become king.

She'd been tight, and it worked well with her buttery soft walls and readiness. Her sex had been dripping. I couldn't hold back any of my sounds when I saw how it wept down her thighs. If this was the fated mate response, I could see why it was so coveted. It was like she was made for my cock.

I blinked again. What was I thinking?

I removed my hand from my length, and my eyes caught on a discoloration. I scented it immediately, but I still raised it to my face to get a better look. Blood. Her blood. I glanced down to my cock and saw that it was also painted in blood.

Fear flooded me when I realized I'd brutally taken a virgin. I felt the blood drain from my face, and a chill swept over me. How badly had I hurt her? I was horrified.

Oh, is your conscience working again? Spine asked flatly, coming back from our haze. The fact that he hadn't been sarcastic meant he was livid. *Congratulations on raping a female, not to mention a virgin. Guess it must be the king in you to demand a virgin sacrifice.*

I grew mad at myself but then allowed rage to replace everything, including my fears. I would not give in to Spine. I would not back down from my stance. I would remain distant. I would put my people first. She was a prisoner, and I'd either use her to find the goddess or kill her.

I redirected my rage to the she-wolf for not warning me that she'd been untouched. Perhaps she'd planned on using a guilt trip to feel some sense of power over me.

You must be constipated because you're so full of shit, Spine snarled.

I scowled at the injured female who was staring at me with large, frightened… green eyes. I hadn't noticed they were green. They were the green of ferns after a gentle misting on a foggy day. A glowing green so vibrant, so full of life, and yet her eyes seemed so dead insi—

"You were a virgin," I said as coldly as possible.

I harnessed all my rage to keep myself together. She looked away. Good. I couldn't tolerate her gaze. I grabbed a cloth and some water to wipe her blood off me. My eyes flickered to the inside of her thighs. Her virgin blood was smeared all over them. I held back a wince and agonized over giving her a damp cloth to clean herself.

Mistakes need nothing, I decided, hardening my heart. I dressed and threw her pants at her, choosing to ignore her struggling. Once she'd donned them, I tugged on her collar to get us moving again. She followed silently, and I worked to steady my emotions.

You hurt her, Zorian. You traumatized her. Let it be known that I hate you for that, Spine said icily.

I was taken off guard. I knew he was mad, but he'd never said that to me before, and it stung. *She is alive, Spine. You should be grateful.*

He didn't reply, and I gritted my teeth in annoyance. We walked in silence until the sun began to set. It was a little jarring to lead a prisoner who turned invisible intermittently as we progressed through the woods. I supposed she didn't know how to control that, or just couldn't.

I decided to stop for the night when we came across a moonlit clearing. It wasn't to give her a rest. It wasn't to give her time to heal. It wasn't to give her time to process. Spine snorted, but this time, it was frigid.

I built a fire that wasn't for her and brought back two hares for dinner, not that I cared if she ate. I just didn't want to carry her if she fainted.

I skinned and gutted the rodents. Once they were thoroughly cooked, we ate in silence and settled to sleep. I held on to her chain, but she limped as far away as the chain allowed to sleep. It didn't bother me in the slightest. It was her problem if she wanted to be cold.

"The same thing applies, Mistake. If you run tonight, I will find you, and you will be punished. The invisibility doesn't hinder me in the slightest. You will not escape, and you wouldn't be able to kill me in time," I warned, then rolled and turned my back to prove my point.

When I closed my eyes, vivid memories of pounding into her flooded my mind. Recalling the fight had my feral instincts prickling along my consciousness, and I felt an urgent need to mount her again. I was grateful my back was turned so I could keep my struggle hidden. I steeled myself and raked my claws through the dirt as I tried to drift off to sleep. All I could do was take deep breaths and think, *Do not get attached.*

Asshole. Spine's insult was the last thing I heard before falling asleep.

⚜

When we arrived at the castle, my soldiers saluted, and I nodded in turn. Some—I imagined they were unmated—stiffened at the sight of the bound female on the other end of my chain. Try as they might to hide it, I could see they were infuriated by my treatment of her.

My beta strode to greet me as I entered the main hall, but he paled as soon as his eyes landed on the she-wolf. His nostrils flared and he fidgeted. "You... found her so quickly, Your Majesty," he remarked, shocked. I noticed an angry shade of red brightening his cheeks.

"Take her to the dungeon, Rudesind," I commanded, letting a small amount of my dominance wash over him. I wasn't in the mood to argue. I handed the chain over to him and went to my chamber to shower. I needed her scent off me.

Once I felt settled, I strode toward my study to see what issues had arisen during my hunt for the female. I flipped through documents that were relatively unimportant and breathed a sigh of relief. Nothing major to worry about—just some territory disputes and requested adjustments to our export prices. I began to peruse the details when my beta knocked on my brand-new door, which was a lovely, passive-aggressive shade of black.

Without asking permission, he walked in and sat across from me. "She's been put in solitary confinement. There were too many issues with our unmated prisoners," he reported stiffly.

I didn't answer, just nodded to acknowledge what he'd said. He sat there, and I could feel his stare. Eventually, I sighed and looked up at him.

"Is that all, Rude?" I asked shortly. I had a feeling it wasn't.

"She does not look good. She's limping, she reeks of blood, and it looks like she's recovering from a concussion and a broken rib. What happened?"

"It doesn't matter. She's in custody now, which was our goal. Treat her as you would the others," I replied, following his microexpressions—suspicion, frustration, anger.

"May I at least call for a doctor?" he asked.

"Do what you will," I said with a shrug. "It matters not to me." I waited for Spine's snort, but it never came.

He stood up and gave me an odd look. It was as if I was a stranger to him. I would warn him to not get attached if he showed more signs of potential disobedience over this female. The beta shook his head, almost imperceptibly, and strode out of the study, leaving me to my thoughts.

Ragna

I was a quivering mess when we approached the castle. Unmated males stared from their nearby posts, and I kept my gaze from theirs. All I could do was focus on the chain links in front of me and steady my breathing. If I looked too distressed, the male soldiers might attack the king, and I didn't want to be the cause of their deaths.

Another tall and brawny lycan greeted us inside, and his eyes locked on mine. I looked away, realizing he was unmated as well. Deep discomfort settled into my belly from all the attention, and I suffered the urge to run and hide. The last time I'd been around this many unmated males was when I was with my pack.

Memories of the banishment flooded my mind, and I fought to keep my tears at bay. I missed my family, I missed my friends, and I missed the camaraderie of my old pack members. I rubbed my nose to catch a bit of mucus that threatened to spill and sniffed as quietly as I could.

The king handed my lead to this male named Rudesind, and I was led down multiple flights of stairs to the dungeon. We passed several guards who confiscated my backpack before the lycan guided me to a hall lined with cells. Torches lit the faces of the prisoners, and every unmated male began yelling for my release. It frightened me, and I kept my gaze locked on the stone floor. I couldn't bear to look at any of the inmates. I didn't want to see what was in their eyes.

Rudesind led me to an empty cell but hesitated. Several inmates nearby were still screaming or pleading, begging for their mate to be spared. It was disturbing instead of heartwarming. This was so unnatural.

I cringed when Rudesind's eyes fell on me. He seemed to be struggling with a decision, but he finally sighed and led me down the next flight of stairs. There was only one door here, and it had a tiny, barred window. A slot at the bottom looked like it was for delivering food.

He watched me limp inside, and I settled onto an old, stained sleeping pad. I winced and held my rib, which was improving but wasn't completely fixed. Poor Trail was working so hard to heal me, but we had too many deep injuries to fix quickly.

I felt the male's eyes on me while I kept mine to the floor. "I'll be back," he said and left, locking the door behind him.

It was dark in the stone cell, the only light coming from a torch outside my door. It wobbled and waned through the little window. I couldn't hold it in anymore. Now that I was alone, I burst into tears, wailing at the top of my lungs. I cried my heart out and couldn't decide what was hurting me most.

All I could think about was what I'd lost, but I'd lost so many things. In several days, I'd lost my freedom and my innocence. It weighed heavily on my soul, and I felt like I was falling apart. What was even left? My life itself? Trail and I were all that was left. She'd been quiet, but I knew she was just as heartbroken.

<hr />

I wasn't sure how much time had passed before I eventually heard approaching footsteps. The door to my cell opened, and an older female lycan appeared, accompanied by the blond lycan who'd escorted me here. She was carrying a large case, and the male had a cardboard box with him.

I curled up tighter, not knowing what to think of my visitors. Was this a doctor, or was this someone brought to torture information out of me? My shaking returned with a vengeance, but the male squatted next to me and laid a soothing hand on my arm.

"Calm, sweet one," the older lady crooned and stroked my head before opening her case.

I stiffed when I saw syringes among the medical equipment. Those could be there for so many reasons.

The male squeezed my arm and whispered, "She won't hurt you. She's just here to check your injuries, ok?"

I nodded and swallowed hard.

The doctor removed my collar, checked my forehead, and pulled up my shirt to look at my ribs. "I smell blood between her legs. She smells like him," she mumbled and then turned to Rudesind. "Please leave for a minute." He winced, then frowned and left the cell.

The female turned to me and helped remove my clothes so she could check my body. She tsked at the bruises on my hips, bottom, and thighs. I flinched when she asked me to spread my legs so she could tend to my injuries. Then she wiped me down, cleaning and sanitizing my private area while muttering curses to herself.

"When did this happen?" she asked. "Yesterday? Two days ago?"

I turned my head away, not wanting to talk about it, but I had to ask. "Yesterday... Did... Did he ruin me?"

"Sounds like you weren't willing, sweet one," she commented with an angry edge in her voice. "And no, he didn't ruin you, though he obviously wasn't gentle. This is nothing you won't heal from. Just give it a day or two. Your wolf will take care of it. Was this your first time?"

I closed my eyes tight and took a deep breath. After a minute, I nodded, and my face flamed from the humiliation of it all. I returned to staring at the wall, wishing I could float away from everything. Rage radiated from the female, but she seemed to calm herself enough to finish tending to my wounds.

"The grand beta will give you a bucket of water and soap so you can get all that mud off you. You were smart to try to hide your scent. I'm sorry that it wasn't enough," she said gently. "Our king... produces results."

Her words broke through my numbness, and I started crying again. I couldn't recall the last time I'd received such kind words. It filled a hole in my chest that I'd tried to forget existed. The female held me and crooned until I calmed.

"Let your wounds air out. You'll get some fresh clothes. I'll check on you tomorrow, sweet one. Until then, rest." She closed her case and left.

I hugged my knees but started when the other lycan entered. He froze for a second, and I cringed, curling tighter to hide my nudity. He broke from his trance and brought in a box, soap, and two buckets of water.

"So you can wash," he explained as he set the buckets next to me. I nodded and accepted the soap he offered. When I tried to lift a bucket, I cried out in pain. My hand shot to my ribs, and I leaned back. Hastily covering my breasts again, I glanced at him in embarrassment. He wore a pained expression, though, not a lustful one.

"Please allow me to wash you. I promise I won't touch you inappropriately. Just let me help you," he asked softly. "Please?"

I looked down at my feet. What did it matter? I felt ruined anyway. I didn't know how I could possibly feel worse about my body. I nodded my assent and crouched by the drain in the middle of the cell. He sighed and lathered the sponge.

I stared at the wall while he tied up my hair. He then gently wiped the mud off my face, taking care to even get behind my ears. I cried when he dabbed at the abrasions around my neck. The silver had pulled off some skin upon the doctor's removal of the collar, and the raw sections were horribly sensitive. He murmured an apology and lightened his touch.

He worked his way down, scrubbing my back and shoulders. He hesitated when he got to my chest and sent me an uncertain look. I nodded and just stared at the opposite wall, moving my legs to the side to give him room.

His breathing was a little shallow as he scrubbed down my chest, my armpits, and around my breasts. Fortunately, my body was in too much shock to respond to his mate touch. His face was blushing in my peripheral vision, and I squirmed uncomfortably.

"It's ok," he said soothingly. "I won't hurt you." I relaxed a little and allowed him to continue his ministrations. He dabbed delicately at my ribs, then finished washing my legs, arms, hands, and feet. Fortunately, the older female had already tended to my private areas, so he didn't need to wash there. He frowned, though, when he did see that I was cleaned.

"Did... he force you?" he asked falteringly.

I didn't reply. I didn't want to think about it or talk about it ever again. I just stared past him at the wall, hoping he'd drop it. He let out a long, grief-stricken sigh.

"I'm so sorry," he whispered.

He washed my hair in silence and rinsed me down with the second bucket of clean water. He draped a large, fluffy towel over my shoulders and pulled things out of the cardboard box. Pillows, blankets, and a number of other comforts I probably wasn't allowed to have were placed on the old sleeping pad. Last, he pulled out several pairs of cotton shirts and pants.

He grabbed the box and stared down at me for a moment before speaking. "I'll have food and water sent down immediately. Let the guards know if you need anything, and I'll make sure you get it."

I didn't respond. I just closed my eyes and put my head down in my arms. Reality felt so very far from here. Perhaps I truly had been abandoned by the Sky Gods.

Chapter 9

King Zorian

An urge to go check on Ragna hit me for the sixth time since the afternoon. I kept pushing away the feeling so I could focus on the documents in front of me, but it was persistent, nagging. I'd also expected my beta to come and chew me out hours ago, but he was oddly absent.

A servant brought the physician's bill to me, and I raised an eyebrow. "She wanted it sent directly to you," the servant murmured, her eyes glued to the floor.

"You're dismissed," I said and perused the invoice. Concussion and fractures were left to be healed by her wolf, while the lacerations were cleaned and treated. My brows furrowed on the last section. She noted that the patient was treated for multiple injuries sustained during what she suspected was a rape, but the patient wouldn't verify. I scowled at the list of injuries, signed the invoice, and called for a servant to take it to the financial manager.

A turmoil I refused to acknowledge swam under my skin and burrowed into my gut. I quivered with the need to destroy everything in my office, but to act out would be to admit that I was emotionally affected by her. I wouldn't feed that. She was nothing.

I tried to keep her as nothing in my mind for as long as possible, but I caved just before sunset. I knew she'd turn invisible soon, and something about that put me into a panic. I couldn't handle it anymore. I told myself

I would go to her cell door to see if I could hear her talk to her wolf about her plans regarding the goddess.

Really? Spine asked, finally talking to me again. *As if she'd talk out loud to her wolf about something like that. That's so stupid. I would laugh if I wasn't so pissed at you.*

I ignored him, and he went back to giving me the silent treatment.

I made my way to the dungeon and walked down the rows of cells until I remembered the she-wolf was in solitary confinement. When I backtracked to the stairs, the movement woke several prisoners who started begging me to free her. They were all one mind about Ragna. I narrowed my eyes and forced my dominance over them to induce submission. They grew quiet and prostrated but shook with uncontrollable emotions, further proof of how dangerous she was. I'd made the right choice putting her into custody.

I marched down the next flight of stairs and stopped to address the two guards. My beta should've verified that these males were mated before stationing them here. I couldn't tell by looking at them since their uniforms covered their necks and shoulders, hiding the stretch of skin where a mate might leave their bite mark. They seemed calm enough, though.

"Any issues with the prisoner?" I asked. One shifted uncomfortably, but they both shook their heads.

"The usual behavior, Your Majesty, but the prisoner is cooperative," the calmer one answered.

"What behavior would that be?" I inquired. Though I could guess, I wanted to hear it.

"Crying, that sort of thing. No issues, Your Majesty."

Maybe I shouldn't have asked. I passed them to peer through the dark cell's window. She was leaning against the right wall, staring into space. It didn't look like she was communicating with her wolf at all, even silently. She looked...

Broken? Devastated? Traumatized? How about despondent?

Shut up, Spine, I growled.

Just helping you find the right word. After all, you did this.

I ignored him and stared at her for a moment longer. She'd been cleaned up and clothed. A tray of food lay on the floor, mostly untouched.

The she-wolf didn't seem to notice my presence either. My gaze then flickered to the high-quality pillows and comforters arranged on her sleeping pad. Deep down in my heart, hidden from Spine, a war escalated. I didn't know whether to punish or thank the beta for providing those luxuries. Unable to reconcile such contradicting thoughts, I curled my lip in a silent snarl and turned to leave.

"Excuse me, Your Majesty? One other matter," the nervous soldier asked, and I turned to face him, raising an eyebrow.

"We've had a lot of, um, unmated soldiers come down to try and... visit. We've confiscated whatever they wished to gift the prisoner, like treats and items of comfort. What shall we do with them? It's become a rather large pile, and we have to clear it out."

He gestured to a table at the other end of the hall laden with fruits, sweets, quality clothing, and a number of other items you'd give a lover. I scowled at it and felt an intense urge to burn it all to the ground. Instead of rending the gifts, I closed my eyes, took a deep breath, and gave the answer you'd give if you didn't give a shit.

"Do what you will. It matters not to me." I then turned and retreated to my bedroom chamber.

You're jealous, Spine accused, and if I were shifted, my hackles would have risen at that statement. Though they'd be Spine's hackles.

I am not, I replied calmly.

Why the fuck can't we just keep her, Zorian? We're the almighty, undefeated, chosen-by-the-people Lycan King, damn it! If there was one female left in the world to have as a fated mate, wouldn't we, of all people, deserve to have her? We've protected our people and been good to them. Don't we deserve something for ourselves?

I will not make myself vulnerable, Spine. That is out of the question.

But we're the best ones to protect her! No one could get to her! We'd just have her reject all the males who work here, and she'd be ours. Then we could spoil her rotten, fatten her up, give her pups... That is, if she ever forgave you.

Spine was chipping at my defenses, and I stumbled in a moment of weakness. With his argument fresh in my mind, I slid into my bed and stared at the ceiling. It was tempting.

I closed my eyes and thought about what it would be like to make love to her—to show her what sex was supposed to feel like. I'd apologize every single day and spend the rest of my life catering to her every need, every desire. I'd put all her pleasures first and never let her feel unloved or lonely ever again. Was I capable of that?

I sighed at the result of such thoughts and slid my hand beneath the waistband of my cotton pants to stroke myself. I pictured her beneath me and what her face might look like as I brought her pleasure. Would she be surprised by how much better it could be? Would she call my name as she got closer and closer to the edge? Would she look me in the eyes or close them when she came? Would she scream or moan?

I was as hard as steel as I pumped away at my length. I thought about her lips, her breasts, and her pussy. Has she been kissed before? Pleasured before? I wanted to know. I wanted to know everything about her.

I moved my activity to the bathroom, leaned against the sink, and fisted my shaft with wild abandon. I grimaced in response to the flood of emotions and sensations that swelled within me. Thoughts of her drowned out everything else, and the pressure built intolerably.

I thought about our sweat intermingling and the smile on her face when I filled her with my seed—if that was what she wanted. I wished I knew what her smile looked like. Would her eyes appear greener with happiness in them?

I clenched my teeth and hissed as I came violently into the bathroom sink. My knees shook, weakening for a split second, and my vision wavered. A long groan erupted from my throat as I pumped out the rest of my load.

I leaned against the counter, breathing hard as I stared at myself in the mirror. I brushed some hair out of my eyes with a wrist and regarded the person looking back at me. The truth was, I couldn't tell if I was looking at a hero or a villain, and that disturbed me. I thought it was the price of being a king, but I didn't like how I felt. Some things were getting harder and harder to justify, and I wasn't used to making concessions after digging in my heels. I honestly didn't know how to backtrack here, and I was getting confused. I felt lost.

I washed my hands and returned to bed, more uncertain than ever.

I thought you didn't have to masturbate, King Zorian, Spine prodded quietly. *Didn't you say you had females for that?*

I didn't feel like looking for someone, Spine, I answered. I was too worn out to fight him.

Yes, because now you've gotten a taste of her, and you don't want anyone else. You got attached.

Leave me alone, Spine, I whispered and buried my face in my pillow.

The answer? It was still no. If I couldn't figure out what happened to the Moon Goddess, and if my people couldn't have their mates, I wouldn't allow myself one either. I couldn't be that kind of king. I allowed myself exactly one minute of vulnerability in the darkness, where there were no witnesses. I sniffed, wiped away the tears, and let sleep take me.

agna

I wasn't sure how much time had passed since I'd been put in confinement. One day? Two days? Three? I probably could've asked the guards, but I didn't feel like talking to them. When King Zorian approached my cell door, I ignored him like I ignored everything else. I felt like an object. Not a person, just a person-shaped object.

He eventually left, and I sighed in relief, free to cry once more. I didn't like confinement any better than banishment. It was too easy to get lost in my thoughts, then go numb, only to have something shatter that numbness and force the cycle to repeat anew.

I was in and out of sleep for a while, distressed and delirious from not knowing how long I'd been unconscious. I didn't even know what time of day it was, and I didn't feel like playing a game with the guards to see if I was invisible or not. I didn't want to ask them. Who knew if they were mated? Would anyone be able to hear me if I screamed?

The growing anxiety from a thousand worries made me desperate for a distraction. I tried playing little games like finding animal shapes in the stones, but it wasn't diverting enough. I ended up singing quietly to myself, hoping it wouldn't attract the guards. It'd been a long time since I last sang. I never felt safe doing it in the wild because I couldn't risk drawing attention to my location.

Though I wasn't a great singer—I was often flat—it was soothing to remember the songs of my childhood. I cherished the songs my mother would sing or the ones I'd learned in school. So, I sang until tears formed in my eyes, and my throat became raw.

I startled from my reverie when I noticed someone outside my cell. It was the beta. I averted my eyes and wrapped my arms around my knees, feeling exposed.

"You have a pretty voice," he said softly. "I'm coming in. I have some things for you."

When the guards followed him in, I panicked and moved to the corner of the cell. The last time I was surrounded by three males...

"Please don't touch me! Please!" I begged and covered my head, but all I heard was the thumping of cardboard. I peeked over my knees and watched the soldiers deliver an assortment of items stuffed into boxes. Rudesind stared at me like I'd broken his heart.

"I'd never let anyone do that. You have nothing to fear, Ragna," he remarked sadly.

It felt extremely weird to hear my name spoken again, almost shocking. I'd been called so many things over the last five years, and—aside from my conversations with Trail—none of those things had been my name. I looked away from him. I didn't know how to talk to the beta. I felt like even talking to an unmated male would lead to trouble, and that scared me.

Rudesind sat on one end of my sleeping pad, pulled a box over, and patted the spot next to him. I stared at him for several minutes, but he just waited patiently with an apologetic smile. Slowly, I moved to the very edge of the sleeping pad, making sure my leg wouldn't brush against his. Then I looked at the box.

"These are all gifts from your admirers, Ragna," he said with a small chuckle and rummaged through the pile to show me what I'd received. I peeked into it and grabbed something I'd never seen before in my life. It smelled good, but what was it?

"That's a pineapple. A fruit," he explained when he saw my bewildered expression. "That one's a little impossible to open with your fingers. Claws would probably work, but... one second... hang on..." A fruit? It looked more like a weapon.

He reached to his side, pulled out a knife, and labored at the fruit to remove a slice for me. After taking a cursory sniff, I bit into it, then slapped a hand over my mouth to muffle a moan. It was delicious, and the tangy juice made my mouth water like crazy. I devoured the rest and licked my fingers zealously. Pineapples were a sticky mess, but I rather liked them. The beta simply laughed and handed his handkerchief to me.

"They were considering throwing all this out or donating it, but seeing as how it was your birthday a couple of days ago"—he shrugged—"I figured you should have it all. It's probably been a while since you had a birthday gift, yeah?"

I froze and stared at the door. My birthday... I swallowed heavily, remembering the day I was banished. "Yes," I replied hoarsely. My throat was tight. "I didn't even know what month it was until now."

He nodded and pulled out various items from the boxes to show me. Not liking him watching me, I insisted on sharing whatever I tried. We made our way through an assortment of chocolates, something called saltwater taffy, and peanut brittle. Every food item was a delicacy to me after years of the bland food I'd hunted or gathered.

Eventually, the beta pulled out some clothes. There were gowns and a sweater, but his attention was drawn to a pair of beautiful, fur-lined boots. He regarded them with a great deal of suspicion and passed them to me. When I tried them on and they fit, he seemed beyond baffled.

"How the fuck did they pick the right size?" he asked, gripping his head with both his hands. He was truly perplexed. "Ragna, I'm not going to be able to sleep tonight over this. There must be a spy among us."

A laugh escaped my lips, and I slapped a hand over my mouth. He looked over with a sparkle in his eyes like he'd won a game. I didn't want to smile. I didn't want to laugh. I was a prisoner, and I'd lost everything. I gritted my teeth, feeling confused and a little angry.

He sat down again next to me and pulled another item from the second box. Handing it to me, he said, "This one's from me. You must be bored out of your mind in here. Happy Birthday, Ragna."

It was a book. I flipped through it, seeing that it was a compilation of mythologies. I knew I'd enjoy reading it. The only book I'd owned since my banishment was the tiny survival guide my father had provided.

"Thank you," I murmured, momentarily shaken by thoughts of family. I might as well ask the burning question that had been on my mind this entire time. "How long have I been in here, Beta?"

"Two days," he informed with a sigh. "I don't know what's going to happen next. I wish I had something to tell you."

Not even the second-in-command knew what was going on with my situation? I wiped my nose before it dripped and rubbed at my tired, swollen eyes. Despair welled up once again.

"I swear I didn't do anything." I whimpered and started crying. "I just... It was my birthday, and then there was fighting, and the females tried to kill me, and..." I sobbed louder, desperate to be understood. I hated this. Why was I locked up? I didn't do anything!

"I believe you," the beta assured quietly, somberly. "Now, I just have to get the king to believe you."

"I'm s-sorry I replaced your m-mate. I b-broke the s-system. I w-want to fix it," I cried and wrapped my arms around my legs again. "I w-want everyone to h-have their fated mates back!"

"I know..." he murmured, placing a hand on my shoulder. I flinched, and he immediately removed it. "I want my mate too. I know something bigger must be happening. We'll figure this out."

"I t-t-tried to s-save m-myself for m-mine b-but..." I didn't know where I'd gotten the courage to open up like that, but it felt good to have someone validate my reality.

"I promise, once this is all fixed, your fated mate won't care. He'll just be so happy to have you. Don't worry about that for one second," he consoled.

"Do you really believe that?" I asked, sniffling and wiping my face, feeling like a pup.

"I'm certain. If you were mine, I wouldn't care for one second," he said with a smile. "I don't think you are mine, but that's where I stand." He shrugged.

"What makes you think that?" I asked, curious but mostly thrilled to have one less person hunting me.

"For starters, I'd never date someone who'd wear this." He held up one of the sweaters and grimaced. The satin bows on it were a bit garish, and another laugh burst out of me. Unfortunately, the happiness I felt also nauseated me. This visit was like a hallucination. Once he left, I'd be alone and lost all over again.

He saw my frown and cleared his throat. "Ragna... One last thing. I know you've been traumatized, but I wanted to tell you that... sex isn't supposed to be like that. It's not supposed to hurt you the way you've been hurt. Quite frankly, I'm outraged at what's been done to you.

"Until the mate bonds are fixed... if you ever want to know what it's truly like to make love with someone who cares about you, I don't mind volunteering for that. You deserve to know that it can be a beautiful experien—shit." He looked at me in panic.

I froze at the mention of sex. Like a chunk of ice, I stared blankly at the opposite wall. What should I say? Thank you? Should I scream because all I can think about are the males who'd attacked me? Should I cry because I felt like a charity case? He was nice. He was kind. He took care of me, but something had stopped my body from functioning. Everything felt rusted into place, and I couldn't move. I was terrified. I felt like I couldn't even breathe.

"Shit, shit, shit," he hissed in concern and squatted in front of me. "Ragna, I'm sorry. I'm so sorry. Come back. I take it all back. You're safe. Forget about all of that. I'm so sorry."

There was a knock at the cell door, and Rudesind jumped, startled. "The king wants to see you both, Beta Rudesind. There's an urgent matter in the main hall by the entrance, and you're both needed as soon as possible."

The beta looked back at me. "Shit!"

Chapter 10

King Borian

I woke up the next day with no idea what to do. I'd already deviated from my plan of killing her, and I was at risk of getting attached to that… she-wolf. I dragged my hands over my face and forced myself out of bed. I showered and dressed then went to take breakfast in my study. As the day progressed, I noticed that my beta was still nowhere to be found. Was he avoiding me?

I trotted down to the dungeon to check on our prisoner. Perhaps seeing her would help me figure out my next steps. When I approached the guards assigned to solitary confinement, I heard voices coming from inside the cell.

"Who's in there?" I growled to the guards.

"Beta Rudesind is in there, Your Majesty. He ordered the gifts we confiscated delivered to her. Something about it being her birthday several days ago." He shrugged.

"You said to do whate—" The other soldier began justifying the order, but I swiped a hand to interrupt him.

"I know what I said. That's fine," I grumbled, distracted by what the other guard had said. I stared at the small window and swallowed. "When did he say her birthday was?"

"Um, let's see. Not yesterday—the day before," the guard answered, nodding in recollection.

The truth was a slap to the face. Trying to keep my movement casual, I turned to make sure no one could see the horror in my eyes.

A feminine laugh burst from the cell, and I snapped out of my reeling. A swirl of rage and joy struck me at the sound of someone else making her happy. Taking a step back, I nodded to the guards and said, "As you were, gentlemen." I had to get away from here.

My chest knotted in intense pain, and I fought to ignore it, along with the other unwanted emotions I'd felt just minutes ago. I didn't know what was wrong with me, but I was hurting—deeply. I leaned against the stone wall near the main hall and pinched the bridge of my nose. I fought to control my breathing, becoming light-headed. Was I having a panic attack?

A commotion at the entryway grabbed my attention, and several males yelled. I ran to see what was happening, and a petite red wolf entered the main hall. Her copper eyes flashed when they locked onto mine like she was issuing a challenge.

I strode up to the strange wolf and barked, "Who are you? What have you done to my guards?"

Your guards are unharmed, her unfeeling voice said over a broad mind-link, and she looked behind her. This was not one of my pack. She should not be able to mind-link me.

I followed her gaze, and every single guard stationed on the way to the castle was submitting. I narrowed my eyes at this she-wolf. This was no alpha either. Something seemed wrong with her.

"What are you? A witch?" I accused, glaring down at her. More of my soldiers poured into the room, aiming their weapons at the small creature before me.

I AM THE SUN GOD! the wolf boomed, and all my soldiers fell to their knees like severed marionettes. *You will bring Ragna here within fifteen minutes, or I will retrieve her myself, and I will not be held responsible for what happens during that time.*

"You dare to threaten me and my soldiers? In my castle?" I thundered and took a step forward to grab the little mutt.

I didn't get within two feet of her scruff before my hand was hit with what felt like boiling water. I snarled and jerked my hand back, cradling it against my chest. It was covered in blisters. I took a closer look at the wolf and noticed a thin layer of thermals rising off her coat. Something was wrong indeed.

I'm on it, Spine announced and began healing my burns.

Do you believe me now, pup? I am over four billion years old. I have a great capacity for patience, but I am losing it quickly over your disobedience. The Sky Gods begged me to give you a chance, but I am seeing that I had good reason to distrust you, the wolf seethed, and for the first time in forever, I felt a sliver of terror. I mind-linked a servant to fetch both my beta and Ragna—immediately.

"They are on their way," I reported flatly, refusing to show fear. I didn't care if this was a god. This was my castle and my territory. If I was going to die, I'd go down with a set jaw.

Wise decision, the wolf said coldly. *For almost five years, the Sky Gods tried to convince me to intervene. They agonized over who could best help Ragna. It always came back to you, but I. Did. Not. Like. You.*

I raised an eyebrow and scrubbed a hand over my mouth. "Pray, tell me why."

I don't need to hold your hand, pup. If you looked at yourself, you'd know why, pup. I saw what you did, and I was not happy, pup. Ragna needs someone who will help her, not hurt her every chance they get... pup.

I wouldn't allow the god to see how much that hurt, but it hurt... a lot. I glanced over at the doorway to see my beta escorting the she-wolf, Ragna. I fought against the brief flare of jealousy that rose in my gut. I didn't like him so close to her, and I loathed that I felt that way. I hated that he'd been the one to make her laugh. Shit, I was distracting myself with nonsense. Fuck!

Ragna's eyes widened, and she ran toward the Sun God.

"Ragna, wait!"

I stepped forward to warn her not to touch the red wolf, but she'd already wrapped her arms around it. Terror struck me at the thought of her getting burned to a crisp, but somehow, she was alright. I nearly fell to my knees in relief.

"Soley!" Ragna cried, sobbing and burying her face in the wolf's deadly coat. I wiped a hand over my forehead, completely thrown off guard. "Soley, I've missed you so much! What are you doing here?"

The red wolf looked down at the female and then back at me. *Why was the Sky-Blessed collared and put in a dungeon?*

"You saw it. She was taken into custody. She's a threat to the kingdom," I answered, reminding the Sun God that He could see everything.

Did you collar her at night? He inquired.

"Uh… yes," I replied, taken aback.

Then I obviously did not see it.

Ok, that was a little embarrassing.

Ragna gasped and asked, "Soley, you're hosting a god just like Hekla, aren't you?"

That is correct, Sky-Blessed. I am the Sun God. Soley was the best fit as my vessel. I have taken good care of her. Do not worry.

"Thank you, Sun God!" she exclaimed and slouched in relief. "I take it you've spoken to the Sky Gods?" Her gaze was hopeful. So far, their conversation was verifying everything she'd told me.

It took a good five years to deliberate, but I am here now, the god informed.

"Oh, thank the goddess! I thought I was abandoned. I'm so sorry I couldn't make much progress. I failed to reach my destinations. I make no excuses…" Ragna cried and prostrated before the god. I felt a pang of guilt.

I watched your travels. I saw what delayed you. It was not your fault. The god looked at me, and it took all my strength to not avert my eyes. *That's why I'm here now. The skies begged me to intervene, and I am here to set things in motion.* A wave of dominance came crashing down around us, and I nearly submitted. I gritted my teeth and stood fast, staring straight into the eyes of the god. I knew that display wasn't even a fraction of their power, and they knew I knew. We had an understanding now.

Ragna, the skies and I have chosen King Zorian to be your champion on your search. I am unhappy with the decision, but ultimately, the Sky Gods are correct. I see now that he is the only one strong enough to carry the burden.

Champion? Burden? What burden? I furrowed my brows and tried to stay focused.

"Wh-why are you unhappy with th-the king?" Ragna stuttered.

I do not like how he's treated you. I do not find him worthy.

"That's... my p-p-problem. He... worries for his people... I don't want anyone to..." She faltered, a range of emotions playing across her strained face.

She didn't want anyone to what? Wait, what? It sank in that she was defending me, and I couldn't believe it. I nearly gaped. I didn't even want to defend me.

You don't deserve her, Spine murmured.

He doesn't deserve your magnanimity. The god growled and sent me a nasty look. *I am here to bless King Zorian with the key to the Realm of the Gods. You may use it to search the Moon Goddess's home for information. You will need to pass through the Realm of the Fae first. It is a rung on a ladder you cannot skip.*

"Thank you, Sun God. I'm certain this will help." Ragna exhaled shakily and wiped a tear off an eyelash. "I'm so relieved to have a better idea of where to start! This means the world to me!"

That is what I'm here for, Sky-Blessed. The god looked up at me again. *Keep your training close to you. Think about motive and strategy. Bring your skills to the field, and you will reap the rewards. Nothing is unimportant.*

Ragna, you will pick up the trail, and King Zorian, you will protect Ragna and offer her passage to our realm. This is the will of the gods. Is our will clear? I do not like to be disappointed. You will find I'm not as forgiving as the others.

"Your will is clear," I said, making sure to keep my face void of emotion.

"Your will is clear, Sun God. Thank you so much..." Ragna's voice trailed off into a whisper.

Come and receive your blessing, Zorian, the red wolf said, beckoning me forward with copper eyes.

I moved toward the god and submitted, making everyone gasp. If this was their will, perhaps my people had a chance. If it could give them the normalcy they pleaded for, I'd show my neck to a beggar. If there was one thing I stood for as a king, it was that my people came first. At that thought, I tried desperately not to think of Ragna.

A wave of heat rushed over me, and I felt my bones ignite. I gritted my teeth and fought the pain, but I'd never experienced anything so excruciating in my life. The marrow of my bones turned into molten lava, and my insides incinerated. I barely made out the words of the Sun God telling Ragna to never leave my side. The heat blossomed into new heights of agony, and I fell to the ground, consumed by ashes and darkness.

Ragna

I watched nervously as the intimidating Lycan King approached the Sun God. I was afraid because the god had repeatedly shown His disapproval. He wouldn't hurt him, would He? I didn't want to be responsible for anyone's death.

The Sky Gods didn't injure us, Ragna. It was a temporary pain.

Oh my goddess, Trail! You're back! I nearly shouted the words out loud; I was so relieved.

I have to say... it is exhausting being your wolf. She chuckled wearily.

I wish I could hug you. Thank you for working so hard to heal me. I know you're doing your best.

It's because I love you. Now shush, and let's watch the Sun God smite King Zorian.

When the king knelt and submitted to the god, the entire hall gasped in surprise. Though he'd hurt me, the act struck a chord. It was a wise decision to try to gain back some degree of approval from the god. An alpha yielding willingly was not something that came naturally or easily, especially if they happened to be a Lycan King. He must have fought against all his instincts to do that.

It's nice to see he's even remotely capable of humility, Trail mumbled. *Wish he'd been that gentle with us.*

I frowned and felt a pang in my chest, not wanting to think about that day. *Just watch.*

The god stood tall and fierce in Soley's body like He was an overlord surveying a battlefield. Copper eyes drilled into King Zorian, who gritted his teeth. After a moment, his face flushed with pain. I took a panicked step forward when his skin grew pink, then red, and began to blister.

My eyes watered, horrified by the suffering required for this blessing. A whimper escaped my lips as several small sections of his skin peeled and blackened. No, no, no, the god was going to kill him! I ran forward when the king fell to a knee and collapsed, unable to help myself.

I shrieked as a single, small puff of smoke curled from his body and dissipated. Why was he smoking? I fell to my knees next to him and listened. His heart was still beating, and his lungs were still pulling in air, albeit weakly.

Burns, burns, burns, burns! I looked up, and when I didn't see anyone who looked like a doctor, I was flooded with anxiety. My mind raced for an answer as I panicked. What had the survival guide said? Cold water!

"Someone, fetch cold water!" I yelled and tried to gingerly pull his clothes from his skin. Shit! I looked around at the soldiers. Some were frozen to the spot, and others had run off, hopefully to find a doctor and cold water.

Would I be punished for undressing him in the hall? I worried about it and finally made a judgment call. I pointed at two soldiers and barked for them to carry the king to his chambers.

My eyes glanced over at the Sun God, who looked very interested in all the chaos. "Will he live?" I asked tearfully, watching the soldiers carrying the large male upstairs.

He has an eighty percent chance of not surviving the blessing, the god informed, regarding me closely. I felt a surge of anger but tamped down on the impulse to yell at a god.

"Why didn't you warn us?" I demanded and started pacing. The need to check on the king was so unbearable that I couldn't keep still.

Because he was the only one who stood a chance, the god answered. *The Realm of the Gods is not meant for mortals. Risking a male's life is worth it to save a goddess.*

I wasn't sure how I felt about that. I bit my lip nervously and worried at my hands. The god gave me an odd look and sighed. *I do not normally say such things as it is against my nature to make calls on uncertainties, but I think he will survive. He is too stubborn, and I hate him too much.*

He will probably make it through just to infuriate me, the Sun God said with a hint of compassion.

I nodded and fell to my knees to embrace the god who was also my friend.

Watch for strangers, Sky-Blessed. Do not let your guard down, and... I heard a touch of a grimace in the god's voice. *Trust in your champion if he lives. Most souls are capable of... defrosting, and his has been blessed by the Sun God. There is no greater heat. Hold fast.*

A team of doctors rushed past me and dashed upstairs. My eyes followed them anxiously.

Go with them. I must leave, the god said through my friend. *Soley will return home safely.* I embraced Him one more time, not caring I was pushing a hug onto an almighty god.

"Thank you," I whispered and raced to track the king's scent to his chambers.

I slowed to a fast walk when I saw six soldiers standing outside his bedroom door. Several did a double take at my approach, and I let a small smile flicker on my face in greeting. One soldier looked particularly exhausted fending off three angry, elegantly dressed females who were demanding to be let in to see the king.

"How is he?" I nervously asked a soldier. I worried at hands that were getting sweatier by the heartbeat, and I tried to slow my breathing. As nervous as I was, this lycan appeared to be three times that. He tried to avoid my gaze and swallowed heavily before answering me. Damnation, he was unmated, wasn't he?

"We don't know. The physicians said they'll come out when they have a p-prognosis, mate. I mean Sky-Blessed! Shit! Sorry! Ah..." He winced, and his face ruddied.

I felt my nose sting and my eyes water. My existence had ruined so many lives. "I'm so sorry. I promise I'll fix the mate bonds. I swear on my life. Please hang in there and be strong for your king, ok?" I put a hand on his shoulder in what I hoped was a genuine gesture.

The soldier let out a heavy breath and nodded, smiling weakly in appreciation.

"And call me Ragna," I said, addressing all the soldiers. Some looked surprised by the request, and others responded with tired, approving smiles. As much as I wanted to distance myself from unmated wolves and lycans, I didn't like the manufactured distance a title created. I longed to make friends, especially now that I had a sliver of hope. All was not doomed. I had not been forgotten by the gods!

"Then I'm Colin," the blushing soldier replied. To my surprise, he opened the chamber door and gestured for me to enter. I skittered past the guards, and he closed it quickly behind me before the other females could follow. I heard their angry protests through the door.

"How come she got to go in? That's the whore who took all the males!"

"Watch your tone, female," a soldier snarled.

"Are any of you the Sky-Blessed?" a different soldier asked.

"No! Of course not," another female growled.

"Then you can be the Hall-Blessed," he replied, and some of the soldiers burst into laughter. I grimaced, feeling like I was going to get targeted for that, but I turned my attention to the scene before me.

I ignored an urge to stop and stare at the extravagance of the suite and tracked his scent toward the bedroom, quickly coming to a halt behind the team of doctors. They were working in a rush, cutting strips of linen, preparing concoctions, and cutting away pieces of his clothing. At the foot of the bed were two servants, and along the inside of the doorway stood several more soldiers.

I noticed eyes on me and realized the beta and the female doctor who'd tended to me were both here. The doctor smiled as she washed her hands. "It's good to see you doing so well, Ragna," she said gently. I didn't feel like I was doing well, but the day's events had made my previous troubles seem more distant.

"The Sun God said he had a twenty percent chance of surviving. How is he?" I asked, drawing my brows in worry and biting my lip. She dried her hands and went back to peeling and cutting cloth from burned skin.

"It's hard to say until we see all of him, but it's good you're here. You're his mate and can try to help him heal." She nodded firmly, not bothering to look up at me as she uttered those words. I shifted uncomfortably.

"Well, we have the fated mate bond for now. It's temporary," I made sure to specify, but she shrugged.

"I'm going to utilize it like any other medical tool, Ragna."

"Wh-what do you n-need me to do?" I stammered, trying to keep my breathing steady. I wasn't sure if I was about to take a step forward or a step backwards.

"Strip your clothes off and get on the bed with him."

Chapter 11

Ragna

It would be nice if we could somehow go an entire day without having to be naked, Trail said. *Of course, there's nothing wrong with being naked, but... you know, it's something I dream about.*

I chuckled darkly at her comment as I undressed down to my underwear. The beta's approach made me flinch, but I quickly realized that he was just offering to take my clothing. He looked sad at my reaction, but I couldn't help it. His offer to make love had sent me into a terrified, uncomfortable spiral. It took him dabbing at my face with ice-cold water earlier to snap me out of it. I was trying to forget about what he'd said, per his begging, but it was just going to take time.

He folded my clothes nicely and placed them in a neat pile on a love seat across the room. The doctor didn't make a comment about my underwear still being on, so I breathed a sigh of relief. I was hoping I could at least get away with that.

I crawled slowly onto the king's bed, feeling tension flood my body from my head to my toes. Part of me was terrified he'd wake up and pounce on me, but as I got a better look, I realized that such an assault was quite impossible. I wiped the moisture from my eyes, staring at the extent of his injuries. Most of his clothes were cut away already, and he was swathed in burns. Some parts of his flesh were outright charred like an overcooked pheasant. The smoky aroma was sickening.

As much as he hurt us, I feel mortified about what's been done to him, Trail remarked, sounding a bit nauseated. *This is a heavy price to pay for getting to the Moon Goddess's home.*

It's a new chapter, Trail. If he survives and makes the effort, I can forgive. It'll be hard, though.

He's still delicious. I don't completely hate your memories.

That makes one of us.

The doctors discussed various parts of his body that were the least damaged, pointing to sections on his arms, ribs, and legs. They turned him onto his side, and I tried to help hold him up from where I was situated. He was damn heavy, and my arms were shaking by the time they were done removing fabric and treating the back of his body. They placed an extra sheet on his side of the bed before settling him on his back, completely nude now.

"We're going to mark sections where you're allowed to touch him, Sky-Blessed. The mate bond should do the rest as he takes energy from you to heal," a short, pale, freckled doctor with frizzy auburn hair directed as he drew dotted lines on the king's body.

I withered from emotional fatigue and said to Trail, *It's ironic how we're sitting here, being asked to save the life of a male who tried to execute us, took our virginity, and then put us in a dungeon.*

Yupper-puppers, Trail agreed succinctly. *But like you said, it's a new chapter.*

Think he'll truly accept our existence one of these days? I wondered.

He'll have to. He may be cruel, but he's not stupid.

I'm not so convinced about the stupid part, I retorted with a suppressed smile. Trail snickered.

"Alright," a tall, tan, and nearly bald doctor said, straightening up and rubbing his back. "We're going to be coming to check on him three times a day, an—"

"A day? How long will it take him to heal?" I asked anxiously, wiping more sweat off my fingers.

"If he survives? Not sure. He's strong and has always recovered quite rapidly from severe injuries, but something as severe as this," he replied and gestured to the length of King Zorian's body, "could very well take days, even with your help. We'll get a better idea tomorrow when we see how he does overnight."

I nodded and furrowed my brows, looking down at the king. "Anything I should do aside from just… lying here?" I inquired quietly.

"If his heart rate goes above this rhythm," the doctor said, clapping at a fast speed, "send a guard to fetch one of us. Several of us will always be close by in the guest wing. So just keep an ear out for it."

"I'll also be stopping by as often as I can," Beta Rudesind said gently, stepping closer with his hands in his pockets. I nodded, not meeting his gaze. "I'll make sure you have everything you need. Fresh clothes, meals, that sort of thing. Just let the guards know, and it'll be delivered to you."

"Thank you," I finally said, not wanting to seem ungrateful.

They laid the last of the cream and bandages down, then filed out of the room. The older female doctor was about to leave when I blurted, "I never got your name."

She chuckled huskily and smacked her palm against her sun-weathered forehead, sending her grey flyaways bouncing. "It's Taisa. Doctor Taisa Egres." She shook her head and left the room, mumbling about old age and brain failure.

Then it was just Beta Rudesind and me. Wiping my cold, clammy hands on the sheets, I shifted nervously, then placed my palms on the king's ribs and left bicep. He was a massive male, and though I wasn't short, my hands looked quite small on him. When the beta brought a chair up to the bed, I swallowed nervously. He wasn't leaving. Why wasn't he leaving?

Trail sighed and mumbled, *What now?*

"Ragna, I know it's difficult, but I really need to know what happened a couple of days ago. I've been agonizing over it, and… I need to know that Zorian isn't as horrible as I'm thinking," he implored, leaning his elbows on his knees and staring at the floor. His hands were subtly shaking, and he clasped them together to still the tremors.

Is it really ok to be having this conversation over the body of a dying male? Trail growled. I had to agree with her, but the beta looked so torn up over it that I caved. If the king he served died tonight, maybe he wanted some closure. I had no idea.

"I can't express how difficult this is to share," I stated, colder than intended. My emotions started shutting down so I could manage this conversation. Part of me threatened to float away, and I almost let it. The beta just nodded and heaved a tortured sigh. Damn it.

"He tried to kill me in my sleep, but I ran. He caught me, I hit my head, and he threw me to the ground, which was how I broke my rib; I hit a rock. Then he interrogated me and took me prisoner. I passed out because I think I was concussed. Later we were stalked by eight rogues, but the king took them all down by himself. The mate bond..." I paused for almost an entire minute, barely able to bring myself to say it. It was so embarrassing, and I hated myself for it.

I tried again, forcing my emotions into a box and locking it. "My body reacted without my permission, and the king went... kind of wild after battle. When he scented it, he demanded I..."

My emotions leaked from the box, and I started crying. Tears dripped onto my bare legs, the tapping sound filling the uncomfortable silence created by my hesitation. "He demanded I s-s-s-submit and... p-p-p-present myself." I'd never had a harder time saying words before, but I felt as much relief as I did embarrassment. "It was brutal. Painful. After, he just threw my pants at me, and we continued walking—like nothing had happened."

The beta ran his hands through his blond hair and closed his eyes. "Fucking alphas." He sighed as if he was completely defeated. "I can explain some of that." He held up a hand when I bristled. "It's an explanation, but it's not an excuse. He thought he was above it, but he wasn't. He should have brought others with him to intervene if violence was encountered, and I'll tell you why." The muscles in my body tensed, but I allowed him to continue.

"Going feral is this..."

"I know what feral is," I interrupted. "My friend went feral once, when someone pushed her buttons repeatedly. She never..." That was a long time ago indeed.

"She never what?"

"She only attacked," I clarified quietly and wiped the layer of tears from my face. It was pointless; they just kept coming.

"So, you don't know about the other kind of feral? Between mates?" he asked cautiously, leaning to meet my gaze.

I shook my head slowly. "They teach you that when you reach eighteen because that's when the Moon Goddess lets you find your mate..."

"And you weren't around for that," he murmured in realization, staring at me. I shook my head again and averted my gaze. "Sounds like you don't know much about heat or anything else between fated mates either." He pressed his fingers to his eyes and sighed. "I need to remember to get Dr. Egres to talk to you about all this. We'll have to speak to your old alpha. Perhaps he thought someone else had already taught you those things before removing you from his pack, but that was a serious misjudgment on his part."

The beta was stuck in thought, looking mildly stressed, so I just waited dully for him to continue. I knew some things. We were educated about sex, and I'd seen wolves and she-wolves couple before, usually in the woods, but I would always flee the area—immediately. Not sure how I would've known if they were feral.

The beta sighed and steepled his fingers under his chin. "Let's just... go over your experience for now. Going feral is this incredibly old and base instinct a lot of males still struggle with. During wartime, populations diminished significantly, so when warriors returned home, they felt compelled to breed—especially with fated mates. It's pure instinct. You know our last war, which wasn't that long ago, took a heavy toll on our population. Your pack is far from where the front lines were, so it seems that you were the least likely to encounter this phenomenon in our generation.

"Since alphas are so strong and—let's be honest here—stupidly hormonal, it's like an overpowering trance. It's very hard to resist and likely nigh impossible with fated mates, temporary or not. He's been so angry about this whole mate bond disaster affecting our kingdom that it probably just fed the intensity."

He winced before saying his next words. "Also, he's made a lot of sacrifices for his people, and I can imagine a part of him was desperate for something for himself. He's not immune to the same frustration everyone else has been feeling, and he definitely won't admit that he's more vulnerable to it."

I didn't know how to feel about it. The context was nice to have, but... he'd still been too cruel. It felt almost unforgiveable. My mind lurched with confusing thoughts and opinions. Then I berated myself a little, suddenly feeling uncomfortable having negative thoughts about a male who may be on his deathbed. I glanced down at the unconscious king, unable to shake my frown through my profound sadness.

"Do you think any part of him regrets it?" I murmured my question, feeling contemplative.

"I don't know. Maybe he will when his anger dries up. He's changed a lot and not necessarily for the better."

I had more questions but decided to leave them for another time. I was quite sleepy. I yawned, and it felt like two anvils were lowering onto my shoulders.

"Get a nap in, Ragna. It's been a trying day... to put it mildly. I'll have some food sent up for you." The beta stood, his brown eyes seeming more at peace. I only wished I felt the same.

I nodded at his words and looked down, needing to figure out how to situate myself for some shut-eye. I laid my head on the king's bicep, placed my hand on his ribs, and slung a leg over his thigh. That was the best I could do. It was awkward, but I was tired enough to pass out in any position. I closed my eyes but started when I felt a blanket being draped over me. I mumbled a thanks to the beta and let sleep take me to the reprieve of unconsciousness.

⚜

True to his word, the beta sent a servant up with a veritable feast. I moved sluggishly from the king to eat at a little coffee table, immediately missing the tingling of our skin touching. I frowned, not wanting to miss the pleasures of the fated mate bond, and shifted all my attention to the food in front of me.

As I ate, I kept an ear out for the king's heartbeat. Halfway through my steak, I noticed his heart rate start to climb, and I froze midbite— listening uneasily. When it approached the speed the doctor had warned me about, I shot out of the bedroom, ripped open the chamber door, and yelled for someone to get a doctor. My alarm scattered most of the guards in the hall, and several ran into each other in their haste to fetch a physician.

I sprinted back into the room, jumped on the bed, and scrambled to the king's side so I could touch him. His heart rate continued climbing, but its acceleration slowed when I got hold of him. What I was doing wasn't enough, and I started crying out of sheer panic. I shouldn't have left the bed!

"Don't you die on me, you stupid, mean... cranky butt!" I hissed as tears rolled down my cheeks, unable to even swear properly. "We have stuff to do! We gotta find the goddess! Augh! I hate you! You're always causing me problems! Trail?"

I'm trying, Ragna! I'm trying to force the energy into him. Ugh, where are the doctors? Trail snarled.

As if on cue, the redheaded doctor and the tall doctor rushed in with their medical cases. The king's heart rate waned, then stopped entirely, and the tingling where our flesh met halted. I shrieked and looked at the doctors, terrified. I'd never felt death occur beneath my hands. The finality of its hush was horrifying.

A doctor climbed on top and immediately started pushing down on the king's chest with both hands, occasionally breathing air into his slack mouth. The other filled a syringe and injected something into him. I had no idea what it was or if it even worked.

I tried to mute my sobbing so I wouldn't be a distraction and began to feel like I was staring from a distance. Others looked into the room to watch the emergency treatment, shocked into silence. Aside from the doctors, it was clear that I was the only other person who could help, and I fought harder to calm myself. Trail and I had to focus. He was my key to the goddess's home!

The doctors switched places but eventually fatigued. One looked over and asked, "Do you think you can take a turn? Don't be afraid to push hard. Two inches down. He has a strong rib cage, but it's normal for breakage during CPR."

I wished they'd picked someone else. They didn't give me time to decline, and the doctor on top moved so I could replace him. I hid a grimace, girded my loins, and straddled the king. I pushed down on his chest the way they had, and one of the doctors shifted my hand placement ever so slightly.

"Breathe for him," a doctor said from his chair, shaking the fatigue out of his arms.

Ugh, he ruined our first time, and now he's going to ruin our first kiss, Trail griped crankily.

Too anxious to reply, I leaned forward, pinched his nose shut, and pressed my lips against his to blow air into his lungs—nothing. I went back to pushing down on his chest and alternated to breathing when directed.

On my fifth forced breath, the mate touch sparked between our lips, startling me. His ribs expanded, and he sucked in air on his own. With his heart pumping again, the doctors rushed to check on him and fill another syringe. My arms were weak, and I stayed where I was, shaking while watching them work. I was too scared to move. Last time I moved from him, he tried to die on me.

I heard a door slam and the beta's voice uttering a hushed, angry protest.

"What is she doing?" a shrill female's voice shrieked.

"Get off of him, you whore!" another yelled, and a hand gripped my arm.

"You can't have him! Out, slut! Get out!" a third squawked.

I twisted in my seat, the king's lap, extended my claws, and raked them into the black-haired female's arm—the one who'd grabbed me. She wailed when my nails shredded deep past muscle and scored bone.

Keeping my claws in her like an anchor, I locked eyes with her. "Get. Out!" I snarled as quietly as I could. "Your king almost died, and you're disturbing him. Get out, or I'll kill you all where you stand. You have thirty seconds." I elongated my canines in a threat, then let a low growl rumble from my chest and throat. Trail announced her presence through my eyes, displaying her support as my wolf. We were the female in charge here.

She tried to tug her arm from my grip, sobbing in agony. When I released her, she fell to the floor. The other two scowled at me with promises of death in their eyes, picked her up, and left. My furious glare moved to the beta, who watched them leave with deep relief.

"They are not to return!" I seethed, showing my canines again and jabbing my finger violently in the direction they'd retreated. The beta shoved his hands into his pockets and nodded enthusiastically. In the back of my mind, I realized I'd just given an order to the highest-ranking beta in the entire kingdom.

"Oh, I agree wholeheartedly. They were threatening to go to their daddies, so I thought I could let them take a peek if they stayed quiet. They did not, however, stay quiet," the beta murmured, his gaze moving toward the king's unconscious face. "How is he?" he asked the doctors, looking concerned but hopeful.

"He's stable again," the tall one answered as he packed his case. "He went into cardiac arrest, but we three got him back. I think he may be on his way to a fever, though. Ragna will have to send for a servant to sponge him when he reaches this temperature." The doctor held out a thin glass cylinder with a red strip inside it. He pointed to a number, and I nodded in understanding. "You'll have to hold this under his tongue for about three minutes."

I held back a sigh as the doctors left. Taking care of my almost executioner was a lot of work.

Hope he gets better soon, Trail grumbled. *I'm going to get cabin fever if we're here more than a couple of days. Scratch that, I already have cabin fever.*

I don't think we've gone this long without shifting before, I realized. *Maybe that's also been contributing to my—our—anxiety. It was bad enough being stuck in a small room.*

This is definitely better than a cell. Though we can't really move far from him, she complained.

I slid slowly off the king to settle by his side, maintaining contact the entire time. I was utterly paranoid about letting go now. Beta Rudesind gave me an amused look. "You sure showed those leeches who's boss." He chuckled quietly, scratching his nose.

The reminder was irritating. "Who are they, anyway? Aside from unhelpful," I asked, my relief slipping into crankiness.

"Marriage candidates, but they certainly behave like mistresses," he replied, and I choked on my spit. Them? Disgusting. Gross. "They're here from neighboring kingdoms, and their fathers are pressuring him to choose a mate. Such is the life of a king. Pretty typical."

"Great goddess, he has a fine selection to pick from," I grumbled and picked idly at the edge of the blanket. The beta chuckled and rested his chin on his fist.

"They're definitely queen material. The one who grabbed you, the tall one with the black hair, she's a dragon-shifter." He watched me closely, like he was looking for fear.

He ain't getting it, Trail mumbled stubbornly. *We've been running from horny males for five years now; we ain't afraid of shit.* That nearly pulled a laugh out of me.

I blinked at the beta's disclosure, then shrugged. It felt weird; I wasn't a shrugger. I just strongly felt the need to express my indifference. "Her flesh certainly tears like a wolf."

He barked a laugh but then placed a hand over his mouth and glanced at the king. Lowering his voice again, he remarked, "You may change your mind if she ever shifts." A cocky half-smile spread across his face.

He's trying to get a rise out of us, that smug bastard, Trail snapped.

"Then I'll rip her throat out before she's finished," I growled maliciously, then froze. "What have I become?"

"I have no clue. Where was this wolf the other day?" He grinned, resting his cheek on his palm and staring at me. Why was he looking like he'd won? That sucked some energy out of me.

"I don't know. I think the stress has finally caught up to me. I wasn't expecting to have to save the life of a male who—" I choked up, frowned, and averted my gaze. For just a moment, I stared off into nothing. Then I shook my head to clear my thoughts and pointed to the table where my abandoned meal sat. "Can you bring me my tray of food? Last time I left to eat, he died."

"Well then." He stood with a smile and returned with my tray. "Let's not repeat that, shall we?"

I needed both my hands to eat my dinner, so I placed my two feet on the king's body while I cut my steak. The beta's quiet laughter finally dragged a chuckle out of me. It did look a little stupid.

"I'm surprised that didn't wake him," I mused. "My feet are very cold."

The beta sobered and sent me a look of warning. "Careful when he wakes, Ragna," he cautioned seriously. "Just remember the whole...

alpha response. He may be a little out of it, so… keep that in mind. Call a guard immediately when he wakes."

I groaned and rubbed my temples with my fingers. "Alright. I hear you."

Beta Rudesind got up and left me alone with the male who hurt me— who was supposed to protect me. It was hard to shake the trepidation.

Chapter 12

King Zorian

Everything was black, but I had a vague sense that chaos was occurring outside of my bubble. The first thing I recalled were tingles on my lips, chest, and hips.

What's happening? I asked the void, somehow knowing I wasn't alone.

I don't know. We were gone, a confused voice answered. It was gruff, animalistic.

Oh. I think something's on my lap, but it feels good. Tingly.

I like it too.

What are those screeching noises? I want them to go away.

They sound familiar…

Yes, they do.

Let's keep the one on our lap, though.

Ok…

Ragna

The night went without incident, but in the morning, his fever spiked. When I called for someone to bathe him, the doctors also arrived to check on his progress.

"His burns are looking much better. Most of the blisters are gone," Doctor Egres noted as the servants with sponges and buckets of cold water finished their ministrations. The king's skin was still radiating heat, and whatever water was left on his body disappeared quickly.

"You've done well, Ragna," another doctor joked as he applied fresh cream to the burns, knowing all I had to do was touch him.

And me, my wolf mumbled.

"If it makes you more comfortable, you can touch anywhere else but these parts." Doctor Egres pointed toward a couple sections that were still quite dark.

Good. Now he'll know what it's like for someone to touch his cock without his permission, Trail remarked demonically.

Trail, no. Just... no, I stated firmly, eschewing the topic with a firm hand.

The beta handed over the book he'd gifted me. I'd forgotten entirely about it. "I should've brought this to you yesterday. You must have been bored out of your mind."

"Ahhh..." I hummed with delight and held it to my chest. "Thank you. Yes, I am going a little stir-crazy." I turned to address Doctor Egres. "When do you think I'll be able to leave?"

She twisted her lips in thought and studied the unconscious king. "Well, probably when he breaks his fever and wakes. Could be as early as tomorrow."

I heaved a sigh of relief and dug into my breakfast. Good. I was not necessarily enjoying my time here. The Sun God had told me to not leave his side, but I had mixed feelings about the king, and this whole arrangement made me uncomfortable. What if he woke and beat me to a pulp for sleeping on his bed?

Or wakes and does something else? Trail said with an audible shiver.

Was that an excited shiver or a disgusted one? I asked. *Please tell me it's the latter.* Trail remained silent.

The thought of him hurting me for sleeping in his bed was a little silly; he knew he was supposed to protect me now. The Sun God was deadly serious about it. Honestly, I didn't think the king would injure me again, but I'd grown to fear the unknown. What would he be like now?

I spent the rest of the day reading, with minor interruptions from doctors and servants. The beta didn't visit as often because the royal duties were piling up, requiring more of his attention. The king's fever spiked again after sunset, and I had to call a servant to sponge him. Unfortunately, I'd forgotten I was invisible and gave the poor young male quite a fright. After I reminded him about the skies' blessing, he calmed and tended to the king.

Trail wanted me to do it instead of the servant, but I was very much against running a wet sponge over his well-defined body. It was hard enough just keeping my arousal at bay. Even glancing at his vulnerable, unconscious face would occasionally stimulate me.

At least I didn't really have to look at him anymore. With the increase in contact points defined by the doctors, I could finally rest facing the other direction if I was pressed against him.

I dozed off facing away from the king with his arm under my neck, my back against his side, and my feet against his shin. The tingling from the mate bond became a relaxing background buzz that pulled me further into a comfortable, dreamless sleep.

⚜

I woke in the middle of the night to find he'd turned into my back so he was hugging me from behind. His head was nestled into my neck, causing goose bumps to erupt all over my body. When his warm puffs of breath brushed against such sensitive skin, my body spasmed involuntarily.

Goddesses! I gasped to Trail, startled. *He moved!*

I'm not complaining, she replied sleepily.

I tried to pry his arm off me so I could roll him over, but he wouldn't budge. He groaned in his sleep and pushed his hips against my butt. Tingles spread everywhere we were touching.

Oh no, I frowned, and my face erupted into flames.

Oh yes, Trail said wickedly.

I tried to scoot forward, but he wrapped his arms around my waist and pulled me against him. He nuzzled back into my neck, and I felt his erection poke against my underwear.

This is not ok, I murmured, wondering if I should call a guard.

This is absolutely ok, Trail argued. *Let the dying male have some fun.*

He's not dying, I snarled. *He's well past that point. Also, he's unconscious. How much fun could he truly be having?*

I let out a quiet, aggravated cry and buried my face in the pillow. My brain might hate it, but my body was starting to form its own opinion. King Zorian pushed his hips against my butt again, sending the head of his shaft along a very sensitive part of my private region. I jerked slightly in surprise. The tingling that traveled through the thin fabric of my underwear was rapturous, and I hated that it felt good. I should be gagging at his touch, but I wasn't.

"Stop that!" I hissed quietly.

He can't hear you, Trail snickered. *And stop telling him to stop! This is great!*

The king pulled me tighter against him, and his large, rough right hand moved to rest on my right breast. His grip was warm and unusually gentle.

Are we sure he's asleep? I asked, bewildered.

This is probably the best fever dream of his life.

The king began to slowly pump his hips into me, grinding his naked shaft along my sex. I glanced down and could see his enormous, engorged cock sliding in and out between my thighs, parting them in an erotic display. He nuzzled more into my neck and took longer, deeper breaths. I held back a pleased moan when his hand massaged my breast over my bra, gripping possessively.

That's it. As soon as he loosens his grip, I'm out of here. He's obviously not dying, and he can heal at his own damn rate, I snapped weakly, wishing my body agreed more with my brain. However, parts of my brain were starting to cave too.

His hips, though moving slowly, dug in harder, and I felt him part my folds through my underwear. The tiniest groan escaped from my lips, and desire kindled within me. A swell of heat also grew between my legs. It was an aching torture I'd never known before.

Maybe sex with him would feel better the second time, Trail suggested. *Look how gentle he can be.*

He's unconscious. Of course he's gentle! And we are not volunteering, damn it, I scolded her. *We're mad at him, remember?*

"Hmm…" The king let out a sighing moan as he rocked his hips into me, slow and steady. His lips brushed against my neck, and a pleasurable shudder racked my body from head to toe, forcing a gasp through my lips. I lost my will to fight when another sensation I'd never felt before grew between my legs. It made me feel like there was an intense itch that I needed to scratch, but it required much more friction and pressure. I became far too curious about it and crumbled.

He continued his slow, torturous pace, making me squirm. I never could've imagined that he was capable of being sensual—even in his sleep. I was incredibly confused and thrown by this discovery. The scent of my arousal blossomed cruelly, and I cringed when I felt my underwear dampen. I prayed that the scent wouldn't wake him. Traitorous body.

Well, if he wakes, that means our job here is done. Let's go out with a bang? Trail joked.

"Mmm… Ragna," the king mumbled in his sleep and shifted so both his hands could rub my breasts in large, demanding circles. My breath hitched, and I froze at his words despite needing to squirm in pleasure. Though he was clearly invading my space, I felt like I was invading his emotional privacy. He certainly couldn't be having a pleasant dream about me. He hated me.

I made a new effort to wriggle out of his grip now that his hands had shifted to my chest, but his palms slid down to my hips, halting my escape with a tight grip. A frustrated sob got caught in my chest because I knew I could fight harder—I just didn't want to anymore.

"Don't go…" he mumbled fretfully and continued pushing his massive, now-lubricated length along my sex. He dragged it back and forth, rocking and pushing until I was a panting mess. My stomach was full of butterflies that worked to tie my abdomen into tight knots. My core became hotter by the stroke, and I squeezed my thighs tight, trying to hold back whatever was growing inside me. The throbbing was unbearable!

"Mmm, that's it." The quietest growl rumbled through his sleeping chest. His body seemed to approve of the tighter space I'd created, and his hips rocked a little faster, causing my mouth to gape from an increase in pleasure.

He pumped against me several more times before he tightened and came against my core, soaking my underwear with his release. In my stimulated daze, I was barely conscious of him tilting my hips back into his pelvis, as though wanting me to welcome his seed. His drawn-out, languid groan into my ear sent my arousal through the roof, and I couldn't hold back a responding moan. I didn't recognize myself or my body's response. What was he doing to me?

His arms pulled me close, and I felt his canines press down on the spot between my neck and shoulder—the marking spot. My mind returned, and my eyes shot open. He was going to mark me! He was going to claim me permanently in his sleep! I tried to push him off, but he wasn't moving. His teeth were about to puncture my skin when I shrieked, extended my canines, and bit into the closest thing I could find—his bicep.

The king released my neck and shouted in either pain or surprise; I couldn't tell. He bolted upright in bed, completely awake, and I fled. I begged a soldier to take me to the beta, and he complied but looked uneasy escorting an invisible person. My face flushed hotly in embarrassment, worrying that they could smell the king on me.

The beta opened the door to his bedroom chamber, and his face went from half asleep to startled when he realized I was there. He didn't know where to look, but he gestured me in and thanked the guards.

As soon as the door was closed behind me, I cried, "I'm not going back in there! I'm not going back, and you can't make me!"

"Woah, woah, woah, woah," Beta Rudesind said and held out his palms to calm me. It wasn't helping. I was in a state.

"He tried to mark me! He tried to mark me in his sleep!" I shouted and wrapped my arms around myself. The beta's nostrils flared, and I could tell he sought me out with his nose. His eyes grazed my shoulder where the king's saliva was and raked down to my thighs where the king's seed was dripping. "I had to bite him to get away!"

He closed his eyes and took a long, steadying breath. "Ah, shit."

King Zorian

I sat up in bed, panting and confused as fuck. I looked over at my right bicep and found the cutest little bite mark. The bleeding had already stopped, and a scab was forming. When I ran a hand through my hair and wiped my flushed skin, I noticed the mild remnants of a fever.

The door to my chamber opened, and my beta strode in to visit. I eyed him warily and sniffed the air around me. Ragna had been here. The air was thick and heavy with her arousal. I looked at the bed and saw signs that I'd ejaculated, injecting fear and uncertainty into my heart. Had I forced her and I just didn't remember? I looked down at the glistening juices on my cock that were definitely from Ragna, and I groaned. This wasn't looking good.

"Fuck," I snapped. "Fuck, shit, fuck." I covered my eyes with a hand and asked, "Rude, what the fuck happened? All I remember is waking up because someone bit me, and that someone seems to be Ragna. What was she even doing in my chamber?"

Rudesind pulled up a chair, and I let my head drop back in aggravation. I was going to be lectured, wasn't I?

"Let me update you on the last couple of days, Zorian," my beta said, resting his elbows on his knees and folding his fingers. "You survived the Sun God's blessing, but you were nearly charred to a crisp. Your heart stopped, but the doctors and Ragna got it going again. Ragna's been asked to stay by your side, in her underwear, this entire time because Doctor Egres wanted to use your mate bond to stabilize and heal you faster. Anyway, apparently you got… more than handsy tonight and tried to mark her in your sleep."

My breathing stopped, and I stared at my beta.

That was real? Spine blurted. *I thought that was just a great dream we were having.*

I would not admit it, but I'd thought it was a dream too—an amazing one. "Fuck," I swore again. "Gods damn it all. Shit!" I gripped my head with my hands and groaned. "Is she ok?" I asked through my teeth, fearing the answer.

"She ran into my room crying with semen on her legs. You tell me," my beta said with a shake of his head. I put my hands back over my eyes in horror. "She refuses to come back in here, but I don't think you need her anymore. You're definitely out of the woods. At least you're awake now, even if you have a bit of a fever."

He leaned forward to place a cool hand on my forehead and nodded. "Oh, and your mistresses tried to attack her, but that was more entertaining than anything, really."

Oh shit. "What happened?" I peeked up at him through a gap in my fingers.

"Ragna was on your lap, in her underwear of course, after doing CPR, and they walked in on that. Your dragon, Princess Asmin, was yelling and tried to yank her off, but our little Sky-Blessed turned into a raging, protective force of nature. Shredded her arm to bits. Ragna didn't like how loud they were being considering we'd almost lost you. She ordered me to keep them out," he said, ending with an amused laugh. "I almost didn't recognize her; she was so pissed. A rogue ordering the kingdom's beta…" He chuckled and wiped away a tear of mirth. "Not that I mind her ordering me—"

"I bet you don't," I muttered lowly before I could think.

Rudesind frowned deeply at me. "I'm not going to give you too much of a hard time considering you almost died, but you really need to sort your shit out, Zorian. Jealousy doesn't look good on a male who doesn't like the female in question. Remember that you were the one who insisted on her execution.

"You've taken a lot from her. You traumatized her, but she still fought to save your life. I can't even mention sex without her freezing up an—"

"Why were you talking to her about sex?" I asked in a frigid, threatening voice, glaring at him and trying to read his face. Rudesind's mouth snapped shut, and a muscle in his jaw twitched. He was very good at hiding his microexpressions when he knew I was watching.

He jumped out of his seat and strode out of the room. "I'm getting your doctors," he said before closing the door. I glared at his exit, and anger bubbled inside me.

This sucks, Spine muttered. *We need to apologize to her.*

Honestly, I'm not sure if I can. I cringed while trying to lie back down on the sheets. The burns hurt like a bitch. I rolled to my side and buried my face in Ragna's pillow. Cloves, nutmeg, and cider. I used it like a drug to calm myself.

What do you mean you can't?

If I go from a raging asshole to a penitent puppy, it's going to seem disingenuous. Not just to her but to me as well. It doesn't... I don't know. I feel like I have to work my way there. I've been mad at her existence for so long; it's hard to just turn off. I'm also still trying to wrap my head around the whole champion thing too. Goddess, I feel like a total mess.

Well, I'm just glad you're being honest with yourself now, Spine said approvingly.

That comment annoyed me, but I held back a retort. My suite door clicked again, and I turned my head to find Doctor Egres and Doctor Medard approaching.

"Good to see you awake, Your Majesty!" Doctor Egres said, placing her suitcase down and opening it to grab some swabs and ointment. Doctor Medard stuck the thermometer in my mouth and began checking a number of things, including my eyes and ears. I was getting uncomfortably sweaty and gestured for the doctor to open a window.

"Looks like you're breaking your fever on your own," Doctor Medard announced, taking the thermometer and looking at it. He nodded, sanitized the glass rod, and stored it. "Excellent. Where is the she-wolf? Ragna? Isn't she supposed to be here?"

Doctor Egres leaned to whisper something into his ear, and his mouth became O-shaped. He cleared his throat, and I felt a blush rise into my cheeks. Damn it. Kings didn't blush.

"Well, it looks like you don't require her mate bond anymore," Doctor Medard said, scratching at his bald scalp. "You should be all healed in a day, I'd wager."

They then worked together to treat my burns with ointment and packed up to depart. "Thank you, Doctor Egres, Doctor Medard." I nodded in gratitude and lay back down to rest.

When it was just Spine and me, he lamented, *I miss her already.*

There's nothing to miss. We've been unconscious this whole time.

Well, I for one wish we'd kept dreaming.

I swallowed heavily and shifted to turn into her pillow again. I slid a finger down my cock to wipe up the scent of her arousal. I brought it up to my nose and inhaled deeply. Saliva flooded my mouth at her smell. If only she was my actual fated mate. How torturous it was to have her here at the castle. So accessible.

Trying to recall more, I thought I'd heard her moaning and panting. A pleased smirk threatened to pull up the corners of my mouth, but I held it back out of guilt.

The front door creaked open, and I smelled one of my mistresses approaching. It was Asmin, and I closed my eyes with a groan. She'd caused trouble, and I didn't want to deal with her drama right now. Why was she bothering me in the middle of the night?

"Your Majesty," she said, crawling onto the bed in her nightgown. I noticed she favored one hand; the other was heavily bandaged.

Spine surprised me with his glee over her injury. *Ragna really did a number on her to protect us. I love a territorial female. That she-wolf is so sexy.*

We weren't actually in danger from her. She was just being loud. Our heart had just stopped!

"What are you doing here, Asmin?" I sighed as she settled next to me. She pouted and angled to give me a view down her nightgown.

"I was just so worried about you, Your Majesty. I heard you woke and just had to... come."

"Your concern has been noted," I replied dryly, wishing she'd leave so I could go back to sleep. I wanted to go back to enjoying Ragna's scent. She was ruining it.

"I just thought maybe I could help make you feel better," she purred in a sultry voice and ran her fingers up my thigh. She grazed a more painful burn, and I growled at her. She mistook my scolding for encouragement and reached for my cock.

I snatched her wrist and put her hand back down on her lap. "I'm not in any condition to play with you, Asmin. I'm tired."

Anger flared in her eyes, and she pushed her dark hair over a shoulder. "So, you're in condition to fuck that whore but not me?" she accused loudly, pointing at the cum on the sheets.

Part of me almost wanted to laugh at her attempt to make me feel guilty. Princesses didn't get to tell kings who they could or couldn't fuck. Pathetic.

"You do not know what you're talking about," I warned. She was walking on thin ice. If she wasn't royalty, I would've had my hand around her throat by now.

She never knows what she's talking about, Spine added.

"The room reeks of that bitch, Zorian!" she spat.

"King Zorian," I snarled, letting my dominance roll over her. She cringed and submitted.

"Yes, Your Majesty," she grumbled, shaking. She looked up again after a minute, furious, and complained, "But look what she did to me!" She held up her bandaged arm. "You know she must be punished for attacking a princess! I will not back down from this insult! My father will hear about this!"

"She's already been punished, Asmin. Drop it," I replied coldly, thinking about how I'd just assaulted Ragna in my bed. If anyone should be exempt from punishment for the rest of their life, it'd be the she-wolf.

"Oh, really? What did you do?" Her face sported a haughty, excited grin, and I dismissed her question with a gesture.

She's a sadistic one, isn't she? Spine noted. *Keep her away from our Ragna.*

Ragna's not ours, Spine.

"Leave. I'm sleeping now," I ordered, glaring her off the bed. She frowned, curtseyed, and left my suite in a huff. I grabbed a corner of my bedsheet, spat on it, and tried to rub Asmin's scent off my leg. I nearly gagged. She no longer smelled good to me.

Chapter 13

King Borian

I was feeling decent enough come morning to prepare for my upcoming absence. I winced slightly as I buttoned up a shirt and pulled on some trousers. The pain was manageable, but the occasional throb pierced my threshold. All I could do was white-knuckle through the pain and dab at the sweat that'd trickle down my brow.

I marched to my study and sat down, grateful my ass was in decent enough shape to sit comfortably. As ordered, servants had delivered a stack of research books on the fae realm from our library, and I flipped through the tomes. I scribbled notes down on a piece of paper, trying to sort out what the next couple months of my life would look like.

I put the pen down and ran my hands through my hair.

We have a lot of preparing to do, but we'll still have to travel light, Spine said thoughtfully.

Should probably get our armor out of storage too. I sighed. *I don't know what to expect, and that's when we need to prepare for the worst.*

I agree.

I made a list of items to have gathered for us. We wouldn't need a lot of rations. I could hunt for us. We'd have to get Ragna's belongings from the dungeon storage because she'd need her weapons. I should bring a coin purse in case we needed to barter. I continued with my list and hadn't noticed that my beta had walked in until he'd cleared his throat.

My eyes rolled up to look at him. "Good morning, Rude. What can I do for you?"

"Are you well enough to be out of bed?" he asked, shoving his hands in his pockets and leaning across the desk to see what I was writing.

"Well enough. It's just pain at this point. The fever is gone," I replied and pulled out another piece of paper to sort out who would cover what duties in my absence. I didn't want everything going to my beta. My normal workload was heavy enough, and I wanted to spread it out to make my absence easier on my staff. Some items were purely maintenance based and didn't require a lot of critical thinking.

"That's good," he said, and I nodded. "I hope you don't mind, but I put Ragna in a guest chamber. I figured the Sky-Blessed shouldn't go back to the dungeon."

"That's reasonable," I agreed. I doubted the Sun God would give me a second chance to live if I threw her back in the dungeon—not that I wanted to do that.

"I also posted two mated guards outside her room, just in case."

"In case of what?" I asked, playing dumb. Gods help me, I didn't know why. Maybe I just needed something to say. Talking about her made me uncomfortable.

"In case any unmated males try to sneak in. Also, to prevent your lovely princesses from murdering her in her sleep," he said with a low chuckle. It hadn't escaped my notice that the emphasis on 'lovely' was heavy and sarcastic.

"I've already spoken to Asmin. I made it clear she needs to drop the issue."

"We'll see if the other two abide by that."

"You seem to have it all handled, Rude. Is that all?" I asked, keeping my eyes on the parchment before me. He sighed.

"Are you going to talk to her? She's... anxious about a lot of things."

"I'll speak to her when I speak to her. I'm busy preparing for my absence," I said coolly, hoping he'd take it as a prompt to leave.

"You're going to be on the road with her for who knows how long. Isn't it time to break the ice? Make amends?" Rudesind persisted.

"I will talk to her, Rude. That's all I have to say," I repeated with finality. I handed him my list of items. "Do me a favor and get the servants to collect these. If I forget anything, I'll go to them directly."

"As you wish," Rudesind said with a bow and left.

Let's go talk to her now. I want to see our mate. I miss her, Spine said excitedly.

She's not... I sighed and gave up. I didn't have the energy for this right now. *Alright, let's go talk to that she-wolf.*

Ragna, Spine corrected, and I let out another withering sigh.

I walked down toward the guest wing and followed her delectable scent until I came to a chamber sandwiched by two guards. They bowed when they saw me, and I knocked on the door. I heard feet padding toward the door and it opened. Her lush green eyes peered up at me, and her face flushed bright red.

"May I enter?" I asked, gesturing past her. She nodded and opened the door for me, keeping her eyes on the ground.

I settled into a chair by a small, round dining table. When my belt dug into a painful burn, I winced and wiped a bead of sweat from my forehead. Ragna rushed to the restroom and returned with a cup of water and a towel. I watched her through lowered lashes as she took a seat next to me and rolled up one of my sleeves so she could rest her hand on my arm.

I felt my body relax under her tingling touch, and the pain of my burns diminished. A grimace flickered across her face, but she pasted on a neutral expression, matching my countenance.

"Good morning, Your Majesty," she mumbled quietly. "I hope you're doing better."

Well, this is off to a great start, Spine said sarcastically.

"I am improved. I've come to inform you that I've compiled a list of resources for our trip and have ordered servants to gather them for us. We'll be traveling light, but we should have all the necessities," I replied in a detached tone.

Holy shit, Zorian, lighten the fucking mood. Tell her last night was fireworks! Thank her for saving us! Anything!

I drew in a deep breath, extremely irritated with Spine's distracting interjections. It was taking all my effort to not turn into a snarling asshole. She made me nervous, and I didn't know how to deal with it. Anger was easy.

Ragna nodded, seemingly lost in thought. I glanced at her hand, and she was subconsciously rubbing her thumb against my wrist. I cleared my throat and continued, "I'm currently situating coverage for my duties while we're gone. It's a lot to sort, but hopefully it'll all be worked out today. I'm also having your personal effects delivered to you. You'll have everything that was confiscated."

She looked relieved, and her eyes flickered up to look at me—but only for a moment. "Thank you, Your Majesty."

She wasn't making this easy.

She's afraid of you, dumbass. You're being cold as fuck. Goddess, you're so frustrating!

I took a deep breath and called her name to get her attention. "Ragna, look at me," I ordered, and her gaze slid from the ground to my eyes. She had such pretty eyes. "My beta brought it to my attention that you were experiencing some distress, some anxiety. Is there anything you wish to discuss? If it's about Asmin, one of the princesses, I've told her to leave you alone."

I noticed that she made a little face when I said the princess's name, but she just shook her head. "I have nothing to discuss, Your Majesty. I'm also not concerned about your... other females."

Ohhh, hohoho, she's jealous! She doesn't like that you've got them to pick from! Spine crowed. *There's hope for you yet!*

Or she thinks I'm a pig, Spine.

I studied her, trying to figure out what else to say. I was running out of ideas. "Why were you headed for the Lunar Coven?" I inquired, wondering if that was something we should still investigate.

"Is this another interrogation, Your Majesty?" she returned quietly.

"No, Ragna. It's just a question. Don't sass me," I reprimanded.

"How am I supposed to know?" she snapped and took her hand off my arm. I couldn't hide my grimace when the pain returned in full force. "First, you want to kill me, then you want to interrogate me, then you rape me, then you put me in a dungeon, and then I have to lie next to you to save your life, only for you to take advantage of m-me," she seethed with furious tears running down her cheeks.

Ah, the dam has broken, Spine remarked sadly.

Ragna paled and fell to her knees in submission, realizing that she'd just said some damn risky things to a king. "I'm s-sorry, Your Majesty. Forgive me! Your beta explained alpha behavior... Forget I said anything," she begged in a hoarse voice.

I leaned on an elbow and scrubbed a hand over my mouth, staring at her. I honestly didn't know what to say. I felt completely unprepared for this breakdown, so I ended up doing the only thing I could think of, which was to get up and leave.

I stopped at the door and turned to her. "Make sure you're rested and prepared for the journey. If all goes well, we'll leave tomorrow or the following day." I opened the door and left her to her devices.

Coward, Spine spat.

Ragna

I stared at the door in shock. I'd flown into a full-blown tantrum, and the king had just waltzed out instead of removing my head from my shoulders.

What kind of reaction was that? Trail gasped, bewildered.

I swear I will never understand that lycan, I replied while rubbing tears from my eyes.

I think his brain is broken? Maybe?

You may be on to something. We still have to travel with... that. I went to the bathroom and splashed cold water on my face. What now? Waiting was killing me.

Maybe we could go for a run? Trail asked hopefully.

That sounds nice!

I opened the door and addressed one of the guards. "Am I allowed to go on a run around the castle? I promise I won't stray. I'm just going a little crazy sitting around here."

The two regarded each other. "We were told to guard your door. Perhaps we could escort you, though we don't have direct instruction to do so."

I frowned. I didn't want to cause trouble. I wish I had asked the king while he was here. "Maybe one of you can ask the beta?" I inquired. "If it's not too much trouble. I'm sorry... It's just been... Never mind." I sighed and closed the door to give up, but one of the guards waved a hand.

"It's time," he said. "I'll go ask. Let me find him."

"Thank you!" I beamed happily, then closed the door. A couple minutes later, I heard a scream and running footsteps outside my room. I opened the door to peek, and four hands seized me. I was gagged with cloth, sprayed with a mist, and yanked violently into the hall, kicking and hollering.

My eyes rolled to the sides, and I saw that my captors were the other two of the king's females. They snickered as they snapped a silver collar around my neck so I was weakened and couldn't shift. I screamed into the gag as the silver bit my throat. They dragged me into a large storage closet and threw me onto the floor.

One of the mistresses was a willowy redhead who would've looked graceful if she wasn't crouched over me, cackling as she tied my wrists behind my back. The other was a sneering, voluptuous blonde who stood with a wide hip jutting out to the side. I blinked through tears, already feeling a bruise on my hipbone as I tried to move onto my side.

The blonde curled her lip and said, "Asmin was forbidden from punishing you, but we've had no such restriction placed on us. There are very strict rules against ordering a princess about and making death threats, especially if you're a filthy rogue mutt. You have no idea the world of trouble you've just signed yourself up for."

I growled a threat, though it was very muffled under the gag.

"Oh, how precious she is." The redhead chuckled darkly. "The puppy is teething."

I scrambled to my feet and tried to kick the redhead, feeling like she was too reckless to be good at dodging or blocking. My judgment was wrong. She grabbed my ankle and promptly snapped it. I screamed at the top of my lungs and writhed in pain, too drained from the silver to fight. Cowards. Cowards!

Why are we always targets? Trail asked weakly. I could tell that this silver collar was much worse than the other one. The nauseating smell of my searing skin lingered in the small room.

They'll find us, I told Trail. *They'll find our scent.*

I hate to say this—Trail panted—*but I think that spray hid our scent.*

"Let's see what she's working with that drives the males so wild. I still think it's witchwork. Sky-Blessed, my ass," the blonde snapped and stepped forward to shred my clothes. I kicked with my good foot and yelled as loudly as I could, but I was tiring fast.

It has now been zero days since our last clothing incident, Trail mumbled, and I felt her presence fade. *Back to the good ol' days...*

"Eh," the redhead muttered, prodding my left breast. "She's passable. Nothing to write home about."

"It's still down to us three to get the king. The reward is one thing, but he's a fine piece of meat. Quite the bonus. It's really too bad we have to make him wait."

"I still want to remove the competition. Not that she is." The redhead scoffed and kicked me in the ribs. I whimpered as pain splintered up my torso, almost blinding enough to make me faint. "Finding her on his naked lap made me want to vomit. I wonder how many males she's slept with to get this far. I say we make her uglier."

She extended a claw and aimed for my face. I struggled, but the other held me down so she could cut both my cheeks. She then drew a long line from the top of one breast to another. I held back a scream and bit down on the gag with my teeth. They would not get the satisfaction o—

The blonde extended her own claws and raked two deep lines down my stomach. That shattered my threshold. I howled at the top of my lungs and tried to scoot away from her, but they held me fast.

"I'm bored." The redhead smirked. "Let's play tic-tac-toe." She carved two horizontal lines across the vertical ones, but it snagged, and some flesh threatened to pull off entirely. The shock from my stomach injuries began to wear off, and the pain blossomed into hot, throbbing, concentrated agony. It was a sensation I couldn't get away from, and I fell into panic. My heart raced as I screamed from each slash. I couldn't bear to look down at my belly, not wanting to witness a possible gutting. Either the gutting would kill me, or my heart would fail from the shock; it was already beating too fast.

"No one's really going to miss you, you know," the blonde said in a low voice. "You're a false prophet. A whore in savior's clothing. To think that you thought you had a chance with the king. It's laughable." She carved an 'x' or an 'o' into my belly, but I couldn't tell through the fire.

Lightheaded and limp, I sluggishly wondered how much blood I'd already lost. How much time did I have left? My life was an hourglass, and they were pulling out sand by the handful.

Please... I prayed to the gods and goddesses. *Please get someone. Please save me.* As much as I had little faith in him as my champion, I prayed to King Zorian as well. *I know you hate me, but please don't let me die. Not like this. Not in such a pathetic way. Let me die on the battlefield. Let me die after saving the Moon Goddess.*

I'd been too confident. I thought I could take on any of these females, but wouldn't they have all been trained in self-defense as princesses? I'd been stupid. I'd let my guard down and should've thought about being outnumbered.

I just couldn't help it earlier when the king's heart had stopped. Their entrance and disrespect had enraged me, almost to where I'd been blinded by fury. I'd felt protective and territorial. I'd let the mate bond cloud my judgment, and now I was paying the price. I hated royalty. I hated their entitlement. I hated that they could get away with murder. I hated that they took death so lightly.

Please, King Zorian, we still have so much to do. I can't die now.

"Damn, Berdil," the blonde cursed. "You beat me. Let's go again. I'll get you this time."

They rolled my stunned body over, and I knew this was how I was going to die. I could feel the blood pooling under me, warm and sticky. My vision blurred as I stared blankly at the wall. They continued carving, but I just felt cold now.

"Bahahaha!" The redhead laughed, though I barely registered it. The voice seemed so far from me. "Got you again, Huzan! Here, let's go again, and I'll show you my trick. Except when you know the trick, we're going to have a stalemate every single time, hahaha!"

They started a new game, and I looked for Trail inside me. *Trail...* I prodded. *Are you gone?* Nothing but silence. *I love you, Trail. Maybe it's time for it to be over. No more rapes. No more assaults. No more females trying to murder us. Maybe it'll be nice and quiet. Maybe the Moon Goddess is just resting somewhere, and we'll say hi on our way out. I'm sorry I kept getting us into trouble.*

I held on to the best memories I could until I faded away, and strangely enough, I wished more of them had been with Zorian. Goddess knew why.

Chapter 14

King Zorian

Something was wrong. I was discussing maintenance with my steward when a rush of uneasiness fell over me. It was similar to the panic attack I'd suffered days ago but much, much worse. My hand tapped anxiously on my upper thigh while the male yammered on about the audience chamber. I scratched my forehead and looked around, trying to discern if anything had changed, but nothing jumped out at me. My heart pounded in my ears, growing louder and louder until I couldn't hear anyone anymore.

I held up a hand to pause our conversation and promptly excused myself. This was too distracting and too bizarre to ignore. Mind-linking the beta, I asked if anything seemed off to him.

Nothing really. Asmin took a bit of a tumble down the stairs a while ago, but she's fine, Rudesind reported.

Where'd she fall?

The guest wing, the main staircase.

I'm on my way.

I sped down to the guest wing, but I had a sense that Asmin wasn't the issue. On top of the uneasiness, nausea sank deeper into my gut with every step. When I reached the staircase, no one was there, so I looked down the hall and noticed that Ragna's chamber door was wide open. No guards were in sight, which was unusual. I jogged down and poked my head through the doorway. One of the guards was frantically searching for something, checking under furniture and tearing open every closet.

"Where's Ragna?" I asked, feeling like maybe this was the source of my unease. He started and jumped to attention.

"My partner went to go ask Beta Rudesind if Ragna was allowed to go on a run around the castle, per her request. Shortly after he left, Asmin fell down the stairs, so I ran to help her. When I got back, the door was open, and Ragna was gone."

This doesn't seem right, Spine remarked worriedly.

Maybe she just snuck out, I reasoned. *I'm not thrilled about that kind of irresponsible behavior—*

Will you just shut the fuck up and listen to my instincts for once in your miserable life? Spine roared, and I was shaken by his ferocity. *GO TALK TO ASMIN!*

I ran down the hall and followed Asmin's scent to her chamber. When I knocked on the door, she opened it with a mischievous smirk. "Hello, Your Majesty," she purred with a curtsey. "What can I do for you?" The princess sauntered forward and walked her fingers up my chest.

Just ask her point blank. Watch her expressions, Spine barked.

I was starting to feel too panicked to argue with him, so I snarled at her. "Where is Ragna?"

I stared intently and watched a brief flicker of irritation and fear cross her features. It wasn't enough, so I had to push further.

"Asmin!" I growled and pulled her out into the hallway. "I'm giving you one chance here! If I find you've done something and didn't come clean, I will end you! It will be a long and painful death! I don't give a shit about the treaty!"

She pulled away and stood tall, pasting a haughty expression on her face. I noticed a flicker of victory—or perhaps satisfaction—pass over her features. That was enough for me. I was doing it. Using an alpha command on royalty was taboo, but I was out of shits to give.

"ASMIN, I COMMAND YOU TO SHOW ME HER LOCATION," I boomed and towered over her, allowing my dominance to crush her. She wailed through her teeth, pointed in a direction with a trembling hand, and I yanked her down the hall. The female struggled to free herself from my grip, but neither that nor her cries of pain fazed me.

She led me back to the guest hall, the last place I would've gone to search, and pointed to the door of a storage closet. Yanking it open, I discovered the other two princesses using a naked Ragna's flesh to play a game. They froze in shock, and I ripped them away from the she-wolf, not hesitating for a second. My blood was boiling, but my mind was clear.

Rude, you are to take the princesses and lock them in the dungeon. Send multiple servants to fetch every doctor they can find and send them to the guest wing, I ordered through the mind-link while dashing to Ragna's unconscious form.

I scooped up her naked form but was startled by the amount of blood dripping freely from dozens of deep cuts. Both sides of her were nearly butchered. Panic surged into me from the sudden gushing of crimson, and I laid her down in the hallway, biting back tears as I ripped off my shirt to cover her stomach.

What happened? Rudesind asked.

They may have just killed Ragna. Hurry, Rude! We're losing her, damn it! Fuck! Fuck! Fuck!

I looked over at the females in shock. "Submit!" I yelled, and they fell to their knees. "SUBMIT!" I screamed, and they lay flat on the floor, sobbing. I pushed down with my dominance, making them wail and press their foreheads into the ground. I wished I could crush them with it— paint the floor with their blood and flattened corpses. "You will not move until Beta Rudesind retrieves you," I seethed and turned back to Ragna.

Her skin was too white, and her heart slowed. Guards circled us, muttering and worrying over the scene. I kept my hands on her belly, trying to stop the bleeding, but I had no idea if I was making it worse. I'd done field dressings before, but this... Dragging my eyes from the red that was everywhere, I noticed that she'd also been forced into a silver collar.

"Get that off her!" I bellowed, and several lycans rushed to remove it.

I prayed that her wolf would be strong enough to keep her from slipping away... from our mission... from life... from me... When the collar was pulled away, I grimaced at the melted flesh around her neck. My gaze then cut to the marks on her cheeks and across her breasts. I tucked my head down so the soldiers couldn't see the tears in my eyes.

I'd already failed as her champion. The Sun God had been right to doubt me.

Briefcases opened around us as doctors crowded Ragna, and then a hand grabbed my shoulder to pull me from the scene. "Give them space, Zorian," my beta murmured and ordered the other soldiers to back off as well.

Then the doctors yelled a contradicting order. "I need as many unmated males as you can find! They need to help stabilize her while we work!" I nodded to some soldiers, and the mated ones raced to gather more people.

Rudesind and I hurried forward and were ordered to crouch on the opposite side to place our hands on her arm. Several soldiers knelt to do the same. More males ran to the scene and squeezed in to touch one of her arms or legs, whichever was closest; it was getting crowded.

Jealousy flared and sizzled as I watched each unmated male look upon her with reverence. The mate bond was such a powerful force to be able to create infatuation between complete strangers. Though I was grateful for the help, the connection was something I loathed sharing.

Returning my gaze to Ragna replaced my jealousy with grief. I held back a sob and made a confession to Rudesind in my moment of vulnerability. "I don't even know her wolf's name. I feel like I should've learned that by now."

You have a terrible memory, Spine scolded. *Her wolf's name is Trail. We overheard her talking at the waterfall.*

Oh... He was right, and I hated myself for forgetting that.

Spine continued, *I suppose I could give you a pass considering she was lounging about under the sun, glorious in her nudity.* I frowned at the accusation, but he wasn't wrong.

Rudesind furrowed his blond brows. "I don't know it either. I wish we could talk to her, but she's unconscious, and she's not part of our pack."

"Maybe we should change that?" I asked, trying to be subtle about wiping my watery eyes with a free hand.

"That'll be her call, if she survives this," he replied bitterly.

"She will!" I hissed through clenched teeth, trying to stay quiet so the doctors could focus. "She survived on her own for years and survived me for a week. She can survive anything!"

Rudesind turned to me in awe. "Was that a moment of self-awareness, Zorian?"

"Shut up and focus on Ragna," I growled, then hesitated. I should mention her wolf's name now, but part of me wanted to keep it all to myself. I'd tell him later. Trail. Trail, Trail, Trail...

I restrained a pathetic whimper as I watched them work on her belly. She'd been butchered in the most sadistically creative way. When they had to dig past her skin, I realized that most of her injuries weren't limited to superficial lacerations. They were deep. Brutal.

When they finished stitching her belly, they bandaged her cheeks and breasts. We worked gently to turn her over so the doctors could treat her back, and I stared—once again—in disbelief at the games of tic-tac-toe they'd carved into her beautiful skin. The other unmated males growled low, their rage just as palpable as mine.

This is unforgiveable, Rudesind seethed through a private mind-link. *What are we doing with them? We can't execute them. That'd start a war.*

They'll be banished and sent back to their kingdoms at the very least. Let me worry about it, Rude. They've all obviously lost any chance they had of marriage.

Good... he muttered. *I didn't like them anyway.*

I sighed. *Rude, they were diverting at first. I admit it was thrilling to see which one was more suitable to rule alongside me. But yes, over time they grated on me. They became too comfortable, but without a mate to produce an heir... it's a lot of pressure. Not just pressure from the other kingdoms to get their claws into my family line but pressure to raise a good king or queen for my people. My people need to be taken good care of when I'm gone. Maybe that's one reason why Ragna infuriates me so. She represents something I haven't found that I desperately need, and it provokes me.*

That's not her fault, Zorian. You need to stop taking it out on her. She has serious physical injuries now on top of psychological ones. She's going to be fragile.

I'm trying. I truly am. I pinched the bridge of my nose with my free hand and squeezed my eyes tight, frustrated with my own inability to communicate. For now, I would have to try to communicate with action. I was probably going to fuck up, but I'd keep trying.

I looked down at her again and stroked her arm with a thumb, feeling the little sparks that—aside from her heartbeat and breathing—told me she was still alive. She looked like she was on death's door, but I had a deep feeling in my gut that she'd survive this.

I glanced around and flagged down a servant. They rushed over, and I said, "Take her things to my chamber. She'll be staying there until we leave. Please provide the most comfortable sleepwear and whatever else she might need." He ran off to execute my order, and my beta peered skeptically at me.

"What are you doing?" he asked suspiciously.

"Doing what I should have done earlier. I've been charged by the gods to be her champion, and I'm going to start acting like it. She's not leaving my sight again."

When the doctors finished sewing, medicating, and bandaging her, I was allowed to lift and carry her to my chambers as long as it was done with extreme caution. The doctors also warned to be mindful of her sprained wrist, fractured rib, and broken ankle. The extended list of injuries was staggering and brought me back to the invoice I'd received from Doctor Egres all those days ago. The comparison sickened me.

Rudesind followed at my heels, but I paid him no mind. I was in shock. I'd been betrayed by females I thought I knew. I'd trusted them, and they proved to be false.

My beta opened the door for me, and I laid Ragna down on the bed. We grabbed the soft pajamas the servant had put out for her and dressed her in silence. I reclined next to her and placed a hand on her arm. Rudesind sat on the other side and did the same. I normally would have been territorial over that action, but I was too tired, too relieved she'd survived to care. If he wanted to help her, I'd let him.

"The mate bond is a strange thing," he murmured, staring at her. "I feel the pull—and it's a significant one—but if I look real deep inside myself, I'm pretty sure she's not mine."

"Oh?" I asked with raised brows. I wasn't unhappy to hear that revelation. I thought he'd been getting a little too close to the she-wolf.

"Mother always said I had good intuition." He chuckled and pushed a strand of cinnamon hair from Ragna's sleeping face. "Don't get me wrong, Ragna's an incredible, beautiful female. She's just not what I pictured. Not even close, really."

"That's interesting," I murmured. "What did you picture?"

"I don't know. It's hard to put into words. When I was younger, I'd daydream about a fierce female warrior who'd conquer the battlefield with me." His faint smile was nostalgic. "Brunettes were also never my thing."

"You said Ragna was fierce with the princesses, though," I mumbled a little defensively. He shrugged.

"Like I said, it's a very subtle gut feeling. Right now, I'd mate and mark Ragna in a heartbeat, but… there's this one percent part of me that's telling me not to. I don't think that's normal for fated mates. They say when you know, you know. Completely."

I nodded, ignoring the urge to rip his head off for even thinking about mating with Ragna.

"Who did you picture, Zorian?"

"Oh, that's impossible to answer, my friend." I sighed heavily and looked up at the ceiling, tucking my other hand under my head. "All I could think of for years was establishing peace and getting the kingdom settled. Then—in the blink of an eye—I was still unmated, and princesses were coming out of the woodwork."

"You must still have a preference. A daydream, no?"

I wiped a hand over my brow, wincing at a burn that throbbed for a second. I cleared my throat and thought deeply about his question. "What this kingdom needs is someone to balance me out and to see things that I miss."

"I'm not asking about the kingdom's preference. Kingdoms don't get fated mates. You're evading the question."

I waved him off with a hand. "I'm exhausted, Rude. I'm still recovering from burns, and I have this little she-wolf to look after now. The weight of being her champion… The shock of what happened… The betrayal. I'm wiped."

My beta nodded, looking slightly ashamed as he stood to leave. "The doctors should come back this evening to change her bandages. Rest. I'll handle things," he said. I thanked him, and he departed from the suite.

I turned on my side, slid an arm around her, and pulled her gently against me, making sure I didn't disturb any bandages. I nuzzled into her hair, taking her scent deep into my lungs. The aroma relaxed me, the bond calmed me, and I tried to shake off my worries, if just for a moment.

"Looks like we're switching roles, little she-wolf," I murmured to her unconscious form. "I'll get you all better, then we can leave and find the Moon Goddess. We'll do it together, and I'll protect you from here on out. We'll make the gods proud."

I clenched my teeth and squeezed my eyes shut from a heavy wave of remorse. "I'm so sorry I wasn't there. I should have protected you. I'm so sorry."

I probably shouldn't have done it, but I peppered the side of her head with soft kisses as tears rolled down my cheeks. Each one was a silent apology. "I'm sorry for everything, most of all for hurting you. Gods, I wish I could talk to you like a normal person. I don't know what's wrong with me."

Keeping myself as close to her as possible, I fell asleep.

Ragna

I felt the pain before I could think of anything else. My hand flew to my stomach and patted around, searching for blood. Prying open my dry eyelids was a slow and painful endeavor. When I turned my face, I discovered that King Zorian was the body sleeping against me. I couldn't find the energy to be confused, scared, or scandalized. He was shirtless, but when I glanced down, I was simultaneously relieved and disappointed to find pants on him.

We're disappointed, Ragna, Trail's sluggish voice mumbled. *Of those two things, we're definitely disappointed.*

Trail... we're not dead. Do you know what happened? I asked and reached to shakily rub an eye. *Gods, how many times have I said that line before?*

I don't remember when they took the collar off, but I felt some unmated give us energy. We were saved in time. She sounded so tired, almost more so than me.

I tried to sit up, but pain exploded up my back and raked across my belly. I froze, gripped the sheets, and screamed silently. The intolerable agony passed, and I relaxed, breathing hard. I looked back to King

Zorian and considered waking him in my growing desperation. A lock of his white hair was flopped over his face, fluttering slightly whenever his breath blew against it. He didn't look like an asshole at all while he slept.

I tried to say his name, but my mouth was so dry that it came out in a hoarse whisper. My throat didn't want to clear without saliva, so I weakly poked him.

"King... Zor..." I coughed, and his burgundy eyes shot open. Leaving my prodding finger on him, I wheezed, "Water..." He rushed out of bed and left the room, returning thirty seconds later with a glass. I tried to shift upright to drink, but I screamed out loud this time, and he gently pushed me flat again.

"Don't move," he warned in a low voice. "You'll rip your stitches." He knelt by the bed, scooped the back of my head with his palm, and put the cup to my lips. I drank about half of it before another wave of pain overwhelmed me. I gritted my teeth and tilted my head back, hissing. When it passed, I went limp and fought to catch my breath, blinking sluggishly and shivering.

"Are you cold?" the king asked but didn't wait for my answer. He quickly moved to the closet and pulled out a thick blanket. I stared at the door he'd swung open, and everything came back to me. The closet. The mistresses.

"Your... Majesty," I gasped as he spread the blanket across my side of the bed. "I remember... something..." I shivered again, this time more violently. I was so cold. It felt like ice water had been injected into my veins.

"Shh," he hushed and placed a large hand over my forehead. I couldn't help but lean into it. Though it was rough, it was so warm. "You don't need to worry about anything right now, aside from getting better."

"Blonde." I coughed and shuddered. "Said something about... a bonus. Waiting..." I made a grab to finish the water, but he repeated his earlier action of helping me drink from the cup.

He frowned while considering my words, then shook his head. "I don't want to talk about them right now. They're not going anywhere, so trust me, it can wait until you're better."

I sighed in defeat. My recollection of it was fuzzy at best. I'd hang on to the details of the memory as best as I could.

"Allow me to clarify that they're in the dungeon. They won't be allowed near you ever again," he said darkly. "They'll be severely punished for what they've done."

"Thank... you." I tried to clear my throat again.

"Well, it's because they've committed basic sacrilege," he clarified, looking away with an expression I couldn't discern. "Attacking a blessed one is an attack on the gods. It's a serious offense in my kingdom." He closed his eyes and shook his head, scowling.

Oh... So it wasn't because anyone cared about me enough to want justice served. It was because of what I represented. My heart caved in at those words, and I felt a tear roll down my cheek. I turned my head so he wouldn't see and wondered if I'd ever find a place where just being Ragna was enough. Not a rogue, not Sky-Blessed, just... Ragna.

Chapter 15

King Zorian

You know, it's like the gods put this perfect opportunity together for you to make amends, but then you just decide to crap all over it, Spine growled in aggravation. *You could have said you had to get revenge because she was important to you or that you'll never let anyone hurt her again as her champion, but no, you decided to say they were arrested because they insulted the gods.*

I was staring at the wall, already furious with myself for allowing those words to escape my mouth. Now I was just pissed, and Spine was making it worse.

I don't get it. You have all these honeyed words for her when she's asleep, but as soon as she's awake, you turn into this... THIS. I don't even have a word to describe you!

Spine, please be quiet. I need to think. She's... I think she's crying. I glanced covertly over, and she was facing away with watery eyes.

"Hey," I said and placed a hand on her arm. "Don't cry. You're already dehydrated. You'll make it worse."

Oh, your bedside manner is just...

There was a knock on the door, and I jogged out to see who it was. I sighed in relief and let a couple doctors in to check on Ragna. They paused and stared at the bed.

"Was she moved, Your Majesty?" one of the doctors asked, but another one leaned over to poke at the blanket over her legs. I looked out the window to verify that it was night. Wait... I could see her now!

"She's invisible at night when out of direct moonlight, if you recall the Sky Gods' blessing described in her file," I reminded them. "As her champion, I can see her now." At least that was my theory. Ragna's eyes flashed up at me in dismay.

Too bad, little she-wolf.

One of the doctors pulled back a curtain and frowned when the moon wasn't currently shining through the glass.

"It's the wrong angle." He looked back to where Ragna was and frowned. "We should avoid moving her to a moonlit space. I don't want to risk ripping the sutures. Ideas?"

"Well, we'll just guide him through changing her bandages. He's done field dressings before," one said and opened their case. I sat on the edge of the bed between the doctors and the she-wolf. Ragna did not look happy with the substitution.

I carefully placed my hands on her upper back and hips to rotate her to a sitting position. She screamed in agony, and I rubbed a thumb back and forth on her upper arm, trying to soothe her. I waited until she caught her breath before continuing. When I reached down to gently pull up her shirt, her eyes widened, and her face flushed with what little blood was left in her. I carefully removed the garment so I could treat her injuries.

I could tell she had the urge to cover her beautiful, full breasts. It wasn't anything I hadn't seen before, and since she was injured, I didn't feel like ravishing her. I just wanted to take care of her. I didn't think there was a way to make her see that, though. She'd assume the worst. I hadn't given her a reason to think otherwise.

Under instruction, I removed the gauze from her cheeks and breasts. I cleaned the skin, sanitized it, and reapplied fresh bandages. I saw the jealousy in where they'd chosen to cut her. Ironically, their actions hadn't made Ragna ugly; it made them ugly.

I frowned when I put a soothing cream on her neck where the silver had bitten her. The injuries had improved but still looked painful. The doctors wanted to leave it exposed to air, so we didn't dress it.

I fought to keep a straight face when I peeled off the giant bandage that covered her stomach. So many emotions flooded me at the sight—rage, despair, relief, disgust. I wanted to rip her attackers limb from limb. I'd seen many upsetting things on the battlefield, but I found the incised games to be particularly disturbing—perverse.

I took great care cleaning and disinfecting the gashes on her belly and back. The smallest touch would make her convulse, and we had to put a towel between her teeth to keep her from biting her tongue. Fortunately, the doctors had a topical painkiller, and she seemed to calm a bit by the time I replaced the last bandage.

Looking at everything I'd treated, I felt an urge to cry. She was a mess, and it was my fault.

"I trust you did a complete job, Your Majesty. We'll be sure to check before sunset instead of after from now on. We'll need to see how she looks tomorrow to give a prognosis," a doctor informed while closing his suitcase. "We're leaving painkillers and supplements by the bed."

I nodded my thanks, and they left. I grabbed a fresh, soft sleep shirt from the closet and helped her don it. She was looking a little faint, so I sent a servant to fetch dinner and gave them explicit instructions to have the cooks prepare a meal rich in iron for Ragna.

I busied myself with building a fire in the bedroom. It'd be a little too warm for me, but I wanted her to be comfortable. After, I heated up water in the suite's kitchenette to fill a water bladder. When I returned to the bedroom, I peeled back the sheet so I could lay the warmer at her feet. I felt her stare on me as I tucked her back in, and I escaped to the lounge until our food arrived.

I ran my hands through my hair, nervous and frustrated with my inability to communicate. My list of things to apologize for was growing, and it was overwhelming. How in the hell was I going to spend weeks—if not months—on the road with her?

The food arrived, and I brought the trays to the bed. Putting mine aside, I cut up little pieces of her steak. "I don't want you sitting up, so I'll help you eat," I stated plainly and held a small bite of meat in front of her mouth for her to grab. I nodded in approval at her obedience when she accepted the morsel, and I prepared another forkful for her. "We'll try sitting you up tomorrow."

"Your Majesty," she began cautiously before taking another bite. "Why am I here?"

I studied the plate in front of me, trying to formulate a response. "You needed an unmated to help you heal," I replied evenly and cut some vegetables into smaller pieces for her.

She received another bite, chewed, and swallowed. "Certainly, the beta could have helped instead. I understand you are not... tolerant of my presence."

"I am your assigned champion. It's my duty. I doubt the Sun God would be happy with any other arrangement." I didn't want her in bed with Rudesind, damn it!

You are really nailing it. Spine sighed, sounding like he had finally lost all faith in me.

I was certain I'd just lost all faith in myself too.

Ragna accepted another bite, and her eyes became unfocused. "When will we be leaving?" she asked after swallowing.

"Once you're no longer in pain, we'll get on the road. I'll be here to help you heal faster. I can work from the bed."

She nodded, and I fed her the rest of her dinner in silence, getting up occasionally to bring her more water. I watched her grow drowsy and fall asleep, then I leaned against the headboard to eat my own dinner, listening to the steady thump of her heart. It had been so slow when I'd found her. She would have died had I not gotten the feeling that something was wrong. I shuddered and finished the rest of my meal. It had been too close. It was enough to give me nightmares.

I put our trays out to be collected and crawled into bed next to Ragna. My gaze was fixed on her face while my hand idly stroked the hair on top of her head. She was still pale but not deathly so, not anymore. I pulled her gingerly to me and fell asleep with her wrapped in my arms, wishing I could turn caring actions like these into words.

Ragna

I woke up screaming and scrambling to get away from the mistresses, crying and begging for mercy. A huge weight shifted dramatically to my left, and I flinched, sobbing in terror. A wave of hot agony crashed over my belly and back, and I nearly blacked out from the intensity.

"Hey! Hey, hey, hey! Shh, shh, shh! You're ok! You're ok!" a low voice said frantically, and I felt a weight on top of me, holding me down but not crushing me. I struggled against it, knowing it was only a matter of time before I was cut again.

A weight leaned against my cheek, and I drew in a lungful of something soothing, delicious. It was like wood shavings and almonds. It was familiar. Pleasant. I was told by the tingles on my skin, the calmness that washed over me, and the scent I breathed that I was safe again. I took in another gasp of air and shuddered, no longer sobbing but still dripping tears.

"They cut me, they cut me up." I whimpered, and the weight on top of me shifted a little.

"You're safe now," the voice by my ear said. "They won't touch you ever again. Ever. I promise. Just relax. You're safe now. I've got you. I've got you."

"Why does everyone want to kill me?" I whispered, lost in delirium.

A long sigh made its way down my neck, and a hand stroked my head. "Not everyone, she-wolf," the voice said thickly. "I know someone who desperately wished they'd never hurt you."

"Who could that p-possibly be?" I sniffed and leaned against the warmth next to my face.

"The Lycan King," the husky voice murmured.

"He hates me…"

"I do no—I mean, he does not. Just wait. He'll prove it to you some day." Lips brushed against my cheek as they spoke. "Come here…" The weight shifted off me, and I was gently positioned next to a warm, hard surface that slowly rose and fell. I heard a thumping inside that reminded me of my pain.

"His hate hurts my heart," I whispered to no one in particular, "like these cuts hurt my belly."

"Then he'll fix it. You'll just need to be patient with him. He's scared too." A hand returned to stroke the top of my head.

"King Zorian isn' 'fraid d'anything..." I slurred tiredly, barely able to stay conscious. "He took onna millun rogues a cuppa days'go."

The surface under me bobbed a couple times, and I distantly heard low, rumbling chuckles. "A million, huh? Guess you should be grateful he's on your side, little she-wolf." A thumb slowly caressed the edge of my ear. "King Zorian is afraid to lose." A long, languid sigh brushed past me. "He lost when he wasn't angry enough, and now it's all he knows. Fear and anger."

"Thas sad..."

"Maybe you can help him, little wolf," the voice said. It sounded depressed now.

"Mmm, how?"

"I don't know."

⚜

I woke in the late afternoon when the doctors arrived. Doctor Egres tended to me this time and tutted as she unwrapped my bandages. I couldn't look down at my belly. I couldn't bring myself to do it. I was so afraid I wouldn't recognize my own body.

"How does it look?" I asked tentatively, turning my head to the side so I could stare at the rest of the room. The king had helped me sit up but had made himself scarce once they'd started removing my shirt. Huh.

"It's actually looking a lot better. The cuts on your belly are about halfway healed, which is great progress!" She cleaned, medicated, and rebandaged my stomach with a more breathable material, then helped me turn onto my stomach. When I yelled from the pain of doing so, King Zorian poked his head in with a deep frown but then promptly left.

I couldn't tell if that was a concerned face or an annoyed face, Trail muttered, irritable.

"Your lower back looks better than your upper back. If you need to sit or stand, get someone to help you. The less you bend, the less stress you'll put on the stitches," she instructed while cleaning and rebandaging my back. "I think you're progressing faster than anticipated because a strong alpha is helping you."

Before she left, I took the opportunity to ask her for help getting to the bathroom so I could relieve myself. My ankle was still healing too. Goddess knew that I wasn't comfortable asking royalty to escort me to the toilet.

Despite it being called the throne, Trail joked, and I chuckled lightly, trying not to jostle my torso and belly.

I returned to bed, and the rest of the day was spent sleeping, eating, and reading. The king was practically waiting on me hand and foot, but I was uncomfortable because his facial expressions cycled only between anger and disinterest. Was he resenting having to do this? If so, he didn't have to go the extra mile to put warmers under the sheets or make tea.

I adjusted my position to read when it became late, and the king brought some paperwork to his bed to peruse. It was so weird to have him purposely and casually sling my leg over his shin to keep our skin in contact. The pleasant tingles were the opposite of his demeanor, and the indifference combined with the mate bond felt like culture shock. I was in a constant state of nervousness and desperately wished I could read his mind. I just wanted to know if he hated me and how much. I wished I had the bravery to push for the truth.

Exhausted from pain and anxiety, I decided to escape to sleep. I didn't want to be awake anymore, so I swallowed a painkiller and some supplements, then tried to lie flat. The king noticed my efforts and reached over to wrap two arms around me to support my back and hips. His gentle placement of my body mixed poorly with his stern expression, and my lips pressed into a flat line of frustration.

His face was quite near, and his balmy breath stroked my cheek. I kept my eyes averted, but my heart pounded against my rib cage with traitorous excitement. Like arousal, there was no hiding your heart rate from another lycan or wolf-shifter. I knew that if I looked at him, I'd just be staring at his lips. I prayed to the goddess to not make my body respond and subtly clamped my thighs together.

When I was in a moderately comfortable position, I snapped my eyes shut and hoped like crazy I'd only have one more day left of this torture.

I woke up screaming for the second night in a row, but this time, I was much more lucid than the previous night. I only thrashed for a moment, but the king saw fit to lean over and hold me in place. Frowning, I pushed slightly against him.

"I'm ok. You can let go. I just had a nightmare. I'm sorry for waking you," I muttered, embarrassed. I blushed furiously at being caged under him, especially with him straddling me. The sight of his muscular chest and shoulders bracing over me was a reminder of how brutally strong he was, yet he was careful not to press on my injuries. This was a far cry from the male who'd thrown me to the ground and collared me.

I tried to call upon irritation to replace the arousal seeping into my blood. Then I struggled to think of all the wrong he'd done me, but I couldn't shake the split second of guilt that flashed across his tired face. He was staring down at me through his white hair, but for the life of me, I still couldn't read him. Did he feel remorse?

The tenderness in his face left, and he rolled off me. "If you rip your stitches, it'll delay our departure," he said in a sleepy but cold voice. As if to further confuse me, he snaked his arm around and beneath my shirt to hold me, avoiding the bandaged areas. The tingling dampened some of the pain, and I breathed a sigh of relief. As if to acknowledge my satisfied sound, he gave my skin a gentle squeeze. Damn this lycan.

Morning brought joy when I realized I was much more mobile and could stand on my own. I wobbled to the bathroom and took a steadying breath before rolling up my shirt. I removed the bandage and gloomily noted that the faded tic-tac-toe marks were still visible. I sniffed and wiped my nose.

King Zorian stepped in quietly and stood at my back, looking into the mirror with me. He reached around and ran a thumb over one of the mostly healed lacerations.

"Your Majesty… how is it so easy for someone to do something like this?" I asked numbly. I couldn't fathom it on my own. "They were laughing. They played games with my skin."

He scowled and shook his head. "Easier than you think for people detached from reality. Some escape pampered childhoods with hearts full of love, but others do not. They don't know pain, so they don't know what limits are. They're sheltered from death, so they don't understand its gravity." His hand stroked a knobby scar. "These will flatten and fade. How is the pain?"

"Much better," I admitted. "I will go back to my room today. Trail can handle the rest."

"No." He removed his hand with his abrupt rejection. "You will stay here until we leave. If you're feeling restored tonight, we can depart tomorrow."

"Why? Why stay when I can just get out of your hair? I know you don't want me here," I protested, and he crossed his arms across his chest. I suddenly felt like I was in trouble.

"You'd be wise not to question your king, she-wolf. It is because I said so," he rebuked and walked out of the bathroom. I placed my hands over my face and groaned.

Bow to your king, Ragna. Don't question your king, Ragna. Ass up for your king, Ragna, Trail snapped in an annoying imitation of King Zorian's voice.

I clenched my jaw and walked after him, deciding now was a good time to tell him what I'd heard during the assault. "Your Majesty?" I called, following the king to a side room that was set up like an office. He sat at his desk and continued writing something he'd been working on earlier.

"Hmm?" he hummed in response, not looking up at me.

"I don't know if this means anything, but I need to tell you what your blonde mistress said the other day."

"She's no longer a candidate for marriage, but go ahead," he murmured, still not meeting my gaze.

"She, or maybe it was the redhead, said it was down to the three of them to get you and that there was a reward of some kind. They had an agreement to make you wait," I recounted, squinting my eyes as I tried to remember everything. I nervously worried at my hands, not sure if he'd dismiss it outright. "I don't know... Maybe I read too much into it, but something about it seemed wrong. You kind of had to be there for the tone..."

The king sat back and stared at me for a while. I fidgeted under his scrutiny, wishing he'd say something already. He finally sucked in a breath and scrubbed a hand over his mouth, his pale stubble rasping against the rough palm. "They're going to be returned to their kingdoms soon, so I doubt any devious plans of theirs could come to fruition now."

I twisted my lips in thought and nodded. At least I'd gotten what I wanted to off my chest.

"Go back to bed. Should we leave tomorrow, you'll be in the best shape to travel if you give your wolf energy to heal," the king ordered while flipping through a new pile of documentation.

"I can't ju—" I began to protest at being ordered to sit around all day, but I snapped my mouth shut. I'd been on my own for so long, I'd forgotten about the pack order for a brief moment, not that I was in a pack. Still, a king was a king. I had little control over my life while I was around him, and I didn't need to give him an excuse to punish me. I had half a mind to submit after my attempted outburst.

"You'll find that you very much can, she-wolf. Now go rest before I command you to," he dismissed with an edge in his voice.

"Yes, Your Majesty." I sighed in defeat and went to read, hoping the book Rudesind had given me would last one more day.

Chapter 16

King Zorian

After I'd accidentally made certain that the she-wolf would resent me for the rest of the day, I thought about the warning she'd given me. Before Ragna had come along, I wouldn't have been able to imagine those three females plotting anything more dangerous than deciding which servant to demoralize during high tea. Now, though... Now I saw who they were, and I couldn't underestimate their capabilities.

A reward could mean the obvious and relatively innocent reward of obtaining power by becoming the queen, or it could mean that there was a third party involved. Had someone offered a reward for a service? That service could refer to the part about making me wait. Wait for what, though? Aside from maintaining the kingdom with me, all that was expected from a future queen were marriage, crowning, and mating. Perhaps they intended to delay in giving me an heir? Were their fathers invested in a conspiracy to take my kingdom?

Or perhaps it was none of that. Maybe it was simply an insane collaboration to remove Ragna out of jealousy. They had every reason to feel threatened. Ragna was beautiful, dedicated, and genuine. She was untainted by the disdain found in aristocratic females. A sneer molded the face as much as a smile. It wasn't impossible that the dialogue was simply meant to provoke, especially with how protective Ragna had shown herself to be.

I hope you're not thinking she's being paranoid.

No. She's not stupid either. She's survived being on the run for five years. I think she can read intent just fine, I replied thoughtfully. *I think if we're quiet, watchful, and patient, we may see someone accidentally show their hand. Until then, we need to focus on the goddess.*

And making Ragna not hate you.

I suppose that too.

Making her love you.

Let's not get ahead of ourselves here.

Making her want to jump your b—

Spine!

I stacked a pile of letters and summoned my beta. Rudesind arrived promptly, closed the door behind him, and seated himself. "What's up, Sun-Blessed?"

I gave him a withering look, then handed him the sealed letters and explained. "These need to go out to the fathers of those princesses. I also need you to send those filthy pieces of trash on their way as soon as possible. They'll whine about having been put in the dungeons, and I'd like to make that day count as small as possible. Also, as much as I'd love to have them wheeled out in an antique slave cart, throw them in a carriage with an escort."

"It's really too bad we can't kill them. I've had dreams the last couple nights about ambushing their carriage and slaughtering them," he mused darkly. "I just can't get the image of Ragna bleeding to death out of my mind. Those females are sick. Sick." He ran both hands through his light hair.

"I've avoided the dungeon because I can't trust myself not to do that very thing, Rude," I replied tersely and leaned back in my chair.

"How is Ragna doing, anyway?" Rudesind inquired. "I haven't checked on her recently."

"Rather well, actually," I said and looked out the window of my suite office. "She wakes up from nightmares but seems calm enough during the day. She was a little sad this morning, trying to wrap her mind around it all. Looked at her stomach for the first time since it happened. It should be completely faded in a couple of days. I'm not going to lie, seeing those markings puts me in a rage."

"I need to know, Zorian," he began cautiously, tilting his head to study me. "Are you going to be able to mind yourself around her when you leave?"

I jerked my head to meet his gaze and glared.

"Don't give me that look," he rebuked. "This is serious. I can warn her about you, but I can't keep you from doing anything stupid."

I white-knuckled my fountain pen until it snapped in half and chucked it angrily into the trash. "I don't know, ok?" I snapped. "I can't even properly talk to her without sounding like an angry, evil overlord."

"Well, I trust you to try, Zorian. I have no idea where her breaking point is, and we're relying on you both to sort the mate bonds out. That's all I can say, but I needed to say it." He stood and straightened his shirt, switching smoothly from friend to beta. "Is that all, Your Majesty?"

I nodded and waved him off to take care of his assignments, feeling deeply frustrated. Ragna was becoming quite the sore subject.

⁂

The day passed at a speed that made syrup seem fast. I managed to sort out all coverage for my duties, and it was just a matter of hours before our departure.

"How are you feeling?" I asked a yawning Ragna when I crawled into bed. I enjoyed seeing her in it every night and dared myself to hope she'd be my mate so it'd be like this forever. It wasn't likely, but that didn't make me covet the fantasy any less.

"I'm fine now, I think. It's only tender when I twist or bend too much, but I'm pretty much back to normal," she answered, turning on her side to face away from me. I frowned but understood why she continued to push me away from her.

"Then how do you feel about departing tomorrow morning? Everything is ready." I lay on my back but kept my gaze on her.

"I'm ready when you are. What's our first destination?"

"The Lunar Coven," I answered and waited for her reaction. It was almost imperceptible, but I saw her muscles tensing. "Since you chose not to answer what I'd asked days ago, I did some research and found it a completely reasonable place to start. I can see why you've been trying to reach it."

Her shoulders shook slightly with her sniffles. "Why are you crying, Ragna?" I asked levelly, trying to keep the nervousness out of my voice.

She shook her head. "I don't have a reasonable answer, Your Majesty. Don't mind me. I'll stop. I just need a minute. I'm sorry." What the hell was I supposed to do with that?

Spine, what the fuck do I do?

Oh, now you want my advice?

Spine!

Ask her again and tell her not to fear you. You just want to know what you can do to help.

"Ragna," I said, and she stilled, waiting. "What is wrong? I am not going to bite you." Frustration darkened my tone, and I winced.

Ok, that came out a touch aggressive, Zorian. Dial it the fuck back.

"My feelings don't matter. I'm just here to do my duty. Apologies, Your Majesty. I'll be quiet." She wiped her tears and adjusted her pillow.

Man, she is pushing you away real hard. Try asking—

Then she doesn't know who she's playing with, I interrupted and took action.

I snarled a warning, and she stiffened. I reached out, snaked an arm around her waist, and pulled her against me. I rolled the back of her shirt up so her skin touched my shirtless abdomen, then rested my head near the nape of her neck and closed my eyes, letting the bond sweep over us. I could tell she was fighting it, but she eventually caved, and her body relaxed dramatically. The she-wolf heaved a long, world-weary sigh.

"Do not continue to test me like this, she-wolf. You are pushing your luck with your disobedience. Your feelings matter if they keep me up," I growled irritably. "If you refuse to answer your king, then you'll accept the mate touch I'm offering and go to sleep. Calm down."

And we have completely tossed the script... Great! Spine retreated to sulk by himself in the back of my mind.

I inhaled her scent and basked in how sublime it felt to clutch her warm, soft body like this. I also made sure to keep my hips away in case my cock decided to get excited. She didn't need to know. It was unfortunate for females that they couldn't hide the scent of their arousal. Terribly unfair. I loved it.

I made a show of adjusting my sleeping position and let my nose brush the back of her neck. I also cracked my knuckles and placed them back down on her waist but on a more sensitive spot. The tiniest shudder ran through her, and I scented her arousal. When she tried to be discreet in pressing her thighs together, I smirked and closed my eyes. I may have just found a suitable, harmless punishment for her after all, and she wasn't even aware of it.

Ragna

Last night was the first I'd been free of nightmares, but I was wide awake before dawn lit the king's bedroom windows. My body had been of two minds all night—tense from the king's hold but relaxed from the effects of the bond. The result was indescribable but not in a good way. It was like I'd slept crooked, but I hadn't developed a kink in my neck.

When I heard the king's deep intake of breath, I realized he was waking. I tried to scoot out of his grip, which tightened momentarily but eventually relaxed. My goal was to take a bath, knowing full well it'd be the last warm one I'd get in a while. When I escaped the bed and sank into the hot water, a languid groan escaped me. Bliss seeped straight into the marrow of my bones.

You'd think lying in bed wouldn't make you so stiff and sore, I said to Trail.

Resting is hard work! She laughed. *Look down at your belly. I want to see how you're doing.* I looked down while pulling myself out of the water a bit.

Better. You're healing so fast. The bonus of having an alpha mate. Get him to cuddle us again tonight, and the marks should be faded completely by tomorrow.

It was not cuddling. He... restrained me, I corrected with a pout.

You need to start listening with your eyes, I think, Trail mused. I frowned and began to scrub days of bed rest off me. There was a long line of feminine products by the tub, and I grinned in amusement as I perused them.

He has such delicate, ladylike tastes. I chuckled.

You know those are for you, Trail corrected flatly. *When did you become so devoted to denial?* I wrinkled my nose and pressed my lips together. I didn't know how to reply. Maybe I was too scared to give him the benefit of the doubt.

When I left the tub, I stared in awe at the clothes left on the bed for me. A tiny squeal of delight snuck past my lips as I gawked at the high-quality cotton tunic and leggings. They weren't just of fine quality. The designs were actually useful! Both would be quick to strip off for shifting. I fingered the three bone toggle buttons on the tunic and marveled at the delicate designs carved into them. My gaze moved to the embroidered symbol of the Sky Gods, and my fingers traveled along the delicate stitching. I smiled, and my heart soared. I'd never received anything so fine in my life.

My eyes fell joyfully on the short, hooded doe-skin cloak, gloves, and sturdy leather boots, but I eyed the lacy, silken underwear with some trepidation and wariness. Otherwise, it felt like a lifetime of birthday presents all rolled into one.

"You have spares as well," the king's voice came from the doorway. I jumped a little in surprise and clutched at my towel in paranoia. He moved far too quietly for being such a large male. "You required outfitting suitable for your position as the Sky-Blessed."

Listen with your eyes, Trail reminded.

He looks emotionless, Trail. I don't understand what you're saying.

Guess I'll need more examples to show you.

"I've also provided a better pack for you. It will hold on better when you shift. Perhaps then you'll be better at catching rabbits." He left abruptly after that. The corner of his lip twitched ever so slightly just before he disappeared. I would have missed it if Trail hadn't pressed me into being more observant.

Was that a smir—Wait, is he referring to... How long had he been watching me that day? I gasped, appalled, but Trail howled with laughter. I blushed furiously and grabbed the new pack that I found at the foot of the bed. It was well crafted indeed, and there was a strap for the bow and quiver, which was lidded and fully restocked with razor-sharp arrows. Rations had already been packed in it. I was being spoiled rotten.

I readied myself, grabbed my belongings, and met the king by the suite's front door. Before leaving the room, I made sure to politely express my gratitude. "Your Majesty, thank you very much for all the lovely items." I held up a hand to keep him from speaking, knowing what he would say. "I understand it's only because of my role, as you said, but I am still grateful and will treasure them. I've never received anything so nice." I was surprised by the intense urge to hug him. It wouldn't have been appropriate, and I was still upset by the way he'd previously treated me.

A muscle in his jaw ticked, and he asked, "Are you ready?" I nodded, and we left for the main hall. Beta Rudesind was waiting for us, and the king approached him to verify some checklist. They shook hands but then exchanged a hug of brotherly love. I was taken aback. Maybe they were old friends as well. Betas tended to have a long history with their alphas because they had to be fully trusted. The role was a huge responsibility.

Beta Rudesind faced me and offered a short, stiff bow. I sighed at his distant demeanor. His offer to make love had me flinching every time he'd touched me platonically. Still, I should really forgive him before leaving. Who knew if I'd even survive this journey?

I reluctantly held my arms out for a hug. He perked up and leaned over to embrace me with a little squeeze. I smiled at the mental picture of his lycan's tail wagging. "Please be safe," he uttered.

"Let's go," the king growled, suddenly sounding cranky.

The beta released me and gave us a worried look. "Both of you return alive."

"I'll tr—"

"We will," King Zorian interrupted and gestured for me to follow.

Waiting for us outside the castle was a carriage. As we approached it, the king frowned and held a hand up to help me into the carriage. I was dumbfounded by the politeness, but I nervously accepted it and stepped in to settle by the far window. He chose to sit across from me, and the carriage began its rumbling, bumpy journey across the stone paving.

"I wasn't expecting to leave by carriage, Your Majesty," I remarked, distracted by the elegance of the compartment. The red velvet cushions were particularly comfortable, absorbing much of the carriage's jostling. Everything was finely crafted too, and I was yet to find a single flaw.

"We'll have to stop a third of the way there. The coven is off the main roads. They do not interact outside of their territory as they are self-sustaining," the king explained and turned to look out the window.

"Also, you are not to address me by my royal title until we return. You may refer to me as your champion since that is my assignment."

I nodded but was uncomfortable with the change. He still frightened me to an extent, and calling him anything less than a king felt dangerous.

He's not going to chop your head off. Calm the pup down, Ragna. Sheesh, Trail chided.

"How long until we leave the carriage?" I asked, dreading the answer.

"Should be a couple days. Then a handful more on foot."

Damnation. That was so upsetting to me. I'd spent years trying to get there. As soon as it became convenient for the king, it was only a matter of days.

Despair assaulted me at that realization. So much time wasted. So many winters spent starving. So many males I'd had to fight off me. All for what? Tears slid down my cheek despite every effort to stop them. It was so unfair. So bloody unfair! I let my hair fall to cover the side of my face so he couldn't see my tears.

"Are you crying again, Ragna?" the king—Champion Zorian—asked. Damnation times two! "Is this what was upsetting you last night?"

I decided it was unwise to avoid answering again. "Yes. I spent years trying to get to a place it'll only take us less than a week to get to. I'm hurting. I feel like I lost five years of my life, Your M—I mean, Champion. I barely stayed ahead of starvation every winter and was assaulted. I was nearly raped countless times, and I was always running. It hurts me deeply at how easy this is for you to achieve. I hope you understand now what a pointless hurt this is and why I didn't want to discuss it. I can't change the past, but I struggle with the pain." I fidgeted after venting, but for the first time, I didn't regret speaking so ardently before the king. I wasn't sure why.

He didn't answer for a while, but I felt his eyes on me. I wasn't sure which of his reactions I would get this time. Would he not respond, change the subject, or snap at me?

He replied measuredly, "Emotions can be strong enough to guide our actions, she-wolf. I know very well how important they are to address. I learned that lesson during wartime. You feel resentment, and it's not unwarranted. All I ask is for you to not let that rancor color the present. I'm here now to make your journey as swift and as painless as possible and will use all the tools at my disposal to do so."

The validation was surprising, welcome. The advice was sound. I grew pensive watching the trees pass, idly wondering when fall would ruddy the forest floor. The champion cleared his throat, and I glanced over at him. He was still staring out the window but looked frustrated, almost angry. His brows drew in as deeply as his breath, and his muscles tensed. Was he going to speak?

Champion Zorian's countenance was stern, but his tone was soft. "I will say this once. For all you've suffered, whether it's been at my hands or others, I am deeply sorry. I... apologize."

Chapter 17

Champion Zorian

It took every ounce of my control to sound genuine. For some reason, the nicer the comment was, the harder it was to deliver without anger. Perhaps this journey would allow for some introspection.

I cut my gaze to Ragna for her reaction. She swallowed heavily and closed her eyes. Then I watched in awe as her body finally relaxed with a long exhale. It was as though a huge burden had melted off her.

It's amazing the power an apology has, Spine remarked knowingly. *Look at how much that meant to her. Was it worth the effort?* At least he wasn't being a smug bastard.

Yes, I said in resignation. *It was.*

Good. Learn from this, and I may start liking you again.

Taken aback, I let out a burst of laughter. Ragna's eyes shot open, and she looked at me in confusion. I gathered myself, straightened my shirt, and dismissed her unspoken question with a wave of my hand. "My lycan said something stupid. Ignore my outburst."

She turned back to the window, but I spied a tiny smile forming on her lips. I did the best I could to control my heart rate at the unusual, beautiful sight. I felt like I was watching a rare flower unfold.

It was surreal how much of the tension had worn away after the apology. Even though the rest of the carriage ride was spent in silence, it was a comfortable silence.

The coachman pulled slightly off the road when night fell so we could camp under a sprawling oak tree. I hunted and Ragna rolled out thin bedrolls and started a fire. While we cooked, I made idle chitchat with the human coachman to pass the time, asking about his wife and children. His family line had been employed at the castle over several generations, and I made a small effort to acknowledge the families who stayed with us—especially the humans.

I kept my eyes and ears open for rogues and predators, but it seemed safe enough to rest for the night. I was a light sleeper anyway.

When it was time to retire, Ragna approached me and timidly asked, "May I make requests since your role has changed, Champion Zorian?" Her tone told me she wasn't thrilled about whatever this was going to be.

I nodded in reply, choosing not to make eye contact, and brushed dirt off my sleeping pad. The reluctance in her green gaze was never enjoyable.

"My wolf requests one last night of healing with the mate touch. She says we'll be completely healed by morning," she explained, fidgeting nervously.

I got up to move her sleeping pad between mine and the fire so she'd stay warm. "You may have the mate touch as you need it, Sky-Blessed," I answered while settling again. I looked up, raised my brows in expectation, and beckoned with a finger.

She lay down on her pad, facing the fire, and placed her heel against my shin to get the contact she needed. I frowned, wrapped my arm around her, and dragged her flush against me, restraining my growl this time. She shuddered under my embrace but didn't complain, and I smirked in victory. It was foolish of me, but I wanted to enjoy her as long as I could. I'd accepted that desire. When we no longer had the mate bond, I'd prove my strength as a self-possessed king and move on the best I could.

Before the coachman climbed into the carriage to sleep, he looked over at us and released a sharp guffaw. I met his eyes and raised a brow.

"S-so sorry, Your Majesty. I was just taken off guard with you cuddling our invisible Sky-Blessed. Your arm's draped over nothing. S-sorry, ignore me," he stammered, desperately trying to hide a wide smile. When he closed the door behind him, his laughter resumed, muffled only a little by the compartment. I grinned, buried my face into Ragna's aromatic hair, and closed my eyes.

"It's n-not cuddling," she mumbled.

We returned to the road at dawn, and it started peacefully, but unease hit me around late afternoon. Ragna was staring at the edge of the woods with a tense expression on her face, noticing what I had.

"Champion..." she whispered, and I nodded.

"I saw something too," I verified and slid open the window by the coachman. "Oswine, turn the carriage about and come to a stop," I ordered. I jumped out of the coach with my pack and kept an eye on the woods. There wasn't any movement now, but the scent of buck urine wafted from the trees. It was potent, and my nose wrinkled from its sting.

Something so concentrated meant that someone was using it to hide their scent. It was such an old tactic. Whoever was out there was either vastly inexperienced or felt it was more important to hide their identity than their presence. You could also go down the rabbit hole of thinking that was what they wanted you to think.

I approached the coachman to deliver my last command. "Oswine, I'm ordering you to return to the castle. We're being followed, and this is where we're disembarking. I think you'll be safe but consider riding through the night." I slapped his knee, turned before he could protest, and opened the door for Ragna.

I crouched over my bag and unfolded my plate armor. "Ragna," I murmured, "prepare yourself to shift. Since you're not in my Royal Pack and can't mind-link, we're going to use two vocal commands. If needed, Spine will give you one whine to stay in place and two short growls for when it's all clear. Do not stray from the plan, and if we're attacked, you're to stay behind him. Is that understood?"

"Yes, Champion."

When I heard her move away from me to undress behind a rock, I snapped, "Do not stray!" She shuffled closer, and I took my clothes off to secure the plate armor. After I shifted, Spine adjusted the metal that relocated smoothly to accommodate his bulk.

Been a while since we wore this stuff. Thanks for having it oiled and getting the straps replaced. I would have forgotten, Spine said approvingly while rotating his shoulder. He turned to face Ragna, who'd already shifted into Trail. The cinnamon-brown wolf with light-green eyes gawked at us, completely frozen in place.

She hasn't gotten a good look at us in this form, Spine said smugly. *Look at the awe in those pretty eyes.*

He crouched down, and before he could fully open his hulking arms to greet her, Trail shot into them and licked furiously at his face. She whined, and her thumping tail was at risk of waggling straight off her body.

Spine! Stop! We have stalkers off the trail, you fucking idiot! Prioritize! Protect our charge! Great gods! I roared, embarrassed beyond belief. Perhaps we should have done their introduction before leaving. Oh, the humiliation...

Spine huffed in annoyance and stood to face the woods. *Trail likes me, and I like her. It's not my fault you can't get along with Ragna.* He stalked forward, and Trail hugged his flank, keeping us between her and whatever was out there.

Can you tell how many are there? I asked Spine.

Not yet, but the urine scent seems too spread out for it to be just one. Ugh, it's like they used a whole fucking bucket. My eyes are going to water.

Then let's hold off proactive engagement.

Agreed.

He veered to keep the dirt road and several rows of trees between us and the activity. We listened intently for any long-distance attacks, particularly the pull of bowstring, but nothing came.

They know we're on the alert. I suspect they'll hit during the night, Spine surmised.

Thank the Sky Gods that she'll be invisible. That should confuse them.

Spine was quiet for a moment. *Unless they know about that and hit at sunset—if she's their target.*

Right. Shit. We'll play it by ear.

Sunset came and went. Spine and I occasionally saw movement across the road, but that was the extent of it. Something, or several somethings, was still stalking us. It was always a blur in our peripheral vision. We couldn't get a sense of the size or shape, which unnerved us. We usually didn't have issues identifying our foes.

We didn't get rusty sitting on our kingly ass, did we? Spine grumbled.

I doubt that's it.

We moved farther from the road, and the stalking stopped after dawn. Spine and I took advantage of the quiet to rest. There was a decent spot by a cluster of trees, and he raked some detritus into a large pile to make a bed. It was musty, damp, noisy, and he absolutely loved it.

Trail also seemed to like it. When she trotted up to curl against him, he snuggled happily into her. His claws rubbed her belly as she whined and nipped at his chin. I sighed inwardly when they eventually settled. My bloodthirsty lycan was behaving like a stupid, bubbly pup. This was going to be incredibly awkward. How could I look Ragna in the eyes after this? I suppose I could also blame her wolf for encouraging him.

⁂

We napped without any issues, and the road was empty upon our return. The stalkers seemed to have left entirely, but the forest was quiet—no birds, no squirrels. There was something out there scaring the wildlife, and we couldn't scent it for the life of us.

It's staying downwind. I hate this. We should consider seeking it out, Spine proposed restlessly. *The sooner we kill it, the sooner she'll be safe.*

Patience, I cautioned. *We need more information. It's not attacking. Keep going and stay alert.*

We felt a gentle nip on our leg and spotted Trail trying to lead us off the road. She stopped and looked up at something hanging from a tree— something she thought worth investigating. When Spine approached the hidden object, we saw it was a strip of cloth stamped with a symbol and some writing.

This isn't good, I muttered and shifted; Ragna followed suit. I rummaged through my bag for a pen and paper, then sketched the symbol to research later.

"What is it?" Ragna asked.

"I've seen this writing before, but I don't know what it means. There are rumors that a cult has been spreading in the northeast. I have people investigating it, but they're not due to return for a while. It's in a remote location." I drew upon anger to drown out my unease. "As you can see, it's completely unacceptable for them to have spread this far west and around the bay."

"Wh-what is this cult about?" she asked, now visibly worried. I felt a fierce urge to pull her against me to comfort her, but she was naked; the combination was a bad idea.

You mean a great idea. Nothing like sex to calm the nerves.

I ignored the horny lycan and answered her. "I don't know yet, but I suspect we'll be finding out shortly."

We shifted again, and Trail followed Spine at a distance so he could hunt. The lycan brought a doe back to her, smug as fuck to have provided for his "mate." Why make her do it when he could?

They gorged on the deer carcass, and I used Spine's ears to stay alert. They rested for about an hour, slipping into food comas before returning to the road. That was when the rogues arrived.

Spine stiffened, and his hackles rose at the group of wolf-shifters and lycans emerging from the woods. They ambled down the road, but we knew bad intention when we saw it. One was in his human form, naked, and I assumed he was the leader.

Two other individuals appeared from the tree line to join the illegal pack, but these were clothed and wearing hooded robes. I couldn't see their faces because of their thin, featureless, wooden masks, and my mind ran through a myriad of reasons for them. It could mean a collective identity, like a cult. The smell that came from them was what really concerned me. If they wanted to hide their faces and scents, they could very well be important, influential individuals, and the scent they'd chosen was deer urine.

"Sky-Blessed," the one wearing a brown robe greeted with a low lisp. "You've found yourself a bodyguard. Only one, though?" He tutted and shook his head.

I shifted so I could address the masked stranger. "State your business and leave. I have some cleaning to do," I growled impatiently and nodded at the rogues. I didn't know who these two were, so they could either offer information or get the hell out of our way. I would've preferred interrogating them, but unless I could defeat the illegal pack before they escaped, I didn't see that happening. Granted, I could track them, but I didn't want to stray from our mission. For all I knew, that was what they wanted.

They definitely knew who Ragna was, and the idea that they were targeting her made me fucking furious. Did any of them know I was King Zorian? If they did, would they still attack? Would they continue to stalk us? I was almost curious enough to test it.

"We're j-just here to p-pick up the S-Sky-Blessed. You're d-dismissed," the one wearing a black robe said to me with a shrug. He or she faked that stutter and deep voice. These two were paranoid—or just thorough.

"But how would you do that without thumbs?" I asked in a dark tone and cracked my knuckles. I had a feeling that intimidation would be ineffective, but I let my alpha dominance push down on them to see what would happen. As suspected, the only ones who flinched were the wolves and lycans. These strangers had to be human. "Are you two—by any chance—handing out memberships?" I inquired. "I've been itching to join a cult." Spine's cheekiness rubbed off on me when we were getting psyched up, and I was itching to tear into some thugs.

I tilted my head and waited for their response, focusing on whatever microexpressions I could gleam from their eyes. Irritation, suspicion, and a flash of concern might've been there for a split second. The one in brown was quite good at keeping their muscles lax, but the one in black was an open book. I still couldn't get enough through those masks, so I memorized their height, gait, and eye color.

"Deliver the Sky-Blessed to us by tonight, alive and unmarked, please. Kill her escort," the one in brown ordered, and the two wandered off the path, as though strolling about their own garden.

"You said you'd stay and help!" the rogue leader snarled. When there was no response, he turned back to me with a frustrated snort. I could see fear in his eyes. Did he at least recognize me?

Our pride is starting to get a little hurt here, Spine muttered. *I'd say we're pretty memorable.*

I laughed out loud. I agreed with that. Not many had hair and eyes matching their lycan's color, especially the white ones. That was more prevalent in alphas.

I invited the leader over, displaying an elongated canine with a sneer. The male charged with his illegal pack and shifted, already provoked. I grinned in excitement as I tore into them, keeping track of every rogue to ensure Trail's safety.

My claws tore out the leader's throat while I swung a wolf into another rogue. I almost wished I'd taken my armor off to get more of a rush. It was slightly less fun without the added risk, but I wouldn't take any chances with Ragna's safety. Besides, I was being entertained in other ways. Their fangs would occasionally miss flesh and clamp jarringly into my plate armor, making them wobble.

I laughed darkly and continued to execute each mercenary. The deaths given were quick; I wasn't a sadist. I was a hunter, a warrior, and I was thriving in my element. My blood hummed brighter with each broken neck and each severed artery. My heart pumped in a roar, and each beat egged me on to finish the next enemy. There were more foes than last time, and the fight carried on longer, but perhaps I was simply savoring it.

This was easy. This was what I knew, and I had every right to do it. Mercenaries like these wouldn't hesitate to kill a pup or a child. With that thought, I slashed brutally into the next lycan's throat, nearly ripping off its head.

I stumbled from the force of my momentum when I realized I had no more rogues left to slaughter. The Sky Gods received my snarling howl of victory. I was alive. I was alive! The rush was incredible, and the high was nearly orgasmic.

Orgasmic... I growled when Ragna's arousal hit my nose, but then I froze.

Champion. Champion. Champion. Champion.

I kept my eyes averted and stepped away from where I knew she was. She'd returned to her human form for some reason, and I could not look at her. If I looked at her, I'd give in to lust. I grabbed my bag and ran away before it was too late. She was safe for now. No rogues left.

They're dead, they're dead, they're dead, they're dead! Champion! I'm her champion! Don't hurt her, don't hurt her, don't hurt her.

Her scent faded when I put enough distance between us, and I dug my claws into a tree with a near-rabid snarl. I threw my bag and armor down and shredded the tree's bark out of madness. Huge chunks of wood cracked out of the tree, and jagged splinters threatened to cut my palms.

I growled loudly and brutally gripped my throbbing erection. Masturbation wouldn't do a fucking thing. If she hadn't been my fated mate—fake or real—I could have calmed myself, but I had no idea what the fuck to do. I was so aroused it almost hurt. My insides coiled and wound like a snake about to strike. I desperately tried pumping at my shaft, but it wasn't enough. My wild body demanded that mate touch, knowing it was nearby. Fuck! How long was this going to take to go away? All I could think about was the she-wolf who'd smelled so delectable.

Her scent wafted over to me, and I panicked. "Ragna, get out of here!" I yelled, unable to risk looking. "Get the fuck out of here! Go! I'll find you later! The area's safe now!"

Footsteps behind me shuffled the leaves. It didn't sound or smell like she was departing. "You stupid she-wolf! Don't you understand I'm trying to calm down? Get the fuck away from me!" I roared, trying to use anger to scare her away.

"Ch-Champion..." her quiet voice called, and I grunted helplessly, fighting all my wild urges. My entire body throbbed in pleasurable agony at her voice, my stomach twisted into knots, and my breathing was as shallow as a summer pond.

"Ragna!" I snarled furiously and jabbed a finger in her direction. "If you don't leave right now, I'm going to fuck you! Go!"

Why wasn't she leaving? Oh gods. My body crumbled from the stress, and I became a shaking mess. It took everything to not turn around and mount her. I sank my claws deeper into wood as if trying to keep myself from flying into a tornado. My forehead pressed painfully into the bark, and a grimace contorted all my face muscles.

Ragna... please. I'm losing the fight.

"I-it's fine... I-I'll help you," she offered quietly. My eyes shot open, and my breath caught. I whirled around to find her submitting to me— waiting. What the fuck was happening?

My control dissolved, and I was lost to her.

Chapter 18

Champion Zorian

I was wild. Savage. I prowled over to the submitting she-wolf, growling. This female was willing, ready, and her generous gesture affected me as much as she did. A hot shudder raked down my body and splintered like lightning, adorning my lust.

My abdomen clenched, and I fell to my knees behind her. I slapped my palms into the handles of her hips and dug my fingers into her flesh. Then I pulled her against me so she could feel my cock glide between her spread thighs and along her sex, making her arousal wet its length. I shook with excitement and slid my hands to her shoulders, then around her back like I was painting my name on her—marking my territory.

I anchored my hands on her hips again and drove my erection along her folds one more time. I wanted her to feel how long, hard, and aroused I was for her. I wanted her to know her power. She had this power over me. She did this to me. She was my aphrodisiac.

Her timid moan was all I needed. I slid a finger down to savor her readiness, grunting in approval as I rubbed just inside her dripping core. She bucked slightly in surprise, or maybe nervousness, but I chose not to admonish her; she'd offered herself willingly. I palmed and rubbed her buttock with my other hand. This was a good female.

I parted her slippery folds, pressed my head against her opening, and nudged inside her. I tilted my head back and clenched my teeth from the agony and ecstasy of joining with her. The ecstasy was heightened by the tingling of the mate bond where we'd joined. The agony was knowing that I'd eventually have to leave her.

I remembered feeling these sensations before, but it was hazy. Had I been with the same female? A memory of a bloody palm came to me, disturbing me enough to try to maintain some control. It was torturous to go so slowly, and my body shook from the effort, but I held on to a chant I recalled from earlier.

Don't hurt her, don't hurt her, don't hurt her.

I pushed farther into her, then withdrew. I entered again, penetrating her a little more before pulling back to her very edge. I slid back inside, moving inch by inch, until I was buried in her snug heat. She had accepted all my pulsing offering—down to the very hilt. Deep satisfaction warmed my groin as she held me in place, affirming her willingness. I groaned lazily and dragged my palms to her buttocks, massaging her round cheeks. Her flesh strained around my girth, and I wanted to give her a moment to get used to me.

I listened for a moment, and she eventually released a soft sigh. The female seemed ok, and that excited me, intensifying my arousal. I dipped my head, squeezed my eyes shut, and bared my teeth. My breath escaped in a harsh growl, and I started pumping my hips into her, dragging and pushing my heavy cock in measured strokes. Her pussy was as soft as melted butter and just as warm. So warm, so tight, and so wet.

I tilted her hips up, wanting to stare at where we were joined. I groaned at the view, feeling my arousal lurch higher. I loved how her swollen sex clenched around me in a tight ring, like she didn't want me to go. I loved the sight of her glistening juices on my cock. The rest of her slick escaped, squeezing out between our rubbing skin to trickle down her thighs. I'd never been so turned on in my life. The only thing that kept me from spilling my seed was the insatiable longing to have more time with this female. My body was on fire. My veins burned, and each lungful of air kindled my need for her.

A fervor ignited, and I jerked her back into my next thrust. Every increase in arousal hardened me more, and I pushed to go as deep as I could, straining her limits. I groaned mindlessly in my indulgence, bottoming out against the soft wall guarding her womb. I loved how it pressed against my sensitive head. Her body took it, stretched for me, and faced every challenge I made.

She was enough, and yet I couldn't get enough. I had to have more. This body felt like it was made for me, and I wanted it all to myself. I wanted her all for myself. She was mine—all mine. When the fervor blossomed into a blinding fever, I snarled, and my thrusts turned into slams.

I caught her pants and whimpers between the slapping of skin. I was spurred on by a tiny mewl that escaped her lips, and my arousal expanded like a wildfire. She was enjoying it. My female was enjoying it! I groaned from deep in my belly and leaned over to fondle her swollen breasts, massaging them while I rocked into her. I nibbled like a hungry predator on her back while I dragged my palms all over her sweaty breasts and belly. She was driving me wild, and I was going out of my mind. All I could see was her. Her scent, her slick body, and her softness were sending my blistering desire sky-high.

She uttered her first cry of pleasure—quiet but needy. Even in the midst of coupling, her sounds were shy. The innocence of it all was too much, and a colossal shudder lurched through my entire body. I reared back and started fucking her as hard as possible. I held on to her hips out of possessiveness and a need to balance myself. I sped up, putting my all into having her. I clenched my eyes shut and grunted ferally with every forceful, dripping slide into her. Oh gods, I didn't want this to end. She was bliss.

I felt the inevitable come to a boil within me, deep in my groin and cock, and as much as I wanted to fight it, I knew it was time to finish. I desperately didn't want to, though. I didn't want to leave, but I had to pull out of her. I hissed and pumped fervently into her pussy, moving faster and faster to reach my peak. Just one more moment in her heat. One more moment. Oh gods, she was perfect. One more...

A tidal wave of pleasure exploded through me, and I shouted out at the top of my lungs, howling to the treetops in euphoria. I yanked myself out of her sweet sex to let my seed spill onto the forest floor between her knees. I grunted and hissed through my teeth with every spurt of release and clung on to her thighs so she wouldn't stumble into my cum.

I groaned softly when the last of my seed dropped, and I moved to pick the she-wolf up so I could lay her down on a softer spot. I collapsed on the forest floor next to her, dizzy with bliss and drenched in sweat. I gasped for air and put a hand over my heart, willing the damn thing to slow down lest I go into cardiac arrest again. I chuckled inwardly at the thought of Ragna having to perform CPR on me again because I'd succumbed from a sex coma.

Ragna.

Ragna!

My mind returned to me, and I paled. Shit. I'd fucked her again! Was she upset? I peered over at her, and she was trying to catch her breath like me, but her eyes were shut tight. I glanced down to check my cock and was relieved to find it clear of blood. Guilt still hung over my head, though. I hadn't forced her, but I was sure as shit she'd felt pressured. Fuck. I'd tried so hard to avoid this. I thought it might've been ok with her in her wolf form. Fuck. Fuck. Fuck!

When the self-loathing stirred, I became worried it'd make me snap at Ragna. I needed to focus and get out of my head. I needed something to do. I reached into my backpack and pulled out my canteen and a cloth. I soaked it and knelt by Ragna. When I parted her legs to clean her, she jerked away and froze. I stopped and just handed her the cloth. I'd wanted to make a sweet gesture, which was normally extremely hard for me to do, but I guess she felt more comfortable cleaning herself.

"Did I hurt you?" I asked, keeping all emotion out of my voice as she turned to tend to herself. I was angry with myself, and I didn't want her to think my frustration was aimed at her. "Are you sore?"

She shook her head and looked away. Her face was a little pale, and I grew concerned. "I'm f-fine, Ch-Champion."

I nodded slowly but wasn't convinced. "Good," I replied flatly. "Thank you." It felt like shit to thank someone for letting you fuck them, but I didn't know how else to acknowledge what she'd done. She'd made an unnecessary sacrifice to ease my suffering. I also didn't think it'd help if I told her that it'd been the best sex I'd ever had. Oh gods, how I fucking hated myself.

I noticed her delicate squirm and a subtle attempt to press her thighs together. She couldn't hide her arousal from me, and I supposed it was a good sign that she needed more. It meant I hadn't completely fucked up her second encounter with sex, like I had with her first. That still ate at me. I wished I could go back to prevent the whole thing from happening. I frowned. How had I softened so much since then? When had that happened?

"Ragna," I called. With wide eyes, she looked over her shoulder at me like I'd caught her stealing from the kitchen. Her heart pounded faster as she waited for my next words. I tilted my head and asked, "Will you accept a reward from your champion for your selfless actions?"

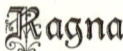agna

Champion Zorian wanted to offer me a reward for my selfless actions? I didn't know how I felt about that. I felt like I should've been offended, but I wasn't. I'd done it willingly, not for payment. I wasn't a prostitute.

When he ran off after killing the attackers, I'd known why. It touched me that he had tried to spare me, but his level of suffering was disturbing, and I didn't like him being alone with it. He'd apologized, and I was starting to care about him—a little.

I'd found him shredding a poor tree to bits, fighting himself so much harder than his last opponents. Running away hadn't been fun for him. It hadn't been a game. He'd taken his role of champion seriously, and somehow that had turned me on more than anything. I didn't owe him anything, so why did I feel the urge to give back? This was no transaction. Still, he'd risked his life. My mind was a mess over the situation, and I ended up considering it when he yelled at me to leave.

I'd made my decision, and Trail had screamed with joy. My gut said the second time with him would be gentler. He had doted on us before, and his words hadn't always matched his actions. Maybe he'd be able to remember me through his haze. That was Trail's thought, at any rate.

I'd still expected an unpleasant experience, but when he'd gotten his hands on me, it had been anything but disagreeable. He'd been wild but had managed to start slow. Instead of pain, I'd just felt the incredible satisfaction of him filling me to the brim. I'd expected a wide steel rod to be the enforcer of pain, but it was like this one had only wanted to spend time with me, as odd as that sounded. Goddess, that sounded odd indeed.

With the fullness came the pleasure, and it had come from everywhere. The age-old, she-wolf's instinctive response to being under a strong male had hit me in full force. Both times I'd been trapped under him, but there'd been a rush this time. Even in his wildness, he'd invited me to join in his pleasure. He'd invited me to experience enjoyable sex. That coming from an alpha alone was enough to make me dizzy with desire.

He'd been centered on me. The snarling, the growling, and the wandering hands had all screamed of his need to possess me, and I had to fight to keep my legs from turning into butter. I'd been mildly concerned when he'd gotten rough, but then I realized he'd prepared me for it, doubling the satisfaction. I had no idea that instinct contributed so much to sex—instinct, handling, and, of course, the tingling from the fated mate bond.

I had been disappointed when he'd finished, but I had no idea why. My instincts had wanted him to fill me with his seed, but I'd known that to be a terrible idea, so I wasn't worried about that, at least not regarding my physical discomfort. My strange disappointment was partially due to how miserably my sex throbbed and ached. I tried to be discreet about my odd suffering, but I knew he'd seen.

I stared back at him as I considered his question. His jawline was tense, but his eyes glinted with... curiosity? Ugh, I couldn't read him at all!

Staring at clever burgundy eyes that were curtained by dove-white hair did absolutely nothing to calm down the ache between my legs. Maybe this reward would distract me from my problem. I didn't really have anything left to lose.

"O-ok..." I answered hesitantly. Without a word, he got up and walked away from me. I blushed furiously at his muscular back and buttocks, but I shook myself free and followed him. When he sat at the base of a tree and patted the ground between his legs, I sent him a confused look.

"Sit with your back to me, Ragna," he ordered.

I did as he asked, but I was very uncertain about this reward. Maybe he would give me a shoulder rub? I hadn't had one since I was a teenager. I'd prefer to be dressed, though.

I waited for him to start, but he pulled me against his chest instead.

What?

He snaked his right arm down my belly, toward my throbbing core, and my entire body tensed. A pathetic, scared whimper escaped my lips. "Ch-Champion this... I can't..." I stuttered, remembering how that male had touched me. Champion Zorian's hand froze, and his low voice hummed into my ear.

"Did someone else hurt you like this, Ragna?"

I nodded. "F-five years ago. Three held me down, and I b-barely got away."

"Point them out if you see them again, and I'll end them," he growled.

"The Sky Gods beat you to it..."

"Good. Don't give them the power to haunt you. They're trash."

Maybe someday it wouldn't bother me as much, and his presence did help. I was torn. This was so strange. "Why is it a reward?" I asked him, lost in my thoughts.

"Because it'll give you release. I got mine, but you didn't. You're all pent up, she-wolf."

"Oh, is that what I'm feeling?" I didn't know there would be complications from letting him have me. "It's uncomfortable."

"If you trust me, I will help you," he murmured into my ear. "It's just me here, your champion. No other male will touch you while I'm around." I tried to hold back a shudder, but I failed. Those protective words plus his breath on my ear made the throbbing so much worse.

He rested his left hand on my upper arm and directed, "If you hold on to my scent, my voice, and my touch, those memories can't have you."

I wasn't certain about that either. I didn't know if he'd ever experienced that kind of trauma. However, I knew that if I didn't try to move on at some point, I might never. It had been years. Maybe I could trust him one more time today and see what happened. Maybe the mate bond would help.

"A-all right," I agreed cautiously.

"Breathe with me, Ragna." He took a deep inhale, and I followed suit. We breathed together, slowly and steadily, so I could relax. When I was calm and heavy, he slid his hand down my belly, caressing my skin until he reached the curls between my legs. I continued my measured breathing, matching the rhythm of his swelling chest.

"That's a good she-wolf," he rumbled and petted downward with the side of his thumb like he was lazily strumming a lute. I jerked nervously when he dipped a thick finger between my folds and stirred, swirling just within my entrance. He hummed softly to soothe me, then removed his finger to slide it upward. I tensed once more from the sensitivity, but when he stroked my arm, I calmed.

I closed my eyes and rested my head against his chest, tilting it in the direction where I could scent him the easiest. This was Zorian, not a brutal rogue. This was my champion, not an evil stranger.

Zorian, Zorian, Zorian. Stay in the present. Stay here with him.

I let out my first moan when he increased the pressure, then alternated between pushing inside and looping around the top. I tensed again when my moan reminded me of the fake one. My champion knew exactly where my mind had gone, and he rubbed my arm before squeezing it.

"You're here with your champion, Ragna. Your champion, your protector, is the one making you moan. He's the only one who'll be making you scream, who'll be making you cry, but it'll all be from pleasure." His breath blew sizzling tingles down my ears, neck, and chest, and I gave myself permission to savor them. I shuddered and ignored everything but his voice. This cold male was being so warm right now, so comforting. It made my arousal soar.

When his left hand slithered over to massage my left breast, I mewled, arched, and spread my legs wide. I did it out of instinct, but an appreciative groan escaped his lips. He pressed firmer as he made diagonal strokes, sliding from the top of my sex to the sides. I panted as that familiar, itchy feeling started building—like needing to sneeze but much worse.

He kept stroking, somehow knowing where to move when I made certain noises. His left hand explored my breast, kneading and rubbing. The sensual massage sent bolts of pleasure into my chest and echoed between my legs. The throbbing was getting worse and worse! I bit my lip, squirmed, and whimpered. What now?

When his fingers accelerated, I gasped. My hands shot out to hold on to something, and I dug my claws in to stay grounded. A pleased growl rumbled out of him, and a heady wave of arousal pushed through me. I groaned and tilted my head back into his chest, feeling like I was being lifted higher. I needed that itch scratched. I needed it scratched! It was driving me mad!

Fingers pinched and pulled on my nipple while a hand focused fervently on my sex, targeting one spot. My stomach tensed, and I felt like something was coming around the corner... like a giant ocean wave. I tossed my head left and right, whimpering and begging for it to come. I wanted it to take me away with it! I needed to be released!

A male's voice tipped me over the edge.

"Come for me, she-wolf," he growled into my ear. His voice was deep, husky with lust. "Come all over your champion's hand. Claim your reward for offering your sweet self to him."

I arched slowly against the warm, hard surface, and then it was there. The wave crashed violently into me and sent my senses spinning. Heat was everywhere, blossoming from my core.

"Ahhh! Ahhhn! Ahhhnnng!" I howled with every splashing wave. A force I couldn't fight, nor wanted to, had control now. Fingers between my legs pushed with every pulse, letting me ride higher and longer. Each surge pulled a noise from me and a buck from my hips. All I could do was writhe to stay afloat.

It wasn't until I was bobbing on the last ripple that I noticed his hands had moved. One arm was wrapped around my waist, and a large hand was stroking my hair. The pets were soft, gentle.

I opened my eyes and waited for the black dots to clear. When I glanced up, I found a delighted smirk on Champion Zorian's face before it was hastily replaced with indifference.

Chapter 19

Ragna

His expression had changed so quickly that I wasn't sure he'd smirked at all. It was so out of character for him. I wish I knew what he'd been thinking about right then. My heart and breathing slowed, but I still couldn't tear my eyes from his. Maybe I could see something in them. No, nothing. Gods, he had scorching eyes, and they always seemed to stare so intently at me. His cheeks had a healthy glow to them now. It made him look powerful—virile.

He blinked several times and lazily searched my eyes as he waited for me to gather my wits. His hand had stopped stroking my hair when his smirk vanished, but I felt his little thumb caress my head. He didn't seem to know he was doing it. I glanced at his lips and thought how odd it was that, aside from his initial treatment of me, we've done everything a normal couple would do but backwards. Kissing wasn't in the cards for us. He didn't need it unless he tried to die on me a second time. Had I been staring at his lips for too long?

Reality caught up to me, and I realized I'd not only given my body to this hulking male, but he'd done something to me that... I couldn't even begin to explain. He'd done that last act with such ease. Oh goddess, I'd practically howled right into his face!

My cheeks ignited, and I averted my eyes while trying to get to my feet. I wobbled and strong, calloused hands grabbed my hips to steady them. My mind flashed back to those hands grabbing those very same spots when he took my body, and I pressed my cold hands to my face, trying to will the blood from my head.

Oh goddess, why was I feeling so embarrassed? How did people do these things so casually? He'd touched my breast, and I had been all bare before him!

Had he liked what he'd seen or was I just... passable? I hadn't really thought about my self-esteem before, but it'd been declining since the attack. I looked down at my belly to trace where the scars had been but froze in shock.

There was blood all over my fingertips. I held up my other hand, and it was the same. Where...? I gasped and looked around, then my eyes fell to the champion's bloody thighs. He was in the middle of wiping his legs down with a damp cloth, cleaning the injuries. I'd raked my claws into him!

"Oh no! Oh great goddess, no! I'm so sorry! I didn't mean to claw you! Why didn't you say anything? I'm so sorry!" I ran over to look at the cuts, feeling awful.

He stopped my approach with a hand. "Calm down, she-wolf. You didn't hurt me. Look, they're already starting to heal." I looked down again. He was right! They were already scabbed. Goodness, alphas healed fast. He pulled his pants up and finished dressing, completed undisturbed.

"I-I'm still sorry," I mumbled, then blushed and hurried to get dressed too.

"It just means that I did a good job," he added with a shrug. I gaped, rendered speechless. It wasn't inaccurate; I just hadn't expected the cockiness! It was additionally jarring to hear it said in such a deadpan way. He grabbed his backpack and headed toward the road, leaving me astounded.

I ran to catch up and wanted to reply, but I didn't know what to say. I guess I should...

"Th-thank you," I murmured, and he nodded coolly.

"You did well. You earned it," he replied. What did one say to that? How did one even do a bad job of getting on their hands and knees? Ah, I was so flustered! My mind was a mess.

I kept stealing glances at him, but he wasn't fazed at all by what we'd done together. He just looked relaxed and was behaving like his normal, serious self. Well, I was feeling very awkward around him now.

Awkwardness aside, whatever he'd done to me had melted a ton of tension off my shoulders. My body felt great, but my mind was still a jumble of thoughts and questions. I decided to try talking to him more since he was Champion Zorian, not King Zorian. I knew they were the same person, but Champion Zorian was much more approachable.

"Was that making love, Champion?" I asked, looking up at him. "Beta Rudesind gave me the impression that it was a gentler thing, but I wouldn't really know the difference."

The question made him angry for some reason. He scowled, and his nostrils flared, making me grimace. Maybe this had been a bad idea.

"No, it's not," he answered harshly. His jaw twitched, and his arms stiffened.

"Oh," I replied quietly, but my curiosity got the better of me. "What is it then?"

"You'll find out when you meet your real fated mate."

I twisted my lips and pouted a little. I guess it was too personal of a question. I was about to apologize when he spoke again.

"It's still sex but... more sentimental. The emotions involved are more... sensitive."

"So, you've never done it either, huh?" The joke slipped out of my mouth before I had a chance to think, and I paled in horror. I slapped a hand over my mouth. That was very much a Trail thing to say, and she was cackling in my head. There was no point in it, and I didn't know why I did it, but I ran like mad until I got to the main road, then put a tree between me and where I expected him to exit the woods.

I yelped when I was lifted off the ground by my backpack, but the champion merely set me down in the middle of the road and continued onward. When he looked back at me with a raised eyebrow, I rushed to catch up. From the side, I eyed him to see if he looked mad, but I only caught a twitch of his lips. I desperately hoped that was him trying to hold back a smile.

When I felt the urge to talk once more, I sighed, then stared down at my boots, kicking the occasional pebble down the road. Being out here made it feel like I was back to my life as a solitary rogue, but now there was someone with me. I'd really missed having someone to talk to.

"I'm sorry I wasn't more helpful today," I apologized, feeling gloomy.

"That's not true. You helped me a lot," he replied, and I realized I wasn't sure what part of the day he meant. I blushed furiously and placed my cold hands back on my cheeks. He couldn't possibly be talking about how I sated him! Indignance swelled in my chest, and I was about to give him a piece of my mind when he interrupted my thoughts.

"You didn't run when I was dealing with the rogues. You didn't distract me. You didn't jump in and try to fight. You didn't get in my way," he listed, counting the points with his fingers. "I knew where you were at all times so I could properly strategize."

Oh, I'd really thought the worst of him for a moment. "So, by just staying out of the way I was being helpful?" I asked, not really sold on that being a terribly important factor.

"You'd be surprised at how impossible it can be to escort a difficult charge," he said while adjusting his pack. "A bodyguard can only do their job if they can trust you to do yours, which is to listen to them."

"But what if I learned to fight better?"

"No, but it sounds like you were kicked from your pack without enough training."

"When I encountered violent rogues for the first time... it's like all my warrior training left my head. I'd never seen action before, so I just ran and never stopped running," I mumbled with a heavy heart. "Rakel was the warrior amongst my friends. I was never quite sure where I fit in."

"Your time will come, she-wolf," he said as if it was a fact. "I'm just bringing you where you need to be. Regardless of whatever or whoever made the goddess disappear, the Sky Gods still chose you and deemed you worthy. It's not a fact to be so easily dismissed."

Great gods, that helped me feel better. Those words, in addition to his apology for how he'd treated me, were really making me grow quite fond of him. I smiled and kicked another pebble down the road.

When we finally settled for the night, I was exhausted. Today hadn't just been about walking, and my body was happily reminding me of that.

Seems like the sex was much better than the first time, Trail noted. *I'm all caught up on your memories. Who knew he was capable of not being a monster?*

Oh, you've been cheering for him this whole time, I reminded her.

I really like Spine, she said, a dreamy smile in her voice. *He's not pure wolf, but he's still perfect. Tall, white fur, and blazing eyes. He's also quite the cuddler. I know he likes me too.*

Smitten like a kitten. Guess we can officially dump Muttons then.

Wish I could talk to Spine, though. She pouted.

They'd have to either mark us or let us join their pack, and neither's about to happen. Sorry... We'll probably shift tomorrow, though! We kinda got delayed by... several things today. You'll get to enjoy more time with Spine. He seems to be a good boy. Enjoy it while it lasts, Trail, I murmured sadly.

Yeah... Speaking of your memories... I'm worried about—

I'm not ready to talk about it, I snapped, and she fell silent.

I stared into the popping campfire as I tried to fall asleep. The champion was on the other side and seemed to be resting peacefully. I, on the other hand, was tossing and turning. I was uncomfortable, cold, and empty. I'd gotten too used to the mate bond and was feeling the absence of my champion's skin. The warm, soothing tingles made falling asleep easy, and I was less likely to have nightmares. Though I could detect his relaxing scent, the purity of it was being spoiled by the campfire.

The only bad thing about fixing the mate bonds was that I'd return to being unmated, and this loneliness would be my life again. Whoever was King Zorian's mate was a lucky female. The goddess would have one in mind for a king. Maybe I'd been fated to them all on accident because there wasn't one for me?

Well, that thought wasn't helpful.

I felt a pang in my chest and rolled onto my other side. Something else was bothering me too, but it was too big. I tried not to think the worst when I'd noticed, and I hadn't wanted to react with his eyes on me. I couldn't bear to think about it now, either. I was just going to keep pushing it away unless it became a problem. I held back a pained groan. I didn't think I'd be getting much rest tonight.

Champion Zorian

Ragna looked ill in the morning. Shadows clung to the thin skin under her eyes, and her pallor was on the green side.

"Are you unwell?" I asked while tying my bedroll.

She brushed my question off with a hand. I noticed with some amusement that she was starting to pick up some of my habits and gestures. "I'm ok. I just didn't sleep very well," she answered, her voice still husky from sleepiness.

"You should have slept with me," I stated with a frown. Why hadn't she? Was she still embarrassed about what we'd done yesterday? Her face had been a tomato all day.

She waved me off again, and I gave up for now. "Let's shift. We have a lot of ground to make up for," I directed, undressing and situating my plate armor. I didn't like going without it now that I knew Ragna was being targeted. Every tool at my disposal was going to be used to protect her.

"Ok. Trail will be happy about that," she said and shuffled shyly toward a tree to undress. I nearly gaped at her. I mean, I'd seen all of her by now. She couldn't possibly be that insecure. From what I knew about wolf-shifters, they were not shy with their bodies. Lycans were the same.

I cleared my throat and tried to remember what she'd just said before I got distracted. "Trail is itching to run?" I asked, waiting for her.

"No, she just won't stop yammering about Spine," she mumbled from behind the tree. I scrubbed my face with a hand, suppressing a smile in case she somehow managed to see. That was going to make Spine an incredibly annoying and smug bastard.

What? Nothin' wrong with her missing her hunky mate, he said with a very audible smirk.

I snorted through my nose and just shifted. He was going to keep rubbing this shit in, so I'd get him to Trail to shut him up. The slobbery reunion between wolf and lycan went as expected, though Trail seemed as lethargic as Ragna.

They're both tired, I reminded Spine. *Maintain a solid pace but keep checking on her.*

Spine loped alongside Trail as they continued down the main road. *What can I say? You wiped Ragna out yesterday.* He sniggered. *Think you'll go back for more when you don't actually need it?*

I considered ignoring him, but I knew he'd keep pushing. *I think you know where I stand, Spine. I'll enjoy what comes my way, but I won't seek it out. All this will end, including you and Trail. The only new thing I'll add is, yeah, this fucking sucks. I'm starting to wish I could keep her, ok? Happy? Go take a victory lap.*

You may think you've only been lying to yourself, but that includes lying to me, and I was getting pretty fucking tired of it.

The denials had been wearing me down too. It felt like trying to use sandpaper to polish a jagged rock. That shit was only going to rip.

The late afternoon brought some rain, which seemed to refresh Trail a bit. A lycan or a wolf would, on occasion, be unceremoniously shoved into mud puddles. I smiled secretly at how much fun the soggy idiots were having. They weren't thinking about anything but the present. That was a muscle I'd never learned to develop very well. I'd always been taught to think multiple steps ahead. Being in the present was a luxury, but it was also a vulnerability.

Maybe thinking several steps ahead was what hindered my connection to Ragna. Maybe I had to be more present. Putting a mask on gave me more time—more time to think and strategize. More time to formulate what to say. But that removed the environment where positive emotions thrived. Laughter, smiling—anything impulsive, really. If I was leaning toward being a total coward and running away, the mask allowed more time for that to occur as well. Was a mask something I could take off easily? Could I put it on just as quickly?

I was giving myself a headache thinking about all this. Was I overcomplicating the matter? It was easier to think I was a raging asshole with anger issues… though those were more like Spine's words for me.

The evening brought the rain down to a drizzle, and we found decent shelter under a dense group of trees. I shifted back and unfolded a tarp to hang over us so we could build a fire, which Ragna started on immediately. I shared the leftover meat with her, and we listened to the canopy's fat droplets patter against the shelter.

The hairs on the back of my neck stood on end when the forest animals went quiet. Ragna froze, and her heartbeat accelerated out of fright. I raised my nose and turned my head in all directions, but I couldn't scent anything. I definitely couldn't see anything. The moisture in the air wasn't helping either, and I had a feeling that whatever it was continued to stay downwind of us.

I stood and walked a few paces out to look up and down the road. Something emaciated slinked into the woods from the road, startling me. It disappeared as quickly as I'd spotted it, and an uncontrollable shudder raked down my spine, accompanying a fear I wasn't used to feeling. Whatever it was, it looked unnatural, unlike any animal I'd ever seen. I backed up, not wanting to get any farther from Ragna—not after seeing that.

I didn't like the look of that fucking thing, Spine growled. *What kind of fucking weird-ass shit was that?*

I don't know. Should we shift and stay on watch so Ragna can sleep, or should I stay in my human form? I asked, never too proud to ask for a second strategic opinion from my battle-hardened lycan.

Stay human so you can at least communicate with her right away if you need to. I really wish you'd just add her to the pack so we could talk.

Alright, I'll keep an eye out. Stay on alert, Spine. I have a bad feeling about that... thing.

I sat down next to Ragna and ordered, "I want you to sleep, and I'll stay on watch. If I get tired, I'll wake you, but I need you to sleep. Remember what I said about listening to your bodyguard, ok?" The part about waking her was a lie. I just didn't want to fight her on the issue. I'd be perfectly fine, and she needed rest.

"What was out there?" she asked, looking up at me with a spooked expression.

"Just some kind of predator," I answered vaguely because if I described it, I was certain she wouldn't fall asleep for a week. "We'll be fine. I'm just staying up in case it wanders too close. I've gone without sleep for much longer. One night is nothing." I threw a little confidence into my cool tone. I needed her to believe me.

Making sure her sleeping mat was between the fire and me, I settled on the ground and kept my eyes on the woods. At least she'd be hidden. I was grateful for the Sky Gods' blessing every damn night.

As she curled up, I stared briefly at the back of her head. I took a deep breath, went out on a limb, and stroked her hair a little. I felt a desire to calm her, and it was as strong as my drive to keep her safe, so I petted her head gently.

It was hard to tear my eyes from her, but I did. I had to keep my gaze on the woods. If it showed up, I was going to rip it to shreds. I couldn't shake the feeling it was here for my ma—I mean, Ragna.

I continued to stroke her damp, cinnamon hair, feeling the bond calm me as well. I knew for sure I was going to miss sweet moments like this—without the freaky abomination skulking about, of course. My fingers occasionally caught on wet tangles, and I wished I had a towel to dry her hair. I didn't want her catching a cold. When she was fast asleep, I pulled her long hair out from under her blanket and tucked the fabric up to cover her neck. There, that was better.

I heard rustling throughout the night. Though the disturbances occurred rarely, they never got closer than several hundred feet. I stayed put, not trusting that thing to lure me away from my charge.

It's testing us, Spine noted. I nodded and continued listening for any sounds or smells I could identify. Nothing.

Patience, I reminded him. It'll show its hand at some point. We won't play into them.

⚜

Just before dawn, when the skies began their preparation for the sun, the rustling approached our location. I jumped silently to my feet, and my entire body tensed. It came within fifty feet of us but departed as fast as it arrived, and the forest finally came out of hiding. It was gone. I let out a breath and finally relaxed. I chose to lie down next to Ragna and told Spine to keep an ear out while I took a brief rest.

I woke when Ragna stirred from sleep. "How did last night go?" she asked while surveying the forest. A shudder rippled through her, and I noticed the little brown hairs on her arms were standing on end. She was still spooked.

"It was uneventful," I reported. "I didn't see anything. You can be calm now—hear how the forest is no longer afraid?" I handed her some cured meat. Her green eyes fell doubtfully on it, and she shook her head. I frowned and offered her a ration instead, which she accepted. She must be more nervous than I thought.

When we returned to the road, a small hand grabbed my arm, and I glanced over to see what Ragna wanted to show me. I followed her gaze to the middle of the road where a rock sat upon a folded piece of cloth. Whatever it was, it'd clearly been left here for us to find, so I carefully removed the rock to study the object beneath.

Just cloth, ink, and parchment... and something like... polish, Spine observed. *I don't smell anything dangerous.*

Agreed, I replied and unfolded the cloth. A letter was inside.

I opened it, scowled, and read it to Ragna. "Ragna, I look forward to seeing you at our mating ceremony. Take this ring as a token of my intention. Signed, E.B."

I looked up at her face, which was frozen in confusion, horror, and shock. She then wobbled, turned on her heels, and threw up on the side of the road.

Chapter 20

Champion Zorian

Ah, shit! Spine said worriedly. I pocketed the note and rushed forward to grab her long hair. Ragna heaved again, but it was just bile the second time. She panted, and her gasps turned into sobs. I dragged my pack over, grabbed the canteen of water, and dripped a little to rinse her hair. Once her strands were clean, I braided her locks in a rush and tucked the end into her tunic collar so it'd stay out of the way.

I slipped my hand under the bottom of her tunic to rub her shivering back. "Stay strong, Ragna," I murmured softly. "I have it easy. I only need to kill, but you have emotional battles to face here." I swallowed and kept rubbing her back, finding it hard to watch her cry now. "You must look at these things as battles. Whoever wrote that won't get you because it's my job to prevent that. Your job is to not allow him to weaken you. Do not let him win. Do not let him dampen your resolve," I ordered firmly.

Ragna let out one last shuddering sob and calmed. "You're right, Champion. Thank you." She rubbed her eyes and sat back on her haunches. I handed her the canteen to rinse her mouth, which she did before speaking again. "I feel like the timing is right. That note and those masked strangers—they're related. They must be," she said while looking down the road. Her eyes seemed a little glassy. "It's rough on my nerves to be pursued so strategically. This is different from before. My stomach just couldn't handle it. Sorry about that."

"I'm pretty sure I've thrown up a hundred more times than you. The battlefield is a nasty place to be," I confessed and patted her shoulder. "Don't concern yourself." She sighed heavily and nodded, then stood so we could leave.

"So just to verify, you do not know anyone with E.B. for initials?" I inquired, standing with her and putting on my pack. She scrunched her face up to think but eventually shook her head.

"No, no one comes to mind, but I never asked any rogues their name when I ran from them," she remarked with a laugh. "No formal introductions at all." A delayed giggle burst from her lips.

"How barbaric," I replied and let the corner of my mouth curl up into a small smile. Goddess, that was hard, but she responded very well to it. She beamed and blushed prettily, then looked away from me and down the road.

Good job, Spine praised. I snorted silently in irritation. That'd been dangerously close to patronizing.

I turned my thoughts back to the letter and dug it out of my pocket to take another look. The initials made me uneasy. *Spine, you don't think...*

That couldn't be Eysteinn. He'd be in no state now to put something like this together. It has to be someone else, Zorian, Spine answered, but he sounded uncertain. *Also, that creature clearly delivered it. No one else was around last night.*

Rage sizzled in my chest at the thought of that male forcing a mating and marking on Ragna. It wasn't happening. Clearly, whoever this was had a death wish. No one took anything from me—not anymore.

Not ever again.

I wrinkled my nose in disgust when I pulled the ring from the envelope. It was a gaudy thing, covered in diamonds and moonstones. I held the ring out for Ragna to look at, but she stopped and took a couple of steps back, as if I was holding a viper. She was more afraid of this than the Sun God Himself.

"I d-don't want that!" she blurted hastily. "Throw it a-away!" Her face was contorted into a troubled, queasy grimace. I hastily retrieved my proffering hand and dropped the ring back into the envelope.

"I'm going to hang on to all this, then. Maybe I can find which shop sold this when everything is said and done. No one will have a claim on you after we fix the bonds," I declared firmly and pulled my pack around to store the troubling items. "No one has a claim on you now as long as I'm around, ok?" As I spoke, I made sure she met my gaze.

"R-right," she replied and shook her arms out to soothe her nerves. We shifted into our wolf and lycan forms and managed a better pace than yesterday. Unfortunately, the rain returned with a vengeance well before dark, and it took us a while to find decent shelter.

We repeated camping under a tarp, and it was when we were heating meat over the fire that the forest fell silent again. Ragna's nerves, already shot, caused her to jump up and squeeze between the rock wall and me. She practically climbed me like a tree, wrapping her arms and legs around my torso while shaking like a baby deer. I listened intently and eventually heard rustling. It must be that creature.

"Is that predator back?" Ragna whispered, hiding her face in my neck.

"Think so," I said, straining my ears.

"What is it, though? Did you ever see it?" she asked. I hesitated, not wanting to lie again.

"I didn't get a great look, so I don't know," I answered truthfully. If it came back tomorrow, I'd tell her about it.

"I should keep watch tonight. At least I have my bow. I mean, it's only one animal. Maybe it's a mountain lion."

"I've never seen you use it," I said in realization, then looked down at her and almost chuckled. All I could see was the top of her head. "Are you any good?" Maybe I could distract her.

"You don't see me use it because I obsessively hoard arrows. I never use an arrow unless it's the only option, and I never let an arrow go unless I'm one hundred percent positive it's going to hit. I only had so many arrows during my banishment. I tried to make more, but the timing never worked out. I'd always get interrupted," she said, and every one of her muffled words vibrated through my chest.

"So, how did you know it would hit?" I asked and stroked the back of her hair. She tried to hide a shudder, and I smirked.

"I had rules. The target had to be within a certain distance if it was a certain size. I never, ever risked uncertain shots, and I salvaged as many used arrows as I could. No, you have to be practiced to be good. I'm not good, I've decided. I'm just... smart about it?"

"You were strategic with your resources. I think you were wise to do so." I nodded as I gazed into the woods, almost wishing the creature would attack so we could be done with its games. I'd rather be thoroughly enjoying Ragna right now.

"Fnanks," was her muffled reply. A chuckle accidentally burst out of me because her voice sounded hilariously congested. Her shoulders shook with light laughter too, and I unexpectedly felt myself relax.

Laughter releases tension. You remember that? You remember laughing, right? Spine teased.

I ignored him and just let Ragna hang on like a squirrel. Eventually, her head drooped, and I placed the she-wolf on her bedroll. I tucked her in and stood facing the woods once more.

I can watch tonight, Spine offered.

You ran all day, Spine.

Ok, how about we take turns then?

That's fair.

I shifted and Spine settled next to Ragna. He crouched protectively by her, and I could feel the heat of his stare on the woods. He was daring something to come and take her. That was the Alpha of Alphas in him, challenging any threat, even if it was an unknown. His ears and nose were constantly testing the environment for any signs of an enemy, but all he sensed was rustling. Him being awake would still drain us, but at least my mind could get some rest. The last thing I needed was hallucinating from lack of sleep. We'd fuel up with calories and hold out for the Lunar Coven. We could sleep properly there.

Spine looked down when he felt a gentle tug. Ragna had grabbed his big, fluffy, white tail and had snuggled into it like it was a cotton doll. We both felt a wave of affection wash over us at her display of... trust? Fondness? What was it? I couldn't even find the right word for it.

I said good night to Spine and tucked myself away to rest. Despite the creature stalking us, I was feeling... good.

⚜

Wake up, Spine prodded tersely, and I came forward to see it was already dawn. Spine had walked us out to the road with our things and

Ragna, waiting only until now to wake me. I looked through his eyes and glared at the rock on the ground. This was a repeat of yesterday.

A folded cloth was under the rock, and I had a feeling there was another letter in there as well. I shifted back into my human body and turned to glance at Ragna. She was looking pale again but seemed more sure-footed.

"Have you eaten yet?" I asked. She shook her head, and I turned back to stare at the delivery.

"Maybe we should leave it," she suggested. "If they see we're not picking them up, maybe they'll stop."

"That's one idea, but it could also provoke them into trying more undesirable tactics," I replied in a low voice while picking up the rock. "I'd rather get as much information out of them now while I can." I sniffed the cloth and envelope. Nothing was different from yesterday, but I noticed the smallest trace of deer urine. Whoever handled this wasn't thorough, or maybe they'd been in a rush.

"I think you were right, Ragna. I smell a little deer urine on this." I opened the envelope and read, forcing the words through gritted teeth.

"Tsk, tsk. Zorian, that ring was not for you. Haven't you taken enough? At any rate, tell MY mate that I'm thinking of her and cannot wait to show her off to every wolf and lycan. E.B."

I almost crushed the note in my fist. I was fuming. I knew in my gut that this had to be Eysteinn. Eysteinn Burchard. It had to be! I brushed hair from my forehead as I broke into a cold sweat. How was this possible?

I wouldn't have expected a male like him to even be capable of leaving his house, Spine said darkly.

He was a male to be pitied, I muttered, staring down at the note.

Ragna walked all around the road, trying to peer into the distance and sniffing. "They watched us open the envelope, Champion. They knew you kept it. They knew I didn't want it." She kept roaming, looking for the eyes we knew must be there. She stopped and blinked at me. "He knows you. He said your name. It sounded personal. You know who he is, don't you?" she asked, not missing a beat.

I folded the note and pocketed it. Taking a deep breath, I ran my hand through my hair and stood up, then gestured for Ragna to walk with me. "There is a possibility that this is from a lycan named Eysteinn Burchard.

The male has had… very bad luck with his mates. If he were to get his hands on you, you'd be his fourth, unless he's had more since the last I've heard."

"And why did he mention you taking something else?" she inquired, looking up at me with her bright green eyes. She looked worried, like maybe I wasn't who she thought I was. Gods, I hoped that wasn't the case. But still, we all had things we'd rather not share.

"He thinks I killed his second-chance mate."

"Did… you?"

I stayed quiet and averted my eyes. I really didn't want to talk about it.

agna

I waited for Champion Zorian to answer my question, and I was becoming pretty concerned about the look on his face. I'd never seen him look scared, but this was close. The crack in his mask was there. His heart pounded, and his eyes were searching the road, but I didn't think they were looking at anything that was there. Those were the eyes of someone who was buried in their memories.

I reminded myself that he was still a stranger to me. I reminded myself that he didn't seem to be the same person who'd tried to kill me under the shady starlight. I didn't actually know who he was. His truths were still just as hidden as they were days and days ago. I knew he must have killed many people, but how easy would it be for him to kill someone's mate without justification?

Was the mate bond the only thing that had kept him from killing me that night? He'd certainly had every chance. If Trail hadn't moved me… would his claws have stopped by a hair's breadth? There was no way to know. I just now realized that he never actually interrogated me after he put me in the dungeon. That was the only reason he'd given for taking me back alive. He must have been at war with himself.

I looked up at him again with truly no idea what he was capable of and if he was a changed male. A sheen of sweat had dotted his forehead, and his posture wasn't as regal as usual. He looked vulnerable. It almost frightened me more than his outbursts because it was so unlike him.

"We don't have to talk about it now," I said gently and reached for his large hand. I took a risk because sometimes compassion got answers sooner than anything else. If he had killed her, maybe he'd already been punished for it. Maybe he'd already punished himself for it. "I feel like I'll need to know eventually, though... if that's part of why I'm being targeted." He flinched when I touched his hand, and I withdrew my arm. "S-sorry."

I stopped in the road, undressed, and shifted into my wolf form. This was the only other way I could offer comfort. I couldn't ask him questions if I was shifted, and we could just focus on traveling. It looked like he needed to work through some stuff, and I wasn't in a rush to know this very moment.

He turned to see what I was doing, and his shoulders slumped a little more. He looked relieved and situated himself to shift as well. I'd made the right call.

When Spine led Trail off the road, I knew we were finally going cross-country like Champion Zorian had said. How many more days on foot? Was it four? I could handle that. I was also hoping we'd lose the mysterious messenger. The only notes I was hoping to wake up to around here would be from birdsong.

The day seemed to go by much faster with the changing scenery. We stopped a little earlier than normal because Spine had found a rather nice place to spend the night. There was a sheltering outcrop on a hill that overlooked a small meadow where a stream burbled a reminder to fill our canteens. Zorian went off to hunt, and I harvested a blackberry bush with wild abandon. They were my absolute favorite. I didn't care how far the berries were in the murder bramble. I would find them all.

With my precious spoils, I meandered down to the stream to rinse them thoroughly, but I nearly dropped the lot of them when a hush swept over the woods. The hairs on my body stood on end, as though saluting the setting sun, and I knew something was watching me. My eyes swept the tree line as I backed up, feeling tiny and exposed. A whimper made me jump, but I realized it had come from me.

I walked backwards at a much faster pace and spied a strange face looking around a tree. It was hard to track its void-like eyes, but I felt like it was looking right at me. I gasped and stumbled over something, falling hard onto my tailbone. I scrambled to sit back up and pulled my pack out from under me. I reached for my bow with shaky hands as a thin, grey creature stalked toward me from the woods.

It looked a bit like a lycan in the way that it walked upright and required a tail to maintain balance, but that was where the similarities ended. I took in its unnatural features and fell back against the outcrop, stunned. I knew who this was.

It was as the mythology compilation had described. Its stone skin was dark grey, pebbled with pale bumps and riddled with pockmarks. There were two craters on an otherwise featureless, ovoid face.

"Wane…" I breathed out the name of this child. Wane was one of the children the Skies had blessed unto the Moon Goddess. Something was wrong with It, though. It looked… wrong. It looked lethargic, emaciated, and unfocused. The godling wobbled toward me on unsteady feet, and I looked down to see that several toes were cracked. A dusting of white powder occasionally fell from the jerks of Its uncertain pace.

A snarl startled me, and the champion jumped down from the outcrop to land between us.

"Stand down!" I growled furiously at him and swiped at his calf to get him to move. "Stop! It's not a threat! That's the Moon Goddess's child, Wane! Sit right down here this instant! I think It's hurt!"

Champion Zorian turned toward me with a dumbstruck expression. I took advantage of his uncertain state and pulled him down next to me. I knew he only allowed me to move him because this situation could very well have been akin to a mouse trying to move a tree. It made me glow for just a moment because that meant he trusted me.

"But this is what's been stalking us for days!" he hissed, and I blinked at his disclosure.

"What?" I whispered in rage, not taking my eyes off the approaching godling. "Why didn't you tell me that It looked like… that? I could've explained it!"

"I didn't want to scare you!" he protested with wide, innocent eyes.

"You scare me every single day, you… you… overgrown tree-piddler!" I retorted childishly while jabbing his stupidly firm bicep with a finger. His jaw dropped.

AAAAH! BAHAHAHAHA! That shut him up! Trail howled.

The godling, Wane, hobbled right up to me, and It jerked several times, like It was having a seizure. I felt my heart break into pieces. How was this godling here? Why was It in such bad shape? A clawed hand reached into a crack on Its chest and pulled out another wrapped letter. It dropped the package to the floor and seized up again, shivering and displacing more pale dust from Its lunar hide.

"Ragna, look at Its armpit," Champion Zorian said lowly and pointed to Its right side. I frowned and narrowed my eyes. There was a small symbol stamped there, but it was being worn away by the stone's erosion.

"Is that some kind of seal? Has it been under a thrall? Remember that design," I ordered and opened my bag to look for what might have kept It from attacking us had It been sent to do so. I pulled the lunaite out and held it up for Wane to look at. The godling zeroed in on the chunk of rock, and I inched forward to lay a hand on Its expressionless face. Its surface was cool and dusty. You wouldn't know It to be alive if It was still.

"Looks like someone took you when they took your mama," I said sadly to It, stroking Its uneven surface for a moment. I elongated a claw and inched my finger toward its armpit.

Oh, great Moon Goddess, Trail begged in a pious prayer, *please tell me your child is not ticklish.*

I closed one eye in a terrified grimace and began to scrape the symbol off with a claw. Wane jerked back, and I tilted the lunaite so it'd stay in Its eyeline. It kept its attention on the rock as planned. My heart was pounding, and sweat trickled down my temple as I reached to scratch off the rest of the image.

The godling settled when the symbol was finally removed. It collapsed to the grass, sending up plumes of white moon dust. My vision watered, and I handed the lunaite to the champion. Tears were falling freely down my cheeks now, but it wasn't from the dust.

"Break off a tiny chunk if you can. I don't know if it'll help to give It a piece of Its mama, but that's what I want to do," I said through a wet sniff as I crouched by the suffering creature. I wiped tears off my face and rested Its bizarre head on my lap. It didn't breathe, It didn't have a heartbeat, and It didn't have a scent, but I knew It was still alive. Its clawed hand gripped onto my boot, almost like It was seeking comfort.

"I think we can safely say the cult is probably involved in the Moon Goddess's disappearance," Champion Zorian's voice remarked as his hand dropped a marble-sized piece of the lunaite into my hand. I held the fragment out to Wane, wondering if perhaps this was the first time It had ever received an offering from a mortal. It was Wane, the Messenger of the Moon Goddess, but It didn't belong here. I wasn't sure how much of Its present state was because of Its kidnappers, but Its fragility was proof that It needed to return home as soon as possible.

Its clawed hand moved from my boot to the fragment. It tucked the piece into a small crater below Its throat and rose awkwardly to Its feet. Taking a wide stance, Wane shook Itself like a wet wolf, sending white powder everywhere. Before I could utter a sound, It turned and raced back into the woods, leaving me with arms extended and lips parted.

"Wha—" I began, feeling surprised and a little disappointed. An errant breeze blew a strand of hair into my face, adding insult to injury. I swiped it away and continued to stare where It had disappeared.

"Looks like It has some unfinished business," the champion murmured thoughtfully and handed the lunaite back to me.

I nodded and looked down at the rock that had come from the sky, turning it over in my berry-stained hands. I wondered if Wane's other parent had known that I'd be delivering a piece of their gift to their child.

Fate is a mystery to us all, Trail said soberly.

Chapter 21

Champion Zorian

I have so… many questions, Spine uttered when I handed the odd rock back to Ragna.

I don't really know where to begin, I remarked honestly. *Ragna just… took control of that entire situation. I feel like I'm still catching up. That was our second god.*

She was very brave t—

Approach that thing? Yeah, she was.

—To snap at you like that, tree-piddler.

Don't you get any ideas to start calling me that, Spine.

Fine. I'll leave that honor to our mate.

I snorted and squatted to pick up the berries that had fallen everywhere. Ragna looked over and slapped her hands to her cheeks. "My berries!" She fell to her hands and knees to collect them, and I backed away from her overzealous claws.

I passed her to pick up the forgotten letter and scowled at it. I could only imagine what rot had been written in it this time. I hadn't expected my mission with Ragna to get personal. To think that Eysteinn, of all people, was potentially behind this madness. It really felt like Fate was playing with us all. I sighed and slid the cloth off the envelope. Same deal. Nothing suspicious about it. I looked over to Ragna and stared at her bottom as she crawled about to collect her scattered snacks.

The leggings were a good choice, Spine snickered.

I smiled a little to myself and sighed. Sure, I was aroused, but that had happened when she'd taken control of the situation. Goddess knew why.

Because you just discovered she'd be a good queen, Spine said in a bored tone.

Did I know that? I closed my eyes and pinched the bridge of my nose but jumped when a hand fell onto my shoulder.

"Oh, sorry!" Ragna gasped and yanked her hand away from me. She looked at what I was holding and sighed. "Can't we just throw that letter away? It's not going to be anything good."

"Let's table it for tomorrow, then. I'll answer your question then as well. Tonight, though... I have so many questions myself." I tucked the note into my backpack. I took to preparing some meat while Ragna went to wash her precious berries again.

"Where did that rock come from?" I asked when she returned, rotating the meat. The dripping fat sizzled and hissed over the crackling fire.

"The Sky Gods gave it to me the night I was blessed. It's lunaite. It came from the moon, and it'll help me find the goddess," she answered with a dark expression. It didn't seem like a night that held fond memories for her.

Wait.

"That's a piece of the Moon Goddess?" I asked, what she'd said earlier about Wane's 'mama' finally clicking. I was absolutely horrified that I'd bashed it with a knife pommel to remove a piece. We'd be lucky if we got our fated mate back after that insult.

Forget that. Just keep Ragna.

"Yeah... I was pretty terrified at first. They said to use it along with tracking my soul scent, which might still be on her. I'm not sure how I'd do that, though. I can't really smell myself. Soley told me once I smelled like autumn."

"Cloves, nutmeg, and apple cider," I listed with certainty, looking up at her while I rotated the meat over the campfire. I brushed some hair from my eyes with a wrist; the breeze was mischievous but enjoyable tonight. It brought her tempting scent toward me in wafts. She had the best damn scent in the world.

Tell her that, Spine encouraged. I kept my mouth shut. Nope, that one was too hard.

She smiled, and her cheeks glowed, but it wasn't from the firelight. "I forgot that you could smell out more details as a temporary fated mate."

"What about me?" I asked curiously. I was always put off by my friends saying that my scent was mild. What did that even mean, really?

She closed her eyes and took a deep breath. For a long moment, she had a dreamy look on her face, and I swallowed hard, certain that my heart had not only skipped a beat but had also fallen down a flight of stairs. "Fresh wood shavings and almonds. It's such a perfect, delicate balance of smells. Not too strong where you can only breathe a couple times before you have to cough but not too weak where you end up sniffing so hard you get light-headed. It's the kind of scent that you could replace air with and smell for hours and not get sick of becau—" Her eyes flew open, and she stammered to change the topic.

I glanced down at the cooking meat to bring less attention to the war on my face. An impossible force to fight off tugged at the corner of my lips, and my mouth broke into a small, uneven grin. I peeked back up to catch her face turning crimson, and she stood abruptly. "I-I'm going f-for a walk!" She jogged off, and I started laughing so hard that I began coughing. The heady scent of her arousal lingered, and I wiped a teary eye. Oh gods, that was extremely flattering.

I don't remember the last time you've laughed and smiled this much, Spine observed.

It feels weird. It's uncomfortable, I confessed. *I feel like I should be mad. I'm just not.*

Consider that a growing pain.

I mulled his reply over while I finished cooking the meat. My emotions didn't make sense to me. I never thought it'd be so uncomfortable to experience happiness. Was I happy? Now wasn't even a time to be happy. Was it? Was there a time for happiness? Did happiness need its own moment in time, or could it coexist with whatever you happened to be doing?

I eyed Ragna as she returned from her walk and handed her dinner. I decided not to torture her over her response and simply ate in silence. After dinner, I lay down on my bedroll and looked up at the blinking stars. It was a nice, clear night and the first decent chance to sleep in days now that Wane had been… freed? I had so many more questions about that.

I chuckled inwardly at Ragna ordering me to memorize the symbol. I had already memorized it, but it was refreshing to see her come to life. I realized, with some surprise, that it was liberating to not be treated like a king anymore. I was glad that Ragna had given me an order. It meant she'd finally seen and accepted me in my new role. I told her that her time would come, and I felt like I'd finally witnessed her in her element. Bold, compassionate, and proactive. I adjusted my pants under the blanket. Who knew that could be so arousing?

Ragna laid her pad on the other side of the fire, and I frowned. "Come sleep with me," I requested and gestured to the spot by my side.

"Wh-wha… Are you feeling ok?" she asked timidly, reaching for her blanket.

"I'm fine. I just haven't really slept in a couple days. I'll rest more effectively with the bond," I replied evenly. I patted the ground by me again and kept my face blank.

"Oh, right. Sorry, of course." She spread the pad out and settled next to me. "You've been keeping watch. I didn't mean to be ungrateful and forget." I watched with a smirk as she scooted her back into me. She knew I was going to pull her over, so she just decided to skip the yanking part. I snaked an arm around her waist and leaned into her warm body, burying my face in her hair. Gods, she smelled so good it made my saliva run. I hoped I wouldn't drool on her hair tonight.

"You handled this evening with the moon's child very well," I praised quietly, staring at what little I could see of her face. My gaze settled on the curve of her cheekbone. This was an easier compliment to give. This was one I could give a soldier. Also, it was easier to compliment when I didn't have to look her in the face. "You took control of the situation and showed a lot of bravery."

"Thank you, Champion," she replied, sounding simultaneously surprised, shy, and pleased. She scooted a bit, and her butt brushed against my erection. I sighed silently to myself and continued my thought.

"You prevented me from doing something unspeakable, attacking a godling, and I wanted to commend you for it. That was a good example of an exception to interrupting a bodyguard. You've impressed your tree-piddler." I said that last part a bit dryly. She wasn't allowed the luxury of forgetting she'd called the Lycan King a tree-piddler. I smiled secretly and vowed to not let her forget any time soon.

She stiffened in my arms and shook from suppressed laughter. "I-I'm sorry!" she apologized while snorting. She held a hand over her mouth. "I don't know wh-what got into m-me!" She snorted again, failing to keep laughter at bay.

"So, Sky-Blessed, pray tell me, what is a tree-piddler?" I asked in a severe tone but grinned into her cinnamon tresses.

"It's, uh, what we wolves call an insecure male who has to piss on everything and mark his territory to, uh, compensate..." she answered, her voice becoming high and squeaky, her answer sounding progressively more like a question.

I let out a tiny growl. "Raaagna," I said in an authoritative, threatening tone. "Are you saying that I, your champion, have something to compensate for?"

Her laughter was cut off, and her entire body cringed. "I, uh... Hmm?"

"I have to assume you're talking about my cock, Ragna," I said into her ear. "I'll ask one more time. Are you saying that I have something to compensate for?" I gripped her hipbones and squashed her ass against my straining erection so she knew exactly what we were discussing. She didn't get to forget what she'd said and play dumb. Joking about an alpha's cock was not a smart move. "You've seen it many times by now, so I'm quite interested in why you've said that," I stated quietly but gruffly into her ear. The flyaways around her ear danced with every puff of air that hitchhiked onto a word.

Though she was intimidated, the air was perfumed by her arousal, and I grinned. Teasing her was my new favorite hobby, though it sometimes resulted in uncomfortably hard erections that I had to tolerate until they calmed.

"I d-didn't mean it!" she stammered, tucking and pressing her legs together. "I... You were just... I was just mad you kept information from me! I want you to trust m-me! I'm not f-fragile!"

Her outburst surprised me. I was impressed that after everything she'd been through and everything I'd put her through, she still wanted to prove herself to me—and likely to herself. Heat blossomed in my chest and abdomen from another spark of arousal.

I wasn't thinking clearly and couldn't pull myself out of the moment. The air felt like it was humming, and we were both getting worked up.

Oh Moon Goddess, how I wanted her right now. I gritted my teeth in agony. Contrary to the mental safeguard I'd put in place, I was about to ask if she wanted to have sex, but she spoke first.

"I noticed that, um... Can you sleep? Do you need me to p-present... myself?"

What?

My heart dropped, and I nearly recoiled from her body. I didn't want her to keep offering herself as a toy to be used. This was my fault. Shit! Shit, fuck, shit! I squeezed my eyes shut and felt light-headed.

"Go to sleep, Ragna," I snapped, ignoring her question and shifting my hips away from her. I was offended by the question but not by her. I'd offended myself because I had unintentionally trained her to do this. Something ugly grew in my belly; it was self-loathing.

After maybe fifteen minutes of us both trying to fall asleep, she spoke up again. "Am I ugly?" she asked in a whisper. Her voice was thick with emotion and wavered ever so slightly.

What? Where did that come from? I was floored she'd ever think to ask something like that.

Why the fuck would she say something like that? Spine snarled.

I don't fucking know. She's exquisite! Actually, she's a little too attractive for her own damn good. It's giving me issues.

Tell her that, he insisted.

No, that one was also too difficult. I'd also never admit that I'd gladly worship her body until the day I died. I had two options; I could either ignore her question out of cowardice or figure out an answer that didn't terrify the shit out of me. I decided to answer it with a question. That would have to do. I could accept being half a coward this time.

"Have I ever given you reason to think that?" I asked in a cold voice. It was so much colder than I'd intended, and I withered, mentally palming my forehead in disgrace.

"I... don't think so?"

"Then stop thinking of things that don't matter and go to sleep. We have another long day tomorrow and will have much to discuss."

Ok, that was harsh, but props on answering this time, Spine sighed. *What am I going to do with you? Augh! You. Were. Doing. So. Well. Earlier! It's a good thing my fur is white because you're giving me a shit ton of grey hairs. Can lycans get ulcers? I think I'm coming down with an ulcer.* He disappeared into the back of my mind, ranting and raving.

I heard her sniff, but she didn't end up crying. I slid my arm back up to rest on her waist again and she relaxed. The blinking stars held my gaze until she fell asleep.

An agonized sigh turned into a pathetic whimper, and I cringed; that was almost as embarrassing as my voice breaking. Thank the gods no one had heard that. I turned my attention back to the she-wolf who was the source of my torture.

"You're not ugly," I whispered and nuzzled into the back of her head. She remained asleep. "You're so beyond beautiful, Ragna. Words can't begin to describe it. I've just realized that it's going to break my heart when I lose you." I held her as though she was a life raft until I ended up following her into sleep.

⚜

I felt better than I had in days when I woke the next morning. I felt like I could do anything! I just wanted to run around and toss boulders! It felt so fucking good to get a solid night of sleep next to a mate. Spine was also itching for a good run toward our destination.

Ragna asked for the envelope that we hadn't touched since yesterday, and I noticed she seemed sick. She was looking a little pale, a little drawn, and I hoped she wasn't coming down with something. It wasn't an ideal time for illness. She opened the letter and fell to her knees. White wolf hair slid out of the envelope along with the card.

"R-Rakel!" she shrieked, sobbed, and covered her mouth with a hand while her eyes flickered over the note. Tears streamed down her cheeks, and I squatted next to her to read over her shoulder.

Beloved Ragna, I'm pleased to inform you that I've gathered some of your loved ones to attend our mating ceremony. I wanted it to be a surprise, but I simply couldn't help myself. E.B.

There was a bloody paw print at the bottom of the letter. A chill trickled down my spine, and I pinched together some of the wolf hair. My nose said it belonged to a female and seemed to be from the same wolf as the blood. Was this friend or family? A deep scowl splintered my face, and I shook my head in revulsion.

Ragna ran away from me to throw up behind the outcropping. I rushed after her and held her hair back again. She heaved over and over, emptying the entire contents of her stomach. Her arms shook, and tears fell freely onto the weeds below her. Fortunately, she didn't get any puke on her hair this time, but I braided it again and tucked it into her tunic.

"Rakel… R-Rakel! That was Rakel… my friend." She sobbed and dry heaved, but there was nothing left for her to throw up. "Oh goddess, is she still alive? Who would send such a thing? Who would do this? My poor Rakel!"

I set my jaw and scooped her up into my arms. She was too distraught to protest—or maybe even notice—me carrying her back to our bags. I sat down and handed her a canteen to rinse her mouth, not letting her leave my lap. She rinsed and spat away from me, then leaned against my chest and started crying her heart out. Her hand fisted my shirt, and she turned inward, like she wanted to disappear into me. I hesitated for a moment, then slowly brought my arms up to hold her to my chest. After a while, I was able to coax her into eating something and get her to put on her backpack. As soon as the bag was strapped on tight, I picked her up and started walking toward the Lunar Coven.

She stared blankly into the woods, and I began to talk. "My mother sent me to stay with her friend in the army when I was a kid. Father wasn't around anymore, and she wanted me to have a male role model, especially since I was from an alpha bloodline. I sorely missed her, but staying with my mentor, who ended up being General Leobwin Warin, prepared me for the army at a far younger age than anyone else from my generation.

"I started off as an errand boy, but I got so side-tracked by warriors who took an interest in training me that I got little work done, which landed me in trouble from time to time." I let a miniscule smile tug my lips at the memories. "It was all worth it, though. When I came of age, I had to start fighting above my age and weight groups at tournaments because no one could challenge me.

"Uncle Leobwin, that was what he ended up being to me, began to put me on missions, and I climbed the ranks like a squirrel would an acorn tree. I was still a little shy, a little insecure due to my age, but everyone seemed to be thrilled with my accomplishments. That is, except for one person."

"E.B.?" Ragna asked distantly, still staring into space. I nodded and continued my story.

"Advisor Eysteinn Burchard," I murmured, not sure if my feelings were leaning toward anger or sadness. "The advisor was very close with Uncle Leobwin, but I had apparently replaced him as Leobwin's favorite. I wasn't sure what that meant, but that's what he ended up telling me.

"Eysteinn took a leave of absence when his fated mate died. Apparently invading soldiers had gotten past our scouts and hit the town she and Eysteinn had called home. He almost didn't survive the heartbreak. We got multiple messages from doctors stating that he was on his deathbed, but somehow, he pulled through.

"After a year, he was cleared for duty, but he'd turned cold. His advice made strategic sense, but they put more civilians at risk. He only seemed to care about the bottom line. The general began to listen to my ideas over Eysteinn's, and that was when his grudge against me became obvious."

I sighed and looked up for just a moment, praying to the gods that Ragna could see past my transgression. I took a deep, unsettled breath and began to answer what she'd asked the other day.

"We'd received intel one day that another battalion had passed through undetected and was on their way to take over a fort that would have given them a considerable advantage in our territory. It would have been catastrophic had they succeeded. The general had sent Eysteinn and me to oversee the interception, and we'd barely gotten our troops there in time before they attacked.

"Eysteinn… he'd smelled his second-chance mate somewhere among the enemy lines," I said, and my voice broke from the oncoming despair. I had to get through this story. Fuck. I blinked tears back and frowned, clearing my throat. Life came back into Ragna's eyes, and she peered up at me.

"He'd smelled his second-chance mate, which is an exceedingly rare blessing as you know, and became frantic. He begged me to call off our soldiers so he could find and get her out of there, but there wasn't time. That fort not only had a full contingent of soldiers, it housed their families. Civilians and merchants had also made that location their home. I couldn't…" I swallowed heavily. "I couldn't justify calling our soldiers back, not even for a minute. I couldn't risk hundreds of innocents for one."

A tear slipped down my cheek, and I tried to rub it off with a shoulder, but I couldn't reach it while holding Ragna. She placed a cold thumb on my face and took care of it herself.

I cleared my throat and looked away from green eyes that'd fixated on me. "A-anyway, the enemy battalion ended up being slaughtered. No one survived our successful interception, not even his second-chance mate. He'd tried to get there in time, but... he didn't make it. He was lucky he hadn't gotten caught in the skirmish and killed outright.

"He went mad for a while. He even challenged and tried to kill me. When I won, he begged me to end his life, but I couldn't. I couldn't do it." My voice became hoarse, and I heaved a depressed sigh.

"I'm going to stop my story there... That should answer your question, Sky-Blessed," I finished and felt the self-loathing return. I would have nightmares tonight. I hadn't allowed myself to remember those events for years and years.

In my peripheral vision, I saw her stare. She stroked my tense frown with a thumb, and my muscles loosened involuntarily. I stopped in my tracks and closed my eyes, letting her touch calm me. I felt her wrap her warm arms around my neck, pull herself up, and hug me in a tight, comforting embrace. She leaned the side of her head into mine, almost in a nuzzle, and squeezed tighter. I could feel her heart thump against mine.

Ragna was hugging me—of her own volition.

A stupid, tiny whimper escaped my throat, and I fought desperately not to cry while she stroked my hair.

Chapter 22

Ragna

I rested my head against Champion Zorian's jaw, brushing his dove-white locks behind his ear. He trembled beneath me, and it broke my heart.

Our heart's not the only one that's breaking, Trail murmured.

What do you mean? I asked. She didn't answer.

I stroked his hair like he'd done for me, wishing I could do more. Whether or not he was responsible for that female's death, accusations like that were hard to bear. They grew into painful burdens over time. All you could hope to do was toss a blanket over it and pretend it wasn't there.

I pulled back to look him in the eyes. I wanted him to understand something, but he was averting his gaze. I gathered my courage and pulled a tactic he often used on me. "Zorian," I stated firmly, and his eyes warily snapped to mine. I softened my tone. "Blame cannot be assigned. One could say you killed her. One could say that the war killed her, or the soldier who stopped her beating heart. Her general killed her. The patrol who missed the invasion; you could say they killed her.

"There are too many factors. The role you played, the action you had to take was as inevitable as a wave hitting a tide pool. The only forgiveness you need to seek is your own, and that's only because of the suffering you've placed upon your body and soul."

I leaned back a little, not certain if I'd just lit a fire or doused a flame. I waited for him to say something, but he just stared at me like he was processing at a snail's pace. Nerves set in, and I squirmed to get out of his hold, but he only responded by tightening his grip on me. In silence, he started walking again.

His eyes slid from mine to the woods around us. He seemed deep in thought, and I sighed. Maybe I had preached too much for someone who'd never seen war. Our individual traumas went deeper than marrow, but they were very different. I'd just thought that a different angle on the issue might be enough to tip the light so he could see better.

I leaned back against his chest and closed my eyes. He needed time to think. After a couple minutes, though, I had to open my eyes because I was starting to get motion sickness.

"Champion, I may puke. Please set me down," I warned and poked him gently to get his attention. His eyes widened, and he slowly eased me onto the ground.

"Are you coming down with something?" he asked. His mask was rickety today, and I could see that he was very concerned. That pleased me, but I didn't let it show. I was certain he didn't want to be readable right now.

"I think I'm just motion sick... I'm ok to shift and run if you are?" I proposed, thinking maybe a run might be good for him and Spine. He nodded, and I—per usual—stripped and shifted behind a tree. I didn't want to draw attention to my body; he still hadn't answered if I was ugly or not. I hated that I'd allowed those princesses to plant that seed in my mind. What did passable mean?

The journey was uneventful, and my concern for him compounded my worry about Rakel. Losing a fated mate could kill you, but surviving losing a fated mate and a second-chance mate seemed impossible. If Eysteinn was holding my Rakel against her will, she was not safe. The champion said he'd lost his chosen mate too. It defied reason that Eysteinn would be sane at this point. All these relationships were too tightly knit. Eysteinn wanted me but had a history with my champion. I was glad I was in Trail's body because I'd otherwise be puking into a bush from all the stress. I'd never been so stressed in my life.

The champion and I settled quietly for dinner. When he finished eating, he started speaking for the first time since morning.

"Eysteinn went on an extended leave when he scraped by surviving his second mate's death. When he showed up again, he'd gone to Leobwin and managed to convince him to let him back into active duty. I don't know how he managed to convince him. Perhaps he'd claimed that duty was the last thing he had left in his life. I have no idea."

I rested my arms on my knees and stared at him as he shared his past. For a large, muscular male, he looked quite small and vulnerable. His vibrant, burgundy eyes looked far away, and I felt an urge to hold him again, but I didn't want to risk him stopping. With Eysteinn returning, maybe he needed this.

"Eysteinn came back with a dark and twisted heart. What was even worse was that he hid it well. Leobwin was glad to see his old advisor contributing, but I was one of the few who first saw Eysteinn play with the war.

"He'd suggest changes here and there that weren't immediately concerning but ended up sacrificing a lot of soldiers and civilians. We could have made the same progress, but he sped it up with blood and in ways that didn't seem directly related to his advice at first or second glance. I couldn't tolerate his underhanded use of human and shifter sacrifice and confronted him about it. He said if I didn't back off, he'd make me regret it. I should have taken that threat more seriously."

Champion Zorian brushed a rogue white lock from his eye with a trembling hand and continued. "We'd heard of enemy movement north of several towns and only had so many soldiers in the area. My mother lived in one, and I was worried about her safety. There was a contingent of soldiers in her town, but Eysteinn had spun this elaborate explanation for why the enemy was going to hit the other town. He convinced Leobwin to remove the contingent from my mother's town.

"I mulled over Eysteinn's strategy, and something about it seemed miscalculated, but I couldn't for the life of me figure out what it was. I spoke up to try to change their minds, but Leobwin was so convinced that he came down hard on me for questioning the decision. I don't know if it was because I was still young and easily intimidated by him, too afraid to push my luck, or simply apathetic from denial that anything would happen to my mother, but I caved and hoped for the best. As invincible as my mother somehow seemed in my eyes, I did try to send a messenger bird out to warn her, but I think Eysteinn intercepted it.

"The soldiers, as decided, were pulled from her hometown the day before it was attacked. Most of the townsfolk were killed, in-including my mother. Eysteinn knew that the other town wasn't their target, and he did what he said he was going to do. He'd made me feel regret, and it ignited a fucking rage inside of me.

"I was furious with myself for not fighting harder. I should have fought tooth and claw to change Leobwin's mind! I should have trusted my gut and called upon every damn spark in me to save those townsfolk! To save my blessed mother!

"In the end, I realized that anger was the only thing that was going to save people's lives. My rage cut through arguments, intimidated people into changing their decisions, and got things done faster. I knew it wasn't healthy, that it was eating me up, but I couldn't stop if it kept people safe from Eysteinn's fuckin' calculating, cold claws!" he snarled with tears in his eyes.

"I had plans to kill Eysteinn after I laid my mother to rest, but when I returned, Leobwin said he'd retired. He'd ran. He killed my mother and ran like a fucking coward! All it did was fuel my anger, and I changed the tune we marched by. I didn't give a shit who stood in my way, not even Leobwin. At that point, no one could physically challenge me either.

"So, I stopped any plans to engage our enemies if the risks were greater than minimal. If civilians were at risk, we either pulled all our resources to remove them or found another way. Because we'd already lost so many lives, we had to fight smarter, not harder. I fought for every single fuckin' one of my peoples' lives! What was a fucking kingdom without people?

"That's what, ultimately, made me king in the end. As you know, the war started because our king's bloodline ended, and neighboring countries saw it as an opportunity to conquer. So, when we successfully fought the invaders off, the people had to choose a new bloodline, and they chose mine. I accepted eagerly because being in power meant I could never let something like Eysteinn happen again," he growled, rubbing a bleary red eye with a knuckle. He stared into the fire like he hated it and remained silent.

"And then," I said quietly in realization, "a she-wolf took all the unmated males and made half your kingdom vulnerable..." I buried my face in my hands. "If anything happened to me after I'd been toured around, or if anyone used me, it would hurt a lot of people. Ah, I see it so clearly now. The entire kingdom would be at risk. It's so much... worse than I thought." I paled and was invaded by the prickling of nausea.

Bile rose in my throat, and I retreated to throw up. My entire dinner departed through my mouth, and I heaved until nothing was left. My head throbbed and spun. I was living a nightmare. When would I wake? I wanted to cry, but I fought it. The very last thing I needed now was a migraine.

The champion rushed over and took care of my hair, rinsing the vomit from it and tucking it away. I dry heaved one more time before I sank down to the forest floor. I understood now why he'd originally wanted to kill me. Though he'd fought for every one of his people's lives during the war, my very existence was simply too dangerous to accept.

"Drink," his voice said gently as he passed water to me. I rinsed out my mouth and drank heavily. Once I caught my breath, I handed it back to him, feeling utterly miserable. He picked me up, unrolled the sleeping pads, and handed me a piece of a ration. "Try to keep this down," he urged in a voice thick with emotion. I nodded and picked at small chunks with my fingers.

After successfully holding down the food, I crawled under the blanket and closed my eyes. I nearly let out a yelp when the champion rolled me over to face him and pulled me to him. He tucked my head under his chin and pressed my body flush against his hard one. His large, muscular arm wrapped around my back in a hug, and he relaxed. His thumb idly stroked the spot between my shoulder blades.

My heart pounded almost painfully, but I was too tired and woozy to feel anxious or aroused from being caged by his large frame. I just let the adrenaline trickle away so I could enjoy his needy embrace. If this is what he required tonight, I'd gladly give it. I was starved for affection, and I would happily pretend this meant something.

⚜

A thrashing force jerked me awake. I squeaked and ducked under a traveling elbow. Wide-eyed and alert, I scooted away from my large champion. Beneath his tangled white hair, his eyes were squeezed tight like he was in pain. He mumbled occasionally and jerked from side to side.

He's still asleep! He's having a nightmare, Trail yapped, as spooked as me.

"Ch-Champion!" I shouted, trying to reach into the danger zone with a toe to poke him awake. "Wake up!" Nothing. I jabbed his rib harder with my toe, but it did absolutely nothing. I crawled over and tried to restrain his arm by putting all my weight on top of it. "Champion! Champion Zorian, wake up!" I shook his shoulder and groaned in frustration at his lack of response.

He's going to hurt himself! I worried over his distressed form.

Kiss him! Trail suggested.

Oh my gods, Trail! If kicking him doesn't work, kissing won't!

I wobbled when the arm I was on lifted, and I fell heavily onto his chest. "Oof!" The air was knocked right out of me.

Kiss him, kiss him, kiss him, kiss him! Trail chanted.

Fortunately, it did not come to that because falling on the champion's chest startled him awake. He cried out in surprise, yelled something unintelligible, and jerked himself into a reclining position. His dove-white hair was a chaotic mess, and his face was glazed with sweat.

"Yeaugh!" I yelled in response, fisting his shirt and squeezing his hips with my thighs to keep from being bucked right off his lap. I managed to maintain a straddle, but his hands shot out to hold on to me as he worked to catch his breath. His eyes were wild and tearful, like he'd just seen a loved one die. He pressed me against him, and his heart was thumping so hard it was like he was knocking on the door to my rib cage.

"You were thrashing," I blurted. "I tried to wake you, but it was like trying to put a hat on a wild horse."

What was I saying? Clearly, I wasn't quite put together either.

He fell back hard, taking me with him in a crushing grip. He seemed extremely distressed, confused, and a little wild. My eyes stared blankly at his chest because all my attention was on his hands, which were roaming all over my body. His right hand eventually snaked up my neck and massaged the back of my head. I stilled and went rigid when his left hand slid down to grab my right butt cheek. I blushed, but when he pressed his erection against my clad—but spread—sex, my face heated up like a teapot. My body throbbed enthusiastically in response, and I cringed in embarrassment.

"Ragna..." He groaned huskily, sounding like he was being tortured in the worst possible way.

"Wh-what? Champion?" I asked nervously. I think I knew what he was going to say.

"I... need..." he began, and his grip tightened like he was afraid to let go. "I... never mind!" he hissed through gritted teeth, and he let go of me. I studied his expression after he turned his bright red face from mine to glare at an oak tree. He was still breathing heavily, and I was certain he'd pull a muscle frowning. Whatever had tormented him in his sleep had shaken him. He was strung much too tight and threatened to break before my eyes.

I slid off his shivering body and removed my leggings and underwear. I lay next to him and hoped he'd understand what I was offering. It was what I thought he'd been trying to communicate. I poked him to get his attention, and when he finally turned his head, his lips parted in surprise. I fidgeted with my fingers and waited. "It's o-ok..." I said. "If it'll help... You're not f-forcing me. I'm offering..."

I saw him war with himself for several seconds as his gaze fell to my legs. With a pained expression on his face, he ran a hand through his hair in frustration. His muscles shook under the strain of whatever he was fighting, and he finally surrendered. "Oh, fuck!"

He tore his clothes off and rolled onto me, settling himself between my thighs. I'd expected him to put me on my hands and knees, but he didn't do that this time. I was terrified to be facing him, but at the same time, I was absolutely thrilled.

He lowered his hips, and I felt the weight of his warm cock settle into my sensitive sex. He shuddered and grinded his hard, silky length against me, sliding up and down in short strokes to wake my body. Heat rose into my face and core as he caged me under him. I'd now have to take what this alpha decided to give.

I stared up at the champion's carved pectorals and abs, then felt moisture drip from my sex when a wave of arousal blossomed in my belly. His body was beautiful, and even though I'd seen it up close when he was unconscious, there was something undeniably electrifying about watching it work hard... inches away from me.

His abs contracted when he slid his cock up, relaxed when his cock pulled back, and I shivered violently at the show. A ragged moan escaped my lips, and I blushed, placing a hand over my mouth to keep quiet. He leaned to his right, and his left hand shot out to pull my hand from my lips. He then reached down between my legs to check my readiness and groaned thickly in approval.

The champion pulled his hips back, and I felt his cock spread the folds that hid my sex. His head parted me and tested how I'd receive his girth. He pumped past my entrance and plunged wetly into the rest of me, displacing the moisture from my core. I cried out but not from pain. He seated his cock deep inside me, buried fully with his sack resting against my outer flesh. I hummed quietly at the fullness, feeling a moment of completeness and that everything I needed was right here with me.

He did not start slow, nor did I have that expectation. I expected him to take what he needed, and that's exactly what he did. His groan was huskier than normal, and I tilted my head up a bit to see if I could catch the expression on his face, but he was too tall, and unless he looked down at me, my view stopped at the bottom of his chin.

He pulled out and drove back into my sex. His hips slapped wetly against my thighs and bottom as I became increasingly aroused. I arched slightly, wishing I had taken my tunic off so I could feel his chest against mine. I hadn't expected to have my own wants when he decided to take me in this position, but the more I saw of him, the more I wanted.

I cautiously reached up to press my hands against his straining abdomen, wanting to touch it, and he jerked in surprise. He groaned ferally, leaned into my hands, and began to thrust into me with renewed purpose.

The long, brutal strokes threatened to push me across the ground, so I extended and dug my claws into the dirt to anchor myself. He slipped a hand into my tunic to massage and explore my breast, then he gasped in pleasure when he tucked his hand into my bra. His cocked swelled more and prodded against my sensitive cervix, claiming my whole channel. Though it was designed to give, his column felt so hungry.

He started panting, and I followed suit, getting caught up in his urgent need for his release. I wanted him to have it so desperately. I wanted him to take from me so he could heal whatever he needed to heal. I wanted to give him relaxation and solace, if only for a moment. My senses were spinning in a delicious whirl of anticipation, and I barely noticed him draping my legs over his shoulders. The new angle felt different, felt deeper somehow, and he drove into me, his gasps and groans getting progressively more desperate as he sought release.

I nearly wailed when his penetrations started rocking my entire body. I closed my eyes and let him take me wherever he needed to go, listening to his desperate breaths and the clapping of skin on skin. His entire body wound up, his muscles drew tight, and he bellowed through his teeth as he came, jerking out to spill his seed. He howled a longing cry with each ejaculation, taut and quivering like an arrow that'd struck a target hard and fast. A long, languid moan escaped him as he spent the last of his desire, and he slowly lowered himself onto his elbows, fighting to catch his breath.

My eyes fluttered open to watch his chest heave to pull in air. He was a work of art. Beads of sweat trickled down his body from his exertion, and I felt a strange, wolfy urge to rub myself all over it. I wanted to be covered in his scent. Trail silently agreed with me.

Champion Zorian continued to keep his weight off me and helped me lower my legs from his shoulders. I winced at how stiff and sore my hip joints were and felt a good deal of relief now that I could straighten my legs. He lowered his forehead to the ground over my shoulder as he continued to recover. He stayed like that for a while, and I began to sense his fear.

Why is he afraid, Trail? I asked, uncertain what to make of this new development.

I think I know too much to answer you, she said hesitantly. *You'll have to get that answer out of him yourself.*

What do you mean? I pressed, frustrated. She'd never withheld anything from me before—at least I didn't think so.

I heard something I wasn't supposed to, and that's all I'm going to say, she answered stubbornly and went quiet.

I was about to move out from under him when he spoke. "I'm sorry," he croaked, his voice tired and raw. I froze. Another apology? That by itself was shocking enough, but why? He hadn't hurt me.

"I didn't… want to use you again."

Use me? "Champion, I offere—" I began, but he pulled away and shook his head while dressing.

"A good male would have declined, she-wolf," he replied flatly. Trail had told me to listen with my eyes. He was afraid, but he was acting cold now. What was he scared of? He sounded angry with himself too. Had I even helped him? More stress meant more nausea. I couldn't handle another day of puking.

I tried to get up but wobbled dizzily and sat back down a little harder than expected. His cold mask cracked again, and he looked frightened. He knelt in front of me and placed his hands on my shoulders, looking straight into my eyes. "Are you ok? I'm sorry. Did that… I mean…" He struggled so hard to find what he wanted to say. He looked as he had earlier when he was fighting a war within his mind. What was going on with him?

He scrunched his eyes tight, scowled fiercely, and took a deep breath. Then he looked gently back into my eyes with his red ones and said, "I should not have spoken to you like that. I'm sorry. Thank you, Sky-Blessed. Thank you for helping me."

Chapter 23

Champion Zorian

I swear to the Sun God, the Sky Gods, and the Moon Goddess that if you open your mouth again, I will find a way to separate myself and kill you. That. Was. Perfect. Do. Not. Ruin. It! Spine threatened frantically. *Don't ruin it!*

I had no doubt he would. I stared nervously into Ragna's green eyes, trying to tamp down the anxiety that coursed through me at… what would I call this? The opposite of pushing someone away from you. Showing gratitude? Or letting my guard down and showing I cared? Ah gods, it'd been so long since I've thought about these things.

All I knew was that she looked hurt by my words, and it made me frantic to change my tune. I was tired of upsetting her. She was so easy to read, and as much as I tried to stop being affected, she wore through my conviction.

I nearly collapsed in relief when her already flushed cheeks pinkened and produced a faint smile. The after-sex glow looked good on her. She looked sexier than ever. "You're welcome." It was genuine—weak, but genuine. I blew out a breath and helped her to her feet, then packed up our campsite while she dressed.

I was also relieved she had volunteered. Dreaming of my mother's death… I hadn't had that nightmare in years. I could never get to her in time and always woke in a state of panic and despair. Burying myself in Ragna for a spell, both mentally and physically, had been such a desperately needed distraction. I no longer felt wound up and about to lose my mind.

I'd treated her so poorly. That had to stop.

We let Trail and Spine take over, and I held my tongue while the two acted like they hadn't seen each other in years. It was a mess of slobber, yipping, and growls. I suppose I should be more grateful of the joys around me.

We pushed hard. We'd been traveling for, wait, it had already been a week? We lost so much time because of that fucking cult. We should've been there by now. At this rate, we should arrive by tomorrow night. I was sure that Ragna was looking forward to a bath and bed as much as I was.

Preferably together, Spine suggested. I wouldn't have an excuse to ask her to join me, but I supposed it would give me something unwholesome enough to daydream about until we got there—a naked Ragna in a bubble bath.

We both passed out after making camp and got another early start. Several hours into traveling, the woods began to feel like a safe space, and I knew we'd finally arrived in their territory. The foliage of the coven grounds was greener, the air was thick with the scent of herbs, and the earth felt slightly warmer beneath the pads of Spine's paws. It almost soothed the ache from loping all day.

We finally spied the lights of the Lunar Coven's main settlement when twilight gave into dusk. The sight was glorious. The settlement was sheltered beneath ancient trees so tall I became dizzy looking skyward. Every cottage-like building had a welcoming aura that made me feel like I was coming home. Even the livestock seemed content in their pens.

We shifted back, and I looked over to Ragna as we dressed. She fell to her hands and knees as though she was terribly out of breath. "I-I made it!" she gasped in disbelief. She looked up at the night sky peeking through the leaves and crowed, "I made it! Sky Gods! After five years, I made it! I made it! I made—" Her eyes went wide, and she fell back onto the ground with an exasperated yell. "They won't be able to see meee!" she wailed, placing her hands over her face.

Holy shit! Spine said. I didn't know if he was referring to her near tantrum or her revelation.

For me, that was when I lost my fucking mind. I plopped my ass down on the grass and started laughing. I gripped my stomach and doubled over with watering eyes. I didn't know what the fuck happened to me. Maybe because it was incredibly anticlimactic for how hard we worked to get here by this evening. Maybe it was seeing Ragna act like a child over something we could probably work with anyway. It would be pretty good proof that she was the Sky-Blessed. I hit the ground with a fist, trying to get air back into my lungs through bursts of laughter.

I wiped away tears of mirth and forced myself to my feet, chuckling. I walked over to Ragna, grabbed her hands, and pulled her up to stand so we could go meet the coven. It was a fight to keep a straight face as she maintained her dramatic, woebegone expression.

We walked down stone paths lit by candle lanterns until we arrived at the Hall of the Lunar Coven. A short lady with large chestnut curls and a pretty, motherly face stood outside the building and waved at me. "Welcome, welcome! You're finally here! Come, come!"

I approached her and held out a hand for her to shake, but she tutted, ignored my gesture, and pulled the terrifying, ferocious Lycan King into a warm hug. This woman, half my size, even deemed it appropriate to rock me a little and pat my back.

What the shit? Spine exclaimed. I was lost for words and had already run out of laughter. *She's going to feed us sprouts! This is the kind of woman who feeds you sprouts! Don't let her do us like that, Zorian!*

I ignored him and tried to focus on the woman before me. "Where is the Sky-Blessed?" she asked excitedly, waving her hands around to find her. She jumped in the air and cried out in surprise but then wrapped her arms around Ragna to return her hug. I scrubbed a hand over my mouth, wide-eyed and at risk of smiling. The act had me noticing how the bristles on my face had grown longer than preferred. Fuck, I needed a shave.

"Come inside!" the woman invited and shuffled us in with a smile.

She led us to a little lounge with a merry fire dancing away in a hearth. Two other women were seated in velvet wingback chairs around a coffee table. The one with the midnight braids had a sly demeanor and a petite build, while the last one was a heavily pregnant redhead.

"How was your journey?" the curly-haired witch asked hospitably, gesturing for us to take the couch while she nestled into the third chair.

I opened my mouth but was feeling very much thrown off-kilter since arriving.

"It was difficult, Mothers," Ragna confessed. "We ran into some cult leaders who wanted to kidnap me, but first, I want to introduce myself. My name is Ragna." I nearly smiled when I saw her pointing to herself out of habit. She was still very much invisible. "And this is the Lycan King, King Zorian, but at the moment, he's my champion and Sun-Blessed. He's been protecting me."

You heard that? She said MY champion. Not THE champion, Zorian, Spine announced proudly. He was reading too much into it.

"Oh!" the curly-haired brunette exclaimed while smacking her forehead with a palm. "I forgot we haven't met yet! I'm so sorry. Divining can be so confusing sometimes!" She tittered and shook her head, sending an embarrassed shrug to the other coven mothers.

"We weren't going to say…" The redhead smirked, then looked at the both of us. Well, she did her best. "I'm Luan," she introduced, then turned to the petite lady next to her.

"I'm Mwezi, and this forgetful one is Senay," the braided mother said with a wicked grin as Senay covered her face in embarrassment.

"A pleasure," I returned politely, nodding in mild deference. Ragna echoed my sentiment.

"So, you need to get to the Moon Goddess's home!" Mwezi said, slapping her hands on her skirted knees to get to business. "That means a quick stop in fae territory. They guard one entrance to the Realm of the Gods."

"But first, refreshments! Oh, you both must be tired and hungry!" Senay exclaimed, getting to her feet. "Zorian, would you like a house brew?" she inquired, raising a lively eyebrow.

I nearly bristled at her casual exclusion of my title, but I took a deep breath and nodded. "That would be welcome. Thank you, Senay."

"Mmm!" Luan interjected, finishing a sip of her tea before holding it up for Senay to see. "Give Ragna what I'm having."

Ragna leaned over and sniffed the air. "Smells good," she said. "Relaxing. It has been very stressful. Thank you very much, Luan."

Senay waved Ragna over to her. "Come on then. I'll show you how to make it!"

Mwezi took a good look at me when Ragna left and grinned. "You two are getting along better. I'm glad to see it." She sent me a very suggestive wink, and I groaned internally. That was… personal.

"I admit that I've forgotten how good your coven is at spying," I said with a tilt of my head and a fist under my chin, aiming hard to change the topic. Neither of these women were trying to hide a damn thing, and it was mildly infuriating. It made me feel weak for some reason, but I couldn't figure out why.

"We've had to keep an eye on things. We were stricken by our goddess's disappearance," Luan remarked. She cupped her tea with both hands as though trying to warm them.

"So, you know we suspect Eysteinn Burchard," I said simply, and they nodded. "I know he wants to mate and mark Ragna, and I can't imagine him not trying to use her as a weapon. If he has a cult at his back, that could amount to a small army. Is there even a point in going to the Realm of the Gods?"

"Yeah," Mwezi said casually, "but I'm not supposed to say that."

"You weren't supposed to say that," Luan reprimanded but did so tiredly. It was as though Mwezi was constantly breaking the rules, and Luan had given up, only replying out of routine. Mwezi shrugged and turned to see Senay returning with food and drinks. Ragna sat back down, looking unwell, and ate the hearty stew that had been placed before her. I looked over in concern and then dug into my own food.

"So, what do we need to do to get into the fae realm? What about after that?" I asked between bites. Every swallow of the stew seemed to rebuild what had worn away during the journey. I healed fast, but there were some aches and pains that had begun to wear me out… just a bit. Perhaps I had gotten soft after taking the throne. I could admit that I missed my grand, luxurious bed, especially when Ragna was in it with me.

"Let's go over that tomorrow," Senay dismissed with a wave of her hand. "You look about ready to fall over!"

I wasn't sleepy, but I looked over at Ragna, who was pale and had her face resting in a hand. "I think you're right. Is there a place we could sleep tonight, Mothers?" I asked respectfully, turning back to face Senay.

"Yes, yes!" she exclaimed and gestured to our dishes. "You may finish those at your own pace in your rooms. Come with me."

Our rooms? Plural? Spine asked with a lovesick whine. What a warrior this one was.

agna

The darkness behind my eyelids spun, and my body lost all sense of direction. Nausea roiled in my stomach, and I heaved. My head tilted to the side to throw up, but nothing came out of it. I tried to move my arms, but I couldn't. Something was burning. Something hurt. A lot of things hurt, including my throbbing temples.

I tried to open my eyes, but they were too dry and resisted my command. I coughed after inhaling some dusty air, which made me dry heave again. I tried to shift to my side, but my wrists wouldn't let me. They hurt so bad. Where was Trail? She seemed gone.

I didn't know how long I was sprawled out, but my wits eventually came back home. Where was I? This wasn't the guest room at the coven. I lifted an arm, but it made my wrist burn. The coven didn't have silver shackles... What was my last memory?

Senay had taken us to the guest rooms. She said I could either stay with Champion Zorian, who had a larger bed, or I could have my own room. I was upset by something that Senay had told me in private, so I wanted my own space to think and process. I remember... I remember... the door opening and a shadow—a shadow but no smell then... nothing. A shadow, no smell, then nothing.

"She's waking," a woman said scornfully. Was this woman going to play tic-tac-toe too?

"O-oh g-g-good!" a deep, familiar voice replied, and shock sizzled down my spine, mixing potently with fear. Oh goddess, I recognized that stutter. It was one of the cult members! I tried to pry my eyes open to see if they were wearing a mask. I could almost hear my eyelids creak from the effort.

"Let me go," I wheezed, coughing and gagging. "Let me go if you don't want puke all over your..." I blinked slowly and looked around the room, which was spinning more than it should. "Lovely... hut." We were in a very small cabin that had seen better days. There were no lights of any kind, not even a lantern. We were all in the dark. I could only hope that being a wolf would give me some advantage if I could get free. This silver, though... I looked numbly at the shackles. My leggings and boots were also gone, and a stinging plant was wrapped around my ankles. I was too weak.

"N-no, I-I'm g-getting ready to b-bring you t-to your mating c-ceremony," the cultist said while gathering items to put into a large canvas bag. Movement through the cabin boards caught my eyes. More rogues. A lot of them. I could smell them, even through my dampened senses.

It was pointless to talk to him, so I tried to run through my options. Would I be carried, or would they let me walk? They'd obviously masked my sce—

Wolf, a voice said in my head, and I nearly flew out of my skin. That was not Trail! *Tired.*

Who is this? I asked, wondering if someone was coming to help. I had no idea how they were linking me, though! Was this a god? It had to be.

Can't fully reach you here. Come to the moon, the voice urged faintly. *Tired.*

I'm trapped! I'll try, but I'm trapped. I promise! I replied. This wasn't the voice of any god I'd met before now. Had Wane gotten home? Was this Wane or someone else?

The voice sighed as though It already knew. *You've been given four thousand heartbeats; make good use of them. Tired. See you soon.* The voice left me alone, and I realized my captors were talking heatedly about something.

"—Sure he honors his promise! How do I know that he will? I've risked everything in betraying my coven!" the woman hissed, leaning into the masked cultist's face. I didn't recognize her. She was just some random woman.

"I c-c-can't promise a-a-a-anything," the cultist dismissed with a shrug. "H-h-he either r-r-rewards y-you or h-he doesn't. You kn-know who y-you're d-d-dealing w-with. Y-you knew th-the r-risks."

The woman shrieked through her teeth and stormed out of the cabin. The cultist muttered to themselves and went back to what they were doing.

Ragna? Trail's voice popped into my head. By the moonlight!

Trail! You're—I paused in my thoughts and looked over at my wrists. The silver wasn't burning me any longer. I cautiously wiggled my toes. The plant had stopped stinging as well. *Trail, I think we've received a temporary blessing. We have less than four thousand heartbeats!*

Trail was on it. *Ok, the moron's turned away from us. I will put my strength into your right arm, then your left arm. The table we're on seems super rickety!*

I'll hop off. Help me yank the plant off, then we'll tackle the cultist as fast as possible.

Tackle, then remove the plants, Trail amended. *We don't have much time. I have no idea what this maskhole is capable of.*

Ok, go! Go! Go! I yelled in my head, trying to psyche myself up. I had no idea what I was going to do, but I had teeth and claws!

I yanked the chains out of the wood in rapid succession, rolled off the table, and bunny-hopped onto the cultist. He let out a scream before I managed to channel Zorian's murder-thirst. I grimaced and ripped deeply into his throat while crying, "I'm sorry! I'm sorry! I'm sorry! I'm sorry!" Blood poured over my claws while my body flooded with adrenaline. My heart slammed so hard against my chest that it risked bruising itself.

The cultist's mauled body slumped to the ground, and tears sprang into my eyes. I'd killed someone. That was a person—a horrible person but still a person. They were living and breathing just moments ago. The finality of it terrified me. That was the last of my innocence, and I hated myself for what I'd just done. I had to, though. I had to, I had to, I had to.

We had to, Trail echoed sadly.

I shredded the plants off and peeked out the window. There was no way my attack had gone unnoticed, but I didn't see anyone. I did, however, hear screams.

I looked at my wrists and scrambled for the cultist's robes. There was a set of keys, and I held my breath while I put them in the shackles, trying one at a time. The restraints fell to the floor, and I stalked out the cabin. My salvation immediately hit my ears.

"Ragna!" the champion's voice screamed. "Ragna, where are you?" I ran around the cabin toward his cry. I was a pile of broken nerves, sobbing in panic to get to where I knew I'd be safe. "Ragna! Ragnaaa!"

I saw my champion standing over a mound of bodies, looking like he was about to explode. He was crushing a rogue's throat but didn't seem to notice the lycan creeping up behind him. The champion screamed my name again and killed the last wolf to his right.

For just a moment, I lost my mind. I fumed at the sight of someone stalking my distracted, terrified champion and ran recklessly to intercept the lycan. Becoming lost to a feral rage, I pounced on the last rogue with a furious shriek. I ripped into its back with claws and canines, and whatever I could reach was what I mauled. I shredded the flesh around its neck in a mad attempt to reach an artery. The bucking lycan tried to throw me off, but I clung fast. It finally collapsed under me, but it was only because Champion Zorian had ripped out its throat.

My champion's wild, flaming eyes bore into mine. His dove-white hair thrashed in the night wind and his chest heaved. He took a step forward, hesitated as though I were some kind of ghost, then snarled and pulled me into him.

His fingers dug into my back, and I sobbed in relief. "Ragna," he growled. "Ragna, Ragna, Ragna! I found you!" He pulled me closer as if I would fly away any second. "I woke up, and something felt wrong!" He gasped, still trying to catch his breath. He flexed me closer with his burly arms and chest. A hand reached up to forcefully grip the back of my head, fisting my hair but mindful not to hurt me.

I buried my face into his breathless chest and squeezed my eyes shut, trying to push away the horror of what I'd just done to survive. I dug my bloody fingers into his chest, never wanting to let go. This was safe. This was good. This was where I wanted to be. I wanted to be where I could feel his lungs fill with air. I wanted to feel his heart press into my palm.

He panted, slouched, and leaned his head down to rest it on top of my head. "I ran to find the mothers, and they knew where you were, but they said they weren't allowed to tell me! Even though they can see bits and pieces of events, they told me they couldn't share most of their knowledge from divining because it might interfere with Fate. Mwezi caved and said you were southwest in a little cabin. It wasn't a lot to go off of, but I ran. I just ran! Whoever took you hid their tracks." A small sob escaped his throat. "I was afraid you'd be gone. I was so afraid."

My heart broke from how worried he'd been, and I nearly started crying again. All I could do was nuzzle closer. I wanted to forget. I wanted to forget it all. Now I knew why he'd reacted the way he had coming out of that nightmare. He wanted to lose himself. I wanted to go to sleep and never wake again, but then I'd never see my champion again. Wasn't worth it.

His hands restlessly checked me for injuries. I winced when he grazed my wrist, and he pulled it up to inspect the damaged skin. "They silvered you. They fucking silvered my Sky-Blessed," he said in a thick voice. To my surprise, he brought both my wrists to his mouth and kissed them. My face ignited into flames. He'd just put his lips on me!

"I can't lose you. I-I mean... before we're done w-with..." He groaned, struggling with his words again.

He kissed my wrist again, then shockingly, started trailing wet kisses all the way up my arm to my neck. I gaped at the change in his behavior. It was startling but... not unwelcome. His last languid lap of his tongue on the base of my neck dispensed hot, carnal pleasure down my body. The muscles inside my sex clenched brutally, like they were pleading to draw my champion's cock into me.

Oh my goddess! My legs almost gave out.

When he noticed my arousal, he released a primal snarl, yanked me off the ground, and pushed me into a tree, wrapping my legs around his hips.

He growled deeply while mindlessly shredding the wood of the tree with frustrated claws. I tilted my head back, blushing furiously as the champion skipped past bloodlust to career into feral lust. I could hear it in his snarls and feel it in his trembling. He was a fully wild and aroused alpha lycan, consumed by carnal needs.

"Never leave my side, she-wolf!" he panted lustfully into my ear. He thrust against me, grinding his straining bulge against the thin fabric of my underwear. "Never leave because you are mine. Mine!"

Chapter 24

Champion Zorian

She-wolf, she-wolf, she-wolf, she-wolf! They had nearly escaped with this female. I found her, though. I'd crushed the filthy packless like the mosquitos they were. Noisy, bloodthirsty, but utterly weak. Pathetic. No one took from me. They were lucky to receive quick executions. I had better things to do, like reclaiming this she-wolf.

I let out a low, vibrating growl as I buried my face into the female's neck and stole a moment of her scent. It stimulated my body and mind more than any aphrodisiac could. It shot an overwhelming, flaming bolt of desire straight into my groin, and I hissed through my teeth and lengthening canines. Saliva pooled in my mouth, and I decided to spread it all over the female's neck. She would reek of me by the time I was through with her, and no one would risk looking at her ever again.

I leaned down and lapped at her skin. My tongue ran roughly over the tiny goose bumps that pebbled her flesh. Her succulence only increased my salivation, and I scraped my teeth along the spot where I'd mark her. I itched to bite down, to nestle both my canines and cock deep into her delectable, blushing body, filling her with my venom and my seed.

The female whimpered and writhed, and I grunted in satisfaction. I rocked my erection against her undergarment and kept it pressed there. Her moisture seeped into my pants, and I shuddered, deeply excited to find she'd soaked through her clothing. She was very ready for me—for me and only me.

I moved the female higher up my body so her hips hugged my abdomen while I opened the front of my pants. My straining cock sprang free of its enclosure, thick and heavy for my she-wolf. My fluid beaded restlessly at the tip in anticipation. I pushed the she-wolf's soaked garment aside and lowered her down to greet my erection. I leaned into her and stretched her folds wide with the head of my cock. With an agonized groan, I squeezed it past her threshold and thrust against the tree with her. I pulled back a little and thrust one more time, bottoming out deep within her sex. She released a keening howl and dug her claws into my chest.

I snarled into her ear and nipped at her neck, but she merely replied with a lustful whine. I gave the she-wolf a moment to get used to me and appreciate the girth I'd created for her. I rocked my hips a little, grinding generously against that spot the females enjoyed so much. Her thighs flexed to bring me closer, and I groaned into her neck. *Yes, she-wolf. Accept all of me.*

I looked down as I pulled back, watching how her shiny, glistening entrance stretched around my cock. I pushed back in, aroused by the sight of her wetness seeping out around my veined, hard flesh. I continued my long strokes, staring at where we were joined. Hot pleasure washed over me and flooded my body with fire.

"You are a very good female," I snarled in a rough, guttural voice. "You please your alpha." She deserved praise. I'd had her before, and she'd always done well. Her sensual body never failed to excite me, and I never grew sick of her. When she was around, I thought of her. When she was gone, I thought of her.

I slid my hands down the soft curve of her hips to dig my fingers into her butt cheeks. Once she was situated, and I had a firm grip, I started pumping into her. I growled at the slapping of our skin. Next to her moans, that was my favorite noise. I rammed harder into her buttery, tight sheath, enjoying the sounds of our joining. I nibbled on the marking spot on her neck, and she spasmed against me, arching and wailing from the pleasure I brought her. I groaned and shuddered at the slick noises caused by her weeping core. The moans, the whimpers, the slaps, and the squelches were an electrifying shot straight to my libido. I slowed for just a moment and breathed deeply before I continued to fuck my favorite female. I wanted to make this last.

"You will not"—I panted ferally—"open for any other male!" I growled and met her eyes for the first time. Her head was tilted back, and her soft lips were parted. Her green eyes gazed up at me through her dark lashes, like she was in a trance, and I was the source of her fascination. Her cheeks flushed red, as though I'd brought a fever upon her, and soft moans parted rhythmically from her throat.

"Respond!" I commanded, pounding harder.

She arched her back again and gasped. "I-I will open only f-for you, Champion!"

"Say it again! Clearly!" I demanded, digging my fingers into her soft flesh and kneading.

"I will open only for you!" she howled as I drove into her. I snarled in approval and felt my arousal swell.

Sweat soaked through my clothes, and I slammed my hips into the female to pin her to the tree so I could rip off my shirt. She lifted her arms and scrabbled at the trunk with her claws to better anchor her position, drawing my attention to her chest. My hands, shaking from adrenaline and excitement, unbuttoned and parted her tunic. I desired her breasts. There was no longer any hiding them from me. I cut her undergarment, and her swollen, sweaty breasts spilled into sight. I moaned as I held them, enjoying their weight and softness. Never had a female had such nectarous nipples. I brushed my thumbs over them, making her gasp and constrict my cock with her sex. I hissed at the sensation and was spurred into moving again.

I gripped her thighs and pumped more aggressively, partially for the pleasure but partially for the show. A growl rose explosively from my chest because the sight of her innocent face looking up at me while her breasts danced for my pleasure was almost too much. I slowed once more, tempted to claw pain into my arm. I wanted to last longer. Never had any female affected me so.

I groaned through my teeth and fucked her as fast as I could. Lust was running as thick in my veins as blood, and all I could think about was claiming this female. I was the only one who could keep her safe. She belonged with me!

"She-wolf! Say you're mine! Say it!" I thundered, leaning down to stare into her gentle eyes while I fucked her. Her lower lip trembled from my forceful penetrations, and she whimpered.

"I'm yours now," she moaned obediently and closed her eyes, tilting her head up sensuously. I stared at her lips as I continued thrusting, enjoying the feeling of her breasts brushing against my chest with every bounce. I gasped and leaned over her as my arousal peaked higher. I shuddered and started slamming into her again. I didn't think it was possible to be harder than I was at this very moment. I was certain I was straining this female to the limit, but she still took me. Every thrust brought me right up against her cervix, and I trembled in excitement. She was mine—all mine!

The she-wolf cried out into the night sky as I did my duty to please her first. With every thrust, I rocked against her opening, making certain I stimulated her well. Her keening wails grew higher in pitch until she came violently against me.

Her walls fisted my member and kneaded my length until I came just as explosively. I howled through my teeth and hissed at the intensity of my release. Her muscles gripped and milked me spurt for spurt. I leaned into her, grinding to her orgasm's rhythm and groaning in ecstasy as her body greedily drank my seed. My hand slid up to massage a warm breast as I leaned toward the female's neck. I salivated and opened my jaw wide to extend my canines as long as possible, aiming for the soft spot between her neck and shoulder to mark her as mine forever. Before I could bite into her blushing flesh, the female screamed and pain ripped across my face.

I jerked away from the she-wolf, blinked, and held a hand to my face. I stared at my fingers, watching blood drip from them in shock. The female scrambled away on the grass, utterly terrified of me. Trying to regain my senses, I shook my head. What was happening? What was going on?

I slowly came to my senses and realized that Ragna was backing away from me. I looked down at her legs and froze. White cum was running down her thighs from her core, and horror coursed through me.

I hadn't pulled out.

"R-Ragna," I begged, reaching out for her. "I'm sorry. I-I lost control!"

"You almost marked me!" she yelled and backed farther away.

"But I didn't! You stopped me in time! I won't do it. I promise! Please, don't run from me! Come here," I said weakly, desperate for forgiveness. Her strained face threatened to cry. "Please, oh my gods, I'm so sorry!"

She wrapped her arms around herself and paced back and forth nervously, her eyes never leaving mine. She looked tortured.

"Ragna, please, I'm so sorry! I didn't mean to. I wanted to pull out. I lost control!"

She shook her head and continued to pace. Her shaking became violent, and she wrapped her arms tighter around herself, as if she could stop the tremors. Even her lower lip trembled with her shot nerves.

"Ragna, please, you have to believe me. I swear…"

"It doesn't matter!" she yelled, stopping in her tracks. "Senay told me in private. It doesn't matter…"

I dropped my arms and felt my heart sink. "Ragna… are you unable to carry pups?" She started crying, and I stepped forward. Oh gods, was this why she had been upset and wanted her own room? She stepped away from me when I got too close. "Ragna?"

"No, Champion," she said in a hoarse voice. "When I said it didn't matter, it didn't matter because I'm already pregnant."

What?

What? Spine echoed me out of nowhere.

I was frozen for a moment, completely shocked. A lump formed in my throat, forcing me to swallow heavily before I could say anything. "Is it mine, Ragna?" I asked, taking another small step forward. I didn't know why I had to ask. The pup could only be mine. I was just too stunned.

She nodded and looked away from me in shame. "Senay verified. It happened the first time I offered myself. You didn't… completely pull out in time. I noticed when I was cleaning myself."

I stepped closer and gently buttoned her tunic, then winced, recalling I owed her a new bra. I could barely think. My head was spinning. "I've failed you, Ragna." I fingered her hand, wishing I had the courage to hold it. "I was supposed to protect you, not impregnate you." I looked miserably at her. "I'm so fucking sorry."

"It may not change anything… The pup will probably miscarry," she said wearily.

"What?"

"Miscarriages are common, plus I'm being targeted. None of this is conducive to keeping a pregnancy," she explained, worrying at her hands. Fear pricked me at those words.

"There's nothing else we can do to... help prevent..."

"Champion, I can be as safe as possible, but that's it." She shook her head and shrugged.

"Zorian," I replied, brushing hair from her eyes. "You're to call me by my name. If you're carrying my pup, I'll not have you address me by a title."

Her shoulders slumped, and she nodded tiredly. I picked her up and began walking us back to the coven. Mate or not, I hoped she would fight to stay the mother of my pup. I was falling too deep to consider anyone else.

⚜

When we returned to the coven, I briefed the mothers on the encounter, and they were already familiar with about a third of it via divining. It was extremely frustrating to have such a powerful source of information nearby that was severely gatekept. I understood the reasoning, but if Mwezi hadn't broken the rules...

I also reminded them to retrieve the body of their traitor and one other if they could manage it. Ragna informed me that one of the cultists had been there, but their body had been left in the cabin. I needed to look under that mask and try to identify them. If it was someone important, I'd have to consider the implications.

I knew Ragna was shaken about killing someone, but I was damn proud of her. I always thought it was easier to fight for someone else than for yourself. I would never forget the murder in her eyes when she tackled the lycan who'd snuck up on me. Something told me she didn't regret that one so much, but then again, I did deal the finishing blow.

I returned with Ragna to my room. It was still the middle of the night, and there was no fucking way I was ever letting her out of my sight again. If she wanted to go back to her roo—

Tough fuckin' luck! Spine snapped, finishing my thought. *We're in daddy mode now!*

Words I'd have never expected a feared lycan like you to say, I replied wryly. I admit, his words put warmth in my chest, and I think for the first time in a long time, we were in harmony.

We wiped ourselves down with a wet towel, too tired to bathe but unwilling to bring the byproducts of the battle between the sheets. I crawled into bed and pulled her against me. She surprised me by turning to wrap her arm over my waist and place her head on my chest. Closing my eyes, I sent a prayer to the gods, thankful that Ragna hadn't pushed me away yet. I stroked the back of her head with a hand and tried to clear my thoughts.

"I'm sorry I scratched you," she whispered. "You don't understand how hard it is for a wolf to say no to an alpha. You told me to tell you I was yours, and… everything was my fault, really."

I reached to feel my cheek. "I'd forgotten. You got me pretty good. That was impressive, surprising an alpha." I sighed. "No. We both had parts to play. It was a rough night to begin with."

"Zorian… you have a queen out there somewhere. I just don't want you to regret marking someone who's not your real mate. It's more important for you than any other shifter to have that."

"And yet I'm the least likely to have that luxury, Ragna. I have royalty pushing their princesses at me from all angles."

And we sent three of those bitches back, Spine reminded me.

"That just further proves my point," she whispered so softly that I almost didn't hear it. "That puts me in last place."

First place, Spine said stubbornly. *No shits given, sexy mama!*

Please don't make me laugh right now, Spine!

"I don't even know what to do if the pup makes it. Try to stay near the castle because they're the king's bastard? I don't even know what that means, but I won't take the pup from you… unless you don't want to be around." I could tell she was getting worked up again. I squeezed her and rubbed her arm to calm her.

"I don't like that word. No child of mine will be called or treated like a bastard. Nothing changes, Ragna. I'm taking care of you now, and I'll take care of you later, with or without a pup." I shrugged gently, mindful of her resting head.

She placed her hand over her face. "Augh, what am I talking about? We have to focus on the Moon Goddess. All this can wait until it's over—if the pup makes it. Sorry, my head's a mess."

"Just so we're clear, Ragna," I tilted her head up and away from her hand to look at me. "I want the pup to make it. I'm not disappointed it happened, but I'm sorry it wasn't planned. I'm sorry about the stress it puts on you."

She stared sadly at me for a minute before replying. "Swear to me that you will not allow this pup to guilt you into making a decision you wouldn't normally make. I can take it. I can survive, but I need your word for peace of mind."

Spine promptly dismissed her insecurity. *Sweet gesture, mate, but totally unnecessary.*

I allowed a small smile to play across my face, only for her. "I think you know that's how I normally function, but I'll bite."

I'll bite too, Spine agreed. *Her cute bum.*

I was glad that she couldn't hear him, and I fought to keep myself from laughing at his stupid interjection. "I solemnly swear that all decisions I make will be genuine and in my best interests."

And she's our best interest, Spine quipped. *Nice loophole!*

We don't need loopholes. Shut up, you hellion.

⁂

We both woke early, anxious to meet with the mothers and move on to the Realm of the Fae. I convinced her to take a bath with me, and I couldn't hear anything for a solid five minutes because Spine was crowing like a rooster who'd eaten a questionable mushroom.

I helped her into the warm water and settled behind her. Her muscles were tense again, which still amazed me after all we'd done together. I took the sponge from her, and she protested shyly, but I insisted on cleaning her. I wasn't sure why, but I just felt like I should? I couldn't place the instinct.

After several minutes of washing her hair and scrubbing her back, she relaxed considerably and hummed in delight. I smiled in satisfaction, and Spine preened. I supposed you could pleasure a female outside of the bed; that pushed an idea into my head.

I made her stand in the tub so I could wash the rest of her. When I reached around to gently scrub her breasts, her heart rate sped up, and I smirked. I worked my way down her stomach, and she tried to tuck herself away with her thighs.

I leaned down to whisper into her ear. "Would you accept a gift from me, Ragna?"

Yes! Yes! Yes! Make her want to staaay! Spine was beside himself today.

I smiled as I watched her fidget. "Um, um, only if you want to..."

Oh, we want to! Spine confirmed.

I eased her down into the tub again and tucked her back against my chest. I wrapped my arms around her and sighed happily. This was another moment I'd remember forever. I slid a hand up to caress her breast with a thumb but did it so lightly that all I could feel were the tingles of the mate bond. My other hand slid down her belly and paused there for a moment. I sent another prayer to the gods that the pup would arrive safely.

I snaked my hand down to her folds and parted them to slip two fingers inside her warm channel. I growled provocatively into her ear, and she moaned delicately in response. She always responded so well to the noises I made. She then melted against me, and I slowly pumped my fingers into her, taking my time.

I started to softly knead her breast, feeling the same thrill I always felt when I touched them. I stroked from the bottom to the side, savoring her weight and graceful shape. I rubbed in small circles up her breast to trace her areola, and she leaned ever so slightly into my hand. I smiled to find her biting her lip, and I nibbled lightly on the top of her ear to make her gasp.

I pinched her taut, darkened nipple gently and started stroking above the entrance to her sex. Now that she was warmed up, I rubbed firmly into the raised tissue, sliding down in different strokes to find the one she responded to the best.

Her moaning became more distracted once I found the winning strategy. Her abdomen tensed, and she arched into my chest. I kept the speed and pressure consistent and watched her face. Her lips parted into a tense, anticipatory smile, and she gasped for air to feed her panting. I leaned down to lap at her ear and neck, growling for her to let go.

"Come for me, Ragna," I murmured, stroking a little harder and faster. "Claim your gift. It's only for you."

"Aaah! Aaahg!" She jerked and bucked into my hand, crying out her release. She whimpered and spasmed with every wave that hit her. Two fingers were working inside her channel, and I extended her currents of pleasure with a thumb, forcing every orgasmic burst to burn longer and brighter. I supported her when she became limp in my arms, panting and blinking slowly. She looked so lovely with that sated glow on her cheeks, and I sorely wished I could see it every day. I moved my hand from her breast to her hair, stroking it gently. When I pulled my fingers out of her, I froze.

"Ragna," I asked, shaking her a little. "Are you bleeding?"

She stood up too quickly, and I had to catch her before she fell out of the tub. It wasn't a lot, but there was a small amount of blood on my fingers that hadn't completely washed away when I withdrew them from the water. I hastily rinsed her off with clean water and snagged two robes from the closet. My heart was in my throat where it absolutely did not belong.

Find someone, find someone, find someone, find someone. I had no idea if those thoughts were Spine's or mine.

I yanked the door open and nearly bowled over Mwezi. I blurted, "I need someone to look—"

"She's fine. It's just implantation. Don't worry about it."

I slammed the door in her face and turned to look at Ragna with wide eyes. Wait.

What's implantation? Spine asked.

I jerked the door open again to find a smirking Mwezi and asked, "What i—"

"Her fertilized egg made it to the wall of her uterus," she said and raised her fists up in mild celebration. "Yay." I nearly slammed the door in her face again. What was wrong with my brain? She raised a finger to keep my attention on her. "It's a little early for implantation, but you are an alpha, and you assholes never do seem to follow the rules." She grinned wickedly. "I like that, though."

Luan strolled around the corner and sighed wearily at Mwezi. "You weren't supposed to say that." She sighed and passed by me to visit Ragna.

I sent Mwezi a questioning frown, but she shook her head. "No, that's just how she greets me." She cackled and walked away. I pinched the bridge of my nose and willed away an impending heart attack. When I glanced back, I found Luan and Ragna in a deep discussion, so I went to finish my bath. Hopefully we wouldn't need to have a lengthy discussion to plan our next move. I was ready to move on from this place. Something about it just... broke my brain.

Sprouts, Spine offered simply. *I blame the sprouts.*

Chapter 25

Ragna

Zorian and I finally got to sit down to discuss matters with the three Lunar Coven mothers. It was surreal being here after five years, not to mention I was with the Lycan King who'd impregnated me and had already attempted to mark me twice. Granted, one of those attempts had been sleep-marking.

Can't believe we're with pup, Trail said dreamily. *I got a little bit of Spine in me!*

If it makes it, Trail. We don't want to get our hopes up.

We'll just make another one! I, uh, don't remember how to do it. We should, uh, ask Zorian to show us one more time. Two more times!

Trail... I chastised.

I suppressed an amused smile with a palm and tried to listen to what Zorian was saying. He was summarizing our trip and showing Senay the symbol we'd found hanging from a tree. Mwezi and Luan leaned over the large study table and frowned. "That's something I haven't seen in a while," Luan commented, scrunching her nose in thought.

"What is it?" Zorian asked, his eyes flickering between the three mothers' faces.

"That's a dampener. It suppresses communication within a certain range. We actually consider these illegal now. Oh, that reminds me. This letter came from your beta," Senay said, going from serious to cheerful in the blink of an eye. She handed a letter to Zorian, and his face grew darker the longer he looked at it.

"Packs have been reporting disturbances in mind-linking..." he said, furrowing his brows and reading further. "The reports started coming in after we left, so this was pretty recent. The mind-linking grew sporadic and stopped working for the most part." He looked up at the mothers. "Would you agree it sounds like the dampeners are the cause?" They nodded, and Zorian scrubbed a hand over his jaw. "A solid warfare tactic is cutting off communication. I would expect this to be followed up with some act of violence. Perhaps they're waiting to get their hands on Ragna." He looked back down at the letter with his chin in his palm.

Uuughhhh, he is sooo smart, Trail said, panting.

Oh, my goddess! Calm your lady bits, Trail! This is serious.

My lady bits are on fire! I just wish Spine could jump on me and ride m—

I cleared my throat loudly and sniffed to try to block out what she was about to say. Zorian's eyes froze on the letter, and he looked alarmed. "The carriage that was escorting the princesses out of our territory was found by our team, who was returning from their scouting of the cult grounds. Two of them were slaughtered, along with the coachman. One is missing."

My jaw dropped open in shock, but a very, very small part of me wanted to smile over their demise. I was deeply ashamed of it. My stomach twisted itself into knots over my messy, tangled emotions, and I ran as fast as I could to throw up in the kitchen sink.

Yeesh, Trail complained. *Our stomach has not been handling stress very well.*

This pup could just fall right out any minute, I replied to her with tears in my eyes.

Well, don't let those bitches kill our pup from the grave! Trail snapped. *Get it together!*

I nodded guiltily and felt Zorian's large arms slide around me in a hug. I heard someone else enter and open a cabinet, but I couldn't smell who it was through the bile in my mouth. "Can I get you anything?" he asked.

"Maybe some of that tea," I answered, accepting the help wearily.

"Luan's already making it."

I sighed and rinsed my mouth with cold water while he rubbed my back. Despite feeling sick, I glowed under his attention. I just wanted to crawl back into bed with him.

Who is this person? Really? Trail asked in wonder. *If you told him he'd be acting like this a week ago, he'd have blown up on the spot. He'd be a pile of dust. Here lies King Zorian, the Lycan Pile of Dust.*

"Who survived?" I asked him, wishing I had the energy to enjoy Trail's antics.

"Asmin, the dragon," he replied quietly and led me to a chair at a large kitchen table. "Considering what you told me after they attacked you, I won't rule out that she was involved in their deaths or the cult." Luan set the tea in front of me with a slice of gingerbread, and I gave her a grateful look. Senay and Mwezi meandered in to join us.

"Fortunately, the other kings aren't pointing fingers yet because this cult has been spreading into their territories as well. It's becoming a transregional concern," Zorian reported, his eyes glossing over the rest of the letter. I waited for Trail's dirty joke because there was too much good material to work with, but she just cackled uncontrollably. I sighed and took a large sip of the tea.

Zorian then summarized our encounter with Wane and drew the symbol I'd scratched off the godling's body. Senay took one look and said, "Yes, that's how they controlled the godling. Another bit of witchwork that's been outlawed. Probably the same little traitor who took Ragna, I'd wager. We'll retrieve the bodies in a little bit."

Zorian nodded but growled. "We'll wait for you, but no one new is to enter this building. No one is to get close to Ragna. Not even for one second. Even if I am here." The mothers nodded amiably, looking completely unperturbed by his aggression. He leaned back in his chair and crossed his arms over his chest. I eyed the contours of the boulders on his arms and fought desperately to keep my arousal at bay.

Trail panicked and rushed out a solution. *Think of gross things! Slugs! Moldy bread! Grandpa's feet!*

I dry heaved, and everyone looked at me. Oh gods, there just wasn't any winning here. When Luan fetched me a glass of water, I hid in it.

"On our side of things," Senay said, "we had a kidnapping and a theft over five years ago. Our lunar temple was broken into, and our own

Key to the Realm of the Gods was taken. We lost some good witches and menfolk that night." She looked sadly at a nail and scraped at a rough corner.

"I didn't know one existed," Zorian remarked, surprised. "But then again, that's probably the point. I imagine that would constantly attract interested parties."

Mwezi shook her head bitterly. "The only of its kind, but we only guarded it, kept it safe. We were entrusted with it by the Moon Goddess generations ago, and we finally failed. It was only intended for emergencies."

"So, that's the only way the cult could have even gotten near the Moon Goddess," he mused aloud, tracing a finger along the grain of the table. "So, how do we get to the Realm of the Fae, and where do I go to open the door to the Realm of the Gods?"

"We've nurtured some doors here to the fae's realm. We have a good relationship with their people." Senay beamed proudly.

Mwezi snorted. "Good relationship? You mean how they look down on us until they just so happen to need something? Snooty wine bibbers."

"Anyway," Luan drawled. "We'll open one for you. Once you arrive, seek out General Belenus and hand him this letter." Luan snatched a sealed scroll out of thin air and handed it to Zorian. Some sparkly dust floated about in the letter's wake, and Luan coughed, waving a hand to shoo it away from her.

"What's this?" I inquired with a smile, reaching up to touch the glittery particles.

"One of our mothers, who shall not be named, saw fit to pull a prank and curse our teleportation spells. Now we have to wait nine more days before it fades." Luan scowled at Mwezi, who suddenly looked very interested in her piece of gingerbread.

"Oh, I think it's great fun!" Senay tittered and ran her fingers through it. Zorian leaned back with a stern expression, obviously not wishing to get glitter on any part of him. He scowled at his hand in disgust, realizing that the letter was covered in it. I laughed at his state of aggravation and finished my tea.

"Is General Belenus mated?" I asked, hoping he was so I didn't have to worry about fighting off another male.

"No, and he may not behave himself." Mwezi grinned savagely at Zorian like she was looking to pick a fight.

"You weren't supposed to say that," Luan sighed dramatically.

"Then no. Find someone else," Zorian snapped.

Luan threw her hands in the air. "Mwezi! This is why!"

Senay just smiled into her cup of tea, content and oblivious to the fighting. "So, the general will take you to the entrance to the Realm of the Gods. You just have to walk through it with Ragna. While you're doing that, we'll work to remove the dampeners, but it's going to take a long time to track them all down," she said merrily.

Zorian looked like he was about to burst into flames, and I put a hand on his arm. Never mind! I hastily moved my hand to his shoulder to pat him. There, that was slightly less arousing.

"We'll go soon!" I said with a smile. "We're so close!"

He grumbled something unintelligible with a deep scowl, then said, "Alright, we'll wait for you to fetch the bodies. Just don't forget the cultist." He turned, leaned in close, and pointed a finger right at me. "You're not to leave my side until they return, and we're out of here. Is that clear?"

I nodded and gave him a little salute. "Yessir!"

<hr>

Zorian was in a dark mood after seeing the bodies. The dead cultist was a human diplomat from Asmin's homeland, the dragon's kingdom. "The wasps have buried themselves deep in the foundation. The sooner we deal with them, the better. The witches will keep his body preserved here for evidence should it be required." He rubbed his temples and sighed. "You ready?" he asked, grabbing his pack and looking over at me.

"I'm ready when you are," I answered, brimming with excitement despite his news. I bounced on my toes impatiently and wondered how many more days it could be before everything returned to normal. I hoped it was less than a week. I was ready for this whole nightmare to end.

A pang hit my heart, almost making me miss Zorian's gesture to leave. He was overdue to find his queen. It was going to hurt like nothing else when our bond broke.

The three mothers led us through a sprawling rose garden and stopped at a large ring of mushrooms on the ground. "Isn't it darling? I call this one the Shroom with a View," Senay said, sighing affectionately at them.

"I liked Zoom Shroom better," Mwezi complained under her breath. Luan shushed her.

"Ok, get on in." Luan motioned for us to step inside the circle. "Oh, and Ragna, try to avoid shifting until you deliver. Bye! Say hello to Belenus for us!"

I opened my mouth to reply, but everything went black before we arrived on a stone platform in a small but vibrant castle courtyard. A wave of dizziness hit me, and Zorian grabbed me to keep me from toppling to the ground. I fought another wave of dizziness when I noticed how viciously the sun baked down on us from a cloudless sky.

Several soldiers in white gold armor stood at the base of the platform, armed with spears but still as stone—almost. The one on the right twitched several times, as though he wanted to turn around to peek at us.

Zorian and I descended from the platform and were met with an approaching group of fae warriors. I glanced up at Zorian, but he didn't seem bothered. I peered back to see who looked the most important; maybe one of them was the general.

"My, my, my, those witches were very accurate about the time of your arrival, Sky-Blessed," the fae in the middle said as he approached with his group. He cut a rather intimidating figure; he might have even been an inch taller than Zorian. I'd have to see them both side by side to know for sure. He had lustrous, sunflower-yellow hair that was swept to the side and gleaming amber eyes. The fae held himself well, being lean and graceful, and seemed to be the type to know that.

He knows he's pretty, Trail warned. *Watch out.*

Augh, yes.

"You must be General Belenus?" I asked hesitantly, hoping I was correct. I knew next to nothing about fae. I held out a hand for him to shake, but he came to a stop and stared at me a little longer than I liked. His eyes dilated, and his heart rate increased. I prayed that he would not become a problem.

"You are most correct, dear Sky-Blessed." He finally reached for my extended hand, and I breathed a sigh of relief, only to tense up when he kissed it. His lips lingered, and he stared up at me through his blond lashes. All the sparks and tingles verified that the Moon Goddess worked here as well. Wonderful.

"Ah, um, please let me introduce you to the Lycan King, King Zorian. He is the Alpha of all our Alphas, the Sun-Blessed, and my champion as decreed by the Sun God." I gestured with my free hand to Zorian, trying to remember every single title he'd ever had to encourage the general to move his attention away from me.

"Ah, yes, we take the Sun God very seriously here in the Summer Court," Belenus said and gripped Zorian's hand in greeting. I couldn't bring myself to look and see if they were doing that male hand-squeezing competition. "A pleasure as always to host a king. Welcome, King Zorian."

"The pleasure is mine, General Belenus," Zorian replied politely but flatly.

"Please relax while you are here, Your Majesty. I will personally make sure that her every need is met," the general added while placing his hands behind his back.

I swallowed heavily and looked up at Zorian. "Do you have that letter they wanted us to deliver?" I asked, balking at the expression on his face. He was trying to hide it, but I could tell he was boiling with rage. The muscles in his jaw were drawn taut. Scratch that. His entire body was drawn taut.

Oh no, it's a penis-off, Trail moaned in dismay. *Someone, bring the hose! We got two tree-piddlers over here!*

Without blinking, Zorian pulled the sealed scroll out of his backpack and handed it to the general. I watched the handoff with moderate discomfort, but it seemed to go well. Zorian did not try to stab the fae's eye out with it.

Ragna, we may need to pull the pregnancy card at some point.

Augh! We should not have to do that, but I will if I have to, I replied with an aggrieved sigh.

The general read the note and nodded. "Everything seems to be in order here." He rolled the note back up and placed it in his pocket. "Now if you'll allow me, I'll show you to your rooms." He held his arm out to me and raised a playful eyebrow, but I frowned.

"I thought we were going straight to the Realm of the Gods today," I protested lightly, thoroughly confused. Zorian moved to stand closer to me, and we waited for his response.

"You will be escorted there tomorrow, of course! Tonight, there is a banquet in your honor! We've known you were arriving for quite some time now," the general said with a borderline roguish grin.

"As gracious as that is, General Belenus, you must understand we're on a mission of great import," Zorian asserted firmly. "It's best we don't delay."

The general overexaggerated a look of being mortally wounded. "Certainly you'd not want to be seen denying our generous hospitality—a gesture of goodwill in hopes of a better relationship with your realm?" He looked certain that his gambit would succeed with great aplomb. Unfortunately, it did.

Zorian looked down at me with a set jaw. A vein I didn't recall seeing before ticked away on a temple. "We can manage one night, I suppose."

"I suppose." I sighed and took the general's proffered arm. Zorian was not happy about it, but I wasn't going to be rude—at least not yet.

General Belenus talked my ear off the entire way to the castle, but all I could think about was a cold glass of water and a nap. I wasn't expecting it to be so hot here. I wiped a bead of sweat from my forehead, and the general gave me a worried look.

"We're almost there, Sky-Blessed," he said and patted my hand. "I'll have refreshments sent up to your rooms immediately." I managed a distracted nod and took in as much of the castle as I could while I was here. Everything was so bright and golden. The architecture was impossibly elegant, and I was convinced that some of the castle's more delicate spires could not have been made without magic.

The interior was as impressive, but the golden molding everywhere was a bit... much. I was honestly afraid to touch anything, even a doorframe. I decompressed a little when the air cooled inside the castle, and I was able to think more clearly. We stopped in front of a lavish guest room, and I nearly gaped at the luxury provided for me. A four-poster bed sat between several balconies dressed in white curtains that fluttered in the breeze. Delicacies were laid out on a table along with an endless assortment of tiny bottles. Goddess knew what those were—perfumes maybe.

"This is your room, Sky-Blessed. I hope it is to your liking," Belenus announced and waited expectantly.

"Yes, it is lovely. Thank you. However, Zorian and I must room together. He is my champion," I answered, looking him firmly in the eyes. The general did not seem perturbed.

"Ah, we do not room unmated together here. I hope you can understand. It's a cultural difference, I'm afraid," he said with a barely concealed smirk.

He can take his cultural differences and shove— Trail began.

I sighed and tapped a toe on the ground, feeling irritation swell in me. "The last several times I've been separated from my champion, I've been kidnapped. I would hope you'd understand the need to flex an exception here." I didn't need to look at Zorian to know he was probably about to commit faeicide.

"You are protected here. It is not our fault your champion failed to prot—" the general began casually, but that was when I hit my newfound threshold.

I turned to Zorian, pointed to my room, and ordered, "Wait in there for me!" I looked up at the general and snapped, "Come with me this instant!" I marched off to find a private place to talk. There was a large balcony at the end of the hall, and I strode as fast as my legs could take me. I shoved the doors open and waited for the general to catch up.

Get him, Ragna! Bite him but not in a sexy way! This will be the only time I'll say that! Trail hollered.

General Belenus swaggered out onto the balcony and grinned. "Couldn't wait to get me alone, Sky-Blessed?"

"Tell me, General. Are you a terrible strategist?" I asked sternly.

"I'm one of the best." He snorted.

"Do you not research those you invite?" I asked a different question.

"We wouldn't have allowed you in the palace otherwise." He smiled and took a step closer.

"Do you often try to provoke your guests into causing a diplomatic incident?"

"Only if my beautiful mate's in the picture," he said and took another step closer. I placed a palm over my face at that answer. There it was, finally.

"You do understand that I'm not your real fated mate, correct? That is what I'm here to correct," I argued with an aggravated huff.

"Who's to say? You could very well be, and I'm unlikely to let you out of my sight until proven otherwise." He shrugged. "Which is why I'm accompanying you both to the Realm of the Gods tomorrow."

"That, dear general, is an atrociously bad idea. I have the most dominant alpha in the world traveling with me, and you have done nothing but provoke him! I don't think you understand how many times he would have killed you today for how you've spoken to him!"

Belenus shrugged. "I could take him."

I couldn't tell who was laughing harder, Trail or me. "So, you're going to make my job more difficult because you think there's a one-in-a-billion chance that we're fated mates?" He opened his mouth to answer, but I waved him to stop. "You know what? I don't care. Do what you want. Just leave King Zorian alone. If you don't, I will call my close and personal friend, the Sun God, to smite your frolicky bum."

Chapter 26

Zorian

Ragna burst through the bedroom door, and I could almost see the irritation radiating from her like thermals on a hot day. She had not been quiet in her reproach of the general, and I'd heard every word through the open doors of the bedroom balcony. She'd been intelligent, passionate, and focused, like a real queen, and it made me horny as fuck. The fact that she felt the need to protect me was cute, but I wasn't threatened.

Liar. You feel so threatened, Spine snorted. *You wouldn't be so murderous toward Belenus if you weren't.*

I ignored him and poured a glass of ice water for Ragna, worried about her fatigue and stress. She accepted it gratefully and downed the entire cup.

"You should rest. I'll make sure to wake you before the banquet in case they have ridiculous demands for how you should look," I said and strode toward the door.

"Nope. You're not going anywhere, Lycan King," she stated, still irritated but less so. I turned with a raised eyebrow, intrigued.

"I need to find my quarters… Sky-Blessed," I responded dryly and shoved my hands into my coat pockets.

"No, you're staying here. He may be the general, but I'm the general of my own personal space. No male gets to decide that for me," she said heatedly and locked her eyes on mine. "Not anymore."

Well, now I was doubly aroused.

She's extra hot when she's confident, Spine admired. I had to agree. As an alpha, I should be at least annoyed with her asserting control, but I wasn't. I wanted to see how far she'd go to get what she wanted. Was I what she wanted?

"I'm taking a nap," she announced decisively and plopped down on the king-size bed.

That nap is taking her, Spine sniggered. *Watch out, nap! Queen Ragna's comin'!* I chuckled quietly and went to pick at the food that was laid out on a table.

I was about to wake Ragna at the time I'd told her, but there was a knock at the door. A fae servant, a little blonde teenager with freckles, held out two white boxes. "Oh, I'm glad I found ye, Yer Majesty. Ye weren't in yer room!"

"The Sky-Blessed demanded a change in plans. Who is the Lycan King to stand in her way?" I said with a shrug and allowed the child to receive a small smile from me. She grinned, curtseyed, and rushed away to complete her next errand.

I placed the boxes on the bed by Ragna's feet and stroked her hair. She was out cold, and now I hated that I had to wake her. I knelt at the bedside. "Ragna, time to get ready," I said in a low voice.

I tried to warn that nap, Spine laughed. *She ain't lettin' go of that fucker!*

I chuckled and tilted my head to stare at her sweet, sleeping face. Her lips were parted, relaxed, and looked very soft. I felt an impulse to kiss her. Instead, I sighed miserably and clutched at my chest from the sensation of heartache. I didn't know it could physically hurt. I compromised and leaned down to kiss the top of her head.

"Ragna, wake up," I urged a bit louder and rubbed her shoulder. She finally stirred and stretched like a cat in the sun.

"Time to get ready?" she asked sleepily.

"Yes, and we just got two boxes that I'm terrified to open."

That got her attention. She sat up and spied them sitting at her feet. She opened the box on the top, and there was a label that had my name on it. "Ah, so they're playing 'Dress the Wolves' for this banquet." Her eyes flitted to me, and she amended it. "And lycan."

She peeked into the next box and sighed, then rolled out of bed and headed to the en suite. Again, why did she walk away to change? "Are you really that shy, Ragna?" I asked curiously.

She twisted her lips in thought and stared at the floor. "I guess so? Those mistresses really got into my head, I guess."

"We'll have to discuss this another time," I said, trying to hide the guilt I was feeling. "Let's get ready."

I put on the formal ensemble that was prepared for me and frowned suspiciously at how perfectly the white-and-gold dinner jacket, shirt, and slacks fit. I was not built like a fae at all, so when did they get a chance to take my measurements without my knowledge? Damned suspicious fae.

I left my hair the way it was. I wasn't putting any of that greasy shit in it. I was at the top of the food chain, and I had never felt a need to impress anyone except for my mother and Uncle Leobwin.

I sat at the table to wait for Ragna, but when she walked out, the table became three-quarters of a table. My claws had accidentally shredded a chunk out of it. Fury and lust were coursing through my veins, and I gritted my teeth through my stomach tying itself into knots.

She looked alarmed at the state of the table. "What happened there?"

I grimaced internally and searched for an excuse. "A weakness in the grain. These fae are wonderful with stonework, but their carpentry is trash." I held my breath, and fortunately, she moved on to the next subject.

Ragna looked down at her dress and winced. "So, is this what fae really wear to dinner? It feels more like... what a dancer might wear."

I grunted a noncommittal reply and tried to lean my elbow on the table. I missed it entirely due to the missing chunk and lost my balance. Fortunately, she hadn't seen as she was still looking down at herself.

The white-and-gold dress basically covered her breasts and privates. The rest of it were layers of gossamer fabric with a texture that reminded me of that sparkly shit that was all over the letter the witches gave me. Elegant and flowy? Yes. Suitable for dinner? Absolutely not. Suitable for the bedroom? Triple fuck yes, but it wouldn't survive the night.

I did not want the general seeing this much of her. "Ragna, should I speak to the general about getting you something different to wear?"

"Honestly, I don't want you two left alone with each other. The general deserves a slow death." She grinned at me, and I noticed her canines were slightly elongated.

Flatterer, Spine said smugly. *Love It.*

A knock on the door interrupted my response to Spine, and I went to answer it. I looked down to find the same servant girl who delivered the outfits to us, and Ragna joined me at the door. The girl grinned and waved up at me. "Ye both look lovely, if ye don't mind me sayin' so," she chirped enthusiastically.

"Ragna looks lovely," I said gruffly but then grinned down at her. "I look handsome, pup."

She giggled and then put on a very professional face for a child. "I'm here to escort the Sky-Blessed and His Majesty King Zorian to the banquet!"

"Well said." Ragna smiled. "What is your name, pup?"

"Bidelia! But I'm starting to like 'pup.'" She giggled again.

"Well then, lead the way, pup," I said in an overly kingly voice. Ragna gave me an odd look, and I tilted my head in a silent question. She blushed and turned to face the direction we were walking.

That was when I caught the scent of her arousal. Interesting. What had triggered that?

Bidelia turned to leave with a little hop in her step, then winced and adjusted the back of her dress. We quickly followed the fae out into the hall and toward dinner. When Ragna's arousal started to drastically affect me, I had to give her a warning. I leaned over and whispered so quietly that only she could hear. "She-wolf, if you don't knock that off, it's going to cause problems. Between General Belenus's advances and that dress, I'm very close to fucking you in this hall for everyone to see."

Her face turned bright red, and she coughed, choking on her spit. She cleared her throat, fanned her face, and made an obvious effort to calm herself. I nodded and fought back a smile.

General "Horndog" Belenus met us at the banquet, making long strides to approach us. He bowed to me and shook my hand, then turned to Ragna. "Sky-Blessed, you look beyond ravishing this evening," he said in a voice that was more sensual than I cared for but not unexpected. I held a growl back when he grabbed her hand and placed a slow kiss on it. Glancing at her face, I was relieved to see her merely tolerating it. He was greatly affected by the mate bond. Fortunately, he was only a general, so h—

"My son, please do us the honor of introducing our honored guests," a melodic voice said above the din of the other guests.

"Of course, Your Majesty," the general replied and led Ragna to the space in the middle of the tables that formed an almost complete circle around the room.

Well fuck, Spine said. *General "Horndog" is a prince.*

We're a king, Spine, I reminded to mollify him, but the news jarred me. I did not like being jarred. A growl slipped from my chest, but it didn't look like anyone had noticed.

We were seated after introductions were made, and—of course—the general was next to Ragna, making small talk. The ladies of the court tried to catch my eye, but I ignored them. Were all fae like this? Then again, maybe I was being a bit of a hypocrite. Lycans were libidinous creatures as well.

I sipped at the wine and tried not to wrinkle my nose. It was too sweet, but at least it was potent. I'd need it to get through goddess-knew-how-many hours of this dinner. Several ladies at our table started boasting about the number of lovers they had to quench their sexual appetites. I had a feeling the discussion was meant to grab my attention, but it only reeked of desperation.

"Tell us, Sky-Blessed," a buxom blonde fae with pouty lips said in a provocative voice. "How many lovers do you have? I can't imagine any with how much traveling you've had to do, you poor thing." The slender brunette next to her nodded along in faux sympathy and batted her eyes innocently.

I glanced over to Ragna and the general, interested in their reactions. Personally, I wanted to kick these fae women out for disrespecting my Sky-Blessed and potential mother of my pup. I was pleased to see some degree of irritation on the general's face, but he also looked amused, which didn't amuse me at all.

Ragna sipped at her water and took her sweet time to reply. I drew a sip from my cup as well, but it was only to hide my smile. This was a power play. She cut a piece of her steak and eventually replied, "Oh, I'm sorry that you've had to go through so many men to find something you like. I only need one male myself."

I swallowed heavily and wondered where she was going with that line of thought.

"I have tasked King Zorian, the Lycan King, the Alpha of all Alphas, also known as the Sun-Blessed, to serve me in that regard. He has endless stamina, he's very skilled, he's creative, and I'm well sated. Actually, I can barely keep up with him. Also, he comes with the benefit of not worrying about diseases, but I imagine you must have very good doctors here," she said calmly and kindly, as though she was talking about the weather.

HOOOLYYYY SHIIIT! Spine screamed. *WE GOT TWO QUEENS IN THE ROOOM!*

Between Spine's deafening screaming and Ragna's beautifully spun comeback, I nearly choked on my wine. I hazarded a glance at the general, and he looked very, very annoyed. I could barely contain my grin at what a beautiful and flattering lie she'd created on the spot.

Hey, most of that was true! Spine crowed.

I quietly cleared my throat and finished my dinner, riding the highest of highs.

Ragna

He's going to kill us for pulling a stunt like that, I said nervously to Trail.

You obviously don't understand that a male's ego loves to be stroked as much as his—

I hear you! I hear you! Please don't make me blush any further at this table. Great goddess!

The general turned to me and offered an arm. "Sky-Blessed, would you do me the honor of taking a little stroll about the garden with me before you retire?"

I hid my dismay and caved. "I suppose I can make time for it," I answered curtly and stood with him. I turned to Zorian and said, "I'll meet you in my chamber later. I shouldn't be long."

Zorian eyed my hand on the general's arm and nodded. The queen called him over, asking to discuss a political issue. At least he'd have a productive conversation to occupy his time.

The general led me to a garden that was—of course—very beautiful. The prettiest section was the water garden where giant lilies bloomed. A tiny dot of light would occasionally enter or leave the large blossoms, and Belenus said, "Those are water faeries. They make their homes in the lilies. You'll see the little lights turn on when the sun sets." I moved my gaze to the sky, and the shadows were indeed getting long.

I started when a hand gripped my arm, and Belenus turned me to face him. "What do you think of my home, Ragna? Could you see yourself here someday?" His expression was hopeful. Like with any mate, I felt the tingles and mild attraction, but it was dull, and I wasn't interested.

"You're getting ahead of yourself, General Belenus. Don't set yourself up for a broken heart," I warned. "Remember the odds here."

He frowned and walked me backwards until I hit a tree. The memory of Zorian taking me against a tree rushed into my mind, and I blushed. That'd been a good night, well, parts of it had been. Belenus's heart raced, and I suspected he'd taken my blush the wrong way. "I haven't found my mate in over a hundred years, Sky-Blessed. What makes you think I won't still want you if you're not my mine?"

"That's something you should think rationally about when you're not high on the mate bond," I answered. He leaned closer to me, and I pushed my head back until it hit the tree with a thunk.

"What if I'm tired of being rational, Sky-Blessed?" He leaned forward, his lips inches from mine. I glanced over at the twinkling stars and the darkening sky. The night shadows were coming to take me away again.

"Then maybe you should rethink your future as a king?" I suggested sympathetically, patted him on the shoulder, and ducked before he could plant his lips on mine. The shadow of the tree scooped me up, and I disappeared from his sight. "I'll see you tomorrow, General, bright and early."

I put some distance between us and watched him look around for me. He didn't look pleased, but he also didn't look like he was about to surrender. He heard my footsteps and said, "You may have someone to relieve you, but if you'd like to try something new, you know where to find me."

I laughed to myself. No, I didn't know where to find him. Not that it mattered.

I returned to my room to find Zorian pacing anxiously on the balcony. His head jerked to face me, and he composed himself. "You're back," he said.

I joined him on the balcony and pointed at the night sky. "He decided he couldn't see me anymore," I replied with a grin. I was very satisfied with how my encounter had ended. I didn't think I'd ever felt this confident in my life. I would have to thank the general later for pushing my buttons hard enough.

Pfeh, Trail mumbled. *That was all us.*

He better hope his future mate is rational enough for the both of them, or this kingdom is doomed, I replied with a chuckle.

Zorian was quiet, and I looked up at him again. Had he not liked my joke? I thought it was pretty good.

"You smell like him," he said softly.

"He tried to kiss me, but I got away." I put a gentle hand on his arm in hopes that he wouldn't go ballistic. "I've had five years of practice for that moment," I proclaimed with a smile. He nodded and wandered back into the bedroom.

"So, tell me, Ragna," he began, sitting at the edge of the bed and crossing his arms over his chest. I tried not to stare at his arms and focused on his face while he spoke. "What did those princesses say that got you so insecure?"

Ah... We were back to this. I sighed. "Nothing detailed, really... They just looked me over and called me 'passable' and 'nothing to write home about.' I've always been a bit shy with my body, but that just made it worse, I guess. Just don't feel like drawing attention to myself."

He nodded as he listened to me, placing his hand over his mouth in his usual thoughtful fashion. He closed his eyes for a moment, then stood and approached me. I grew nervous when he cupped my face and looked me over.

"Let's start here, then," he said without emotion. "Your hair is sleek, shiny, and healthy. I love how the sun picks up tiny bits of copper in it, like they're little hidden gems. Your brows are set and match your personality very well because you're driven and focused. Your eyes are remarkable and remind me of freshly watered ferns on a foggy day. They glow with life.

"Your nose is well proportioned to your face, and I particularly like how your little nostrils flare when you're upset," he said, then hesitated when his eyes fell to my mouth. "Your lips look soft and are expressive. They dazzle when you smile but are even better when you laugh." He tilted my head up a little. "Your chin makes you look strong, like you're not going to take anyone's shit anymore." I laughed at that but stopped when he gave a playful warning growl. "Your ears are perfect. I don't have much to say about them other than I've enjoyed nibbling on them." I squirmed a bit at that, and my toes curled in my shoes.

His hands went to the neck of my dress, and his eyes sent me a silent question. Heat rose to my cheeks, and my belly clenched from nervousness. What if he didn't like what he saw when he took a much closer look at the rest of me?

What are you saying? Trail admonished. *We are beautiful. Now give him a show! Daaance!*

I nodded shyly and averted my eyes. Zorian slipped my dress over my head, and I heard his breath catch. He released the quietest groan and ran his hands along my shoulders. "Your neck is slender, and your collarbone is exquisitely crafted. I love the dip in the middle the best." He slid his hands down to my wrists. "Your arms and legs are strong, a testament to your survival in the wild. Your mind and spirit, by the way, are just as strong because of that. Your fingers are long and delicate. If I didn't know any better, I'd say you were a musician."

He knelt before me, and that was when my nerves utterly possessed me. His hand reached to trace the contour of a breast. "Your breasts are perfect, Ragna. Not too big and not too small. They're soft, proud, and generous, more than enough to fill my hands." He traced a lazy path down my stomach and landed on my hips. "Your abdomen is strong and lean, but I hope to see it round with my pup someday." Oh goddess, I squeezed my thighs together and tried to pray away my arousal.

His hands pulled my underwear down, letting them fall to the floor, and he ran his fingers through the curls between my thighs. "And all this down here… it's such a pretty picture. I've never seen prettier. You're like a little rose framed in cinnamon." He stood and walked behind me, which made all the hairs on my body stand on end. He traced a finger down my back. "You have lovely musculature back here. Your shoulder blades are elegant and sturdy." He slid his palm down to cup my bottom, and a violent shudder raked down my spine. "You also have the most perfect ass I've ever seen—round and firm."

He wrapped his arms around my waist and whispered in my ear. "So, Ragna, who do you believe more? Someone who's spent hours studying your body, or several bitches who were too jealous of you to see straight?"

I couldn't say anything. I was a completely stunned tomato. What surprised me the most was that I wasn't thinking about being embarrassed. I was just deeply pleased and extremely aroused. My toes curled again, and my heart did several flips when he let go of me.

"You smell good, Ragna," he murmured. "No female has smelled better." I knew that was the bond talking, but I'd take it.

He came around to my front again and towered over me with his arms crossed over his chest. "I can smell your desire, Ragna, and it seems to me that since you've tasked King Zorian, the Lycan King, the Alpha of all Alphas, also known as the Sun-Blessed, to serve you, I should probably start... right... now."

I knew this would come back to bite me in the ass, I said to Trail.

Mm, yes please!

"I-I just said that to shush those women," I stammered as he backed me toward the bed.

He tilted his head and gave me a serious look. "So, you're saying you lied in front of royalty? Oh goddess, Ragna, that can't be true. You're better than that. Did you also lie about how good I was?"

"N-no!" I said when I ran into the edge of the bed.

"So... just to be clear, you don't want me to do this?" he asked as he leaned forward to kiss my neck. His lips were soft—sensual. I gasped, and my legs weakened.

"Or this?" His hand moved to caress a breast, and I jerked in surprise.

"What about this?" he whispered into my ear and slid a finger between my legs to rub against the spot that tortured me so. My legs gave out, and I fell onto the bed, pressing my thighs together to try to relieve some of the ache. He leaned over me and tilted his head. "So, what do you say, Sky-Blessed? Do you still wish to rescind my task?"

I peeked through the hands that were covering my flaming face. "No?" I whispered.

"I didn't catch that, Ragna." He narrowed his eyes.

"No?" I repeated a little louder.

"Was that a question, Ragna?"

"No!"

He knelt between my legs and spread them. "Then I live to serve, Sky-Blessed."

Chapter 27

Ragna

Zorian pulled my shoes off, grabbed my hips, and dragged my bottom to the edge of the bed where he spread my legs wide. I clamped my lips shut to muffle a shriek of dismay, then covered my face with my hands. This was too embarrassing!

"Z-Zorian!" I protested when I peeked to see his head between my legs. "D-don't look! Faces don't belong d-down there!"

"Mine does," he murmured smokily and turned his head to trail kisses up my inner thigh. I bucked my hips, not expecting that part of me to be so sensitive. He repeated the sensual maneuver on the other side until I was a heated, panting mess. His saliva cooled in the night air and prolonged the tingling that I felt from his mate touch. I was quickly forgetting about how much his face didn't belong down there.

My hips twitched, and my thighs tensed when he ran his rough fingers down my painfully throbbing folds and spread them. Something smooth and warm ran up between them, and heat flooded my core, squeezing an aroused moan from my lips. Oh, my goddess, that was pleasurable! What was that?

I looked down and blanched to see him lapping at my sex. I squeaked in horror at this foreign action and tried to wiggle away, but he held on to my hips and growled. The vibrations sent a broiling wave of arousal through me, and I groaned through my clenched teeth at the new sensation.

"Don't move, she-wolf," he snapped.

"Is th-this making love?" I stammered, feeling very self-conscious.

"No, this is oral sex, Ragna," he answered gruffly, his heated burgundy gaze rolling up to meet mine. "Don't think—feel."

Easier said than done! I thought to Trail.

Wheee! Do something I would do! she replied and disappeared into the back of my mind to give me privacy.

Zorian ran his silky, searing tongue up my folds in rhythmic strokes, like how his fingers moved when he pleasured me. I was so stressed about my core weeping on his face, but I tried hard to shut my brain up like he'd ordered.

As if he'd read my mind, he paused in his ministrations and said, "Relax, Ragna. Your flavor is as beautiful as the rest of you." I peeked to see him staring hungrily at me while he rubbed his thumb into the swollen, throbbing flesh at the apex of my sex. The seductive look in his red eyes, plus the pleasure I received from his stroking, was almost too much for me.

A colossal wave of arousal swirled into my belly and blossomed between my legs. My breasts ached, and my breath caught. I softly called out to him and slid my hands down the bed in a pathetic effort to reach this enticing, virile male.

He leaned back down to continue licking, but his eyes never left mine, and mine never left his. Oh goddesses, this was too hot—too hot! I wanted him! My legs started shaking, and the itch that needed to be scratched started growing within me. I whimpered and writhed, trying to keep still but finding it quite impossible. I needed his arms around me! My whimpers turned into whines as I begged for release. The waves swelled when there was a knock at the door.

I froze and stared at the door.

Zorian stood and raised his voice, irate. "What is it?"

The door opened, and General Belenus looked in, his eyes scanning the room, obviously looking for me. I didn't know how he expected to spot an invisible female.

"I did not say you could enter, General," Zorian admonished with a scowl.

"Where's the Sky-Blessed?" he asked, not bothering to respond to Zorian or provide a reason for calling upon me at such a late hour.

"Well, she was supposed to come, but she got interrupted," Zorian answered with a dangerous edge to his voice. I blushed fiercely at the wordplay, hoping the fae wouldn't figure out that he was—in fact—the interruption. He crossed his imposing arms and asked, "Can I take a message?"

"No…" the general said while taking another look around the room for me. "I'll see you both tomorrow. Good night, Your Majesty." He frowned and left. Zorian strode to the door and locked it with a snarl.

"Fucking idiot!" Zorian growled.

I let out my held breath and collapsed. I was a hot-faced, panting mess, and he looked apologetically at me. "I've got you, Ragna." He returned to kneel between my legs, but I protested.

"No! Come here," I whined, backing up on the bed and squirming. I was going out of my mind without his body next to mine. I held my arms out and said words I never thought I'd say to this male. "I need you, please. I can't take it anymore. I feel so empty without you. Please, I need you inside!"

Oral was nice, but I wanted more. I needed more. His mask dropped completely, and he looked shocked. I guess this was the first time I'd demanded sex from him. I was too wound up to care what it looked like. I was burning alive, and I needed all of him to extinguish me. "Zorian, please! I want you!"

At that last beg, the fire in his eyes ignited. He ripped his clothes off, jumped onto the bed, and crawled up my body like a stalking beast. He caged me under him, spread my legs, and nudged the head of his cock into my opening. He was already as hard as steel!

"Ah, ready so fast!" I gasped as he slowly squeezed his cock past my threshold.

"I'm always ready for you, Ragna." He groaned huskily into my ear and kissed just beneath it. He groaned again as he pushed his cock deeper into me. I was so turned on by his words and physical response that I wished I could release on the spot just to escape the exquisite agony.

I slid my arms around his ribs and gripped his back, trying to urge him to get inside me faster. He shuddered and pumped his hips a couple more times to sink in the rest of the way. I released a long, mewling moan.

Ah, I was full again! I felt so complete. I wrapped my legs around his hips and arched into him. He stilled and breathed heavily into my neck, giving us both a moment to revel in the agonizing perfection of how our bodies locked together.

I placed my hands over his shoulders to try to move him back a little so I could take in his unmasked face. He seemed to understand what I wanted and shifted a little to meet my gaze. He continued to look surprised by my forwardness, but after his eyes searched mine, his face softened. I moved his pale hair aside and placed a hand on his cheek. In that moment, I discovered something new. I saw more in him than I thought he had—tenderness, attentiveness, patience, and, surprisingly, deep longing. He no longer looked imperious, detached, or heartless. This was an unwrapped, exposed Zorian. He'd been hidden away since the day we met.

He continued staring at me as he slowly started rocking his hips. I took a deep breath and released a long, lazy sigh, pleased by the strokes stretching my channel. He lowered himself onto an elbow, which brought him closer to my face, and caressed my hip with one of his large, calloused hands. He rubbed my skin in leisurely circles, and I unwrapped my legs, running them down his thighs in an unspoken response. I wanted to feel him with everything I had.

He grinded sensually against my sex with every push in, mindful to roll his determined groin into the throbbing, swollen spot above my entrance. I whimpered quietly and arched into him, wanting to feel his hard chest move and flex against my breasts. He breathed out in a rush, and his head sank next to mine so we were cheek to cheek. His hand slid up my side, over my ribs, and cupped a breast. We gasped simultaneously, and he brushed a thumb over my nipple. It ached like the rest of my breast, making me squirm under him.

He moved down my body a little, taking shallower strokes into my sex to do so, and latched on to my nipple with his mouth. I jerked slightly and whimpered when he began to suck and pull at the sensitive skin. I had no idea; I had no idea it could feel so good. I had no idea the pleasure could run so deep. It streaked down my abdomen and belly to swirl into my sex, which throbbed harder and clenched around his cock. He groaned into my breast while he licked, suckled, and pulled. His mouth was hot and wet—eager. Both his hands moved to fist the sheets, white-knuckled and shaking.

I tilted my head back and held his head down with both my hands. His pulls made me clench around his girth, and he groaned every single time. Each clench sent flaming pleasure through my body, and I almost couldn't breathe through them.

He released my nipple and licked up my breast. When he reached my upper chest, he paused and took a deep breath. "Your pheromones kill me, Ragna," he whispered, almost to himself. He kissed up my neck from there, and I gasped when he grazed my marking spot. Electricity sizzled through my nerves, and I bucked up against him, so overwhelmed with pleasure that I could cry.

"Z-Zorian," I whimpered, not knowing why I had to say his name.

He hesitated, then kissed farther up my neck and moved to trail them along my jaw. They were slow, seductive, and made my toes curl. I was slowly going out of my mind. I wanted more. I needed more. He placed several more kisses on my cheek, and my heart began to pound in my chest. I was certain it had already been beating like a drum, but this was when I really noticed it. I tensed as his motions slowed. He leaned his head back down, pressing his cheek to mine again as he continued to glide his cock in and out of me.

He was frozen again. I could tell he was afraid, but I didn't know what to do. I wrapped my arms around him and tilted my head to give his cheek a little kiss. He sucked in a ragged breath and swore quietly. I kissed his cheek again, putting as much affection into it as I could. I hoped he could sense that I didn't want him to be afraid—that he could be himself with me.

He slowly turned to face me, and I brushed his white locks away from his magnetic eyes. I could see the fear in them, but the longing still lingered. He leaned in to place another tentative kiss on my cheeks, then one on my chin. He looked up into my eyes, and I held my breath. All I could hear was the pounding of my heart, which yearned for him with a devastating intensity.

He slowed and stopped his rocking. Leaning on one elbow again, he cupped my cheek and leaned closer. He was an inch away, and I could feel his breath on my mouth. He glanced down at my lips, and I parted them without thinking.

Zorian leaned in and pressed his warm, soft lips against mine.

Zorian was kissing me.

My mind and body centered on him, and I returned his kiss. The connection I felt with him was unfathomable. It was as though he'd wrapped his soul around mine and brought us to a plane of boundless joy and eternal pleasure. Several tears dripped down my cheeks as I pulled him closer. My chest was so full. So full. My heart had been throbbing hungrily, but now it was sated. It was filling up slowly with every moment his lips remained on mine.

I felt his tongue press gently between my lips, and I timidly opened my mouth. He plunged his tongue in and groaned loudly. His hips moved again, pumping into me as his tongue invaded my mouth. I eventually learned the rhythm of his tongue and kissed him back but let him lead the dance. He explored my mouth sensually, licking and stroking. His devouring kindled a fire in me that burned unlike any other. It was passionate but not wild. It was heated but not aggressive.

He took longer strokes with his hips and groaned longingly into my mouth. I replied with a whimper and wrapped my legs around him again. He rocked and grinded into me, adamant about bringing me pleasure, and I cried out into his mouth, grateful to be muted by his kiss.

"Ragna, I... I..." He moaned, struggling once again with his words. He sped his hips up, and I arched into him, gripping the back of his head so I could feel his lips on mine again. In and out he slid, and I writhed beneath him, completely overwhelmed by the entire experience. Tears ran down my cheeks as I kissed him with desperation.

"Ragna, I... lo—" he gritted through his teeth, then closed his eyes and kissed me again. He moved faster, grinding heavily against me and bottoming out before pulling his cock back to plunge in again.

I sensed the wave coming around the corner, and the waters around my feet rose in anticipation. His mouth clamped back down on mine when I howled in ecstasy. My body jerked, my hips bucked, and I released violently. I dug my fingers into his shoulders and felt my core clamp like a vise on his cock. Waves rippled through me, and once again, my channel stroked his release out of him. A growling howl was liberated from his chest, and he hissed, grunting as I milked his seed from him. He grinded against me to prolong both our pleasures, straining and shaking with every ejaculation. Our panting was synchronized, and I responded to his groans with moans of my own.

Once the last of him was spent deep inside me, he rolled onto his back and pulled me with him. I wiped tears away and clung to him, terrified that I'd wake any moment to find that this had never happened. He held me tightly and stroked my hair with his other hand; I loved it when he did that. My head rose and fell with his heaving lungs. His heart thrummed in its cage, calling out to mine.

"That... Ragna," he said breathlessly. "That was making love."

Love... I realized with a stab in my heart. Breaking the mate bond would be the worst day of my life because now it meant breaking my heart. I was falling in love with Zorian.

Zorian

I woke to a she-wolf's feet padding hastily to the bathroom, where she ended up puking into the sink. I rushed after her with a glass of cold water, not liking how much the pregnancy was already affecting her. It was too early for this sort of thing, wasn't it? I knew it was harder on females who had to bear an alpha's pup, but I'd never seen it firsthand.

I brought her back to the bed, where I coaxed her into eating the blandest food I could find from the table. It was still an hour away from sunrise, so we decided to get dressed and make sure everything was packed before crawling back onto the bed.

I pulled the corner of a pillow over my shoulder and encouraged her to rest her head on it so she'd be more comfortable. She wrapped an arm around my chest and closed her eyes. After I'd made love to her last night, my heartache was worse than ever. I'd almost told her how I felt, but I just couldn't get the words past my lips. I was such a coward.

So... Spine's voice popped into my head. *Last night was pretty wild.*

I placed the palm of my unanchored arm over my eyes and said, *Once she told me she wanted me, it was pretty much over, Spine. My fight is just... gone. I don't think I can walk away when all of this is over anymore.*

And I don't think you should, he agreed. *Forget princesses and whatever other mate you think might be out there. I don't think there's anything politically wrong with you taking her as a chosen mate. I still think she's our fated mate, though.*

What makes you think that? That's a little too good to be true, don't you think?

She doesn't respond to others like she responds to us! She's hardly ever aroused around other unmated. You don't see her smellin' extra excited around General Horndog, do you? I mean, I'd love to toot my own sexy horn, but I think it's because we're her actual mate.

I looked down at her sweet, resting face and dared to hope that maybe Spine was right.

I'm always right.

A servant fetched us to eat breakfast with the general, and we departed the castle for the Realm of the Gods. Like at breakfast, the general tried to stay as close to Ragna as possible, but for some reason, I wasn't really bothered by it anymore. Spine was right; she didn't respond to him much at all, even when he kissed the back of her hand. For all intents and purposes, his touches should affect her as much as mine. There was only so much of the mate bond one could ignore.

The general led us to a tall, heavily guarded tower, and Ragna whimpered when we entered. She looked forlornly at the spiral stairs. "We're walking up to the top?" she asked, brushing beads of sweat from her brow. It was another hot day in the Summer Court.

General Belenus nodded and grinned, holding out a hand. "I could carry you if you wish."

Ragna accidentally backed up into me and turned to meet my gaze. "I'm a little light-headed, Zorian. Would you mind?"

BAHAHAHAHA! SUCK IT, GENERAL HORNDOG! Spine crowed, and I nearly winced from the volume.

I scooped her up into my arms. Carrying her was as easy as arousing her. Ragna was strong, but I was damn glad she wasn't too proud to ask for help when she needed it. The general fought to keep a neutral face and spun around to begin his ascent. I smirked into her hair once his back was turned and followed his lead.

"Thank you," she whispered, placing a hand on my chest, and I hummed in response.

There was a raised stone platform at the top, flanked by several pedestals. The sun baked down on us, and I had an uneasy thought about the Sun God landing and slaughtering me for accidentally putting a pup in Ragna. Then again, if the Sun God liked Ragna so much, maybe He could drop the temperature here a bit.

A cool breeze passed by the top of the tower, and Ragna sighed in relief.

Sun of a bitch, Spine sputtered.

I lowered her down to the ground, and she blushed, looking up at me through her eyelashes. My heart clenched painfully, and I tried to clear my thoughts. I gestured to the platform and looked at the general. "The door?" I asked, and he nodded, not bothering to add a fucking ounce of helpful instruction. Fighting back a growl, I took Ragna's hand and stepped onto the platform. I didn't know what I was doing, but I was the fucking Sun-Blessed, so the door better damn well respond to my authority.

The view around me distorted as a thermal column ignited beneath my feet. I felt like I should've been scalded, but my skin was cool. I only felt the strokes of the thermals, like wind across my skin. I looked down at Ragna. "You ok?" I asked, and she nodded, albeit nervously. I was nervous as fuck too, but I'd be damned if I showed it on my face.

I thought about the Moon Goddess's home and hoped this would take us right there. I'd settle for a location farther away so long as I knew which direction to go. The space before me distorted further, and I couldn't make anything out, but I felt like the door was fully opened. I trusted the sensation, pulled Ragna against me, and strode through the threshold.

The air around us immediately cooled, and our feet touched down onto springy moss by a creek bed. I heard the general enter behind me, and I fought the urge to growl again. He really was coming across as a stupid, clingy, lovesick puppy.

Occasionally, when I'd blink, I'd notice a different landscape for a fraction of a second. It was blurry, bright, and felt beyond comprehension. I realized that this environment, what we were seeing, was made for guests. I was a little concerned that the glimpses of the Moon Goddess's true environment were a sign that She'd been away for too long. The illusion should hold, right? What would happen if it didn't?

We followed the creek to a thatched cottage, and my nose picked up the scent of deer scat. The whole area was a little slice of wolf and lycan perfection, really—woods to run in, game to hunt, a creek to drink from and a quiet, quaint cottage in the middle of nowhere to hide away with your mate.

"This is Her home," Ragna said and rushed ahead. I stayed close behind her and kept my eyes open for danger. If Eysteinn had been here, then I didn't quite trust this house yet.

"May I go first, Ragna?" I asked before she reached the door. "I would feel better if I went in first. Would you allow me that?"

She paused and stepped away from the front door. "That's fair," she responded thoughtfully and waited for me to pass. I entered to find that the cottage was exactly what its exterior suggested.

Cozy as fuck! Spine admired.

Indeed, I replied, stalking from the clean, organized kitchen to the living room. The Moon Goddess certainly liked Her wicker furniture. I narrowed my eyes when I noticed some haphazard repairs to broken windows and furniture. Had someone been here after Her kidnapping? I caught the faint scent of a person, but I didn't think it was a shifter.

I toured the rest of the first floor and found nothing else that was particularly out of sorts, so I waved for Ragna to enter. I'd taken several steps up the stairs when my ears caught the sound of an extra heart beating nearby. It was fast—afraid.

I turned to Ragna and the general and put a warning finger to my lips. I crept up the stairs and followed the heartbeat to a closet in the bedroom. "We're not here to hurt you," I called out through the door. "The Sky- and Sun-Blessed are searching to save the goddess."

"Sky-Blessed?" a young man's voice asked through the door. "Ragna's here?"

I furrowed my brows and looked back to the doorway where Ragna was. "We weren't expecting anyone to be here. Who are you?" I asked, not wanting to unleash danger on the future mother of my pup.

"My name's Koray. I was taken from my home years ago. The one who stole me just… I didn't go back with him. I couldn't bring myself to do it," the voice said tiredly, and I heard the truth in his heart. The truth was sadder than I expected.

"Open the door, Koray. Come and meet us," I said, trying to add some gentleness to my voice and stepped back to not crowd his exit.

A young man, probably several years younger than Ragna, cautiously came out from the closet. I imagined his hair had grown since he'd been stuck here because it was long—long, shiny, and black like a starling. His royal-blue eyes widened, and he balked when he saw me, but I backed up with my palms facing outward.

"We will not hurt you, lost one," I said gently and held out a hand for him to shake. "I'm King Zorian, and it's an honor to meet another Key."

Chapter 28

Ragna

"Y-you know about me?" he asked, accepting Zorian's firm handshake as he looked at us in astonishment. He did a double take when he noticed the general behind me.

"The theft from the temple," I mumbled to myself, looking down at the ground. My eyes darted back up to the young man in delayed realization. Had the Summer Court already fried my brains? "That was you! Oh, the mothers will be so happy to know you're ok!"

"They still remember me?" he asked, and a pang hit my heart.

This poor kid, Trail sighed.

"Of course they do, and you'll be returning with us," Zorian stated firmly. "We'll get you home safely." He was being quite gentle with this young man. He'd been surprising me a lot lately, like when he was being playful with that pup at the fae's palace. I had a sudden urge to find a place to be alone with him.

I was startled out of my fuzzy thoughts when the young man crumpled to the floor and started crying in relief. I dashed over to wrap my arms around him, hoping I could do something to soothe his battered soul. "Was it Eysteinn?" Zorian asked, gritting his teeth through the advisor's name. "Did he take you?"

"He tried to take me back, but he had his hands full with the Moon Goddess. When I opened the door, I kicked him through it and shut it behind him. I couldn't allow him to use me to get back into this realm again. I had to lock myself in. He's too... unstable. I was too afraid to return. What if he had people waiting for me?"

Zorian crouched and put a hand on his shoulder. "That was very noble of you, Koray. Not even some of my bravest soldiers could've made a sacrifice like that. You have a warrior's spirit."

Koray rubbed a bloodshot, weeping eye. "Her child, Wane, begged me to open the door, so I did. I guess they went to help Her. Then the Sky Gods came by, and They showed me how to survive here... Said help would eventually come, but I'd lost hope..." He turned to me and added, "Don't worry, Sky-Blessed. I won't try to claim you as my mate. I'm aware of your situation. I actually have much to show you in Her workroom."

I was deeply touched and stood quickly, excited for him to lead us there.

"I can read people very easily, Koray, and you're going to grow up into one hell of a man," Zorian said, helping Koray back onto his feet. The young man stopped by Belenus for a moment and nodded stiffly in recognition. "Prince Belenus... good to see you again," Koray's voice held the shadow of a grudge, and I was shocked to see that Belenus had gone extremely pale. He was looking at Koray like he'd died and come back to life.

"So, General, you helped Eysteinn enter the Realm of the Gods?" I heard Zorian ask Belenus as Koray led me up another flight of stairs.

"I did not know he was about to kidnap a goddess," he snapped.

"Did you also not notice he had a child in distress?" Zorian followed up, growing angry.

"He said he was just a new slave boy, to not pay attention to him."

"If your people were more knowledgeable about ours, you'd know we'd abolished slavery over a century ago," Zorian informed him with a low growl. I didn't want them to start a fight here, and I was getting anxious.

Belenus slammed his fist through the wall next to us, making Koray and me nearly jump out of our skins. Zorian waved for us to continue. "We'll be right behind you," he said flatly. Belenus had shut his eyes and was near hyperventilating.

I reached to hold Koray's hand, and we continued upstairs together. I could still hear them quite clearly, though. This house could offer no privacy for two booming voices.

"I regret it, ok?" the general hissed. "When I learned Eysteinn had returned to your realm without the boy, I never stopped thinking about it! It kept me up for bleeding months! Was he starving? Was he dead? Did a god keep him? But I couldn't do a bloody thing about it! The boy had been the only Key, and he was beyond the locked do—"

Koray had ushered me into the door at the top of the stairs and shut it quickly behind him. Their voices were immediately cut off, and the room was blissfully silent. "I'm so sorry about that," I said to Koray. "That couldn't have been easy to hear. Do you want me to tell him to leave the house?"

Koray simply waved it off with a hand. "No, I don't want to let him waste my time. Here." He led me to a huge table in front of an equally massive round window, and I squinted my eyes to try to make sense of the object in the distant sky.

"What... Koray, that's not the moon. Is that...?"

"Yeah, that's our home, Ragna. That's our planet. We're on the moon."

Oh great goddesses, I'm going to faint. Catch me, Ragna, Trail moaned. I could only stare at my planet. I was transfixed and utterly discombobulated. A prickling urge to vomit swelled in me, but I successfully suppressed it. I swallowed heavily, then looked down at the mysterious object before us.

We were leaning against a circular table that was probably about as long as I was tall. The surface rippled like water, but it wasn't wet. Tiny pieces were scattered all over the surface and deep into its inky depths. I couldn't tell if the pieces were petals, leaves, seed pods, or something else that was entirely new or as old as time. Every single piece seemed to have the same symbol on it—except for one. I looked closer at the unique one, and I just knew it was me.

"This is me," I said to Koray, pointing at the piece.

"And all of those other ones are the unmated men—and males." He twisted his lips, staring at the table in disquietude. I looked among them, wondering if I could find Zorian's, but it was such a mess in there. Hundreds upon thousands were scattered carelessly, without a thought for their happiness. Perhaps more than a million. How many unmated males were on our planet? I couldn't fathom it.

"And Eysteinn did this," I said, feeling an urge to start removing the pieces. I wouldn't, though. I wouldn't know what I was doing, and I wasn't about to mess with a goddess's tool.

"With the fervor you'd expect of a madman," Koray muttered and gestured for me to sit at a writing desk. He opened a tome, turned it to a bookmarked page, and set it before me. I gasped and placed a hand to my mouth.

Zorian and General Belenus walked into the workroom, but I paid them no mind. When Koray went to speak with them, I tuned out their conversation. My eyes blurred with tears as my fingers brushed over the beautiful illustrations of Hekla, Soley, Rakel, and me. I pushed the book farther up the desk to prevent rogue tears from tainting the skillful creation.

I sniffed and read about the four of us. Our little sub-pack, we were the most compatible vessels for the gods and goddess to use. They all knew about us. Hekla and Soley weren't a surprise; I'd seen them both carry gods in their flesh. Who were Rakel and I meant to host? I was pretty sure that the voice I'd heard at the cultist's cabin wasn't the Moon Goddess.

Oh, right, Trail remembered. *They said to meet them here because they couldn't reach us.*

The Moon Goddess wasn't here, though. That meant Rakel was the Moon Goddess's vessel. That's why Eysteinn took her! I rubbed mucus off my nose before it could drip, and I sniffed again. Who was the last god?

I placed my chin in my hand and flipped through several more pages. Most of the writing was not in a language I understood. Perhaps not even the goddess could translate those concepts for us. I wiped more tears from my eyes. Gods, I sorely missed my friends, and I was desperately worried for Rakel.

I scented Zorian's approach, and he laid a calming hand on my shoulder. I pointed at the illustrations and looked up at him. His eyebrows raised, and he nodded slowly, scrubbing a hand across his mouth.

"Rakel is the Moon Goddess's vessel, Zorian. That's why Eysteinn has her," I said hoarsely, though I didn't know why my throat was so scratchy—I hadn't started wailing yet. "I'm just trying to figure out mine now." I rubbed my temples tiredly. I was getting a headache, but I was glad to be here and get some answers. "If I have another resource at my disposal, we could strategize around it."

He wiped a tear from my cheek and moved closer. "You're starting to sound like a queen, Ragna." Zorian slid his large hands up my arms to massage my shoulders. I blushed furiously, remembering the last time I'd thought I was going to get a back rub. I'd gotten a very different reward instead.

"The general and Koray went back downstairs. Koray's generously offered to make us some lunch," he said by my temple before moving down to suckle on an earlobe. I tried to reply, but the words got stuck when a moan bullied its way past them. My head fell back against the chair, and I let out a long, weary sigh. His touch was melting some of my anxiety, and I basked in him like a snake on a hot stone.

"You must be so stressed, Ragna," he murmured in a seductive voice. "I'd do anything to pause time and take care of that for you."

I shivered, and my body flushed with excitement. "I-if only."

Zorian's hand slipped between the buttons of my tunic and plunged under the bra to cup my breast. A deep shudder raked through me, and I whimpered from the sudden invasion, thanking all the gods that there were no other shifters in the house who could smell how turned on I was.

"We might not have the time to have me serve you properly, Sky-Blessed, but I'm not useless in a pinch," he growled.

As if to punctuate his point, he gently pinched and pulled on my nipple. I gasped and squeaked from the shooting sensation that traveled straight to my core. Zorian moved from my ear to kiss down my neck, and my toes curled so tightly that I wondered if they'd ever straighten again. His hand massaged my breast in slow circles, and he trailed warm, wet kisses closer to my marking spot. My stomach twisted with agonizing pleasure, and I squirmed on the chair.

When he shifted to get a better angle, I knew I was about to be vanquished. He reached around with his other hand to rub my throbbing sex through my leggings, and I squeezed my thighs together, not sure if I wanted to trap his hand in there or block his advance.

He moved more aggressively than he had before, and I wasn't sure I could get to where he wanted me to go in time, but when he clamped his lips down and sucked mercilessly on the marking spot, I was blindsided by a tsunami. My eyes rolled back, and I slapped a hand over my mouth to stifle a scream. He grinded his thumb against my sex to push me deeper and deeper into the waters of my release. Distantly, I heard a pleased growl rumble through his chest.

There was a knock on the door to let us know the food was done, but I was still writhing from his explosive gift. I nearly fell out of the chair, but he caught me, hoisted me up into his arms and said, "Let's go feed you, mama wolf."

Oh gods, what am I doing? We can't keep doing this anymore. I need to prepare myself for losing him, I sobbed to Trail. *I'm already in too deep!*

Maybe we won't lose him, Trail pondered. *Maybe he's our mate. We still haven't run into anyone else who affects us like he does. He's different.*

The not knowing was a painful sickness, but getting my hopes up to only have them dashed? That might kill me outright.

❦

After lunch, I returned to the goddess's workroom to search for more answers. Zorian never left my side for more than five minutes at a time and occupied himself with some books that had him completely absorbed. It'd hit me occasionally that I was on the moon in the goddess's home, and I'd be struck by an astounding combination of fear, excitement, relief, and wonder. Just being here was almost too much to process.

My mind tired, so I dragged the chair to stare out the large, round window with the tome in my lap. I started when I felt something press against my back and realized Zorian had slid a pillow behind me to make me more comfortable.

"Thank you," I blurted, a little stunned, and he went back to his book. My eyes watered at the thoughtfulness. Who was this male? He'd hurt me, but now he treated me like royalty. I wiped a tear away and stared out the window again, trying to block out the painful throbbing of a heart that was falling in love. Falling in love in an impossible situation.

I wondered what the goddess would think of that. I reflected on what I knew about Her while I looked at my world in the sky. The goddess. The Earth. I tilted my head and considered its story from the mythology compilation. The Earth was the goddess's parent. A drifting celestial being had collided passionately with the Earth, and they created the Moon Goddess.

"It's you," I realized in a daze. The answer was right in front of my eyes. "I'm your vessel, aren't I?"

The planet didn't reply. It just sat in the sky like a taciturn sentry. I stared at it, trying to figure out why the god had asked me to come here. I needed Koray.

"Do you need something, Ragna?" Zorian asked, abandoning a book on the couch cushion.

How... how did he know? "Uh, I was about to get Koray to ask some questions," I answered, a little stupefied. He jumped up and strode out to find Koray, and I was glad he'd left because I was certain I had an incredibly weird, idiotic expression on my face. How had he known?

Koray returned with Zorian and offered me a happy smile. "Hi, Sky-Blessed. You wanted to see me?"

"Yes, I..." I turned to look at the planet and then back down at the book. "I'm trying to figure out something, and maybe you'll know since you've been here so long." I sighed and took a deep breath. "I think I'm the vessel for the Earth God, but when It spoke to me on the planet, It sounded so faint. It told me to come here, but I don't know why. Is there anything here connected to the Earth God? I know It's Her parent."

He pondered a moment before replying. "There's a large clay jar with some dirt in it on the fireplace mantle," Koray guessed, looking thoughtful. "I thought maybe it was for a potted plant, but now that you mention it, I'm reminded of an urn you'd keep ashes in."

"Hmm," I hummed and went downstairs to peek at it. Belenus was napping on the couch, so I tiptoed past him. I reached to grab a plain but beautiful clay urn, but the surface buzzed against my palms, and I nearly dropped it out of surprise.

Oh my goddess, that was close! I squeaked to Trail.

That is no urndinary pot, Trail quipped, but we were both too terrified of dropping it to be amused. I brought the heavy container to the dining table and looked inside. True to Koray's words, there was plenty of dirt in there, along with some rocks and detritus. I even spied a couple earthworms poking about the soil. There was moisture in the urn as well, as if someone watered it regularly.

Koray and Zorian seated themselves at the table to watch. No voices came from it. I leaned over the top and said, "Hello? Earth God?"

Put your hand in it, Trail suggested. *That will be the last time I ever say such words.*

I was just about to, I replied tentatively. I parted some of the dirt so I wouldn't squish any of the earthworms. "Excuse me, little wigglers. Just popping by for a visit," I murmured apologetically to the tiny critters.

My entire body throbbed, and I gasped. Stumbling dizzily, I reached for the table to keep myself upright. Zorian shot up and was by me in an instant, holding me steady. A cleansing wisp brushed through my veins into the rest of my body, pairing well with Zorian's touch to relax me.

You finally reached Our daughter's home, Ragna.

I realized that the voice I'd heard before was actually two voices. They were synchronized so flawlessly that I hadn't noticed through their weakened state.

"Earth Gods?" I asked aloud, wanting to include the others so they could hear at least half of the conversation.

Now We are. The being from the sky forsook Her corporeal body and stayed with the Earth God after Our daughter was born, They explained.

"Do you know where She is?" I asked, unable to believe I was finally making progress after all these years. I felt like I was dreaming.

The region you're from. We feel Her in the mountains with Our grandchild, where the cliffs kiss the bay, They answered. I repeated that excitedly to Zorian.

"Do you know where that is?" I asked, bouncing on the balls of my feet with excitement.

"Yeah, that's close to where I sent my soldiers to investigate the cult. I assume my beta would have already sent troops over after the princesses' bodies were found," he answered with a thoughtful nod.

"Earth Gods, why couldn't You speak to me on the planet?" I asked the urn again.

Someone hung something upon Our branches that made it hard to talk. We tried to reach you, but it made Us tired, They explained. *But it is clearing up.*

"The mothers of the Lunar Coven did say that they'd be removing those, but it'll take a while. It's forbidden witchwork. We think the cult wanted to silence communication among the packs."

Until that magic is cleared, We cannot talk to or use you without what is in this container. Reach inside and take a piece of Our heart. We gave it to Our daughter when She left home so She'd have a piece of Us with Her always.

I swallowed nervously and dug my hand in deeper, promising to give the precious memento back to the Moon Goddess. It felt wrong to take it from here, but if we needed it to save Her, then it had to come. My hand touched something larger than a pebble, and I delicately lifted the heavy object from the earth. I shook dirt from it and studied the dark-grey rock. Its color and pebbled texture reminded me of the cast-iron pans my old pack used for cooking. It was perfectly still, but vibrations pulsed into my hand like a heart, which fascinated me as much as it unsettled me.

"I swear to keep this piece of Your heart safe, Earth Gods, then return it to Your daughter," I promised, brushing a little more dirt off it, making sure the excess returned to the urn. "Do you know why Eysteinn, the lycan who took Your daughter, needs me as his mate? He took the Moon Goddess's vessel to bait me—not that I wasn't going to rescue them anyway."

We can only guess he knows you're Our vessel, and We're his biggest threat. If he takes you as his mate, it might make it difficult for Us to kill him. He knows raging parents would do anything to retrieve their child. He can try to keep separating you from Us. He hides behind Our daughter and keeps Us from Our vessel. Nothing like this has happened before. He is sick. He plays a doomed game—facing the gods.

"But why pair me up with so many unmated?" My mind was buzzing with questions, and I savored the rush from finally getting some answers.

That is Our daughter's specialty. Once you find Her, perhaps She could explain, Ragna.

I nodded, trying not to feel disappointed. I'd gotten a lot from coming here, and I should be grateful.

As it is safe here, Ragna, Our vessel, would you receive Our blessing? the gods inquired. I perked up, and my heart skipped from exhilaration, ravenous for any help.

"Yes! I would accept your blessing!" I said a little too loudly, startling poor Koray.

There was silence for a moment, and I clutched the Gods' Heart nervously. *Ragna,* They finally said. *You are pregnant.*

"Y-yes, I am. It's King Z-Zorian's," I stammered nervously. Why were They asking about that? I trembled, and Zorian moved closer, pulling me against him in a protective embrace. I reached up to grip his shirt like it was a security blanket. "Wh-why do you mention that?"

Because if We bless you, you will lose your pup. Do you still wish to accept the blessing?

$\mathfrak{C}$hapter 29

$\mathfrak{Z}$orian

I'd been feeling optimistic about the conversation Ragna had been having with the pottery until she placed the Gods' Heart on the table like it'd burned her. With a stricken face, she stepped away from the table, her face frozen in a shocked grimace. I knew that face; she was about to cry.

"I need," she whispered, "a moment... some time..." I wasn't sure if she was aiming that toward Koray and me or the Earth Gods. She stumbled up the stairs, and I heard the bedroom door close. I had a dark feeling that this was related to our pup, so I told Koray we needed privacy and followed her to the bedroom.

I entered to find Ragna curled into a tiny ball with her hands on her head. Her eyes were wide, like she was facing an impossible decision. I locked the door behind me and rushed over, not happy to see the potential mother of my pup in such distress. I crawled onto the bed and lay down to face her, grabbing one of her hands from her head and kissing the knuckles.

"Hey... Hey, hey, hey," I said quietly, trying to get her attention. "Ragna, look at me. What happened?" I tucked her hand close to my heart and regarded her tortured face. "Ragna," I repeated and reached out to cup her face. "Talk to me."

Her green eyes finally flickered to mine, and they brimmed with tears. She opened her mouth to speak, but she still seemed frozen with fear. I could hear her heart pounding at a rate I wasn't happy with, so I rubbed my hand along her arm to get her attention. "Ragna, breathe. You're going to get dizzy. You need to slow that heart down a bit. Can you do that for me? For the pup?"

She started crying and said, "They offered a blessing, but They realized I was pregnant and warned me that if I accepted it, it would kill the pup!"

I sucked in a harsh, ragged breath as fear washed over me. I didn't know what to think. I could see how she needed time. I needed time. What did this mean? What would...

Holy fuck! Save Spine, Junior! Spine cried in panic.

Spine, quiet for now.

"It's good They warned you, Ragna," I began cautiously. I needed to hear more of her thoughts before I spoke. This was... We were... Everything was so fragile right now. "Speak your thoughts as they come, Ragna. It will help you process."

I wiped away a tear that had been hanging on to her eyelash for dear life while she stared at me. "How do I decide what's more important, Zorian? How do I know what I need to succeed?" She began to echo her thoughts with a face that broke my heart. "Is a pup worth more than a goddess? But sacrificing a pup for a goddess sounds like something She'd never forgive. It's barbaric. But She's a goddess. What would happen if... we were to fail? What if we failed because I didn't accept this blessing?"

She choked on a sob and dug her fingers into the blanket. I didn't think she realized her claws were out because she was shredding the material. Ragna grimaced and clenched her eyes shut, as though the emotional pain brought physical agony. Her canines were elongated too. Her body was in survival mode.

"Ragna, calm... calm," I murmured and continued rubbing her arm. "Just talk to me. Breathe. Let's go through the options. Why would you accept the blessing? There are a lot of 'what-ifs' attached to that decision."

"I'd accept it to have an edge against Eysteinn," she mumbled, her crying slowing to just a couple of sniffles.

"Well, Eysteinn has no gods on his side at all, Ragna. Worst-case scenario is he has a small army and a witch or two. I have a very large army, decent relationships with neighboring kingdoms, and all the gods are on our side. Do we truly need another blessing?" I asked, studying her poor, swollen eyes.

She looked uncertain then and gazed past me to think. Her mind had gone somewhere else. Perhaps she was talking to Trail. A minute went by before I switched the question. "How about the second one, Ragna? Why would you choose to keep the pup?" This was the question I truly wanted answered.

Her eyes returned to the present, and she gazed at me with an expression I couldn't quite decipher. "It nauseates me to think I'm sacrificing a life for a power. It feels... wicked, like something a cult would do."

I remembered when my plan was to kill Ragna so my people could have mates again. It was too close for comfort. The way things had turned out... I couldn't be more relieved.

"Also," she said and looked down into the blanket, staring unbothered at the shredded material under her claws. She picked at it for a minute, and I could sense her fear. It hung over her like a heavy, abusive fog. I recognized it because she'd brought me out of it before—multiple times. The last was when we were making love, and I wanted to kiss her. I'd frozen, but she'd released me with her sweet kisses on my cheek.

I cupped her cheek and leaned forward to kiss her forehead, then laid my head down so we were nose to nose with closed eyes. "Take your time," I murmured, stroking her soft cheek with my thumb. She let out a long, withering sigh and finished it with the tiniest, quietest whimper I've ever heard.

"Also," she repeated in a wavering voice, "the pup will be the last of you I'll have."

My eyes shot open to find her already looking at me with watery eyes and trembling lips. Did she have real feelings for me—after all I'd done? I couldn't let this go. "It doesn't have to be the last," I whispered, feeling my heart clench painfully.

"What does that even mean?" Her brows pulled inward like she was fighting a sob.

"We... could be fated, Ragna. Even if we're not... you could be my chosen... if you wanted." I couldn't believe I'd gotten those words out of me. That was fucking monumental. That was more difficult than any battle I'd ever fought. It was more nerve-racking than facing off with the most dominant alpha. I tried to keep it together, but I felt myself break into a cold sweat. "We could... make another pup." I didn't prefer that option, but a good king put all on the table for review.

I wasn't sure how I thought she'd react, but I hadn't expected her to deflate and stare hopelessly at me. "Why do you think we're fated? And why do you think you'll still want me after the bond breaks? The general told me the very same thing. You're all looking through tainted glass."

I frowned and growled. "Don't compare me to the general, Ragna. That deeply upsets me." I rubbed my eyes and looked at her again. "The bond doesn't rearrange your face, Ragna. It doesn't change your personality. It doesn't suddenly give you qualities that I lo—like in a female. It just intensifies what's already there. It's there to let you know that you found the right one so you can stop wasting your time with the wrong ones.

"As for your first question? You tell me. What did you experience when we touched for the first time? Forget the monstrous shit I did for a second. What did you feel? What did you sense?"

She put her hand to her quivering lips as she contemplated. "I smelled your scent... wood shavings and almonds. I felt the tingles, and they were intense. They felt... really good. I was scared you'd scent my arousal..." Her voice faded with embarrassment as she spoke.

"Ok, now how about any other unmated males? What was meeting them like?" I asked, allowing her to look away if the topic embarrassed her so much.

"Just some tingles, a little automatic arousal but... underwhelming. I couldn't really make out the details of their scents," she murmured, curling a little tighter like she was trying to reject the truth.

"That doesn't tell you anything, Ragna?" I asked her and reached to stroke her hair.

"I just thought it was because the bond was spread out unevenly among everyone," she admitted slowly.

"No, I don't think so," I said, shaking my head. There was something we were both avoiding, and that was how we felt about each other. We danced around it but were too afraid to touch it. I grabbed her hand to hold it in mine, and we stared at each other for a while. I was terrified to go first. What right did I have to ask her to stay with me? I'd abused her. Try as I did to make up for that, I couldn't erase the past.

But I wanted her so. I wanted her so much it hurt. My heart had been in a vise for days, waiting to discover which way the handle would turn.

I kissed her knuckles softly and asked, "What do you think of me, Ragna?" I waited for the handle to turn in the wrong direction. I waited for it to crush me.

"I can't answer that," she replied, blinking away tears. "If I say what I want, and it doesn't happen, it will kill me." She blinked away another tear, scrunched up her face, and cried, "It will kill me!" She buried her face into the bed to escape reality.

I think I had my answer, and the vise let up the pressure on my heart. My lungs released my held breath. My mind cleared. "Do you want to know how I feel about you?" I asked gently and rubbed her back in slow, soothing circles.

She shook her head and came up for air. "No, I couldn't... I couldn't handle. I... can't. I can't..." She was a mess for words, just like me when I tried to share my feelings with her. I kept rubbing her back and stared sadly at her tormented figure.

"Then do you want me to show you how I feel about you?" I asked in a softer voice, moving my hand behind her head. She stared uncertainly at me.

"What do you me—" she began, but I pulled her to me and pressed our lips together. My cupping hand kept our mouths locked, and I wrapped my other arm around her waist to squeeze her body into mine. I poured all my love into that kiss, wishing she could feel every drop. Wishing she knew that I'd always be there for her. Wishing she could believe that I'd do anything for her.

Her hands rested timidly on my chest and slowly gripped my shirt. She opened her mouth, and I deepened the kiss, wanting to give her all I had. Maybe, just maybe, she could detect my love for her between my lips. Maybe I could show her enough to give her hope... so we could both fight harder.

She pulled back first, rosy-cheeked and short of breath. Licking her lips, she whispered, "I... I'll decline the blessing. I'll believe in my own strength."

I crushed her into my arms, not wanting her to see the tears of joy and relief that sprang into my eyes.

agna

I was a nervous wreck after Zorian's physical confession and got completely stuck in my head. I reluctantly pulled myself from his sublime, affectionate cradling and hurried downstairs to reject the Earth Gods' offer. I had to do it as soon as possible, for Zorian as well. I needed that crossroad removed from my life.

Hello, Ragna, the voices of the Earth Gods said in unison.

"Hi, Earth Gods. I… have to decline the blessing. I hope You are not offended, but I simply cannot bring myself to do it," I confessed, drained from the whole ordeal.

We are not offended. You don't want to lose the pup of the male you love. That is wolf nature. Our daughter would greatly approve, so We approve, They said magnanimously.

It was shattering to hear someone else speak of my feelings for Zorian. Keeping it locked inside me had made me feel safer, but now it was a bleeding wound I hadn't received yet. I cringed at the stinging pain in my chest and changed the topic.

"Why did it take so long for you to find me, Earth Gods? I was traveling for five years," I asked through the gods' heart.

It was pointless until We knew where Our daughter was. We suspect that the lycan used a witch to keep Her in poor vessels until he placed Her in the right one. We can't find Her if She's stuffed into an incompatible body.

A chill seeped into me, and my grip on the stone tightened. "What happens when a god is placed in a… poor vessel?" Did I want to know? Did I really?

They die. They are destroyed from the inside out.

I sat down hard in one of the dining room chairs. "H-how long does it take the poor vessel to d-die?"

Ragna, don't ask these questions, Trail begged, deeply upset. *I don't want to know! You don't want to know. We don't need to know!*

About a month, the Earth Gods answered. I placed a hand over my mouth to muffle a sob. Was that about sixty? Had sixty wolves been used as sacrifices to keep the Moon Goddess trapped? Had sixty wolves burned from the inside out so Eysteinn could… what? Mate me? No. Whatever all this was, it was much bigger. I ran to the sink to throw up my lunch.

I panted between heaves and closed my eyes, fighting tears. I didn't want to cry! I wanted to get angry! We were going to get justice for those wolves. Eysteinn would pay for their deaths!

I was startled from my reeling thoughts by Koray wandering into the kitchen. He pulled some light snacks out and gestured for me to eat. He must have heard me.

"Thanks, Koray," I said gratefully after rinsing my mouth. I eased myself back into a chair and sucked on the corner of a cracker. I froze and eyed the cracker suspiciously. Where did Koray get these?

"The pantry refills," he volunteered with an empathetic expression of disbelief. "Yeah, I know; it's crazy." His head turned, and we both watched Zorian descend the stairs at a brisk pace.

"I think we're good to go," I told him. "There's no need to stay here any longer. I got everything I needed… and then some." I sighed and continued to nibble on the mysterious moon cracker.

"Alright," he said and slid a glass of water over to me. "Get something in your stomach, mama wolf, and we'll wake the general. He's had a shitty day."

I was surprised to hear sympathy toward General Belenus. Whatever they talked about must have cleared the air. I was dying to ask, but maybe it was best I stayed out of it.

Zorian stood behind me and rubbed my shoulders soothingly. His new nickname for me was sweet, and it made me feel closer to him, like we were proper mates. The thought of anyone calling the brutal Alpha of Alphas "papa lycan" was a whole new level of comedy, though. I couldn't do it. I'd die laughing.

Koray looked from Zorian to me in pleasant surprise. "Congratulations! I wish you a safe delivery, Sky-Blessed." He raised his glass of water in a toast, and I smiled, mirroring his sweet gesture. I was growing very fond of him, and I hoped that he'd get a mate just as sweet. He deserved it.

I told Koray and Zorian everything I'd discussed with the Earth Gods. It was going well until I got to the very end, where I shared the distressing news about the poor vessels. Koray looked sick, but Zorian froze, and his mask returned.

"Zorian?" I asked, hesitantly reaching for his hand. He turned and stormed out of the house. Koray and I stared sadly at the table, listening to Zorian yell and scream outside in despair. I wiped tears from my face, feeling horrible for triggering Zorian's trauma. Eysteinn continued to kill his people under his watch. Part of me wished that I hadn't told him, but he needed to know. That was the curse of being a leader.

General Belenus walked in, obviously startled awake by the commotion. He looked at us, then out to where Zorian was raging. A tree fell near the house, and I jumped in my chair. Great goddess, that was close!

I told Belenus everything that had happened, and his features turned grim when I mentioned the sacrificed vessels. I stood to go to Zorian, but Belenus shook his head and eased me back into the chair.

"I'll talk to him," he said calmly and walked out of the goddess's home.

"What is going on with those two?" Koray asked, and I raised my palms in the air.

"Don't ask me. They're both army males. Maybe they bonded over a shared love of military rations," I suggested, laying my head on my arms. My joke belied my self-loathing and the anxiety I felt for Zorian. "We're going to leave soon, Koray. If you have anything you want to pack, now would be a good time to do it." I gave him a supportive smile, and he jumped out of his chair to race upstairs.

Belenus and Zorian returned without mentioning the incident. Zorian grabbed his bag and was ready to go, but he looked miserable. I timidly approached him, hoping he wasn't mad at me. His eyes softened when he saw the worried look on my face, and he kissed the top of my head. I nearly melted in relief and fell forward into his chest with a thud. He let out a weak chuckle. Today had been too stressful for us.

We walked out, and Koray offered to open the door back to the fae realm. It wasn't at all how Zorian opened the door. A slight breeze brought something strange; everything within three feet of us turned a shade of blue, like we were out at night. My eyes burned when I glanced at the brilliant sunset landscape outside the moonlit circle. The contrast in brightness was painful, so I rubbed my strained eyes and kept them on the dark-blue ground. I was more than ready to leave the Realm of the Gods.

We passed through the door, and I was bombarded once more by the heat and light of the Summer Court. It was getting late, so we agreed to spend one last night in the fae realm. Belenus escorted Zorian and me to a guest chamber and promised to send up some food. He had no qualms this time about us sharing a room.

Zorian collapsed onto the enormous four-poster bed. I crawled after him but settled his head on my lap, where I idly combed his white hair with my fingers. I didn't know what to say. Eysteinn was a monster and had found a way to keep hurting Zorian.

"What can I do for you?" I asked gently as I stroked his soft hair. His brows were drawn in, and his eyes were shut tight, like he was trying to keep nightmares at bay. He slowly opened his eyes and looked down at the palm of his hand. He stared at it for a while, and I tucked his hair behind his ear so I could gaze at his beautiful, strong, tanned cheeks and jawline.

"Do you really want to do something that would help me? It would help me a lot," he asked, his eyes not wavering from his hand.

I kept stroking his head and hummed. "Of course I do," I answered and stroked his cheek with a thumb. I was getting too affectionate. Goddess help me, I couldn't help it. This male was a magnet for my love. It was too hard to fight.

"Let me make you pack, Ragna. Let me bring you into my lycan pack. I want you to join the King's Pack." His countenance was calm—his tone decisive.

Trail gasped.

"Wh-why would that help?" I asked nervously. That would make it harder to run away if my heart broke.

"Because then I could protect two more wolves, or a wolf and a lycan, whichever our pup is. I failed to protect sixty wolves, and it's eating me alive. If you won't have me as a mate after this, Ragna, then at least you'd have my pack to protect you. I want to make sure you're cared for if you won't let me do it personally."

I was speechless and moved beyond belief. Was his affection so unconditional?

Trail growled at me. *I know you're scared, Ragna, but I'm getting sick of you second-guessing our mate.*

When the males got bonded to us, the people we thought we knew tried to kill us! Kill us, Trail! Bonds are dangerous! They change people! Do you really know for a fact that Zorian won't go running off if his fated mate shows up? Are you so certain he won't leave us in the dust? I snapped back at her, and tears threatened to spill.

"Fighting with Trail?" Zorian asked, and I realized he was looking up at me. I nodded and rubbed my eyes. He reached up to tenderly cup my cheek, and my mind cleared a little.

"I'm giving my trauma too much power again," I murmured to myself. I stared down into Zorian's beautiful red eyes and sighed. "I accept your invitation into the King's Pack."

He still appeared tired, but his face lit up at my words. He jumped off the bed and dragged me to the balcony where the sun was setting. Ah, here? Goddess, this was romantic. A cool breeze meandered around me, taking the edge off the summer heat. Zorian stood tall and straightened his hair, which made me burst into laughter. He regarded me with incredulity, but amusement glimmered in his eyes.

"Sorry." I cleared my throat and stood tall. The tiniest smirk graced his lips before he put on his kingliest façade and claimed one of my hands.

"Do you, Ragna Rhydderch, promise to allow the King's Pack to spoil you and your pup rotten until the end of time?"

I protested instantly. "Those are not the traditional lines for initia—" I tried to pull my hand away, but the male's grip was like stone.

"I believe there is only one king on this balcony, Ragna. Are you challenging me?"

"N-no!" I sputtered, waving my free hand in a horrified denial.

"Good. Now we have to start all over again." He released an irritated—but playful—growl.

"No, it's ok. I remember what you said! I accept the spoiling of myself and my pup," I recalled hastily, wanting to get through this initiation with my sanity intact.

"Do you promise to allow the King's Pack to provide for you and your pup and ensure your safety?"

"I promise to allow the King's Pack to provide for me and my pup and ensure my safety."

"And finally, if there is a matter that causes you unhappiness, do you promise to bring it to the king's attention and not suffer in silence?"

Oh goddess, that one was sweet.

"I promise that if something is causing me unhappiness, I will go bother His Majesty." I pouted, failing to hide my smile. Zorian wrinkled his nose and rocked his free hand in deliberation.

"I suppose that's good enough," he said with a wry expression. He cut a line into the palm of his hand with a claw, and I cut a similar line into my palm. Finally, he took my bloody hand in his.

"I, Alpha Zorian, accept you, Ragna Rhydderch, into the King's Pack."

I felt a glowing, warm tether fall into a spot within me that had been collecting cobwebs and tears for far too long. I stumbled and grabbed at my chest. Warmth. Belonging. More comfort spilled into me, and I realized it was Zorian. He just stood there, holding me and welcoming me home. It felt so right. Maybe he was my fated mate after all. Could I allow myself to be vulnerable?

I looked up at him, feeling breathless from hope and desire. He leaned in and brushed a rough thumb under my chin, tilting my lips up toward his. My heart thumped ardently when I spied the affection, longing, and tenderness in his burgundy gaze. Was he going to kiss me again?

Trail! Are you there? a new, gruff voice said in my head through a pack mind-link. Zorian and I had frozen in place, nearly nose to nose.

Oh my goddess, is that you, Spine?

Holy fuck! We can talk now!

I cannot wait to see you again, my big, bad, dominant, alpha daddy!

I don't care what we gotta do to figure it out. I'm going to do so many nasty things to you!

Zorian's eyes went wide.

Oh! Do tell!

First of al—

"Spine!" Zorian roared. "Take it to a private link, for fuck's sake!"

Chapter 30

Zorian

Well, Spine had absolutely fucked up the mood. Here I was, laying my kingdom at Ragna's feet under the glow of a fae sunset, when he comes charging into the local pack mind-link looking to get horny with Trail.

I sighed and scooped Ragna's beautiful body into my arms. The only thing that was making me feel better was her, and I was worn down to the bone. I pulled the bedsheets back and set her down on the floor. I removed all my clothes and placed my hands on her tunic, sending her a silent plea through my eyes. She unbuttoned it without a word, and I helped her undress. She didn't seem stressed or confused; she just let me lead her.

I slipped into bed and held my arms out for her, once again asking for her help. Her face softened, and she slid into my embrace, allowing me to hang on to her as I desperately fought to keep from crying. Crying because I'd become king to never allow something like Eysteinn to happen again. Yet he happened. It wasn't something like Eysteinn. It was Eysteinn. I'd failed. I gritted my teeth and squeezed my eyes, trying to will away the tears. I failed.

I felt better when we woke. Ragna had held me all night without saying a word. She let me cry and bleed out the pain until we fell asleep. Maybe I would have been embarrassed a week ago, but I was just grateful for her now.

General Belenus escorted us to the stone platform in the courtyard where we'd arrived. "Are you certain you still wish to come with us, General?" I asked, adjusting one of the straps on my backpack.

He nodded and jerked his head in Koray's direction. "I want to personally make sure this kid gets home in one piece."

Belenus had been really fucked up yesterday. After he'd broken down over feeling responsible for Koray, we butted heads over Ragna. It wasn't surprising; we were two dominant males. We were two leaders with thrones hanging over our heads instead of beneath us to carry our weight. It was different for Belenus, though. He'd be forced to marry in less than a month if he didn't find his fated mate. The queen, his mother, had lost patience with him. Apparently, a hundred years was too long for her. On top of that, his intended was a beautiful but corrupt monster.

I felt for him, I really did, but he would not get the mother of my pup. I would also not have my offspring grow up in the fae realm. When I asked him what the queen would think of her son marrying a she-wolf carrying the Lycan King's pup, he nearly collapsed. Ragna had been his last hope and one he'd thought was too good to be true, so he'd pulled out all the stops. He was right; she had been too good to be true. Before he'd collapsed into a depressed sleep, I promised him that if he put the work in, he'd always have an ally in the lycans. It was all I could offer. He wasn't a bad man, but he did have more growing up to do.

"Do you know if there's a fae gate that's close to where we need to go, General?" I asked. "Perhaps we could get dropped off before you return Koray?"

The general strode to one of the soldiers guarding the gate and held his hand out expectantly. The soldier relinquished a regional map. I stood next to the general and searched for the location Ragna had shared.

"There." I pointed to a gate. "That's almost on top of it. Can we be dropped off there?"

"Easily," the general replied evenly. He passed the map back to the guard and marched up the stairs to the platform. I clutched Ragna close, remembering how wobbly she'd gotten last time. The same black void closed in on us and dissipated.

We stood on a high, grassy clifftop, surrounded by a circle of small tree stumps. I tightened my grip on Ragna when she wavered for a moment, then I marched to the edge of the cliff, unable to believe what I was seeing.

At the very bottom of the cliff was a lantern-lit entrance, where dozens of cloaked figures were coming and going. I squatted to stay out of sight. None of them seemed to bother with masks, which made sense if they thought they were the only ones here. What really shocked me was the entire small army of my men that was hidden on a cliff just below us. What the fuck? My eyes landed on my beta, who was bent over in a deep discussion with one of our generals.

Beta Rude! I hissed in a mind-link. *What is going on? Why are you here with an army?*

My beta's head shot up, but he couldn't find me, so I threw a pebble that conked him on the head. He grabbed his head, mouthed an "ow!" and looked up in surprise. I waved sarcastically at him and waited for his reply. Ragna stuck her head over the edge of the cliff and waited with me.

Hi Beta! she chirped impishly over the pack link to him. Rude looked doubly stunned and held up a finger so he could get his bearings.

Oh gods. Ok... Two things! the beta began. *Our troops returned from the investigation to report that a small army has been developing here, so we're here to wipe them out.*

Ok, but why are you here, Rude? I asked, not knowing why he had to personally lead this raid. That was work for our ranked officers.

I frowned when I felt my beta switch to a private mind-link. What was going on here? *I got a note back from the Lunar Coven from a coven mother named Mwezi. She said I had to be here for the raid.*

She's known for interfering even though she's not supposed to, but her actions have always been for our benefit. I would lean toward trusting what she said.

Well, here's the thing. Our soldiers returned with some wolf fur, hoping to identify who was being held there. They could see restraints and cages, but only one seemed to be occupied—at least, alive.

Pain flooded my chest. Sixty bodies. How many had been laid to rest? *Ragna said her childhood friend was taken by Eysteinn. We verified she was the Moon Goddess's vessel. Rakel, her name is. She should still be alive.*

Ah, he replied, but I sensed he wasn't telling me everything.

What is it, Rude? What aren't you saying? I pressed, more curious than annoyed.

I don't know yet. I examined the hairs, and I felt I needed to be here. Mwezi just gave me a better excuse to do it.

Huh. *Alright, well, what's your plan?*

We'll hit at nightfall, but we're trying to sort out a distraction. Zorian, Asmin is in there—willingly.

What? I roared, and Rude winced. He paced nervously and ran his fingers through his blond hair.

Yeah, she's quite cozy with Eysteinn, actually. He cringed, as though expecting lightning to strike him. Oh, the betrayal ran deeper than words could ever express. The thought that I'd also once shared the same female with Eysteinn made me want to vomit. My claws dug into the cliffside, and rage shuddered through my bones. By the time I was done with Eysteinn, not even the gods would be able to identify his remains.

"When are you attacking?" General Belenus asked from behind me. I growled and scooted back from the edge, still livid.

"We're going in toni—" I froze when two wolves trotted around a narrow pathway on the mountainside. Ragna scrambled to her feet and raced toward them. She tackled the red one I recognized as Soley and brought the black wolf in for a nuzzle. I got up and walked over to the reunion with Belenus and Koray, really getting the sense that the gods were looking aggressively over our shoulders.

The she-wolves shifted into their human forms, and they all embraced. "What are you doing here?" Ragna squealed quietly to the two young females.

"We went looking for Rakel after she'd been taken. I can't believe you're here too!" the midnight-tressed female said, and little Soley nodded aggressively. Their youthful, firm, feminine parts jiggled from their enthusiastic motions, and I turned to see how the non-shifters were handling the casual wolf nudity. Oh, this was going to be brilliant.

General Belenus's face was bright red and frozen in fear, but when he saw me glance at him with a raised eyebrow, he swiftly turned his back to the females. Koray was also staring at the naked females, gaping but not in fear. He looked like he was having the best day of his life. Belenus smacked him upside the head to make him turn away, and I covered my mouth, trying to hold my laughter over the general's extreme embarrassment.

The she-wolves were unaffected by the drama regarding them. Ragna was the only shifter female I'd ever met who truly shied from exposure. Fae women were graceful and charming, but I doubted the general was prepared for the thrilling, wild enticement of she-wolves. I was almost convinced he wouldn't be able to handle one.

"So, King Zorian," the general said, clearing his throat and adjusting his pants discreetly. "You said you'd be joining the raid tonight?"

"Yes, General Belenus," I answered flatly, having the absolute time of my life right now. I crossed my arms and waited gleefully for it.

"If needed, I'd be honored to offer my sword arm tonight. The Moon Goddess is important to us fae as well."

I bet he'd be willing to offer another body part too, Spine snickered.

Oh, there you are. Are you done talking smut with Trail? I thought you'd never come up for air.

Pfft, never! I just wanted to watch the she-wolves take the general down a peg or two.

"The Lycan King accepts your generous offer, General Belenus," I said, hiding a smirk behind a hand.

Koray's hand shot up in the air. "I volunteer as well!" he stated quietly but enthusiastically, trying to turn around to get another peek at the she-wolves.

Ragna

We hiked down to where the beta's army was hidden from the eyes of the cult. Soley held my left hand while Hekla gripped my right. I almost felt complete sitting in the quiet camp with my she-wolves, but Rakel's absence was so very loud. Once we'd settled into a corner, it had taken me over several hours to tell my she-wolves what had transpired. I whimpered with deep homesickness, and they embraced me once again, cooing and humming while petting my hair.

"Rakel's the only one I hadn't seen since my banishment, but I missed you all terribly," I shared, squeezing their hands tightly. "How did things go at the pack after... after the first year passed?"

"Quiet," Soley answered. "No one wanted to take any mates. Wolves were scared. Some thought we were being punished for something or that the gods had outright abandoned us. There'd be a pup or two outside of matings, but it's like time froze for our pack. Your parents are fine. They're sad, but they're fine. We visit them often." My eyes watered at their thoughtfulness, and I hugged them both with abandon.

"I can only hope that by this time tomorrow, it'll all be fixed," I whispered.

"If not tomorrow, the next day," Hekla countered soothingly. "It will happen. We have too many strong elements on our side to lose the fight."

"You are so levelheaded, Hekla. If only you both had travelled with me. You could have helped me keep these males in line." I sighed dramatically and rolled my head in the direction of Zorian, Rudesind, and Belenus. Koray had always behaved. He was exempt from my playful scorn. Hekla laughed and eyed the men.

"I wish! This really is the most attention we've received from males since the Moon Goddess disappeared," Soley informed, leaning over to speak in a low, conspiratorial voice. "I would otherwise never be so brazen!"

"I'm really enjoying how much these non-shifters are suffering over absolutely nothing," Hekla said, leaning back to take another look at Belenus and Koray.

"Well, it'd probably help if you two got dressed," I replied with an entertained grin, knowing that would not happen. "My offer of my spare tunics still stands, my she-wolves."

"We definitely are not interested in getting dressed if this is the reaction we get," Hekla said, arching her back in a seemingly innocent stretch and sighing. I heard Belenus choke, and I spun to see him sputtering over his water canteen. We desperately fought to hold our giggles.

"Maybe wait until after he drinks, Hekla, or we'll be a male short for tonight," I admonished.

"You might be a male short anyway, if Hekla gets her way." Soley gasped, unable to catch her breath through tears of mirth. She sent a wink over to Koray as she giggled, who blushed fiercely but looked much more excited than Belenus. The chuckling was starting to make my stomach sore. Oh, how I missed these two females. Soon Rakel would join us. I would make that happen!

I got up when Soley and Hekla decided to go torture General Belenus. They skipped up to him and started asking questions. A point system of who could get the most direct eye contact, if at all, had likely been established. Underneath all the gaiety, the game was just a distraction. It was almost unbearable sitting and waiting for nightfall. We wanted to save Rakel right now! It itched fiercely under our skins.

I wandered over to Zorian and Rudesind. "How goes the preparations?" I murmured.

"Not brilliant," Zorian said. "It's too hard to get a sense of the inside layout. If there was more than one entrance, it might be easier, but it's too risky sending a soldier undercover. Koray's familiar with witchwork, and he knows several ways they could detect an intruder."

"I coul—" I began, but Zorian interrupted me.

"I know what you're about to say, but I really don't want you going in there alone," he interrupted and placed his hand on my arm. His brows were drawn, forming deep creases in his worried face.

I sighed and placed my hand over his. "Do you remember, Zorian, what you said to me a while back? You said that my time would come. Well, my time has been here for a while now, and I need to do what I'm meant to do. And guess what? If I'm captured, you have the perfect distraction right there!" I smiled up at him, trying to comfort the massive lycan. He looked scared, but I could see the acceptance and respect in his deep red eyes. We were here for a larger purpose than either one of us.

I went through my bag and grabbed only what I needed. Zorian hovered anxiously, seeming quite keen to stick by my side now that I'd be going into the cult's hideout alone. I attached the quiver to my belt and strung my grandfather's bow. I held the lunaite and the Earth Gods' Heart in each hand and considered them. I needed both, but what if I got caught? I didn't want to lose them. I glanced up at Zorian and twisted my lips in thought.

"I need you to tell me if this looks weird or suspicious," I said and moved to a more private location. I placed the lunaite into my bra under my left breast. The Earth Gods' Heart went into my bra under my right breast. "Can you tell I'm hiding things in my bra?" I held my arms out so he could get a good look. This was absurd, but so long as they didn't strip search me, it should work.

Zorian came forward with an inscrutable expression and grabbed both my breasts through my tunic. "I meant by outward appearance." My face heated, and I swallowed heavily, looking up at him for a response.

"One minute. I'm just trying to get you your answer," he said seriously. I stared up at him as he continued to grope me. He'd put on a face that suggested he was thinking, but I knew better. His cock was doing the thinking for him.

"Well?" I asked, getting progressively more aroused. I'd have to squeeze my thighs together soon if he didn't stop. The moment I detected dampness between my legs, he backed me into the rock wall and slipped a hand into my clothes to wrap his tingling fingers around my breast. When he stroked my nipple, my core throbbed, and I bit back a groan.

He leaned into me, practically dripping with tension. "Do you even realize what I'm going through right now—as a fucking alpha? Allowing the unmated mother of my pup to stroll right into the enemy's arms?" he said through clenched teeth, his dark, fiery eyes burning into mine. "My body, this alpha in me, is screaming and clawing at me to fuck you until your sweet sex overflows with my cum. It wants you to reek of my scent. It wants me to hold you down and dig my canines into you, penetrating your flesh and marking you so deeply and completely with my venom that there's no chance anyone could take you away from me," he growled into my ear, puffing out frustrated breaths.

"I-I'm sorry you're suffering so," I replied on a breath, trying not to pant from his intensity. I held a whine back as his invading hand rubbed in little circles. "The gods ch-chose us for a reason, Zorian. Trust me to do my job like I trust you to do yours." Shockingly, he sighed and withdrew his hand from my tunic. I was expecting him to turn into a sex-crazed alpha for a moment. This was unusual. He fell to his knees, wrapped his arms around my waist, and rested his forehead against my belly.

"Don't get hurt, Ragna," he begged. "Just... don't get hurt. I couldn't take it."

"I'll be fine. Everything will turn out fine," I comforted. "We'll get everyone their mates back. All will be as it should... but I have a question."

He tilted his head up to look at me with a concerned frown. "What's that?"

"Who are you?" I asked, unable to keep the smile from ruining my straight-faced inquiry. He buried his face into my belly and laughed quietly, his broad shoulders bobbing with his chuckles. He tightened his grip around my waist and nuzzled into me.

"I don't know," he groaned. "Just a foolish lycan who didn't know a good thing in a she-wolf when he saw it right away. A king prostrated and at a subject's beck and call. An alpha submitting to an ex-rogue. Just a dumb male who doesn't deserve the kindness shown to him by the mother of his pup. I'm so sorry, Ragna. I'm so sorry for every injury I've given you. I hate myself for it."

Great goddesses, how he's changed. I ran my fingers through his hair and thought of words spoken not that long ago. "Zorian, you remember that god who hates you?"

I felt him tense, and he nodded, mumbling, "The Sun God... wish I could forget." I scrunched my nose and fought to restrain a giggle.

"He told me to trust in you. He said that most souls could defrost. I don't quite see it that way—you being frozen, I mean. You just had a deep, bleeding wound that took a long time to start healing. You were always this male, Zorian. Your anger was a cast to protect the broken bones of your heart. Know that I forgive you. I wish for you to stop apologizing for what's already transpired. Will you grant my wish?"

"I would grant anything for you, Ragna," he said quietly. "This may be the hardest one yet, but I will grant it." He looked up at me with affection and longing. It wasn't just written in his gleaming red eyes. His whole face, his whole body, was laying every last ounce of his sincerity at my feet.

He got back to his feet, cupped my face, and placed his alluring lips on mine. I sighed and closed my eyes in rapture. This was true bliss. His warm lips pressed and massaged against mine as though he spoke of his devotion. The more I kissed him, the more I was pulled into the dream of him being my fated mate. I couldn't speak of it now to him, but how could this be anything but? Whether or not I was ready to take the risk, I already loved him—hopelessly.

Chapter 31

Ragna

Everyone was huddled in a circle, discussing problematic scenarios, like what to do if they set up a dampener and disrupted mind-linking. Since I was supposed to let Zorian know if I got captured, I relied on the link to work. The Sky Gods even borrowed Hekla to say they'd risk coming to find me if a dampener was created.

Once night arrived, and I covered my scent the best I could, Zorian escorted me down a path that would lead me straight to the cult's front door. When I turned to say a short goodbye to him, he cupped my face with both of his large, rough hands and growled quietly. "You go in there, and as soon as you get a sense of the layout, you come right back out. Is that understood?" His burgundy eyes were a vicious purple in the blue cloak of the night. I nodded and gave him one last hug. He squeezed me tight, huffed in frustration, and let me go with a worried, unhappy face.

I stuck to the cliff walls, making sure I was strictly within the starlit shadows. I found it ironic that the moon's very glow could sabotage the rescue of its goddess. I listened near the door and waited for whoever was about to come out to do just that. A hooded cultist popped out and closed the door behind them. Sensing no one else nearby, I opened the door and squeezed in as fast as possible.

I let out a quiet sigh of relief. Now that I was indoors, I was safe from the moon's sabotaging rays. Now I just had to avoid bumping into bodies.

I tilted my head back in awe. The inside of the mountain was carved into a large chamber that could fit hundreds of individuals. There were ramps of stone that curled up along the wall and fed into dark hallways. Several torches burned in sconces, but most of the light seemed to be from small, bright flames that required neither wick nor wax to burn— obviously witchwork. I followed the flames farther into the chamber and noticed large, circular pools of water toward the end. Several individuals were standing at one pool or another, and a chill trickled down my spine when I noticed images in the water. Were they scrying? What were they watching?

One tall woman, who absolutely reeked, stirred a primal fear in me, and I decided it'd be a bad idea to get closer to these people if they were witches. I had no idea what they were capable of, but I felt very exposed, and I backed away with a spooked, pounding heart.

The rock under my left breast grew warm when I moved toward the right ramp, and I wondered if the lunaite was reacting to the goddess's proximity. She must be in this direction. I wanted to take it out, but I didn't want to risk losing it.

Yes, this is very odd, Trail said. *Navigating with your bosom. When I think about natural dowsing rods, I'm not imagining the female of the species.*

Welcome back, I said with a silent chuckle. My face wanted to contort into a smirk because that's what I imagined Zorian's face doing.

Sorry, she said bashfully. *I hope you didn't think I abandoned you. We started talking and just… never stopped.*

Not at all. Your happiness is my happiness, Trail, I said. It was mostly true. We both had our own needs. That was just life as a shifter.

I reached the top of the ramp and looked down the dark hallway. It was riddled with doors that hinted at these being private chambers. At the end, it seemed to open into another large space that split into two ramps. I grimaced, hoping that this place didn't end up being an awful maze.

I tiptoed down the hall and looked over the edge of the path. The decline spiraled down into what promised to be a detention area. The lunaite was getting warmer, and I decided it was time to leave. I had a good enough idea, and the goddess was definitely here somewhere.

I spun around and nearly walked straight into the tall, cadaverous woman. I held my breath as she stood still. Her subtle, sickly trembling forced her massive tangle of black hair to jitter like it was a dying animal. Could she hear me? Smell me?

Not even Trail risked speaking to me, her terror as palpable as mine.

I stared into her bloodshot eyes as they drifted. They slid from where I had been looking to where I was standing. I bit back a whimper and wondered if she could hear the movement of my jaw clenching. Her gaze drifted up until it looked straight into my eyes. Electricity splintered up my body from sheer horror. She could see me! No one had ever been able to see me!

She screamed rabidly into my face, sending spit flying, and grabbed me by my hair. I was taken completely off guard and terror throttled me, nearly making my bladder release. How had she seen me? She yanked me down into the dirt and proceeded to drag me along the floor by my hair. I extended my claws and slashed at her arms, but my hair was too long, and I couldn't reach her. I tried to sever my hair, but she jerked me violently, opened a door, and threw me into a small, damp chamber. I landed on my belly, and the wind was knocked out of me.

Zorian! I yelled, my wits catching up to me. *Someone saw me! I think it's a wi—*

Ragna, she's grabbing somethi—

Ragna? Wh—

My shout, Trail's warning, and Zorian's interjection were disrupted when she crawled onto my back, ripped my tunic, and smacked her palm down between my shoulder blades. I grimaced and seized as my body heated, like something had stoked a fever. My head swam, and I tried to claw the woman off me, but I couldn't reach. She let out an ear-piercing shriek, and cultists swarmed into the room, grabbing me by all my limbs. I writhed and mauled whoever I could reach, but if I sent one person away to bleed out, another came to replace them just as fast. My leggings warmed and dampened. Had I peed myself?

I was dragged out of the room and taken to the pools in the main chamber, my bow and quiver thrown unceremoniously to the side. The area swarmed with pure madness. Cultists rushed every which way, streaming from the bowels of the hideout like termites. They poured through the only door to leave—to where the roar of battle raged.

My eyes caught on some very large rocks that I swore hadn't been there earlier. I narrowed my eyes and realized that Wane had managed to infiltrate the building through all the chaos. The godling had cleverly rolled in mud to look less... lunar. Now It was inching Its way up the ramp through the throngs of distracted, cloaked figures.

A deep, delighted gasp echoed in the chamber, making all the hairs on the back of my neck stand on end. A large male marched down the other ramp with a delighted expression on his face. He wasn't as tall as Zorian, nor as bulky. And though he was muscular, he looked unhealthy, like he'd chosen one day to dine solely on rotten meat. His dark hair was aged with smears of grey at the temples, and his greedy grin stretched his trimmed, salt-and-pepper beard.

When the cavern air shifted and blew his scent to me, it confirmed my suspicion. This was a lycan. This had to be Eysteinn Burchard. I had no doubt about it. "Hello, Ragna," he greeted in a honeyed voice. "Caught sneaking in?" He chuckled and walked right up to me.

My nose twitched; I could barely keep myself from snarling at the filthy lycan who'd severely hurt my male. I was pushed closer to one of the pools, and Eysteinn nodded at the witch who'd exposed me. The frightening creature came forward and crouched at the pool by my feet. She leaned down to do something to the water, but I couldn't tell what.

"You look lovely tonight," Eysteinn said and raked his gaze down my body until it landed on my sex. He frowned. "You're bleeding, Ragna."

I looked down and gasped.

No...

Oh goddess, no!

It hadn't been urine. It had been blood—a lot of it. "No!" Tears sprang into my eyes.

I became wild.

I thrashed. I screamed.

I fought to reach the decrepit woman so I could gut her. "You killed my pup! I'll kill you! I'll rip you to pieces! You're dead! Do you hear me?" I sobbed and writhed, unable to get free.

A hand wrapped around my arm, and the tingles brought more bile into my throat than pleasure. "Calm yourself, mate. We'll make another pup tonight," Eysteinn murmured into my ear. I turned and snapped at him with my teeth, barely keeping my sanity intact. My teeth and claws lengthened, sore from distress and itching to kill.

Eysteinn glanced at the door, listening to the sounds of battle leaking through it. He smiled, and I felt a spike of uneasiness. Zorian said he was a nasty strategist, and I didn't like the look on his face. "Bind and gag her," he ordered, still staring at the door. "Connect to the unmated now. Leave out the ones outside."

I stopped struggling when they stuffed a gag into my mouth. I was worn and needed to rest a moment. I tried the pack link, but it was missing. I tried to reach the Earth Gods, but that option seemed muted as well. I was on my own until the king's army broke through the line of cultists. I knew I didn't have the luxury of waiting for that to happen.

The witch backed away from the pool, releasing an unsettling clicking noise that made my skin crawl. The pool flickered to life, and I felt eyes on me. I couldn't see them, but I could feel them. Hundreds of thousands were on the other side. Eysteinn grabbed my arm roughly and pushed me to the edge of the pool. I braced myself, but he merely leaned me forward, forcing me to look into it.

"Hello, every unmated in the kingdom! Good evening. If you don't recognize me, my name is Eysteinn Burchard. If you recall, I've served you all during the last war. As you can see here," he said, fisting my hair and pushing me closer to the water, "I have your fated mate. This is Ragna, and she's your only fated mate, but she's in my hands.

"I'm here to serve you again. The Moon Goddess has left us, and it's time we renounce Her ways. You think She was there to bring you joy, but it was all manipulation. Fate and Her conspire against you. It matters not if you don't believe me.

"I will generously allow you to have your last chance at a fated mate if you gather at the capitol and take over the castle in my name. If you fail on the first day"—he sneered and began unbuttoning my tunic—"you will all watch me rape your mate." He pointed to the blood between my legs and tacked on a disgusting lie. "As you can see, I am not a gentle lover. Any subsequent days that you are unsuccessful, I will remove a finger or a limb from her."

He yanked on my hair, making me groan in pain through the gag. "Do you hear that noise?" he yelled into the pool and pointed at the door. "Do you hear that fighting outside? That's a pack I just destroyed for choosing to defy me. Your communication is down, and you have no time to look for us, so I suggest you decide very fast if you want the last fated mate to live or die!"

The pool dimmed, and he let go of me, causing me to fall into the dirty water. I turned my head to stare up at him, telling him clearly with my cold eyes and dead heart that he was going to die tonight. He barely reacted to my heated glare and turned to a cultist whose robes smelled faintly of deer urine.

"Move the vessel to the secondary location and get more men to secure the front door. If any of our own try to get back in, kill them." The cultist bowed and rushed off to complete his tasks.

I looked back up to the retired advisor and saw what Zorian had seen in the male—someone who only coveted the bottom line. Of course he'd let his own men die. There were only hundreds of them.

Eysteinn yanked me off the floor, threw me over his shoulder, and retreated up the ramp. I writhed my hands in their bindings, but the rope stung and weakened me the more it dug into my flesh. I kicked off a boot and tried to claw him, but he merely grabbed my ankles in one hand and continued walking, unfazed.

I snarled through the gag, feeling torn between going into a blind, pointless rage and biding my time. I was suffering, and numbness was trickling into my nerves. Soon, I wouldn't be able to feel anything. I couldn't think either, and I knew that if I was going to survive, I needed to be able to think.

I couldn't see in the direction he was going, but we seemed to pass through a hidden entrance to another hall. He opened the door to a chamber, and an ugly, familiar shriek assaulted my ears.

"Why the fuck did you bring that whore in here, Steinn?" Asmin's voice screeched. It grated painfully like claws on metal sheeting, and I winced. "What the fuck!" she yelled as Eysteinn gently lowered me onto the bed. I felt the mattress stir and finally saw the irate dragon-shifter at the foot of the bed, nearly hyperventilating. "Why the fuck is she on our bed?"

"Because I'm about to mark her, female." Eysteinn grunted and turned to face her. "Are you staying to watch?"

"Mark her? I thought you were going to mark me! Why are you talking to me like this, Steinn?" she asked warily, nervousness weakening the bite of her anger.

"Talking to you like what? Like the whore I used you for?" Eysteinn taunted. "You think I'm keeping you around? You couldn't even do your job properly. You just had to get yourself kicked out of the castle! I told you to keep an eye on Zorian and make sure he only ended up with one of you three—but no! You just simply couldn't resist getting into trouble.

"I can't believe you three almost killed the key to my entire fucking plan, but that's what happens when you hire entitled little pups, I guess." The words looked like they'd slapped her. "You think it was easy to find unmated royal ninnies willing to go along with my plan? You think you've earned your place back in my bed by killing off the other two? You're dead wrong." He laughed coldly. "You never had a place to begin with."

"You s-said you'd make me queen!" She lurched forward to grab his arms in desperation.

I rolled off the bed and made a dash for the door, but the advisor scooped me up like I was a disobedient puppy and laid me back down on the bed. Fuck! Fuck! Fuck! I swore at him in my head with every curse I'd heard pop out of Zorian's mouth.

"You promised!" she screamed when he didn't reply.

"Sometimes adults don't do what they say," he returned in an amused, patronizing voice. "Now, if you're done making a fool of yourself, get out so I can finally claim my fated mate. She's much prettier than you—and definitely smells better."

A muscle in Asmin's cheek twitched. She looked like he had just run her through with a sword. Emotion drained from her face, and she glided out in her filmy nightgown like an improper, proper princess. Her sudden change was so out of place that it made goose bumps break out across my skin. Somehow, she seemed more dangerous now.

The door slammed behind her, and Eysteinn began to undress. I rolled slowly to the edge of the bed and sat up, watching him as he watched me. I was wary, but he was calm. When he began to drop his pants, I made another bolt for the door, but he caught me again, somehow not tripping on his pants. He held me down this time as he finished undressing, and I tried to gut him with my feet. I only managed a light scrape, but he pulled his abdomen back before I could sink my claws in any deeper.

I struggled even more when he began to undress me. He ripped my tunic and bra off, which sent the priceless stones tumbling onto the blankets. He kept me pushed down with a hand on my chest and picked up one of the stones, raising an eyebrow in curiosity. "No doubt you'll have to tell me what these are later," he murmured thoughtfully, as though he wasn't about to rape a female, and then he leaned over to store them in the chest at the foot of the bed. Fuck! Fuck! Fuck!

He yanked my bloody leggings and underwear off, and I felt a new wave of despair hit me. My pup. My pup... Zorian's pup. Our pup. Our pup! Tears flowed down my cheeks, and my heart writhed with agony.

"Whose little bastard was that anyway?" He grunted as he fought to grab my ankles. "Zorian's? Where's that brat anyway? I thought he was supposed to be protecting you." He chuckled, and I felt like he was toying with me. He knew I'd lost something precious, and he was gloating.

"What a joke, making him your bodyguard," Eysteinn said, laughing heartily. "Couldn't even save his own mother." I wasn't surprised he'd said it, but that didn't make it any less chilling. I felt nausea roil in my stomach. Oh gods, I better not puke with this gag in my mouth. If things could get any worse, that would be one of them.

"I gave up saving my females, you know. That is, until now. I think you're going to be a little harder to kill, yes?" He finally grabbed one ankle and was now trying to grab the other. "You probably heard I had a chosen mate, but don't worry, she's not around any longer. She's quite dead. She's actually the reason you're my mate. It was such a beautiful trade, really."

I almost stopped fighting him out of pure shock when his words hit home—a trade. He laughed and almost doubled over when he saw my face. "Oh, come on, it's practically poetry!" he admonished with a grin. I gagged when he caressed my ankle with his thumb. "Alright, I'm not a monster. I didn't know putting the Moon Goddess in her would kill her until after I got to the goddess's realm. I made sure she was as comfortable as possible until she expired." He shrugged, like we were having this conversation over dinner.

It was insane. I was looking straight into the mouth of insanity, and he hid it so well with his demeanor. Zorian must have been unbelievably perceptive to notice this before Eysteinn had completely lost his mind.

Anger unfolded inside me.

I was furious for the innocents he'd gotten away with killing—the soldiers who could have been protected, the civilians who should've never seen the battlefront come to them, and those he'd sacrificed to house the Moon Goddess.

The anger unfurled into fury.

I'd gotten mad for Zorian and for our lost pup, but when was I going to get mad for me?

My fury bloomed into rage, but somehow, my mind cleared.

I made a show of gagging like I was about to vomit. He raised a brow and regarded me with suspicion. "Are you trying to trick me, little mate?" he asked, his lips curling into a smile, but I could see his uncertainty. I gagged again and allowed that to trigger actual nausea in me, which was still extremely easy to do. Eysteinn's eyes flickered down to my bloody sex and how I'd stopped fighting his advance with my legs.

I dry heaved, and he was convinced. He fumbled for my gag.

"I, Ragna Rhydderch, reject you, Eysteinn Burchard, as my fated mate!" I shrieked at the top of my lungs. Eysteinn recoiled, stunned from the agony of rejection, and I lashed out. I brought my knees to my chest so I could get them in front of Eysteinn. I put my left foot down at the base of his erect cock and used my other foot to forcefully bend his phallus over it. His cock broke with a popping sound, and he released a gut-wrenching scream.

He stumbled back and fell off the bed, roaring and clutching at his fractured dick. I jumped off the bed and agonized over how he was clutching onto the chest that contained the lunaite and the Earth Gods' Heart. I didn't have time. I remembered my words to Zorian. I was going to believe in my own strength.

First of all, I knew I wasn't a warrior. I needed to buy time. I kicked at Eysteinn's exposed leg tendons to sever them both with my claws. It wasn't clean, it wasn't pleasant, and it took me a couple tries because he was squirming too much. After crippling him, I fumbled awkwardly at the door with my bound wrists and escaped the private chamber.

I didn't take a last look at Eysteinn to enjoy his suffering. I didn't have time for pleasure. I wasn't sure if I could feel pleasure ever again. I wasn't sure if I'd be able to feel anything again. Zorian might, though, and I left Eysteinn alive as a gift for him. I had to get to the Moon Goddess. I had to find Rakel.

Chapter 32

Ragna

My feet slapped on the cold stone floor as I ran down the hall, desperate to find something I could use to free my bound wrists. The walls were too smooth, and there weren't any sharp rocks to be found. When I came to the door of the secret passage, I tried to hook and twist the binds off with the handle but realized that wasn't going to work either.

I bolted out the door and arrived upon a morbid scene. Screaming, yelling, and crying filled the air as thickly as the scent of death. Cultists and witches rushed chaotically in the main chamber, trying to move or save scorched bodies. Most were fighting to secure the door, which was bending under a prevailing force.

The burned bodies… Asmin had been responsible for them; I was certain. I scowled at the site where she'd held her tantrum. These would have been her people too. What a nightmare of a queen she would have made. Between her and Eysteinn, they'd have no one left to rule.

I looked to my left and regarded the ramp I'd left unexplored. I could probably find a weapon in the chaos of the main chamber, but I didn't want to take the chance. I was too vulnerable, naked and bound like this. I dashed up the ramp and found another hallway, then started throwing doors open at random, finding nothing more exciting than spare beds and pairs of slippers. I ran back down the hall and turned right. The doors to a storage room were left ajar, and adrenaline spurred my tired muscles.

I shuffled past stacks of rations to find racks burdened with swords. I sobbed in relief and leaned into a blade to slice my bindings. They snapped, and I groaned in alleviation. My wrists had deep, chaffed burns, but at least they worked and were free. I snatched a sword and ran out with it, planning on ditching it as soon as I retrieved my bow.

I scrambled through the panic to retrieve my bow, which had remained abandoned on the ground. I buckled the quiver around my naked hips and raced to where I'd last sensed the Moon Goddess. I knew they'd moved her, but I was hoping to find Wane first. When I spied the caked mud the godling's scuttling had shed, I swallowed a sob and followed it like a beacon.

I noticed Asmin's scent too late, and I was shoved onto the ground where I ended up rolling down the ramp. I hissed at my skinned elbows and knees but quickly jumped to my feet. Asmin would pay for that. She was about to pay for a lot of things.

"You're a fucking walking nightmare, you greedy whore. You took them all! You took everything from me!" Asmin screeched crazily from her hiding spot against the wall. Her form swelled as she shifted, and I remembered what I'd said before to Rudesind. She still bled like a wolf.

I didn't bother responding to Asmin as she shifted. I just loaded an arrow onto the bowstring and waited. The coldness in my heart was the only thing keeping me from panicking. I remembered that I still had rules, and they didn't apply any less to dragons.

Asmin huffed black smoke when she finished shifting. Her black dragon was quite large, maybe the size of a small cottage, but that only limited her movement in the area. That was one advantage. The downside was that her flames were going to suck out a lot of the air here. I couldn't rush, but I couldn't take my time. Anxiety pierced the numbness and swirled into my pumping adrenaline, almost making me sick.

She stalked awkwardly down the ramp and spat a jet of fire at me. I ran away from the broiling air, knowing that, if anything, I was great at running away. I'd been doing it for years.

I skirted a swipe of her claws and headed for her flank. Taking a huge risk, I launched from her tail onto her back. I expected her to buck me off—which she did—but that was fine because I wanted the higher ground on the upper ramp.

She snarled and spat short bursts of flames, trying to follow my dodges. I screamed through my teeth when one volley got too close to my calf and singed flesh. It took every ounce of self-control to keep running and not pause to look at the damage. The pain was near blinding as working muscles pulled against the injury, and tears sprang into my vision.

I had to find the right spot and the right time. If the conditions weren't good enough for a reliable shot, the fallout would be devastating. I turned to face Asmin and noted that she struggled to stay on the ramp with her bulky form and large wings. Her right wing flapped manically to keep her from tumbling off the edge, and the left wing was too cramped against the wall to help balance. This was it. I just needed to get close enough on her next fumble.

She roared in frustration and spat another line of fire, but I spied her slight recoil from the extra effort she'd put into it. She'd gotten sloppy, and I had to take part of that flame to make the shot. I ran down the ramp and jumped through the least scalding fringe of her searing projectile, clutching my bow close to protect its waxed string. My left shoulder and arm screamed from the licking flames, but I landed on my feet and caught her wobbling as she tried to track my movement. She clamped on the corner with a claw and lost her balance.

This would be my hardest shot yet, but I felt it was the closest to a sure thing I'd ever get. She'd recover if I missed and bite me in half. I pulled the arrow back, watched how her head bobbed, and released, aiming for where her eye would be next.

Asmin let out a deafening screech when my arrow buried itself in her left eye, and she tumbled off the edge to land on the lower level. I raced down after her while nocking another arrow, knowing I only had so much time before she'd heal, and I'd be dead. Asmin shifted back into her human form, horror-stricken at her injury. She screamed while she prepared herself and yanked the arrow from her bleeding socket. It was genuinely tragic that she had to learn about pain and consequences right before she died.

She whirled to face me and screeched at the top of her lungs. She was saying something, but it was completely unintelligible, and I wasn't interested. I got as close as I dared before I released my arrow into her head, killing her instantly. I wished I could have given her a less gruesome death by piercing her heart, but it was a smaller target. I was not a good archer, so I had to be a smart one.

I walked to her body and looked down at the dead female, forcing myself to acknowledge what I'd done. I'd disliked her immensely, but that was stored in a separate box from my sympathy. "I'm sorry, Asmin. I'm sorry your life ended this way. I wish you had chosen to use your status to help people. Perhaps you will in your next life. Good luck."

I sighed miserably, feeling my soul get one death heavier, and ran back up the ramp to find Wane's trail of dried mud, which I'd spied on the upper level. I jogged down a hall that declined into a longer, darker tunnel. There weren't as many lights down here, probably because the tunnel wasn't regularly trafficked. I slipped through another door that looked like an exposed hidden entrance, turned around a corner, and found Wane trying to break down a door.

"Wane!" I gasped and hobbled up to It, gritting my teeth through another wave of excruciating pain hitting my leg. I still couldn't bring myself to look at it. I knew there had to be blisters at the very least. I also had no idea how bad the burns were on my arm and shoulder, but I didn't think they were as seared as my calf.

The godling's head snapped over to look at me, then back at the door. I tried the handle, but it was locked. Needing to verify before I put any more precious energy into this barrier, I pressed my nose to the crack under the door and took a deep whiff. I sneezed violently, but I caught her scent. Rakel was behind this door!

I released a strange, sobbing laugh and focused on the problem at hand. If I forced the handle, would it break? I paced in frustration and ran my fingers through my hair. Tears welled in my eyes, and I tried to tamp down a rising panic attack.

I tried everything short of using my bow to pry open the door. I stared miserably down at my grandpa's shortbow. Was it worth it? My indecision was interrupted by running footsteps, and I turned to see the brown-robed, deer-pee cultist running toward me. I nocked an arrow and drew it, but I didn't want to kill again. My soul was already too burdened by death.

The cultist studied my shaky aim and my pained expression, then surprised me by holding his hands up to squeeze past, not taking his eyes off mine for an instant. Once he left my sight, his running footsteps were terminated with a scream. The scent of burning flesh wafted down the hall toward me, and I blanched. No... No, no, no! Asmin was dead, wasn't she? I'd shot her in the head!

Wane made a strange, grinding noise, as though talking through Its rocky joints, and ran down the hall toward a fiery light. "Wait!" I hissed, taking a hesitant step after It. "Careful!" Wane couldn't be hurt by fire, could It? Rocks only got scorched, right? A familiar scent broke through the foul, smoky odor, and my hesitation turned into deep relief.

"Hekla! Soley!" I called, gestured the wolves over to me, and collapsed in their presence. Wane followed and hovered over Hekla's wolf, Eventide, like an elated pup. "I can't... I can't get this open," I gasped and scooted to lean against the wall. I hazarded a glance at my leg and grimaced at the dark, blistering burns. The very center was black—charred. My adrenaline was wearing off, and the pain would soon arrive in full force.

The Sun God's vessel, without breaking stride, walked right through the door, and His radiating heat cut through the metal like it was butter. The might of this celestial deity was staggering. I shouldn't be surprised by His power, but my mind just couldn't catch up to my senses. Perhaps it was the combination of the might being channeled through Noon's tiny wolf body.

I passed through the molten hole and limped over to embrace a very alive but very unconscious Rakel. I cried into her fur. I'd finally found her. Both of them.

I shook Rakel gently and called to her. "Rakel? Moon Goddess? I'm here. I found you. Please wake up!" I worried over her still form and avoided touching the silver collar and shackles that were covered in warped, odd symbols. Her fur was singed, and the flesh around the silver was a mess of peeling, black skin. I scooted closer and hissed from a deep, biting sting on my kneecap. I jerked my leg back and looked down to find that she was lying on a mat made from the same plant I'd been bound with both tonight and the night I'd been stolen from the Lunar Coven.

"What is this stuff?" I asked the gods who stood on either side of me after shifting.

"Aconite," the Sky Gods answered. "A lot of it. This amount combined with all this silver would probably kill any other wolf but is probably only enough to keep the Moon Goddess and Her vessel paralyzed."

"I need to get this silver off, then I can roll her off the mat," I said tiredly. I turned to the Sun God to ask Him to melt the locks, but He either read my mind or was way ahead of me because He moved closer and looked down at her neck. With surgical precision, the god heated the collar's lock until it glowed and sagged. He delicately used Soley's little claws to push and scrape the thick molten silver onto the ground until the collar could be removed.

I extended my claws as much as possible and freed her neck from the restraint, flicking it far away to hit the cell wall. We repeated the process with all four shackles and slowly rolled Rakel's polar wolf off the mat. Of our little sub-pack, she was the biggest, and it took some real effort to flop her free.

I crouched over her and stroked her snowy fur. "Rakel? Goddess?" I asked, frowning at her comatose state. Wane nudged me and dropped the tiny piece of lunaite I'd given It days and days ago. I gasped and snatched it up to show the Sky Gods.

"Could this help? This is a piece of the lunaite! I gave it to your child a while ago... Wane seemed... sick at the time," I asked, hoping that our forest encounter had happened for a reason.

"Put it in her mouth. Contact with her moon should give her strength," the Sky Gods proposed. I carefully pried Rakel's maw open to set the small stone on her tongue like a pearl. I stroked her fur once more, willing her to heal and wake.

"Please be ok," I whispered, feeling my eyes sting. "I miss you, Rakel. I love you, Rakel. Moon Goddess? We need You more than ever. Please come help Your pups, Your children. They're suffering so much without You. I'd give You my strength if I could," I begged, overwhelmed. "Everything I have left!"

I wasn't sure how long I sat there, but the body beneath my loving pats finally stirred. Rakel's golden eyes opened and rolled to discover us. Her eyes met mine, and she slowly sat up on her haunches.

"She says it is good to see you too, one of her bravest," the Sky Gods conveyed.

The Moon Goddess leaned into me. I gave in to the surreal moment and returned her embrace, falling into deep, racking sobs as my broken heart tried to absorb all the love she had to give. Soon, all would be fixed... except my pup.

Zorian

Spine made one last push and burst through the door with a victorious howl. Cultists and witches on the other side scattered like ants, panicking from something we hadn't caused. The inside was a complete mess with smoking bodies strewn about the floor. Combined with the lingering scent, I had a pretty good idea who had been the cause of this. Why would Asmin turn on Eysteinn? She'd be a serious threat to Ragna if he couldn't control her.

Spine cut through the cultists with a one-track mind. We were on the hunt for two things—Eysteinn and Ragna. Beta Rudesind was on my left, and General Belenus was on my right. Koray followed behind us, keeping a sharp eye out for witchwork and traps. We mowed through Eysteinn's warriors, and I was trying to decide with Spine which way to go when a third voice popped into my mind.

We've found Ragna, the Sky Gods said, and relief shuddered through Spine's body. *We also have the Moon Goddess. Hekla, my child, and the Sun God will escort them back to you. I must leave. Starlight preserve you.*

Thank you! I cried out to them, hoping they heard it before they departed.

Spine then caught a whiff of someone we hadn't scented in a very long time, not since our mother was murdered. He was boiling, starving for vengeance, and turned his head to see a grim Eysteinn stalking down a ramp. His eyes immediately locked onto ours, and he smiled. Despite his poise and the mad glee in his eyes, he wasn't looking good. His face was ashen and strained painfully with every step he took. Someone had gotten to him first, and he reeked of Ragna.

Had he touched her? Spine roared, lunged in a blur, and slugged Eysteinn in the face, sending the old advisor into the rock wall.

Eysteinn laughed and wiped blood from his broken nose. "Oh, what do you know? My nose is bleeding as much as Ragna's pussy."

What the fuck did he do? I screamed to Spine. The gods had her, but they hadn't told us her condition. Had he raped her?

Spine saw red.

He lunged for the lycan, who managed to dodge and rip into Spine's ribs. Spine kicked off the wall and raked his claws across Eysteinn's belly, but it was too shallow to gut him.

"Don't worry. I told her it'd be ok, that we'd make a new pup after I marked her," he said with a leering grin. Spine's hackles shot up in fear and rage.

No, he couldn't have! I shouted at Spine. *He's just provoking us. He wants us to make a mistake!*

He's dead. He's fuckin' dead! THE MOTHERFUCKER KILLED OUR PUP!

Spine snarled and lunged again, but Eysteinn just laughed, grabbed a passing cultist, and flung him into our approach like a fucking human shield. The cultist's scream was cut short, as all screams ended if they started in my lycan's path.

A number of Eysteinn's men continued to fight at his side, but a good amount turned tail and ran. Rudesind and Belenus chipped away at the cultists, slowly carving a path to the other lycan for me.

Koray had found an abandoned sword and engaged a witch—one that resembled a corpse more than the dead bodies piling around us. Before I turned away, Koray swung the blade and lopped the witch's head clean off her shoulders. Her head splashed into a shallow pool, muffling her last, breathless shriek.

Koray staggered from exhaustion and let his guard down for one second too long. I couldn't get there in time, but Belenus did. The fae general shoved the young man away and tried to block the cultist's sword from an awkward angle. His sword slipped, and the cultist stabbed into his right side. Belenus roared and backhanded him into the ground, where he then drove his sword into the man's heart. Koray was shaken but alert again, and Belenus started cutting down the closest opponents to prevent them from being swarmed.

Eysteinn noticed Belenus's injury and his distracted protection of the younger man. He parted through his men like a shark through water, eager to target bleeding prey. Spine pushed harder to get to Eysteinn, mowing cultists down to find a shortcut through the masses. Spine roared a command to Rudesind, who happened to be closer, and he noticed Eysteinn's new target. Belenus barely caught the lycan's approach in time and blocked his claws with his sword.

In an incredibly stupid, brave, and risky move, Koray ducked under their arms and pierced Eysteinn's belly with his blade. Eysteinn stumbled back into Rudesind, whose fist sent him flying toward me. Spine grabbed Eysteinn's coat and used his momentum to slam him face-first into the wall. I could hear the brutal crunches of the lycan's facial bones shattering upon impact.

The cultists fled. No one seemed to think their cause was worth their lives.

I shifted back into my human form and yanked the cult leader off the floor. He was in a mild daze and struggled weakly to rip himself from my grasp. He wasn't going anywhere soon. The male was a mess. No words could describe the horror that was now his face.

I heard running footsteps and looked up to see Hekla, Wane, and the Sun God escorting the Moon Goddess's vessel and my beautiful female. I staggered in relief, but then my eyes fell to her thighs, which were covered in dried blood. Her eyes were distant and despairing.

Had we really… lost…?

Spine screamed inside me. He howled and shrieked, but all I could do was stare back at her and join her agony. Everything inside of me deadened, and I looked blankly down at Eysteinn's pathetic, writhing form. I had considered a slow death, but now I just wanted him gone. I was tired.

"Traitor," I declared in a cold, detached tone. "For murdering my mother, for touching my female, for sacrificing the king's soldiers and civilians, you're sentenced to death. I'd rip your heart out, but you don't appear to have one." I proceeded to dig my claws into his neck and tore out his throat. Eysteinn's empty shell fell to the ground.

I spat on it.

Everyone was silent, but I didn't want to spend one more minute looking at his remains. I scooped Ragna into my arms and strode away without a word. Before we left, she had me take her to Eysteinn's chamber to retrieve her relics. We reclaimed them and left that fucking hellhole.

I was numbly satisfied with how we were cleaning up the area. Our soldiers were in pretty good shape, and they were busy arresting any cultists who'd surrendered. We hadn't lost many, but I'd still grieve every death. There really was no victory in war—just death, pointless death. I held Ragna closer for a moment to ride out a particularly stinging wave of emotional pain.

We gathered at the camp, and I sat down, clutching Ragna possessively in my lap. The Sun God approached and summoned Koray. *Koray,* the Sun God commanded, *remove this dampener from the Sky-Blessed. It is new magic. I cannot touch it.* How could Koray remove...

"So that's why we can see her?" my beta asked.

"You can?" I blurted, wrapping my arms around her and verifying it was still very much nighttime. We weren't in the moonlight either. I nearly growled at the other males as I covered her, unwilling to share her nudity with anyone else now. I needed to find her a shirt; I only wore my armor. Rudesind nodded with averted eyes and dipped his head in submission, likely noticing my changed behavior around her.

I adjusted Ragna's body in my lap so Koray could look at the complicated stamp that marred her lovely back. He stared intently at it, narrowing his royal-blue eyes while resting his chin in a palm.

"This is incredibly complicated," he observed in a dark tone. "I've never seen one like this. It must have taken years to design, which wouldn't surprise me if it inhibits the very gods." He frowned and traced his fingers along the symbol, starting from the outside lines and working his way toward the center. He removed a line on occasion and would pause to think before continuing. It was like he was solving a complicated maze puzzle. "That witch in there, that wasn't a normal witch, either. She was something much more feral—older. I wouldn't be surprised if she'd created this."

Koray let out a satisfied hum, and the symbol evaporated. Ragna crumpled against me, as though she'd been using the last of her strength to carry the burden of that magic on her back.

Rakel's polar wolf gazed around the campfire at us. We weren't looking our best, to put it lightly. Belenus was getting his wound bandaged, and Spine still hadn't spoken to me. He'd locked himself away to grieve.

Sleep, My children, She said softly. *We will talk in the morn.*

I cleaned, clothed, and tended to my precious, injured female. Once she was properly bandaged, I wrapped us both in a blanket and begged for sleep to take us away from here. Anywhere but here.

Chapter 33

Ragna

The Moon Goddess led us to the nearby woods in the early golden morning so we'd be away from the deaths and the bitter memories of the cult site. Zorian and I still hadn't spoken, at least not with words. We conversed in touches of comfort and affection. I knew he was as devastated as I was about losing our pup, but I could tell that he was immensely relieved and grateful I'd survived. He'd held on to me overnight like I was his last source of sustenance.

Rakel's wolf, Wax, sat down between two trees and waited for us all to settle. Hekla and Soley shifted back into their human forms and settled down together, with Soley leaning her head on Hekla's shoulder. She seemed tired after hosting the Sun God for so many hours yesterday.

Zorian kept me in his lap, and I curled up, wanting to escape into his possessiveness. Belenus, Koray, and Rudesind settled between us and the naked she-wolves, but the non-shifters looked too exhausted to be flustered by them. Rudesind was as stalwart as ever, attentive and alert like a true beta, or perhaps he was just fascinated by the goddess before him. We all were.

First of all, thank you, my beloved children, for answering Fate's call. All has gone according to plan, the Moon Goddess said.

"What do you mean by 'according to plan?'" Zorian asked from behind me, sounding as disquieted as I felt. He tightened his grip around my waist, and I returned his squeeze.

I work with what Fate offers, My son. Fate has a plan, but I push and pull at events when I can to make Fate favor My children. It may seem cruel to you, sons and daughters, but Eysteinn's very existence has allowed for individuals to meet when they would not have otherwise. My kidnapping was an unfortunate necessity to bring together warriors, rulers, defenders, and allies.

"You planned your own kidnapping?" Koray asked, shocked. Mixed feelings floated around our group in murmurs.

In a manner of speaking... It was not optional if I wanted to keep my wolves safe, the goddess said patiently and lovingly. *None of my she-wolves here have birthed yet, but a mother would gladly sacrifice for her children. Fathers too. In the grand scheme, these last handful of years will see to my wolves' survival for generations to come and save hundreds of thousands of lives in the future.*

We were all a little stunned, and no one seemed to have any questions. I knew my mind was too fuzzy to think straight, and my senses were spinning. My eyes stung horribly when she mentioned mothers, though. Zorian seemed to know somehow and kissed the top of my head.

I must return to my work this very minute. I have much to fix and suffering to reduce, but all is as it should and will be.

"And the bonds will all be fixed?" I asked, needing to hear it for myself. I couldn't believe it was all over. It was all finally over!

Yes, my resolute, most dedicated daughter. All will be as it should, she answered, and I sensed her departure. I scrambled off Zorian's lap and dashed to Rakel, tears flowing directly from my overburdened soul. Rakel shifted back in time to receive my embrace, and we were dog-piled by Hekla and Soley, who were also sobbing in bone-deep relief. We held Rakel close and worried over her state. She'd lost weight, a little of her muscle mass, and was still healing from the deep burns around her neck, ankles, and side.

"Ragna," Rakel cried and nuzzled her forehead into mine. "We've been so worried about you all these years. I can't believe it's all over. The nightmare is over! We're all together again!" She hiccupped, showing a vulnerability I've never seen before in her. She had traumas to heal now, and it would take a very long time. I could only hope that she'd have a strong, loving mate by her side to help her heal.

Almost as if triggered by that thought, a thick cord felt like it was yanked out of my soul, and I stumbled backwards, crying out in pain. I collapsed onto the forest floor, clutching my chest. When I heard a deep, male groan, I turned my head to discover Rudesind reeling and clutching at his chest.

Zorian and my she-wolves were helping me up when I heard Rudesind exclaim, "My bond to Ragna—it's gone!" His eyes locked on to mine with the wildest relief. They also expressed sympathy and gratitude. He ran his hands through his hair and rubbed his eyes, but then froze.

"Rude?" Zorian asked, concerned. "Are you ok?"

Rudesind ignore him, and his eyes moved to Rakel. His nostrils flared, and he took an aggressive step toward her. I glanced at Rakel and realized what was happening. She'd frozen too and was staring right back at him.

"Mine!" Rudesind growled softly and strode up to her.

"Mine," she breathed and ran to meet him halfway. They collided. She jumped into his arms, and he clutched her obsessively, as though she was a dream, and he was about to wake. My heart warmed as I watched my dear friend, Rakel, nuzzle into the beta's chest. She seemed desperate for the comfort he was already providing.

Her muscles relaxed, and a calm swept over them both. He carried her to settle against a tree with her in his arms. She buried herself into his large chest, and he closed his eyes in pure bliss, looking like satisfaction and peacefulness personified.

"Congratulations, Rude," Zorian said with genuine warmth and affection. "You two deserve it." Everyone else echoed the sentiment but didn't offer any handshakes, sensing that their moment was too precious and intimate to approach. I was surprised he hadn't hauled her off somewhere private, but he probably wanted to be here until we dispersed. He was a true, dedicated beta. He could handle both.

Another cord snapped in my chest, and I spasmed through the soul-deep pain. Zorian held me tightly so I wouldn't injure my burns further with my thrashing. This time, I spied Belenus doubling over in pain, grabbing at his battle wound as though he thought that was the cause.

Hekla wasted no time running up to stabilize him. "Mine!" she proclaimed with a feral grin, staring up at the towering fae who suddenly looked terrified. His skin, usually tinted with the subtlest amount of gold, flushed as he stared down at the equally imposing—and very naked— she-wolf. His foot lifted, and I couldn't quite tell if it was to take a step forward or backwards, but I chuckled quietly all the same.

"Don't worry, Mr. General," she teased. "I won't bite… until you're ready." She flashed him another impish grin and reached out to shake his hand. Belenus looked taken aback by the formal gesture and accepted it, but he'd fallen for her trap. She yanked him forward and ensnared him in a hug. She met my eyes and smiled the happiest smile I'd ever seen on her face.

I sighed, slumped, and my heart practically melted to see my very best friend find her fated mate. Belenus had been a pain at first, but he was a good man, and she'd whip him into shape. The poor fae didn't stand a snowball's chance in the desert. Little did she know, she'd be a queen someday. I couldn't wait to discover her reaction to that little fact... but I'd leave it to her new mate to break the news.

She moved to his side and held his hand, sensing he was stunned and needed a moment. He'd hoped to get his mate by coming back with me, and he certainly got that. He turned to look down at her, and I spied the most subtle relief and adoration in his eyes. I muffled another giggle, noticing his trousers were also being affected by their fated connection.

My eyes looked up to see Soley's reaction to all this, but she was just staring at Koray, and he was glancing back at her. I think she knew, and I held my breath, waiting for the third severance. It was like Fate had wrapped Its immediate attention around all of us. A third cord snapped, and I screamed through my teeth. Zorian rocked me, murmuring in his soothing voice, but I couldn't make out what he was saying. He kept firm contact with my skin, doing what he could with the mate touch. I panted for air, desperately wanting to pass out and sleep, but I didn't want to miss this.

Soley's eyes suddenly locked onto the blue-eyed Key from the Lunar Coven like he was a delicious hare in a trap. She strode confidently up to Koray, leaned over cutely to look up at him, and asked, "Mine?" Her adorable follow-up growl also sounded like an inquiry, like she was asking him to dance.

Koray leaned his head back in mild surprise and replied, "Uh, h-hey there, Soley?" A corner of his mouth curled up in pleasant surprise, but he looked completely at a loss for what to do. He glanced at everyone else, as though asking for help, but Soley reached up on her tiptoes to force his gaze back on her.

"Yes! Mate!" She jumped to wrap her arms around his neck and pulled him down for a long, joyful kiss. His body was frozen for a moment, but then his hands found Soley's sides and wrapped around her waist. They seemed to lose themselves in each other, and an aroused groan escaped Koray. He stilled again when he realized they were not in a private space and retreated from Soley's lips. He laughed nervously and was about to say something, but Soley pulled on his arm and ran off, dragging him with her and giggling.

I placed a palm to my face, closed my eyes, and chuckled weakly. Soley was a very submissive wolf, and I wondered if being with a non-shifter would give her room to grow. Between today and yesterday, she already seemed much bolder, but I hadn't been around to see how much of that had previously been developing. I was certain he'd be good for her, though. Koray had been steadfast from the very beginning, and I knew he'd always put her first.

Zorian moved to kneel before me. He took my hands in his and gazed at me in earnest. He seemed nervous but resolute. His brows were set in a firm line, but his red eyes became soft, warm, and full of hope. I tried to move onto my knees to face him better, but I hissed in pain and seated myself again. My burned calf and skinned knees were not a fan of the forest floor. Zorian steadied me by placing a hand on my shoulder.

"No, don't move. You'll aggravate your wounds," he said worriedly. He knelt closer to my side so I didn't have to go to him, then he gripped my hands and ran his thumb over my knuckles, studying my face. I watched him with uncertainty, waiting for what he was about to communicate. I had a seed of hope in my heart, but who knew if that would come to fruition.

"Ragna, I want you to know that... whatever happens with the mate bonds," he began and sucked in a long, deep breath. "I still want you. Fated or chosen, I don't want anyone else as my mate but you." He looked down at my hands as I was flooded with an array of emotions.

His piercing burgundy eyes rolled up to meet mine again, and he added, "I love you, Ragna. I love you so much, and I'd do anything to make you happy. I've fallen so deep. Would you... accept me as your mate?"

I was in shock. He still wanted me? Even after I'd lost our pup? I was so worried that he no longer wanted me after I'd failed to keep it safe. I guess I felt that I didn't have much else to offer. I was stunned and put a hand to my parted lips. Tears of joy ran down my cheek, and I struggled to my feet because I wanted to stand to accept him. I hadn't felt our bond break, so maybe we were fated! This was what I had been holding on to this whole time. My heart was practically glowing with joy. We could start fresh now that everything was completed. I could breathe in a new chapter with the male I loved.

Once I was standing, I hesitated slightly, realizing I hadn't felt any other bonds break yet, and a sense of dread came over me. Everything seemed quiet... like the calm before a storm. Not even the ferns in the woods bobbed under a small breeze.

I looked up as Zorian's happy, hopeful expression faltered. He looked concerned at my trepidation.

Pain.

A pain unlikely anything I'd ever felt hit me. It wrenched me so hard that my entire body and soul went numb for a moment. It wasn't one cord snapping from my soul but millions. Hundreds were being yanked out at a time, like a pup ripping out handfuls of grass from the dirt. If it had just been one, it would have left behind a sore spot, but it hadn't been. It was more, and I wasn't sure my body, mind, and soul would survive the assault.

I toppled forward with a scream, and Zorian caught me, looking into my face with wild, terrified eyes. I desperately searched his body for the mate touch, but I couldn't find it. I ran my hands over his chest, his arms, and his face, but there was no tingling, no sparks, no soothing, no pain relief! I panicked. It was like I had suddenly gone blind. Where was our bond?

"Z-Zorian!" I sobbed, and he grabbed my face, trying to hush me. His mouth moved, and I assumed he was telling me it'd be ok, but I couldn't hear him clearly. I needed my mate!

I staggered again as more bonds snapped. I was barely aware of everyone surrounding me, trying to hold me while I writhed in agony. "Z-Zorian! M-maybe she had to take it to g-give it back—like a reset?" I asked him weakly, desperately. He continued to hold me steady, and I tried scenting him, but there was nothing, just a mild version of what I used to know.

I stared into his eyes, trying to will the bond to return. "I was so sure!" I sobbed. "I was so sure we were fated!"

"Hey, hey, hey, it's ok! Remember, I still want you! I love you, Ragna!" he reminded, looking genuinely scared now. He gripped my arms tighter, forcing me to keep looking at him.

I screamed again and again from physical and emotional pain. Every bond removed was like a rejection. I felt like a skeleton that was being squeezed for blood. It was maddening, and I was losing my grip on my mind. My eyes were clenched so tight that the muscles screamed in pain. Dots danced behind my eyelids as if they were taunting me.

Was I even worthy of love? Was I even given a fated? What could I possibly have to offer anyone? I was no genius. I was no warrior. I couldn't do anything on my own. I'd fumbled embarrassingly for years. I barely scraped through the last couple of weeks. I couldn't even protect my own pup.

I was spiraling.

All I could think of was rejection.

That was a stupid decision to go into the cultist den. I was a stupid female—a stupid, undeserving female. Stupid, stupid, stupid. Zorian could do better than me. I let him down, and I hurt him deeply. Hurt him so bad. I'd never forget the look on his face when he saw the blood on my legs. I loved him too much to ever hurt him again. His queen was still out there. She wouldn't do something so stupid. Stupid, stupid, stupid.

The pain was unbearable.

The fear was endless.

The snapping cords made my body heat up, and I keeled over to vomit. I coughed, dry heaved, and my vision blurred. "I'm sorry, Z-Z-Zorian. I don't deserve your love... I'm going... now," I said weakly and struggled to stand. People around me were yelling, crying, and grabbing at me, but the sounds muffled further, and the world darkened like the burn on my leg—black and curling. I was an empty, broken, and burnt shell.

Then I was nothing.

orian

I watched helplessly as Ragna started dying right before my eyes. Tears streamed down my face, and I cried to the gods for help. Even Soley came running back with Koray. I wouldn't be surprised if people had heard Ragna's blood-curdling screams from halfway around the world. Rudesind and Belenus held her arms down to keep her from thrashing while the she-wolves tried to help me calm her. At some point, her eyes opened and became glassy. It was clear she couldn't see or hear us anymore, and her heart slowed. I sobbed. I did everything I could think of, even splashing water on her face. Nothing stoked the coals of her heart. We were losing her. I was losing her.

Before her heart stopped entirely, Ragna sat up abruptly, startling everyone. "We had to hibernate her and Trail. They're asleep now," she said, and I almost thought I had gone mad. What was she saying? Had I heard right?

"It is good to hear from you again, Earth Gods," Soley said, but her mannerism was different. Was this the Sun God speaking through her again? I looked back at Ragna. Was she acting as a vessel now? "It seems that the Sky-Blessed succumbed as expected. No wolf could survive that."

"I imagine you're taking her now?" Hekla inquired. Was this the Sky Gods? Were they all acting as vessels now?

"Wait, no, no, no," I said with my hands out, trying to slow the conversation. I was on the edge and very close to having a panic attack. "Why are you taking her? Wher—"

"We are taking her to heal. We will build a burrow, a nest, a womb, and nurture her back to health. She will sup from the best of the earth and drink from the purest spring. Our daughter asked Us to perform this fated task when it happened. It has happened now." The Earth Gods stood with Ragna's defeated body.

"How long?" I asked with a sore throat, wiping tears from my burning, swollen eyes.

"Until she passes her final test," the Earth Gods said and began to walk away, as if there was all the time in the world with which to complete this task.

"Can I visit?" I begged, already feeling like I couldn't breathe without her. I couldn't feel the bond, but I needed her. She was my everything.

"No," the Sun God said, standing next to me to watch Ragna's departure into the woods. "I, along with the other gods, will follow her progress."

"Is… there a way I could get updates?" I asked, hesitant to even mention the word 'favor' around a god that would love nothing more than to incinerate me where I stood.

"I will make a consideration. You have already suffered sufficiently," the Sun God replied. I didn't dare look at Him in surprise. Did that mean I could earn His forgiveness eventually?

"Thank you," I said humbly and tried to tolerate the pain of an anxious, impatient heart. I wasn't sure how long we stood there, watching Ragna wander farther from our sight. It wasn't until she disappeared entirely that the Sun God spoke again.

"Ragna is still pregnant," He announced flatly. "I would not normally share this, but you've completed your task as a champion—even though I never asked you to impregnate your charge... pup. Your reward for doing what I've asked is time spent not suffering over something that is untrue."

Shock struck me hard and fast but blossomed into warmth. I fell to my knees and placed my palms on my cheeks. Happy tears streamed down my face, replacing the old tracks of the despairing ones. "Our pup is still alive?" I croaked, unable to believe it. "It survived the bleeding? She didn't miscarry?"

In the back of my mind, Spine wept. He didn't say anything, but I knew he was listening. Listening and crying. I swallowed hard and tried to be his rock.

"Pups," the Sun God corrected, and a joyful sob escaped my throat. I placed my hands on my knees and tried to slow my breathing. "And of course they survived; they are too stubborn to die. It seems to run in the family," the Sun God remarked dryly. "If I couldn't kill you, Alpha of Alphas, what chance did that pathetic cult have with your unborn?" I groaned silently but couldn't contain my chuckle. I sniffed and looked down at my hands. These large, calloused, barbaric hands would be holding fragile pups in a matter of months.

"H-how many?" I knew I was pushing my luck with all these questions, but I couldn't stop myself. I was riding a high. A high I desperately wished I could share with Ragna.

"Leave some mysteries in your life, but I hope you're prepared for a litter," the god answered. I couldn't tell for the life of me if He was amused.

Bliss. I laughed and wiped my eyes. I could barely think straight. "I wish I could tell her," I choked out, knowing how much it would mean to her. It would lighten her burden. It was all I ever wanted to do once I'd gotten my head out of my own ass.

"She has a last test to pass. If she passes, she will come home, and you will tell her."

"What happens if she doesn't?" I asked. Dread crawled back into me.

"Then she'll disappear from your life forever."

$\mathfrak{C}$hapter 34

$\mathfrak{R}$agna

I woke feeling as though my mind was using its legs for the first time. My joints felt so stiff that I struggled to move even a finger. Muscles shook more violently than a newborn foal, and even my eyes were crusted shut. I moaned at the discomfort of simply being in my own body.

A confusing tactile experience was also occurring under my heavy form. My fingers curled around clumps of moss, leaves, soft green twigs, and feathers. I tried to move my hand to rub my eye, but a tiny, wet hand did it for me. I jerked, startled, but the little hand was adamant.

I could finally open my eyes and discovered a beaver watching me. It was chewing on a rolled-up lily pad and staring like I was a source of entertainment. I couldn't help the weak smile that spread my lips over the sweetness of such a creature.

It is good to see you wake, Ragna, the Earth Gods said.

Where are we? Trail moaned tiredly.

We've provided a space for you both to heal, the gods replied. *You will be able to leave when you're ready. As the Earth Gods, We work most with the heart and the hearth. You'll find this warm cave with a bed, a small waterfall to drink from and bathe with, vegetables and fruit straight from My earth, and warm sunshine to nourish your body and soul.*

"Who are these little ones?" I asked, watching another beaver waddle into the cave.

They are My volunteers. All the animals here mate for life, and I've allowed their partners to stay here with you as well. These beavers have built your bed and have assisted with the garden. They are good, sturdy servants of Our will.

I suppose we won't eat them, Trail joked weakly.

"Thank you," I said to the busy rodents as I struggled to stand. "Earth Gods, how long have I been asleep?"

A little over a week.

Oh, Goddess...

Spine must be so worried, Trail lamented, suddenly fretful and restless in my mind. A severe pang hit my heart when I remembered Zorian. I missed him so much, and for a moment, I nearly forgot how to breathe. I wished he was here. I wanted his arms around me.

"We... W-we're not their fated, Trail," I whimpered tearfully and stumbled out of the cave where I fell to my knees and vomited bile. Oh gods, I had hoped that would stop after the miscarriage. My body must still be in shock. I turned toward the first thing I saw, a crisp and sparkling waterfall.

None of these animals are fated mates, Ragna, the Earth Gods informed. *Love does not require the intervention of Fate. Look at how their lives please them. They are more than enough for each other.*

My eyes searched the rest of the space, finding several owls and eagles with white crests sitting in a fruiting loquat tree, pressed close or grooming their better half. A pair of cranes fished enthusiastically together at a busy pond, and the beavers had retired to the garden to pluck carrots from its depths. I didn't know if the Earth Gods helped me see it better, but all these animals radiated happiness and satisfaction.

I rinsed in the waterfall with Zorian at the center of my thoughts. He said he wanted me. He said he loved me. Would that be enough, or would I always question my worth? Were my concerns valid, or would I be sabotaging my happiness? I sighed, but somehow, I wasn't emotionally exhausted. Maybe my rest had been more restorative than I thought. A week was a long time to be unconscious.

My eyes fell upon a pile of plants at the base of the pool. As though reading my mind, the Earth Gods explained their presence. *Those are natural soaps. The beavers brought them so you could cleanse your body while you cleansed your heart and mind.*

"They are good to me," I murmured softly as I watched them work. I bathed and a beaver led me to a soft mat in the sun. I sat down to dry and traced the fine woven plant fibers with my fingertips. "You and your mate have made beautiful things here. I am grateful. I wish I knew how to repay you."

They and their offspring are repaid with protection. I have a pair of coyotes that guard their den, but I intervene if something is beyond their scope.

These are good gods, Trail remarked with awe. *I think it's an incredible honor to be Their vessel, to be honest. I can hardly believe all we are seeing.*

I think so as well, I agreed.

I have one question for you today, Ragna. Then you will rest and be ready to receive guests tomorrow, the gods said.

I lay down on the mat and let the sun seep into my chilled, quenched skin. "I am ready for your question," I said, but my mind was fixated on my guests tomorrow. Would Zorian come?

Do I have poor judgment? the Earth Gods asked, and nervousness poured into me faster than sunshine.

Please, for the love of the Moon Goddess, say no. I cannot handle these gods' wrath on top of losing our pup, Trail said mournfully. Our pup… for a blissful moment I'd forgotten about our loss, and I felt deep guilt over that. I needed to focus; the gods had asked me a question.

"I cannot imagine you ever having made a poor decision," I answered truthfully.

Yes or no, Ragna, the gods reprimanded. *That was a yes or no question.*

"N-no!"

So, you agree that choosing you to be my vessel was a good decision, They said, and I hesitated. It went against how I valued myself, but I was not wiser than any god.

"I would be forced to by that logic," I replied but winced. It had come out a little more rebellious than I'd intended.

Yes or no, Ragna.

"Yes!"

You will think about that for five hours today, Ragna. That is a command from your gods. Do not disobey, They bade, and I nodded in deference.

"Yes, I will," I promised and worried at my hands. Why did this feel so much more difficult than fighting a dragon? Remembering Asmin, I checked my body for injuries. I was completely healed.

The next morning began the same as the day before. The beavers laid a feast of vegetables at my feet while the eagles, owls, and herons brought gifts of small rabbits and fish. I was startled when a loquat walked along the stone floor all by itself. With a bewildered expression, I leaned forward and discovered it was being dragged by two enthusiastic termites.

What in the name of... Trail sputtered.

"Thank... you?" I picked up the loquat and gawked at their retreat. They absconded as if they were a couple who lived life on the edge. "Earth Gods?" I asked, wanting to—no, needing to—know more about what I'd just witnessed.

They snuck in, the gods replied shortly, clearly not wishing to divulge more.

Familiar voices rang out from the hidden entrance to my sanctuary, and I jumped to my feet. When Hekla, Soley, and Rakel filed in, I flung myself at them. A part of my heart sank when I realized Zorian wasn't there, but I was still over the moon to see my precious sub-pack.

"Ragna!" they all said at once and clung to me. Warmth spread through me as I absorbed their affection. I was expecting tears of joy, but my eyes refused to weep. It was as though they'd rested enough and wished to stay happy.

We settled in my cave, and I shared my feast with them. Hekla gutted the fish, Soley skinned and prepared the rabbits, and Rakel happily cooked whatever was ready. No one let me help, so with a perky heart, I sat on my nest and chewed on a carrot.

"I must know how you and your fated mates are doing—especially Hekla. Hekla, is Belenus still terrified of you?" I inquired with a giggle. Hekla grinned as she ripped out the spine of a fish.

She raised her chin. "He is simply not used to a strong, confident female who wishes to ride him like there is no tomorrow. Augh! He insists on 'courting' me properly, and I can't get him to change his mind! He hasn't even kissed me yet. I am so horny!" she complained, but she couldn't hide her grin. As much as she griped, I could tell her heart was enraptured.

"Soley's already kissed hers." I grinned, teasing the little she-wolf. The redhead fell on her back and kicked her legs in delight.

"And what a good kisser he is!" she yelled at the top of her lungs, as though needing the actual sun to hear her. "Oh, I cannot wait to mark him. I have no idea how he'll mark me, though. He has very human teeth. We will have to sort it out. I can't jump him either because I will be too tempted to bite and claim him. I want it to be at the same time! Ah, but how I fancy him... Mmm, fancy, fancy, fancy!"

We all burst into laughter. I doubled over, barely able to breathe. "S-Soley, you have turned into quite a bold and lusty wolf!"

"She keeps telling us what a monstrous 'key' he has—not that she's seen it," Rakel snorted.

"Hey!" she protested and pouted but just ended up giggling.

"And you, Rakel?" I asked eagerly. "Rude is a very good lycan. He helped me a lot when Zorian was being a complete m—" I frowned and corrected myself. "When he was deeply injured and confused."

Spine is Zorian, Trail reminded me. *Spine told me how much he fought Zorian for us and how much Zorian fought with himself. Like you said... not a monster. Made horrible decisions but not a monster. Injured deeper than marrow. Confused, hurt, and alone but not a monster. Everyone gets another chance if they make the effort, and he did. It was why we loved him.*

My heart stumbled just thinking about Zorian, and I realized everyone was watching me sit in my thoughts. "Sorry! Trail was talking. What did you say Rakel?"

"Oh, I was just waiting for you. I could tell you'd withdrawn." She smiled kindly. Rakel was gentler now. Her time in captivity must have made her more vulnerable than ever, and it was odd to see. I just hoped it didn't interfere with her dreams to rise in the warrior ranks. She needed more time.

"Rudesind has been very good to me." She sighed, staring at the cooking meat. "He is waiting for me to be ready. It's rare, but we occasionally rest together. It helps with the nightmares." She smiled and rotated a section of the rabbit. "You'd think he'd be scary as the grand beta, but he is just a big softy."

"But is he a biiig hardy?" Soley asked impishly, splaying her arms wide, and we all ended up in stitches.

"S-Soley! You're killing me!" I gasped.

I wished I had said that. That was something I would have said. Damn it, I am getting slow! Trail whined, but she whined between fits of laughter.

When my she-wolves were done cooking, we moved to eat under the sun. Just as I was thinking the meat could use some salt, a chunk of the stuff came wobbling along the ground toward us. We stopped speaking and ogled the approaching seasoning.

"Mated... termites..." I explained with a wave of my hand, as though the concept was a well-known fact, and the termite lovers disappeared to do goddess-knew-what next.

Must have been a small wedding, Trail quipped, and Rakel snorted.

"You'll get there, Trail. You warm up those funny bones," I laughed. Hekla and Soley sighed as they looked at me, unable to hear my wolf now. "I know. I'm sorry we're not in the same pack anymore." I picked up the salt offering and worked on crushing it to season the food.

"We'll always be pack in here," Hekla said, placing a fist to her chest. Soley nodded with a thoughtful smile.

"So, our gods have questions they wanted us to ask you," Rakel stated, sprinkling some of the salt on a fish filet.

"The gods sure have been curious lately. I got an odd one from the Earth Gods the other day," I mumbled pensively and bit into a piece of the juicy rabbit. "Mmm, Rakel, perfectly cooked!" I praised.

"So, the first one is kind of a continuation from the one you got yesterday," Hekla began, fixing her umbral stare on me. "So, you agreed that the Earth Gods' decision to choose you as its vessel was a good one. The Sky Gods wish to know why you are a good fit to be a vessel in regards to your physical and mental strengths. You are not allowed to disparage yourself in the answer."

I blanched, feeling horribly put on the spot.

Oh dear, that's a big question, Trail laughed nervously.

"Oh gosh," I swallowed heavily and shifted uncomfortably. It was hard to accept the Earth Gods' words, but it was even more difficult to analyze them. "Um, I guess I'll start with physical strength?" This was going to be hard. The very first thing I wanted to say was self-deprecating. "I've become a very good runner over the last five years, so I have excellent endurance. I've learned to be stealthy and quick. I'm quite practiced at evading capture.

"For mental strength, I suppo—I mean, I've found smart alternatives to limitations. I keep an open mind, so more solutions are available to me. I enjoy reading and can use other people's knowledge to inform my decisions. I try to foresee complications." I twisted my mouth and looked away in deep thought. Was that enough?

Hekla nodded, then turned to Soley. "I got the second one!" she chirped, raising her hand. "The Sun God wishes to know how those qualities lend themselves to a queen's duties, which is to protect and serve her people."

I blanched. Oh, the gods were really hitting me with some hard ones.

They actually all do, Ragna. Break it down, Trail encouraged.

I never thought of a queen benefitting from physical strength. That was a bit new. I placed a finger on my chin and stared at the grass. "A queen must remain safe so she can maintain her people's safety. If an assassin were after me, they'd have a hard time catching me because of my stamina and evasiveness. I'd be impossible to find at nighttime, which is usually when assassin's work. On a different note, I can tour the kingdom and be around my people more because I don't tire easily. It'll let me see problems in person.

"For mental strength, if my people encounter limitations, like with space or resources, I can brainstorm alternatives, and I'm open to other people's opinions. I've always figured that the more people come together over a problem, the sooner you'll get a good solution. Since I like reading, I'll be expanding my knowledge base constantly. The more I read, the more useful I'll be. Since I think about things in advance, I can be proactive for my people... so I can protect them before they have a chance to get hurt."

I stopped there, feeling like that was a thorough answer. It also made the thought of being queen a little less scary.

"I think you'd be a perfect queen," Hekla said with a shrug. "And I'm not just saying that."

"Agreed," Rakel said. Then she tilted her head and gave me a smile. "Finally, with all that in mind, the Moon Goddess wants you to explain how you're the right mate for Zorian."

My heart sank at this last battle I had to fight. I'd lost so many bonds that rejection was too present in my mind, but I knew that it was false. I knew Zorian wanted me. How would I sort my mind out over this? I placed my hands on the sides of my head, trying not to panic. Soley got up and sat behind me, scooting to wrap her arms around my waist. Hekla gave me a supportive nudge with her fist.

"I'm the right mate because I love him," I whispered. I began to shuffle through my qualities to provide a better answer, but Rakel interrupted me.

"That was the correct answer," she said with a knowing smile and took another bite of her fish. "The goddess wasn't looking for anything else."

With a surrendering whine, I collapsed dramatically against Soley, and she giggled, barely able to hold up my weight. I rolled off her and picked at some cabbage. I felt like I should be overwhelmed, but I wasn't. Still, thank the gods the questions were ove—

"I have my own question, Ragna," Hekla piped up, leaning her face into her palm. "Why aren't you your own friend?"

"What do you mean?" I asked, confused but a little intrigued.

"I mean, why don't you look at yourself and think, 'I should help that person out. I should tell her she's smart, pretty, and strong?'"

I was taken aback. That was a good question. Why didn't I treat myself like I treated everyone else?

"Fear," I realized slowly. "Fear gets in the way."

"And you do know that you have nothing to fear with Zorian, right? I mean, you know that."

"Right," I murmured and furrowed my brows. I didn't know what else to say. Not a whole lot of my fears were based on facts. I needed more time with that.

Hekla just blew our minds.

A lot of things just did, I replied and came to another realization. *It's not my fault the pup died, Trail. We knew it could happen. It doesn't mean we'd be a bad mother or mate.*

I honestly didn't even realize when we stopped being paranoid about it, she replied. *We must move on. Can we go home now? Zorian will help make more.*

Tomorrow morning, I decided. *We'll go home tomorrow morning. He's waiting for us.*

And he's our chosen. Him and Spine, yes? Trail pressed anxiously.

Yes, I said, in a bit of a daze but meaning every word. *He's our chosen. We're worthy. We... we will make a good queen. We will work hard.*

Yes, you will, and I'll be there to help with whatever you need, Rakel chimed in, and I smiled warmly at her. I was glad she would be staying at the castle. We could help each other adapt.

And I will be there for you. Whatever you want, I'll make it happen, I promised Rakel.

Cuz we'll be queen! Trail announced.

Don't let Trail become a dictator, Rakel snorted.

Nah, I'm only interested in dick t— Trail began, but I interrupted her.

I don't know where you're going with that, but please stop. I have a feeling that one is going to be weirder than normal.

I chuckled at Trail's raucous laughter and finished my dinner. "Where are you going now, Soley? Hekla?" I asked, grateful to be done with the terrifying questions.

"Belenus needs to sort out some stuff at home in the fae realm before he takes me there," Hekla sighed, pouting and poking the dirt with a stick.

"I'll bet he does," I mumbled to myself. Little did she know, he had to get the castle ready to receive the next future queen.

"Belenus also wants Koray to come to the fae realm for a little while to improve his sword fighting," Soley moaned. "I don't think I'm invited because I'll be a distraction."

Hekla leaned back onto her palms. "He just wants Koray to be able to protect you better. He means well, but I agree with you. It sucks to be away from your mate!"

"But where will you be when he returns? Are you both going back to the Lunar Coven?" I asked.

"Yes! I'm excited about it. I've heard there are books as far as the eye can see!" she said with a grin. "And I can see pretty far!" That she could. She was a fast reader too, and I wondered how long it'd take her to conquer their library.

My she-wolves left several hours later, and I hugged the bundle they'd given me to my chest. I didn't have any spare clothes, so they'd brought me some. The garments I'd slept in for over a week simply wouldn't do, especially for meeting Zorian.

We could arrive naked. Sneak into Zorian's room and just wait on the bed? Trail suggested mischievously. I smiled, and my face warmed. Why did I still blush? For goodness' sake.

"Even if we're not fated, his nose is still good enough to scent us before we'd get that far!" I laughed and allowed myself to feel warm and fuzzy. I didn't think I'd be able to sleep tonight. Part of me just wanted to leave now.

We could. We don't need to wait for anything. I think we're healed. I think we've got what we've needed from this sanctuary.

You are ready to leave, Ragna, the Earth Gods said, and I started a bit, not quite expecting Them to jump into my current thoughts. *Your last task is to walk back as Ragna. You may not shift until after you've found Zorian.*

That's an odd one, I remarked to Trail. *I'll heed your order, Earth Gods. Though, which way is the castle from here?*

You'll see when you leave.

Alright... That would have to do.

orian

Every single day without her was a fucking struggle. I still loved her. I still desperately wanted her. If my supposed 'fated mate' arrived tomorrow, ready to be a queen and have pups, I'd still reject her on the spot. Ragna was it. No one else could hold a candle to her.

I'd kept up my duties as king, but I fought to keep my sanity when I was alone… without her. Sometimes it felt like she'd just been a dream, and then I'd panic, and Rudesind would run in with Rakel to remind me she was real. Those were the hardest moments to bear.

The Sun God told me she'd woken up a couple days ago, and it took everything in me to stay away from her sanctuary. Not knowing when she'd return was killing me. I didn't think I could hang on much longer.

Let's go visit her sanctuary. Let's just sleep next to it or something. I can't take this anymore! Spine shouted, crumbling. *She has our pups in her belly. I need to be near them, Zorian. I need to protect them. I'm going mad!*

I'm going mad too, I mumbled wearily, running my hands through my hair and closing my tired, swollen eyes. *I miss her so much it hurts. It physically hurts.*

So, let's just fucking go! Who gives a shit? We won't bother anyone. Let's just be nearby. Please? Spine begged, and I saw no reason to argue. I agreed with him.

Alright, let's… go.

Chapter 35

Ragna

When I stepped out of my sanctuary, I saw that the castle was only a mile from where I stood. My heart leapt in my chest when I realized I'd be seeing him so much sooner than expected. Peace of mind made me take the first steps forward, and elation had me breaking into a run. I giggled like a child as I ran as fast as my legs could take me. *Zorian, Zorian, Zorian!* Each pump of my heart chanted his name like he was what flowed through it.

Then I noticed it.

I was slapped by a scent that I'd been obsessed with for weeks, and it almost brought me to my knees. Too adrenalized to falter, I ran faster and took in deeper sniffs, my nostrils flaring in disbelief. It couldn't be! It'd been taken, hadn't it?

I ran up a hill and saw white hair crest the peak of it. A handsome face came into view—one that was usually hardened with sternness. It was now filled with youthful wonder.

"Zorian?" I screamed, and we collided like lightning and thunder.

Sparks and tingles erupted.

He crushed me into his brawny arms and planted his lips on mine, as desperate to melt into me as I was to him. The fated mate touch flared brighter, as though trying to bind us together. I clutched Zorian as tightly as I could, digging my fingers into his hard back and pressing as much of myself against him as I could. He growled into my lips, and when I returned the noise, he slipped his tongue in to play with mine. I moaned and my claws extended with every pull of his lips and sweep of his tongue. My canines stretched and straddled his tongue, triggered by his flavor.

He groaned and released my lips with a snarl. I saw the wildness in his burgundy gaze, and it called to the wildness within me. I was too confused about how all of this was possible, and I couldn't think, so my brain switched into a different mode.

We ripped each other's clothes off, growling and snarling in our fervor. All I could see was my male. He was a good male—the very best. I'd needed him. I'd missed him.

My male wasted no time. He lifted one of my legs and slid two fingers down my sex to plunge into my channel. I whimpered and arched into him, impatient for his larger member. He withdrew his fingers and groaned into my ear, the silky strands of his white hair caressing my cheek. "Such a good female. Always so ready for your alpha."

A violent shudder raked down my body, pleasured by his praise and aroused by his dominant tone. "Always, my alpha," I replied to my strong, protective male. He snarled and lifted me to hover over a commanding, throbbing cock that glistened with pre-cum. I gripped my male's shoulder with one hand and guided his impaling length with another.

I held my breath as he parted my entrance, squeezing slowly past to seek the depths of my channel. As usual, he stretched me almost too wide, but I stayed calm, knowing he'd be careful. I knew he'd never hurt me again. He lowered me along his length, pulling me closer to him. His hips started moving, and a wave of arousal curled into my belly, making me clamp down on his erection. I whimpered at the feeling of him rubbing past my inner muscles, and he groaned in response. He finally yanked my hips roughly to his and buried himself to the hilt.

"Faster, my male," I urged, wanting him to go wild with me, and his eyes snapped to mine as if I had no idea what I'd asked. He dug his fingers into my hips and butt and started sliding me up and down his length. When my legs got a better hold around his hips, he lifted me higher and yanked me back down to slam against his pelvis, bucking to deepen the impact.

I leaned into him, panting and gluttonous for his attention. My male was deeply pleasing my emotions now. He held me high this time, like I was a precious object, and I reveled in the thought of an alpha putting a female above him. Another wave of arousal hit me, and I arched my back, crying out my joy and satisfaction, sharing my euphoria with the sun and skies.

"You are so good to me, my male." I gasped toward the clouds, eyes half-lidded under the late afternoon sky. I wasn't seeing it. I wasn't seeing anything. I could only feel. He growled louder, and I felt him harden more within me. His thrusts pushed his head against the back of my channel, kissing my cervix with every fervent stroke. I writhed and started pulling myself into his thrusts with my ankles.

"I. Will. Fuck. You. Anytime. You. Desire. My. Female!" He grunted rhythmically, and I responded with a long whine. My alpha would let me be greedy! My core clenched again as arousal blossomed through my system. He felt so good in me—so full, so warm, so right. I never wanted to be apart from him again. It wasn't right to separate us. If I could, I'd keep him buried deep inside me forever.

I clung to him when he crouched and lay down on the dirt, still connected to me. I was sitting on his lap now, but when I moved to place them on the ground, he snatched my ankles and planted my feet on his flexing biceps.

"My female will not touch the dirt!" he growled and reached for my hips again. He gripped me and jerked me down on his lap. I yowled in pleasure, scrabbling for his arms to maintain balance. His hips jerked to slap up into me, sending little shockwaves of ecstasy into my belly and chest. Everything was a carnal delight. He wanted me. He needed me. He pleased me. I pleased him. It was overwhelming in the most gratifying sense. Just thinking about it made me throb with desire.

He sat up, tilted my hips down, and grinded my sex against him. "Oh!" I cried out, and my head lolled back from the exquisite, deep, itching pleasure. I could almost hear the waters of my release coming. The tide swelled up to my ankles and knees, and I nearly started holding my breath before the waves swallowed me whole. My belly clenched as I waited with anticipation for the sea to take me away but not from my male. Never take me from my male.

My legs shook, and my male groaned, hungry for my surrender. "Come for me, my female. Let your alpha please you. Come on my lap and cover me with your sweetness." He said in a low, guttural tone that dripped with voracity. "COME," he commanded in his alpha voice, and I howled a euphoric cry in response, having never been so aroused in my life.

I was crushed by a wave of release that hauled me from almost all my senses. I jerked back with each swell of satisfying, carnal bliss, and I barely felt the hands on my hips that pumped with each pulse of my channel. "Pups, my male. Fill me with your pups!" I begged, scratching blindly at his chest.

I heard an aroused groan as my butt slammed down onto his lap. My male roared his release through his teeth and held me as he spent his seed against my cervix. I whimpered as my channel throbbed around him, rubbing ropes of his seed out to feed my womb. More, more, I wanted more. He grunted in agonized delight with every spurt I urged out of him. The waves of my release fell into a steady, rolling tide as he ejaculated one last time.

He caught me as I dropped my legs and fell limply against him. We were gasping, desperate to get air back into our fevered brains. My mind cleared, and I sank into his embrace, nuzzling into his delectable, sweaty neck.

"I love you too, Zorian," I confessed softly, as though our last conversation had never been interrupted. He choked on a sob and wrapped his arms tighter around me. "I came back to accept you as my chosen, but somehow, the bond came back?" I closed my eyes and savored the mate touch that had returned with a beautiful vengeance.

"Thank you, Ragna," he said, sniffling. I felt a tear drip onto my shoulder. "Thank you for forgiving me. Thank you for loving me. Thank you for choosing me." He buried his wet face in my shoulder.

"Will you mark me today?" I asked shyly. "I don't mind if you do it on accident this time."

He tilted his head back and laughed. I grinned into his chest and nuzzled, loving the sound of it. I remember the first time I'd heard it and thought it was a handsome din. It was even better now.

"Yes! Nothing would make me happier, my queen-to-be," he answered, kissing the top of my head with reverence. "Let's get you home first."

Home...

Home, Trail echoed. *It's been a long time since we could say that.*

Wherever Zorian is, I declared emotionally, *is our home now.*

And Spine, Trail agreed. *Though he is acting weird. He is anxious. He wants to get back to the castle as soon as possible.*

I think we're all looking to settle into some quiet comfort for a while.

Zorian refused to let me walk home, especially after I realized my cotton pants wouldn't stay up after our hasty undressing. I didn't complain when he carried me. I couldn't think of anywhere else I wanted to be. When I wasn't with him, all I could think about was being in his arms, listening to his heartbeat, and feeling his lungs rock me against his chest.

He carried me into the castle, and I couldn't keep the grin off my face when I saw how much more relaxed the soldiers and servants were. Some smiled or bowed their heads in gratitude. I wondered if any of them had found their fated mates since I'd been gone. Short of being with Zorian, nothing would make me happier than that.

As we approached the wing of the castle where his chambers were, he paused in front of an adjacent door. He looked down at me and swallowed nervously, but it was an excited kind of nervous.

"I have something to tell you," he said, slowly setting me down on my feet. I held my pants up with a small laugh and looked up at him in anticipation. "I didn't know this before you left. It wasn't until the Earth Gods took you away that the Sun God informed me..."

On those last couple of words, he opened the door to a large... nursery?

I was surprised. I didn't know what to think or say as I studied the extravagant and well-supplied room. It was nice of him to think about our future together, though I was still a little raw about the miscarriage. I was about to ask what he meant by informed, but he got to that first.

Zorian tilted my chin up, and his eyes locked on to mine. "You didn't lose the pups, Ragna," he stated, reaching to hold my free hand in his. "You're still pregnant."

Trail and I gasped in unison, and I brought my hands to my mouth in shock, barely noticing my pants falling gracelessly to my ankles. Zorian bit his lower lip to hold back a laugh, but all I could do was stare up into his excited and loving red eyes.

Ahh! Now I can finally talk about it! Spine screamed. *We're gonna be parents, Trail! Daddy Spine is gonna rock your world after they're born, mama wolf! Just you wait! Paw massages for days! Late night feedings? Leave them to Spine! Poopy diapers? Euh... leave them to Zorian!*

I started laughing and crying at the same time, but then I paused and looked up at him in surprise. "Pups? Plural?"

Zorian

A proud grin spread across my face at the surprise in her sparkling green eyes. I could hear her heart thump like a rabbit's, except hers was from awe and elation. "Yes," I chuckled and grabbed both her hands, not wanting her to hide her pretty face. "The Sun God said to prepare for a litter—whatever that means."

"Litters don't run in my family!" she exclaimed. "Do they run in yours?"

I shrugged. I'd never really been that interested in my family tree. "Not sure."

"Litters are four at a minimum!" she informed, swooning slightly, and I steadied her with a low laugh. She looked up at me through her pretty eyelashes, nervous—as if I'd be intimidated by so many pups.

Woah! Spine interjected. *We are potent!*

"We're not scared," I assured firmly, making sure she met my gaze. I eased my lips onto hers to offer a soft, gentle kiss. She relaxed against me and sighed. I could feel her tension drain away and evaporate. I would have gladly claimed her without the fated bond, but I was grateful it had returned so I could give her everything I had to give.

"Ragna, you have many months to go. Your pups are not coming yet," an amused voice came from the doorway. We turned to see Rakel smiling, gesturing to Ragna's fallen pants.

"The string broke!" Ragna defended and giggled, pulling her pants up while waddling over to give Rakel a hug.

"I knew you would pass the test, My daughter," She said.

"Ah, Moon Goddess, are You well? What test? The questions?" Ragna asked anxiously. I moved to wrap my arms around her and kissed the top of her head.

"I am well. Yes, you had to find your self-worth, Ragna. A queen without that cannot focus completely on her people. A mate without that can never truly love with all her heart."

I was curious about all of this. I'd have to ask her for the story later. Ragna leaned into me and nodded. Her response to the goddess was solemn. "The questions... Just being asked them helped me find the answers. Fear was blinding me to many things. Thank you, Moon Goddess."

"I'm curious why the fated mate bond didn't come back right away," I stated, hoping She could fill in the gap there. The goddess tilted Rakel's head and smiled.

"There are two answers. You could probably guess them both," the goddess prompted.

I furrowed my brows. Current events fed one answer. "Did you delay it so her near-death wouldn't hurt me as well?" I guessed, frowning. That seemed selfish. I wouldn't have wanted the bond removed just to spare me some pain. I could have soothed her with it.

The goddess nodded, staring at me thoughtfully. She knew what I was thinking. I was certain of it. I did not approve of Her decision to remove the bond, and that thought seemed to bring a smile to Her face. Would She ever stop testing us? I restrained a cranky growl.

"And the second?" the goddess urged. I sighed and buried my face into Ragna's hair.

"Your turn," I grumbled to my pregnant female.

"My self-worth," Ragna murmured, then spoke louder. "Knowing I'm right for something is stronger than being told I'm right for something. Fate could say I'd be a good queen, but I'd have a hard time accepting it if I didn't believe in myself. I wouldn't do as good of a job. Fate could say I'm meant to be with Zorian, but if I felt unworthy, I'd always be pushing him away."

"Don't push me away," I grumped, and she broke into laughter at my childish surliness. I tried to fight a smile, but her lilting giggles defeated me.

"You are both ready to be optimal rulers now," the Moon Goddess nodded in satisfaction. "You've grown much, Zorian, and you've healed well. Your mother is proud of you, as am I."

My heart stilled for just a beat, and my eyes watered at the mention of my mother. Was she watching? Was she resting or waiting for reincarnation? I didn't have the courage to ask, and she likely wouldn't say.

The goddess held up a finger. "One more thing. I have a reward for Trail and Spine," She announced, then placed her hands behind her back. "They have both shown to be some of my most dedicated children for they fought desperately for you to come together, as you were meant to be."

Damn fucking straight. You were such a nightmare, Zorian. A real pain in the a—

Shh! Trail shushed him. *I want my reward. Be a good daddy, and I'll make you happy later.*

I cleared my throat and side-eyed the goddess in embarrassment. Did She still think that after hearing their interchange? The goddess pressed Rakel's lips together and raised her brows. Was She trying not to laugh? I was good at reading people—not deities.

"After Ragna delivers your pups, Trail will be able to shift into a lycan when she wishes, and Spine will be able to shift into a wolf when he wishes. This blessing symbolizes love knowing no boundaries. Zorian and Ragna, there was a mountain between you, and they helped you climb it. Trail and Spine, you have done well." She raised a hand in farewell. "Until we meet again, my children. My pups."

I braced myself for it. This was the calm before the storm.

Holy shit!

Oh, my goddess! Trail squealed. *We're going to be able to do it!*

Gonna get so freaky!

Do lycans have that feel good spot that Ragna has?

"Trail!" Ragna protested, shocked.

I'm just going to have to show you, mama wolf! Spine said to Trail, missing Ragna's outburst.

I'm 'lycan' the sound of that, big daddy!

Can't wait to wolf down what you got!

"Spine! This isn't a private mind-link!" I admonished. They were much too excited to hear me.

'Howl' we ever choose which form to do it in first?

Don't matter, gonna make yo—

Please, Spine! I cringed, running my hands through my hair. *I'm begging you!*

"We're going to have to deal with that... for the rest of our lives," Ragna said, pointing in a random direction with a red face and a stunned expression. I couldn't tell if her gaze spoke of horror or amusement, but it was definitely saying something. I groaned and pulled her close.

"If we are going to suffer, we'll suffer together," I laughed into her neck, nuzzling. Our beasts were still us, and as embarrassing as they could be, I thought it was a good sign that their passion burned as brightly as ours.

I looked up to find Rakel gone, so I linked Rudesind and told him I wanted to hold Ragna's coronation as soon as possible, as I'd be marking and mating her tonight. I turned my attention back to my fated mate, satisfied that my best friend and beta was taking care of business.

I took Ragna's hand and guided her to our bedroom, our suite. She ran around excitedly at the changes I'd made to make her more comfortable. Even though the Sun God hinted there was a possibility of Ragna failing her last test, I had moved forward with the thought that she would pass and return to my side. The alternative was unacceptable, so I got ready to spoil her rotten like I'd said I would. She ran from the closet where all her new clothes were to where I'd had her grandfather's bow fixed up a bit and restrung.

She squeaked when she ran to the secure display case that contained her lunaite and the Earth Gods' Heart. "Ahh! I forgot to give this back to the Moon Goddess!" she yelped, pointed to the heart and turned to me in dismay.

I shrugged. "She'll be back, Ragna. You can give it to her next time, or I could take you to visit her." I grinned and crossed my arms, flexing them a little. It hadn't escaped my notice that she liked it when I did that.

She blushed, averted her eyes, and laughed nervously. "Right, right...
You can just take me to the moon."

"And back." I smirked and stalked up to her. She fidgeted and looked
away, pressing her thighs together.

"Still so shy, Ragna?" I asked and tilted her chin up to look at me.
"You weren't so shy in the woods earlier."

"I don't know! I'm just nervous I guess," she admitted, trying to cool
her heated face down with her hands. The long, dark lashes framing her
vibrant eyes fluttered with her flustered motions.

"Because I'm going to mark you?" I asked, rubbing her forearms
soothingly with my hands, enjoying the tingling between our flesh. "Is
that why?" I leaned down to draw in her scent. Oh, how it pleased me.
Cloves, nutmeg, and cider.

"Mm-hmm," she hummed, nodding. I slowly moved her back to the
bed, placing soft kisses where I planned to sink my teeth.

"Because I'm going to take you as my queen?" I lifted her up, climbed
onto the bed, and laid her down with her head on a soft, silky pillow. She
hummed again, and I reached under her shirt to palm her waist. "Gods,
I can't wait to see your belly full with our pups," I groaned through an
aroused, tight abdomen. I leaned down to kiss her stomach, nuzzled her
skin, and took a deep breath. "I can barely scent our combined smells,
but it's there. Great gods, that's the sexiest thing I've ever scented." She
squirmed under me, and her desire flooded my nose, overpowering all
other smells.

I shuddered and slid my hands up her ribs, pulling her shirt along
with my thumbs. I slipped my tongue past my lengthening canines and
licked up her torso until I ran into that accursed female undergarment. I
was tempted to rip it off, but I promised I'd spoil her, and I didn't want
to destroy anything she liked. I slipped my hands behind her, unhooked
it, and pulled her clothes over her head, leaving her beautiful and bare
below me.

A longing moan escaped me. All this would be mine soon, just like
all of me would be hers. "You are so beautiful, Ragna," I murmured and
traced a line down the side of her breast. Little goose bumps textured her
skin, and her heart broke into a lope.

She reached up to tug on the bottom of my shirt. "We must be fair,
Zorian, my male," she complained. "I need my eyeful as much as you do."

I grinned excitedly, pleased to get a compliment. I enjoyed them as much as anyone else. "You like what I have to offer?" I asked, raising my arms so she could remove my shirt.

She threw it onto the floor and flushed as she looked me over. "You are very virile. Just looking at your muscular arms and chest, your abdomen, it is a problem when we are in public," she admitted with an embarrassed grimace, and I laughed heartily, glowing from her admiration.

Ragna continued, stroking a finger along my collarbone. "You are very handsome, Zorian. I am fortunate your heart now matches your body. Strong and beautiful."

My grin widened, and I leaned down to kiss her. "You flatter me," I pressed my lips softly to hers, feeling my heart fill with love and affection.

"I could compliment you daily, but I'm worried it'd make you swollen-headed," she said into my lips. I smirked at her innocent words, grabbed her hand, and held it to my clothed erection.

"I'm afraid it is much too late for that, Ragna," I murmured back into her lips, letting our mouths brush as I spoke. I released her hand so she could retract it, but retract she did not.

"I'm ready, my love. Please make me yours forever."

Chapter 36

Zorian

When she called me her love, my heart softened, and my cock hardened—more. I groaned when she gave my shaft a squeeze over my pants. I'd tucked it off to the side because it'd gotten too long to stay below the belt, and she growled in frustration when her fingers couldn't quite reach it from around the hem. I smirked down at her focused face as she worked to unbuckle and slide my pants down my thighs.

"What an eager thing my female has beco—Ahh!" I began, but Ragna gripped my cock when it sprang free of my clothes. She palmed it and felt its heavy, engorged weight, testing it the way I did with her breasts. I groaned in pleasure as she explored it, dabbing her fingertip to gather some pre-cum and slide it down my length. She licked her hand and returned it to my cock, making it more slippery. I gritted my teeth and shuddered. I had not expected this with how shy she'd been acting minutes earlier. She kept this alpha on his toes.

She looked up at me through her eyelashes and asked, "Do females put their faces down there as well?"

I moaned when she stroked my length, trying to use my pre-cum to make it slippery. "You mean oral?" I gasped at her massaging. "Uh, some do. Some don't."

She frowned at my vague reply. "Do you like having a female's face down there?"

"Only if the f-female enjoys it," I grunted, leaning slightly into her hand on her next stroke.

"What does she do?" she asked, squeezing a little harder to encourage an answer.

"What you're doing now but with her mouth," I groaned, closing my eyes and enjoying her touch. "Why are you asking all these questions?" I felt her hand leave my cock, and a pathetic, embarrassing whimper escaped my throat. Ah gods, what was this female doing to the Lycan King? I felt her smaller hands push against my chest, and I rolled off her, sighing and letting her have her way.

The weight on the bed shifted, and I opened my eyes to find her ripping my pants and undergarments off the rest of the way. My brows shot up when she straddled my legs and leaned over to lick the tip of my cock.

"Ragna, you don't have to d—" I protested but gasped when she interrupted me again to slide my length in between her soft lips. "Oh, fuck!" My hips twitched, bucking slightly in response to her actions, and I gripped the sheets on either side of me.

She slid down as far as she could take me in, gagging slightly, then pulling back up to release me with a slurp of her lips. "You don't have to go so far," I groaned. "If you must, you can add your hand."

She hummed and slid me back into her velvety, soft mouth, adding her hand just below it to cover more of my length. My head tilted back, and I let out a breath I didn't know I was holding. My legs shifted slightly as she began to pump her head, using her saliva to lubricate her hand. She pushed down with her lips and hand and squeezed her grip when she retreated. I desperately tried to keep my writhing to a minimum as she continued this pattern, but she was doing too good. She was doing far too good of a job.

I white-knuckled the sheets and heard them tear under my claws. I needed to stop this before it went too far. I desperately wanted my next load to be for marking her. I was getting impatient.

"Ragna," I gasped and tried to urge her off with a knee, but she stuck fast to me. "If you don't stop, I'm going to explode into your pretty little mouth," I warned. Trying to scare her away didn't work; in fact, it made things much worse. She suctioned on, and I could tell she was getting more aroused. Ok, intervention time. I growled and moved her back to her pillow, making her frown.

"You didn't enjoy it?" she asked as I crawled over her, but then she arched when I pushed the head of my cock between her folds.

"Oh, I most certainly did, but I'm getting impatient to make you mine," I growled into her ear and rolled my hips to pump my spit-covered girth past her opening. I stared hungrily down at my female, her breasts bouncing slightly with each push into her tight channel. She shuddered and moaned under me, then slid her hands up and around my ribs to clutch my back. With the help of her arousal, I glided in, parting her gripping walls to bottom out in her sex.

She pulled herself up against me, and I wrapped my arms around her, keeping my weight off my pregnant female with an elbow. She sighed a long, beautiful, soft sigh, and I nuzzled into her neck, enjoying our moment of closeness. The first joining was always the best; it was a reminder of how deeply I missed her when we were apart.

I moved my head to brush my lips against her cheek, kissing it like I had the very first time we'd made love. I kissed my way over until I reached her lips. I hovered over them for a moment and waited for her eyes to open. They fluttered open, and she glanced through them at me, wondering why I'd stopped. I supported her head, looked into her sparkling green eyes, and said, "I love you, Ragna."

Her eyebrows drew into a tender expression, and she whispered, "I love you too, Zorian." When I heard what I'd been dying to hear again, I pressed my lips slowly and softly to hers, offering everything I had to give through that kiss. I lowered her back down and continued kissing her, rocking my hips to ease in and out. She moaned into my lips and ran her nails down my back, this time careful not to claw me — not that I minded.

She kissed me with what felt like kindled devotion, overwhelming me. I broke from her lips and gasped into her neck. "Gods," I squeezed my eyes shut and basked in her love and affection. She radiated it for me. "Gods, I love you so much." I gasped and kissed her again. Just as love swelled into my heart, arousal flooded my groin, and I realized that being in love was more of a turn-on than anything I'd ever experienced in my life.

I boxed her head in with my forearms and slid my tongue between her lips. My entire universe was centered on her. I synced up our rhythm, plunging my tongue into her mouth at the same pace as my cock. I smiled into her lips and rolled my hips a little faster when I noticed her wiggling under me.

I groaned at how her buttery walls gripped me tighter every time she became more aroused. "You feel so perfect," I murmured into her ear, gently pulling on her lobe with my teeth. When her sex squeezed me again, I grunted and started peppering her neck with tingling kisses. I slid my right hand down her chest to cup her breast and rubbed in large circles, occasionally massaging into her nipple to make her squirm.

Her legs slid seductively up my thighs to wrap around my hips, and she put pressure on my butt every time I slid my cock into her, like I was a horse she was trying to spur. I buried my groan into her shoulder and quickened my pace per her demand. Who was I to deny my queen?

She moaned, mewled, and whimpered with each thrust, trying to buck her hips up to meet mine. Arousal splintered and grew throughout me at the wet slapping of our flesh. I slid both my hands into her hair, fisting it, and responding to her lustful calls with my own guttural ones.

"I love you," she whimpered into my ear. "I love you, I love you, I love you, I love you!" A wave of pleasure rode a shudder from my chest to my groin. Gods, those words sent me spiraling. I grunted and took a deep, steadying breath, willing myself to hang in there until we were ready.

I thrust harder into my female, angling my throbbing member so I could grind against her. Her pealing wails became more desperate as I worked my hips into her. I loved being the cause of her cries. I was addicted to creating them once I knew what she sounded like. I also craved making her orgasm; there was no sweeter face on the planet than hers when she found her bliss.

She hung on tight as I rocked heavily into her sensitive bundle, forcing keening mewls out of her panting mouth. I felt her stomach clench, her limbs shake, and her body lock up before she went over the edge.

I couldn't hold back.

We were slammed nigh senseless from our climaxes. She howled, and I snarled as her channel milked my cum right out of me.

Fighting tooth and claw to stay focused on our goal, I leaned down to lick where her neck met her shoulder and clamped down into her flesh with my teeth. My canines penetrated her marking spot, and she screamed underneath me, writhing from another intense orgasm I'd just triggered. I injected my venom deep into her with my canines to change her chemistry, marking her so no one else could ever have her. Her whole body would tell the world that she belonged to the Lycan King. No one would dare touch or harm her ever again.

I jerked and cried out in ecstasy when she mirrored my action, piercing the flesh at my marking spot with her sharp wolf canines. Carnal heat rolled through me as her mark seeped into my very being. It was there to claim me as hers. It was there for her pleasure. It was there for her safety, and it was there to tell all the females out there that they'd better fuck off if they valued their lives.

We were a mess of sounds and limbs, writhing and hanging on to each other for dear life as our bond brought us to new heights of pleasure. Our markings had sealed our fated connection, and we were tied together forever. I felt not only her skin, her breaths, and her pulsing flesh around my cock, but I could also feel her joy, her excitement, and a profound sense of completion. Our emotions whirled between us, wrapped tight in euphoria.

I wasn't sure how many times I'd spent my seed in her, but our bodies eventually calmed, and I collapsed next to her, taking her with me to lie on my heaving, sweating chest. She held me as tightly as I held her, nuzzling like she couldn't get close enough. I was radiating happiness. I finally had my precious fated mate and rightful queen.

"I can feel your emotions. You're so happy," she whispered, and I hummed a response, still breathless. Her voice was full of awe as she continued, "We finally did it. We worked together. We accomplished our task."

"Fell in love," I added, catching my breath.

"Got pregnant first," she chuckled. "All backwards."

"I liked you before then," I grumbled under my breath. "I just didn't know how to deal with it."

"If what you say is true, you definitely didn't know how to." She laughed and wrapped her arms around my neck, kissing me soundly. "We already know we make a good team, Zorian," she murmured and nuzzled my nose sweetly. "I'm really looking forward to doing some good as a queen by your side."

I gazed over at her lovingly, cupped her soft cheek, and kissed her in return. "Me too, my love."

Queen Ragna: Two days later

The coronation went by in a haze, and I knew I wouldn't remember much of it. Trail and I were terrified of being in front of thousands after our five lonely years in solitude. We had conditioned ourselves to avoid people, so the number of eyes on us was daunting. My mate, King Zorian, felt my terror through the bond and sent soothing thoughts over to me. I was not sure what Spine had been sending Trail because she became a flustered and distracted mess about halfway through the ceremony.

What I remembered the most was my mate's face when he placed the Queen's Crown on my head. This lycan looked upon me as though I was his sun, his stars, his moon, and the ground beneath his feet. His heart now radiated love. The outcome of our challenging journey had been worth the suffering.

I believed in second chances now. I'd gotten one, and so had he. We had survived events that seemed impossible to grow past. I would say that I felt lucky to have gotten here, but to be honest, I had worked for it. We had both earned our happiness.

With Zorian at my arm, I managed not to trip on my gown descending the stairs. As soon as we arrived at our banquet table, I was approached by a familiar sobbing. I glanced up sharply to see my mother running toward me, glowing with pride and covered in tears.

"Mother!" I shouted and ran into her arms. She held me close and wept. My heart simultaneously broke and warmed to see her. Seconds later, another pair of arms wrapped around us, and I scented my father. I tried to hold it back, but my eyes started leaking too.

"My little Trailblazer," my father said, choking on his emotions. "It's so good to see you again. Your mother was so worried."

I pulled back to look at them, dismayed to see they'd aged more than I'd expected while I was gone. There was more grey than there used to be, and it felt like my fault. "I'm safe now, Mother," I comforted and squeezed her arm. I turned to my father and said, "I brought honor to Grandfather's bow. It's still with me."

He beamed. "Then it did what it was meant to do. Take down any bears?" he chuckled. For a moment, I felt the urge to brag about having slayed a dragon, but that was too dark for me. I wasn't proud of it.

"No bears." I shook my head. "I'll tell you all about it when things settle."

Zorian approached and held his hand out to my father. I saw my father struggle between submitting and aggressively sizing up my mate. Somehow, he still felt the need to protect me. Zorian broke the tension by allowing him to see the smallest smile. My father gave him a wary look after that and took his hand.

"Welcome to the family, Your Majesty," my father grunted. I burst into laughter. Gods help me, I didn't know why this scene was so funny, but I doubled over, wheezing. My crown flew off, and I managed to snatch it out of the air before it hit the ground.

Perhaps we have finally lost our mind, Trail mused. *We need a vacation.*

I wiped tears of mirth away to find everyone staring at me. I waved them off, pretending I didn't just bust a royal gut for no reason. My mate chuckled and turned back to my father. "You are both invited to join the Royal Pack if that is something you desire. You will always have a place in the castle."

I was touched by his offer and was about to say something when another familiar voice interrupted. "Trying to steal my pack members, Your Majesty?"

Zorian turned to shake hands with my old alpha. "Good to see you again, Alpha Erik," my mate said. "How is your pack faring?"

"Much better now, thanks to your efforts," he answered with a submissive nod of deference to Zorian and me. He put his hands behind his back and said, "If you don't mind me saying so, I'm proud of you, Queen Ragna. You took on an overwhelming task and succeeded. Your exploits have spread across the territory. I am... relieved that you survived your ordeal. It was not an easy decision to remove you from my pack."

I nodded in understanding. "It was the only thing you could do. I harbor no ill will."

I'm queen now. Am I allowed to hug an alpha? I asked Zorian, glancing over to him. I had no idea what the etiquette was for a queen. My mate turned, and I saw his shoulders shake from suppressed laughter.

I don't know how to respond to that. You're the queen. Go for it. That's fine, he replied, his humor present through our mind-link and bond. I could almost feel his laughs in my belly.

I held my arms open for the alpha, and his eyebrows shot up in surprise. I stepped forward and gave him a squeeze. Hesitantly, he hugged me back and patted me on the shoulder before letting go.

Zorian was more composed by the time I'd stepped back, and we all settled down to eat. My she-wolves sat on the other side of the table with their mates. Rakel and Rudesind mostly sat in silence, sending shy little glances to each other. The beta would occasionally give her an affectionate rub on the back, and she'd relax. She clearly had a long way to go in her own healing. I couldn't imagine what she'd been through.

Hekla was making a show of finding her food quite pleasurable, sucking way longer on her silverware than necessary. Poor Belenus was constantly clearing his throat and adjusting his pants, trying not to meet her gaze when she'd fork a sausage. Zorian and I were close to bursting into laughter at the two of them. Belenus had been so confident with me, but Hekla had torn through his defenses somehow. It was only a matter of time before they collided like an inferno. I was half-tempted to lock them in a tiny room to finally be done with the sexual tension.

By order of the queen, Trail barked with laughter.

And the king, Spine added. *I order thee to mark already, for all our fuckin' sakes!*

I snorted into my food and nearly choked on it. Zorian patted my back, also red-faced from our beasts' commentary. I wiped a tear from my eye and glowed when my mate pressed his lips to my cheek. Ah Moon Goddess, I was so happy.

Soley and Koray were just a delight to watch. They were obviously smitten, giving each other bites of their food and sneaking kisses. Their happiness warmed my belly like a glass of wine, not that I could have any. By early evening, Soley had leaned her head against Koray's shoulder while he stroked it and chatted with the other guests. I was doing the same with Zorian, almost unable to believe that all of this was real.

My friends and family were seated with my mate and me on the day I became queen.

What a trip, Trail marveled.

The mistake turned into a happy accident, I said thoughtfully and turned to press my lips against my mate's eager ones. My mate, my king, my everything. Whatever love I sent to him, he returned tenfold. The Moon Goddess was right. All was as it should be.

The End

𝕬uthor's 𝕹otes

Why this Book was Written

Dear readers,

When I was young, I was sexually assaulted. Later, I was targeted by another pedophile. I survived a traumatic childhood, and decades after, I found a psychiatrist who referred me to a DBT program. That was when I began the process of healing. Honestly, at that point, I thought I'd been beyond all help, but dark thoughts shocked me into choosing to live.

I've made progress, but I shy at being touched by certain people. For the longest time, I didn't even realize that the discomfort, anxiety, and nausea I felt wasn't a normal reaction. Whenever I'm intimate with someone, I need to keep my eyes open to make sure they're who they're supposed to be. Otherwise, my mind will put someone else there. Sometimes my skin crawls because I remember what it's like to be touched without consent. Parts of my body can't be touched without me feeling like something is wrong, which leads to nausea and dissociation.

I've been dipping my feet into exposure therapy for a while, but it's difficult. Currently, I don't feel like there's a whole lot I can work with, and I've also been juggling some medical problems that keep me from the rest of my life.

I got very depressed, and the things that normally brought me joy stopped doing so. I needed a new way to escape. I needed a new outlet. That was when I started writing. *The Mistake and the Lycan King* was my very first book. I've taken no creative writing classes, and whatever grammar I didn't learn from public school was painfully self-taught.

I turned writing into my exposure therapy. I gave my story everything I needed to meet some feelings head on. I put it on a website to interact with readers because I didn't want to go through it alone.

I pulled out everything that was raw inside me and placed it into the story. Then I wrote whatever I wanted after that. I let my imagination pour out and worked at the pages like an artist sculpting a figure from a dreary old boulder.

I didn't go into this planning on publishing, but with the encouragement of my readers, my shifter family, I went ahead and aimed for the Sky Gods.

⚜

Zorian: He represented my struggle with my assault. The anger, the self-loathing, the self-blame, the helplessness, the excuses, the denial. Spine was the spine of Zorian's character, his heart and humanity. He was there as contrast to show that Zorian's side was what was injured. Zorian wasn't broken or a monster; he was injured. I'm not broken. I'm just injured.

[Calling myself broken, unless I have an actual broken bone, for example, is an exaggeration like catastrophizing, and it makes my SUDS, subjective units of distress, rise. Stopping exaggerated thoughts really helped my mental health.]

I was angry. I was angry for so long, and I needed Zorian to be who he was. I needed him to hate what he'd done. I needed him to wish desperately for growth. I needed his drive to improve to spur mine.

The quote below from Zorian was from a very specific moment in my life (a handful of years ago after starting therapy) where I felt genuine contentment for the first time. I was so used to telling people I was sad or depressed when they asked how I was. When someone asked me how I was, and I was actually having what I'd heard of was a good day, I almost couldn't be honest about it because it felt too alien. It felt uncomfortable to be happy because it was almost like my body didn't have a place ready to put that emotion. My body wanted to reject it and go into denial. It was also the beginning of separating a good/bad day from moments in the day that were good/bad. Needless to say, it was a very confusing chapter of my life.

"My emotions didn't make sense to me. I never thought it'd be so uncomfortable to experience happiness. Was I happy? Now wasn't even a time to be happy. Was it? Was there a time for happiness? Did happiness need its own moment in time, or could it coexist with whatever you happened to be doing?"

⁂

Ragna: She was my therapy. She was someone who looked at the larger picture and thought about how things could be better. She defended Zorian in front of the Sun God because she didn't want to be the cause of anyone dying. She looked to heal, not to punish. That's how I progressed, and still progress, through therapy. I focused on healing, not on hurting the ones who hurt me. Whenever I feel hate over my trauma, it makes me sick to my stomach. There's no peace there.

The anger I held for a little over two decades wore on me. It made me sick, and it wasn't until I learned to forgive that I began to feel better. I needed Ragna to take me through that with Zorian. I needed them both to find understanding, acceptance, and forgiveness together.

By the end, their relationship is healthy and thriving. It's where I hope to be someday with my body and mind.

⁂

Sex: For part of the sex exposure therapy, since I had no partner who could help me, I had not planned on writing as erotically as I did. When I pushed it past my comfort zone, it allowed me a microscopic view of the sexual act, and the more I pushed it, the more comfortable I felt about it. It doesn't have to be realistic to help. Sometimes it helps to be less realistic. It depends.

The fact that both characters were part beast also made it easier to digest the rawness. A fantasy realm helped put it at a safer distance too. I found myself kind of bumping around in the dark with this novel, pushing and prodding at what elements felt helpful.

Could I write about someone's breasts being touched without me feeling like throwing up? Turns out I could, and it got easier over time.

I've been cautioned through therapy to make sure I'm not cueing up too much to handle, but my therapist sees it as a valid exercise. I'm careful with it, but it's more of a release for me than not.

∗∗∗

Second chances and growth: I believe in second chances and that every case must be assessed individually to see if a second chance is safe or not. Some people are too dangerous to be given second chances. We all have our own ideas about what that threshold is. Everyone's feelings are valid, and I leave decisions to the experts.

That being said, there's a reason why we have programs that help reintroduce people back into society. People can be and are rehabilitated all the time. I buy my bread from a company founded by someone who turned their life around after jail. They also support second chance employment, which means hiring whoever is good for the job, regardless of criminal history.

People can heal and give back to society. I have no regrets about how I've built and developed Zorian's character. Someone's past does not always decide their future. My past does not decide my future. I hope I can be comfortable and feel safe in my own body someday.

∗∗∗

My regular commenters and readers know who they are. You've been there by my side from the very beginning, and you could not possibly understand how much I needed you when you came along. Thank you from the very bottom of my heart. I didn't have to go alone as I'd feared.

Starlight preserve you,
Asha Nyr